THE WIND IN THE FOREST

"Mrs. Fletcher writes historical fiction at its vital best. In this, her ninth novel of America's past, she deftly threads Hillary's romance through the turmoil of Tidewater-backwoods civil strife."

—*The New York Times*

"Has the ring of truth and a fine vigor."

—*Saturday Review*

"After all her writing on colonial Carolina, Mrs. Fletcher retains a fresh sense of the period and of the men and women who had to take sides in a truceless struggle."

—*Chicago Sunday Tribune*

THE WIND
IN THE FOREST

By

Inglis Fletcher

*This low-priced Bantam Book
has been completely reset in a type face
designed for easy reading, and was printed
from new plates. It contains the complete
text of the original hard-cover edition.*
NOT ONE WORD HAS BEEN OMITTED.

THE WIND IN THE FOREST

*A Bantam Book / published by arrangement with
Bobbs-Merrill Co., Inc.*

PRINTING HISTORY

Bobbs-Merrill edition published October 1957
2nd printing . . . .October 1957
Bantam edition / August 1975

*Bantam Books are published by Bantam Books, Inc. Its trade-
mark, consisting of the words "Bantam Books" and the por-
trayal of a bantam, is registered in the United States Patent
Office and in other countries. Marca Registrada. Bantam
Books, Inc., 666 Fifth Avenue, New York, New York 10019.*

PRINTED IN THE UNITED STATES OF AMERICA

Dedication

To my dear Grandson
JAMES CHENOWETH FLETCHER
*Who is twelve years old
and is growing up in the strong
and vigorous State of North Carolina*

A NOTE
ON SOME SOURCES
... WITH GRATITUDE

The controversial figure of the Royal Governor of North Carolina, William Tryon, was developed from his own letters and records of the Battle of Alamance.

The character of the little known Harmon Husband, of the Regulators, came out of his tracts:

Remarks on Religion	1761
Impartial Relation	1770
Fan for Fanning	1771

The character of the young missionary preacher, Member of the Society of Friends, was suggested by the memoirs of Catherine Phillips, published 1798.

Inglis Fletcher

. . . O ye Daughters of Jerusalem! . . .
He will come in the Time when it shall please
Him, and be as a Wind in the Forest among
the trees.

—From a pamphlet by Harmon Husband,
    published in 1761 as he began the decade
    of Carolina years that led to Alamance.

Contents

Foreword

Some years ago when I wrote *Raleigh's Eden* I devoted a small section to the Battle of Alamance.

I was new at writing historical novels and I used as source material a history that was not of the period. That was a mistake, for I treated in a manner I now know to be inadequate two men whose contest makes a complex, important (though little known) episode of our history.

Subsequent reading has given me a different idea of the Regulators and, I trust, a somewhat better insight into the strange nature of Harmon Husband, the quiet man who had somehow a passionate eloquence that could move and direct men, the believer in the Quaker principle of non-violence who stirred dissension, invited violence and raised revolt because he also believed in justice.

In like manner I have come to know more of the enigmatic, endlessly fascinating William Tryon, who does not really deserve the anathema pronounced by the Regulators. Their early courageous understanding of a great American attitude and principle did not prevent their making judgements which sober study revises as it increases their stature and promotes their deserved celebrity.

Tryon and Husband faced each other in a series of dramatic meetings which in 1770–71 led to the military action at Alamance. In a sense each was a victor, as (I hope) you will understand completely in the tale I've set down here. Yet I suspect you will hear most clearly the voices of Richard and Matthew Caswell, and of Adam

Rutledge, who mocks any claim that I "created" him by striding boldly into any work of mine to which he is attracted. The Caswells are quite real to history, and the planter Rutledge—you may think and I should like to believe—is as real as the concepts and attitudes gathered into the word "American." You are the inheritors and successors; they are your elder country men.

They are you—yesterday.

While I am not quite ready to agree with historian Benson Lossing that Alamance was the first battle of the American Revolution, I can with Josephus Daniels regard Harmon Husband and the Regulators as among those ". . . making straight the path for patriots who took the next step that became the War of Revolution."

As at Lexington and Concord "embattled farmers" stood and fought, so at Alamance the farmers, trappers and scouts, the men of the Carolina back country, moved toward freedom. The action at Great Alamance Creek deserves wider attention. It's causes were embodied in the greater causes of the American Revolution.

This is not a history, however, but a novel. Incidents that do not distort the large facts have been used as they add to the story line and dramatic unity of the novel. I assure the reader I've made only a few minor changes in the order of events. Honest fiction may speak truth as well as fact. But its yield of truth sometimes depends on a (strictly limited) liberty with time. No liberty may be taken with the larger truths. Once or twice it has served the purposes of truth to bring together in time related events that were in fact a little apart. Their effect and meaning are not altered. Their impact on the reader is, I think, rather increased. A truth made up of many facts may thus be the clearer.

To single out an example here would risk attaching a false value to it when the reader encounters it in the story. We have now to follow a story of many exciting truths—and the story begins here.

Inglis Fletcher

Bandon Plantation
Edenton, North Carolina
May 1957

Path to Sandy Creek

The path which led from the village of Hillsborough to the farms of Sandy Creek was seldom travelled; on the vaguely marked trail the grass was high and wet with rain. Delicate branches from the high brush along the creek arched over the pathway, their fragile yellow blossoms catching the first slant rays of the sun.

It was May of 1768 in the County of Orange in the Royal Province of North Carolina. Spring storms had passed over the land: the thunder of the Western discontent had rolled like the muster of drums; the lightning of their anger had illuminated, burned, struck into contrast the wide districts of the Tidewater and the country of the hills.

But on this morning there was a certain peace, a thing fragile as blossoms—a light like the dawn which banded the country. Then from the east, from the direction of Hillsborough, sounded the drumming of hoofs.

A mockingbird flew startled from the brush; and a grey, thin branch was still springing like a whip when, seconds later, horsemen galloped down the trail, snapping the brush aside. There were seven riders in all, and the rising sun now gleamed on their swords and glinted from the metal of their guns.

The leader of the file was a captain in the militia. His uniform was dirty, and the collar of his shirt was pulled wide. His square, stolid face had the stubble of a two-day beard. He was followed by a fat tavern-keeper from Hillsborough who jostled uncomfortably on his mount.

His short legs angled outward to the stirrups. His hair was matted to his round forehead with sweat.

The hoofbeats shattered the dawn, seemed to hurry the rising sun which illumined Sandy Creek and the features of the other riders. A thin, fish-eyed clerk leaned forward on his mount, urging it onward with a series of oaths. Two pistols were jammed into his belt. Behind rode a murderer—recently paroled from the Hillsborough gaol—whose permanent reprieve was contingent on his actions at Sandy Creek. Three ragged young privates of the militia, their coats unfastened, their faces lined with weariness, completed the file.

The captain in the lead reined his mount at a sandy patch of ground near the creek's edge and raised his hand in signal to the others. He wheeled his tired mare to face them. One by one they drew up while the captain stared down the path in the direction from which they had come, straining his eyes down the swinging archway of branches as if he expected another rider.

The tavern-keeper stretched, yawned and reached his fat arms around to try to rub the small of his back. The mare which he rode was flecked with foam. All the horses of that crew had been ridden too hard; they blew and whinnied.

"I'd be glad to hang every Regulator myself after this ride," the clerk said. He wiped the back of his hand across his lips. "If the Colonel wants it I'll put the rope on 'em all by myself."

The murderer had leaned forward and slapped his mount gently on the neck to quiet it. "By the Lord, he's a brave man," he said to the captain. "I wonder why he stays a clerk?"

The clerk's face was flushed for a moment, then it returned to its usual cadaverous white. "You've Colonel Fanning to thank that you're out of the gaol. I'd mind my tongue if I was you. I might forget who you was and mark you for a Regulator when I put out the warrants for arrest."

"Warrants! Who's ever needed a warrant in this county?"

"Now, Bill, hold yer temper down," a private said. "Just let him tell me. That's all I want. Who needs a warrant? Have we got one for this Harmon Husband? Well, have we, Mr. Clerk?"

The clerk looked to the captain for support. "I guess the Colonel's got one."

"In a pig's eye, he has. Look at me when you talk to me. Don't go pretending you're a man and then try to back out."

"The Colonel's coming."

The group fell silent and waited as Edmund Fanning, Colonel of Militia, Judge, Register of Deeds, Assemblyman of Orange County, close friend of Govrnor William Tryon—in short, the man of power at the Courthouse in Hillsborough—appeared at the end of the archway of brush and cantered his roan toward them.

The horsemen were impatient to be done with their work, for they had spent the entire night riding from Hillsborough to the farms of Sandy Creek in order to arrest the leaders of the Regulators—a group of farmers and frontiersmen who had sworn not to pay the fees and taxes levied by Colonel Fanning.

The Colonel reined his horse before them. He carried himself with the dignity and imperiousness of a Royal official. He was well dressed—his blue coat and white breeches had been tailored with care. His tricorn hat gave him a look of court dignity—a dignity which could not be found in his puffy cheeks, his aquiline nose or his pouting lips. His eyes were quick and marked him as a man of some shrewdness, but, above all, as a man without scruples. When he spoke, it was with the accent of a gentleman of culture, though he had been born in the Colonies and had served his Governor, William Tryon, as an able and willing supporter in the backwoods regions.

He pointed down the path with his riding crop. "You'll find the immoral Quaker at the farm at the end of this path." He glanced from face to face to see that he was understood. "I believe you've all seen him in Hillsborough. Captain Hart, you're responsible for bringing him to me." Colonel Fanning paused thoughtfully and then added, "Our hanging will be in Hillsborough—not in this back country."

"Within the hour, Colonel."

"Within the half hour, Captain."

"Yes, sir." He saluted, turned his horse to the trail again, glanced back once to see the Colonel dismount and approach the stream for a drink. Then Captain Hart spurred his mount forward, and the band of men followed him toward the Sandy Creek plantation of Harmon Husband.

Farmer and political pamphleteer, Harmon Husband, sat on the high stool before his pine desk. He touched the feather of his quill pen to his cheek. He had been pronouncing words aloud to determine their best effect. He was searching for the rolling sounds that would catch men's spirits. It was his written word, he knew, that could give them reason, but it was the sound that would fire their hearts.

He smiled thoughtfully. He had been a student of words as far back as his youthful days in Maryland when he had walked his Grandfather Kinkey's farm, repeating over and over the Apostle's Creed or a passage from the Book of Common Prayer—supplications that had rolled with smooth undulation from his tongue.

Those had been the good days of the Lord, he thought; and it was pleasant to turn back the pages of his mind. He thought of the first sermon of the new rector of St. Stephen's Parish in Cecil County, Hugh Jones: "The Lord shall come with fire." Hugh Jones, the Oxford graduate, had preached many a sermon in St. Stephen's, but none was more clearly remembered. None had so deeply affected Harmon's life, for it was on that day that the world of mysticism was opened to him. Hugh Jones had done that for him, had made a wedge in the sky; and another great man, Whitefield, had bared the whole heaven for him.

Harmon Husband was a tall, thin man. He had an awkward appearance as he sat at the desk, yet he could move with the lithe grace of a forest animal. His features were craggy but clean-cut. His eyes were grey under his broad brow and there was a certain faraway look in them. His unruly brown hair was continually escaping the queue, giving him an untidy appearance which caused his wife, Amy, constant embarrassment. Now he drew his eyes away from the window and the spring fields. Again he studied the paper on his desk:

A BILL OF RIGHTS

The Lords Spiritual and Temporal, and Commons; Pursuant of their several letters and elections, being now assembled in full and free representation of this Nation; for the vindications and asserting of their Ancient Rights and Liberties, declare . . .

He threw down his pen in disgust. There he was again —carried away by words. These were phrases that many of his friends among the Regulators could not even understand.

He remembered so vividly what his kinsman Benjamin Franklin had said to him on his visit to Philadelphia: "I'm afraid, Harmon, that you're overpowered by the majesty of words. You've read Milton, no doubt; I can hear the echo of some of his lines. But, Harmon, a man appreciates those grand phrases only after study and reading. A man who gives his soul and body to the fields all day may not be captured by a Milton. If you really want to be a political pamphleteer, well and good for that. But you have to speak to the hearts of plain men, of simple folk who work, who work much more than they bother to think. You must say what you have to say in the simplest language so they'll understand— and remember."

Harmon sat at his desk and remembered. He remembered the way Franklin had looked over his narrow spectacles and said, "You want to convince folk that you say the truth? Then tell them plainly, Harmon. Forget your Church-of-England childhood, and forget your Whitefield." He had smiled then. "Come now, Harmon, keep your mind on your Quaker training—simplicity of speech, speech to the heart, is best. Indeed, it's the only weapon."

Those words came back to him with an increasing conviction. He tore up the paper on the desk, although paper was pitifully scarce, and began again:

A Bill of Rights

It is the right of the subject to petition the King.
Freedom of speech is the right of all subjects.
Excessive bail ought not be required.
No excessive fines ought to be imposed, nor cruel
or unusual punishment be inflicted.
A jury of peers is the right of *every* man.
Election of Colonial officers should be free.
Fees paid for the Register of Deeds to Sheriffs
    and Officials should be kept to legal amounts as
    prescribed by law.

Harmon Husband looked thoughtfully at the list of grievances and then wrote a final sentence which he underscored twice with his pen:

All protests should be put forth valiantly—according to law and without violence.

Captain Hart of the militia of Orange reined his horse and motioned for his men to wait in the broad yard before the plantation. He swung down from his mount, loosened his sword in the scabbard and strode forward to the long, low front porch. He rubbed his hand over the stubble of his beard as if to give himself courage. In two quick strides he was up the front stoop and facing the door. He raised his fist, hesitated, and then hammered it against the wood. He glanced back toward his men, then along the porch; he pounded again and shouted: "Open in the name of Colonel Fanning of Orange!" At the sound of approaching footsteps he rested one hand apprehensively on the hilt of his sword.

Captain Hart was not prepared to see a young woman at the door of the Husband household, and he stepped slightly back, surprised. She was dressed in a simple grey Friends costume. Her soft, blond hair had a lustrous quality in the morning light. The grey dress was enhanced by a fichu of soft white mull, which accentuated her firm, well-drawn figure. Her face seemed to reflect an inner serenity, compelling and pure. After she had opened the door to him she let her hands drop to her sides in a defenceless gesture; but when she spoke, her voice was clear and unafraid. The captain, staring at her with a mixture of anger and admiration, scarcely listened to her words.

"What do thee wish, sir? Thee has no need to pronounce the Colonel's name to gain entrance. Thine own is enough."

Captain Hart was confused. He had not expected to be received this way. Had the door been barred, had he been met by an armed man—by the Lord, had he even been spoken to with insolence!—he would have known what to do. He dropped his hand from the hilt of his sword and walked forward brusquely, rudely pushing past her even though she tried to step out of his way. He surveyed the long front hall silently, then turned abruptly toward her. He noted again the pleasant curve of her hips and the lines of her legs. She looked at him without fear, without hate, and with a certain pity as if she understood the workings of his mind.

"I want that damn Regulator," he demanded, feeling that the words might conceal his inadequacy and his slippery thoughts. "You bring him here!"

She seemed almost to smile, and then she shook her head slowly and answered, "Thee must be weary, Captain. There is no Regulator here. May it be that thee has lost thy way and come to the wrong home?"

"Don't take me for a fool!"

"But I don't."

"And don't lie to me." His voice rose in anger. "I came for Harmon Husband, and, by God, I'll have him!"

"But there was no intention of lying to thee, Captain. This is the home of Harmon Husband, but thee will not find him a Regulator."

"Get him," he snapped.

"My uncle is working at the moment, Captain, and I would not . . ."

The captain tensed; his right arm came half up as if he might strike her. "Did you hear me?" he barked.

Her cheeks reddened, but she made no effort to move away. Her gaze seemed to penetrate him.

The door to the right of the hallway opened. A tall, thin man appeared, holding a quill pen in his hand. He spoke even as he opened the door. "Niece Charity, what

is the sound———" He looked up to see the captain of
the militia and broke off his question.

"Aye! You're the one. I've seen you often enough in
Hillsborough."

Harmon Husband puzzled his brow for a moment and
walked slowly forward. "What is it you wish, sir?"

"You're under arrest."

"I don't think that I understand . . ."

Charity interrupted him and, turning to the Captain,
said, "Has thee a warrant for his arrest?"

The captain pivoted. "You'd better learn to hold your
tongue."

She repeated the question. "Has thee a warrant, Captain?"

He stiffened, his nostrils dilated, but his hand remained innocently at his side. "Aye, there's a warrant!"

"Then thee will let me see it?" She continued to speak
with the same quiet passion in her voice that had first
disturbed the captain.

Harmon Husband had advanced into the hall and he
put his hand on Charity's shoulder as if to calm her.
"Peace, Charity. If the Captain says he has a warrant,
we'd do well to believe him."

Angrily, the captain said, "You're dressed for riding
now. Let's be going."

Husband turned away. "I'll be with you as soon as I
speak with my wife."

"You'll be with me now," the captain said. He called
from the doorway, "Ashly, Morton, dismount!" The fat
tavern-keeper and the clerk swung down from their sad-
dles.

"There's no need for that," Harmon said. "My wife
and Charity Allen have no desire to see your men."

The captain raised his hand to restrain the two men
who were advancing toward the house. He unsheathed
his sword to make the capture look bolder before his
men and motioned Harmon Husband to the front door
and the stoop.

Two of the privates had brought a horse from the stable, already saddled for the journey. They grabbed Husband rudely and tied his hands with a leather strap
which they had found in the barn. They boosted him

onto the horse. The clerk reluctantly put the two pistols back into his belt, having had no excuse to use them. The murderer laughed openly at him, then took the reins of Husband's mount to lead it.

When Charity Allen and Amy Husband reached the front porch, the last rider was disappearing in the thickets beyond the barn. Amy stood helpless, her hands to her sides. She clutched a small purse of money which she had hoped her husband could use for bail. Her face seemed tired beyond its years, and when she turned to the younger girl, there were tears in her eyes.

"Charity, Charity," she said softly, "they take him for a rebel, for a warring man—but he's none of that. You know it to be true." Her voice broke for a moment. "You know he's not a Regulator. It's that Fanning . . ."

"Harmon has written pamphlets for the Regulators," Charity said.

"But he's not one of them. He's not for war!"

"Thee and I know it," Charity said. "But Colonel Fanning can't trouble himself with the truth."

"And what will they do with him now?"

"Have faith, Amy." Charity left the desparing woman on the porch and entered the house.

"Where is thee going?"

"To dress for riding" came the reply.

Amy turned toward the door without hope. "Thee can't do anything in Hillsborough."

"No" came the voice again. "I can do nothing alone. But there are those in the hills who would help him. I can pass the word to them."

Amy glanced again to the brush beyond the barn which still swayed gently where the riders had passed. A goldfinch darted downward, resting on one of the branches—and a door was closed in the wilderness.

The fort which had been constructed in the village of Hillsborough to hold offenders against the law, against the Crown, and against the honour of the gentlemen who ruled Orange, especially Edmund Fanning, was surrounded by a heavy guard of militiamen. The streets of the town were patrolled by armed guards.

The evening passed slowly for the Colonel as he wait-

ed in the home of the secretary to the Governor of
North Carolina. William Tryon's secretary, Edwards, sat
opposite Fanning at the large dining-room table. He was
bald, his face thinner than Fanning's, his dress less elegant. When he spoke it was with an air of deference to
the Colonel and Assemblyman from Orange, the close
friend of his employer. His serious countenance belied
the tone of his voice, for he did not approve of all of
Fanning's actions.

"I should hang him now," Fanning was saying. "Justice Lloyd has just issued the warrant for me, so everything seems in order. I had him charged with inciting
riots. That *could* be enough to do away with him."

Edwards rubbed his chin thoughtfully, then reached
for his glass of port. "It might be a dangerous move,
Colonel."

"Dangerous! I say it's damned dangerous to let him
stay alive. Haven't his writings stirred up the county?
Nay, even the Province? He's had the effrontery to send
word directly to the Governor that we cheat the people
on their court fees. He claims I steal land deeds!"

Edwards allowed himself a slight smile. "Don't you,
Colonel?"

"By God, Edwards, are you going against me?"

"No, no," Edwards hastened to say. "Not against you,
Colonel. That would be a rather foolish thing for me to
do. You know the Governor's mind far better than I."

"Thank you for that observation, Mr. Edwards."

"But you've also seen his requests," Edwards continued.

"Sir?"

"I'm referring only to his letters in which he says that
he knows the farmers are being charged exorbitant court
fees—and that he disapproves of it."

"Then such affairs should be between the Governor
and me, should they not?"

"Yes, Colonel."

Fanning rubbed his eyes and yawned. He drummed
his fingers on the mahogany table, and then he stood up
peremptorily and walked to the window. He pulled aside
the curtain and pushed the shutters wide. The heavy
curtains and the shutters had muffled the street sounds,

but now the noise broke into the solitude of the room. Outside in the streets he could see torches. Fanning let the curtain fall back into place and returned to his chair at the table.

"You've noticed that there seems to be a near riot in the streets?"

"I have," Edwards answered.

"Doesn't it bother you?"

"No, sir. I suspect it's a riot of your own making, Colonel. When I see that you have no worry, then I have none."

"Edwards, you surprise me," Fanning said candidly. "I hope your new assistant may be less perceptive. I'd prefer not to have all my plans known to hirelings."

Edwards ignored the final insult and said, "My assistant will be a man from the coastal plains. He may still be perceptive, but I assure you that he'll be symphathetic toward you. Loyalty to the Governor breeds a sympathy with you, sir."

Fanning was looking toward the curtained window again, and when he spoke the words were directed more to himself than to Edwards. "No, it's unfortunate that I can't afford to order Husband hanged. I *should* be able to—" he leaned back in his chair and frowned—"but there are some things for which it is best not to take responsibility. Anyway, by midnight the hanging will have been done for me."

"The riot is part of it?"

Fanning glanced at Edwards. There was an edge of annoyance in his tone when he said, "Of course. Captain Hart has my permission to take the prisoner from the gaol and to lead him through the streets. The riot will be at its peak—a riot against the violence of the Regulators." He turned his hand over and examined the narrow palm. "The rest is a matter of course."

"I can't say that I approve of your actions, Colonel."

"I don't ask your approval, sir."

"But . . ."

"And there's nothing you'll do about it."

"There's nothing I *can* do."

The futility in Edwards' voice caused the Colonel to look at him in amusement. "Quite right, Edwards, there's nothing you can do. Oh, I suppose you could speak to the Governor about it all sometime, and you might even mutter something about its illegality. But it wouldn't bring back the dead, would it?"

"No," Edwards said wearily.

"And there'll be peace in Orange for a change."

"Do you really believe that, Colonel?" Edwards reached for the port to fill his glass again.

"Certainly I believe it, Mr. Edwards. I *must* believe in something. You hold me too cheaply, sir. A man must believe in something."

"Yes, I suppose so."

It was nearly midnight when a young corporal pounded on the door of Isaac Edwards' house. Fanning was still sitting at the great dining-room table. His eyes were focused on the heavy red curtains, as if to open them meant to command performance of a play which he had written, to demand the hanging scene which he had devised. He was author and audience of his success.

Edwards opened the front door himself, having sent the servants away to bed. The breathless militiaman in front of him said, "Colonel Fanning. The prisoner demands to see the Colonel. He's here, isn't he?"

"Just a moment." Edwards shut the door and returned to the dining-room where he gave the Colonel the message.

"Damn it!" Fanning exploded. "You knew I didn't want to be involved in this! There was no need to let him know I was here." But even as he spoke he had risen and taken his cape from the bench by the wall. He met the militiaman at the door, spoke with him briefly and then walked with him into the street, leaving the door wide.

There was a multitude of torches in the streets. The sounds of strident voices slashed through the night air. Colonel Fanning followed the corporal toward the square west of the gaol, the center of disturbance. Fanning could tell by the shouts that the prisoner had already been taken from the gaol. He only hoped that Husband would be hanging by the time he reached him.

"Colonel Fanning! Colonel!" The plump tavern-keeper trotted beside him.

"Don't bother me," Fanning said angrily.

"But, sir, you don't understand," the man persisted.

"I understand you haven't finished your work. That's enough, isn't it?"

"Sir, you'll see that we . . ."

Fanning ignored him, and pushed his way into the crowd that ranged in a great circle about a central figure on horseback. Five militiamen surrounded the prisoner, their guns lowered.

Harmon Husband was seated backwards on the horse. His legs were strapped about the animal, his hands bound behind him.

"Here's the Colonel!" someone shouted. A path was made for Fanning through the press of men.

"We can't do it!" whispered a voice beside him. He turned petulantly to see the sweat-soaked face of Captain Hart.

He glanced icily toward Hart and then back to the prisoner. "What is it you want from me, Husband? Permission to stir up more riots?"

"No. I want my release."

"Release! You're guilty of inciting riots. There'll be no release!"

"I've had no trial."

"And you'll get none."

"I have a right to trial by jury."

Colonel Fanning placed his hands on his hips. "It would seem to me, Husband, that the good people of Hillsborough have already found you guilty. Arbitration, not jury trials—isn't that the custom of you Regulators?" He paused, then said with a touch of drama in his voice, "I wonder if these good people could be dissuaded from hanging you this moment. The Lord knows you ought to be!"

"Aye! That's the word," someone shouted.

"Take him to the tree!" yelled the tavern-keeper.

But for the most part the crowd about the prisoner was silent. Quickly Fanning scanned the mob, half masked by the night and the shadowy smoke of the torches, and felt a menace in its quietness. Suddenly he realized that too few of the faces were familar to Hillsborough. The men about the prisoner were from the back country. Somehow the cry had been let loose in the hills beyond his village.

The back country men were there, and the spirit which had driven them did not matter to him. He did not picture the spreading of the word of Husband's capture: the farmers who left their ploughs, the strong hands which gripped rifles from wall-pegs, the lean frontiersmen who mounted horse and drove hard on Hillsborough with a single thought in mind—to save Harmon Husband.

"Why don't you let him go?"

Another voice: "Ought to put Fanning up there."

"Cut the ropes!"

Fanning felt the temper of the crowd and shouted quickly, "Husband! You say you want your release?"

"Aye! He does!" someone shouted.

"Peace!" Fanning shouted. "He'd have his freedom if one of our militiamen hadn't taken him from the gaol." He glared at Captain Hart. "Justice Lloyd is preparing a release now."

"Well, set him free."

Fanning walked back and forth along the fringe of the torch-lit circle. "Husband, if you're returned to Sandy Creek, do you swear to incite no more riots? Will you swear not to support the Regulators?"

"I'll not concern myself with your fees, if that's what you mean."

"Will you stop aiding the Regulators?"

"Under duress I'll promise that. But I reserve the right to meet with my friends to speak my own heart."

"You've heard his oath?" Again Fanning looked the mob over. "He swears to cease inciting riots. He swears he will not support the Regulators. I'll take the man at his word."

Harmon Husband listened as his promise was distorted. He was about to object, when Fanning shouted suddenly, "Release the prisoner. Release him! I accept his word."

There was no chance to make his objections heard

above the shouts of the crowd. The smoke of the torches stung his nostrils. He felt the cords being cut loose from his wrists. He was helped down from the horse, and the press of men was about him. But Husband knew many had turned away discouraged. He knew that many had heard only Fanning's restatement of his promise, and that they felt they had been betrayed by the man whom they had come to save.

Fanning was close by him, watching as he stroked his numbed wrists. "You're lucky, Husband. I should add this mob as another crime against you."

"Do you think you silenced *all* of those folk?"

"Enough of them."

"We'll be heard, Colonel Fanning."

"When?" he snapped.

"In the hour of our own conscience, sir."

Fanning had already turned away. Words from a madman meant nothing to him.

2

Hillary Caswell

The country of the coastal plain was full and rich with late autumn. The Speaker of the Assembly of North Carolina, Richard Caswell, reined his horse and pointed his riding crop to the south. A wedge of geese were flying across the leaden sky toward the great pocosin which bordered the Alligator River. Even as he pointed the long wedge split into several smaller groups, and with a great crying and honking they settled slowly. Caswell's proud bay pranced nervously, impatiently.

"The geese must be over the lake now," Caswell said. "It won't be long."

The handsome young man on the roan beside him turned partly in his saddle. He had the easy grace of a man accustomed to the saddle, and his bearing and dress were those of an aristocrat. "Three miles, would you say, Cousin Richard?"

"Just about. Certainly no more, Hillary. Then you'll be at your new home." Richard hesitated for a moment as he studied the face of the younger man. There was a certain tension in the features, but finally the lines relaxed, and he smiled.

Richard continued, "I imagine you'll find Manor House to your liking. But you'll have so many names of cousins to learn that you may not be steady for a while. They're good folk. I suppose the lads will forgive you the fact that you're from Maryland—and I'm certain the lassies will."

Hillary Caswell laughed. "Now, Richard," he said, "how am I going to have time for them? You know the course I've set for myself."

"True, true. I know." Richard frowned slightly as he spoke. They moved their horses forward and rode single file along the trail which would eventually lead them to Manor House.

Once, after they had passed the most dismal edges of the swamplands and emerged from the cool darkness into the brazen glare of sky, Richard drew up his mount again. "Hillary, you're positive that you want to pursue this idea of joining the Governor's staff?"

"Pursue it? For the time being I have no choice."

"You're the last man who should say that. You've a plantation in Maryland, and your father left you land here in North Carolina. There's no reason you should spend your time in politics."

No, Hillary thought, there were no reasons except a promise he had made. It was a promise which bound him, even though the pull of the land, the feel of the rich, dark earth, was strong in him. Those thoughts of the land had caused the tension in his features. He shrugged away his desire.

Richard was speaking again. "I know Governor Tryon fairly well, Hillary. Remind me to speak to him about your position. Isaac Edwards definitely accepted you as his assistant, didn't he?"

"He accepted me last year—but you know I wasn't able to begin while my father was sick."

Richard nodded quickly. "Yes, yes, I understand that. But this position—you're to take it up following Christmas?"

"Before, if I should choose. With the Assembly meeting I should think that Edwards might have need of me."

"No doubt of that. Still . . . Well, I just don't understand. I'm not convinced that politics can ever be a profession in itself. I may be Speaker of the Assembly—but I'm a planter first. And I've watched you, Hillary. You love the land too much to get your heart full of New Bern and all the small men *that* world admits. Be a planter—then a politician. What would be your objection to that? You might love the land so much that you'd never go to New Bern."

Hillary smiled and dismissed the argument as easily as he could. Richard Caswell's observations were too accurate for comfort.

They had crossed a small, rough-hewn bridge and turned into a long, curving avenue of cedar trees when Richard called over his shoulder, jokingly, "Perhaps one of our young lassies at Manor House can convince you to settle on your land here. They've a charm that I'm afraid the Governor lacks—for all his virtues."

Hillary smiled, but it was only a reflex to the jesting tone of Richard Caswell's words. His mind was on the tumble and puzzle of recollections called up by the word *father*. It had been only a month! He remembered the long talks which he and his father had held together— the preciousness of life as his father lay dying.

He would never forget the words that had passed during those hours. Onrushing death had sharpened both men's senses: each hour had been rich—those were the hours to be filled with memory.

"Now, son, I want you to think seriously about politics." Lawrence Caswell had been calm as he spoke though the pain which bit into his chest made him blanch. On the verge of death he spoke as reasonably as if he lectured on Maryland's history, as though he digressed on the late-summer weather. "It gives me a good feeling to know that in spite of what happens to me— and I suppose we both know what will—that you'll pursue your plans with Edwards. You remember when I visited Cousin Richard at Kings Town? I told Edwards then that you had an aptitude for those affairs. I meant it. I can feel it. And then, you might never be a proper planter. . . ."

"Never?"

"Now, son, I wouldn't be willing to say 'never,' and sometimes I have to admit that I've seen you with the look of the land in your eyes. Made me think of your Uncle Matthew—" Lawrence Caswell was racked with a sudden spell of coughing—"but there's time for that. There'll be time."

His last night was in no way different from the other evenings of his life. There was no bitterness in his heart toward parting, and he would not show the final pain of living even as he lay weak and pale in the giant four-poster bed with Hillary sitting by his side. The conversation had turned again to Hillary's future.

"I always wanted to live in North Carolina," his father mused. "But I never could bring myself to move. Still . . . I wanted more than just this plantation; I wanted to be a complete man! I thought I could break free from living on day by day in the same round—oh, it's hard to explain, but I wanted to be in everything, a part of everything. That's the way a man *should* be. Few men can reach that goal, though."

Lawrence Caswell breathed heavily. Hillary touched his hand to his father's frail shoulder, to quiet him, to keep him from talking. Nothing would stay the old man, for he knew the end was near and there was no time left to spare himself pain.

"Few men can go beyond the routine of everyday life," Lawrence said. "I've known some who did . . . and I envied them. Your Cousin Richard is one. And I met a man in Tyrrell County called Rutledge. He's a complete man, Hillary. But I . . . I couldn't be everything. I could be only one thing. I've been a planter, no more than that—" Lawrence paused to gain his breath —"but no less, either—no less," he repeated proudly. "I want to see you hold a position in government for a while; I want to see you . . ." The sick man's words had trailed off and he full suddenly asleep.

Hillary waited by the bedside numbly, and later, when Lawrence woke again, it was to resume the same conversation, briefly.

"There'll be time for planting someday, my son. But promise me, Hillary, promise me you'll try the state before the land. Promise me that one thing!"

Without hesitation Hillary had said, "I promise." His father never guessed of the pain in his son's heart when he spoke those words, never knew of the sorrow Hillary felt at his promise to leave the land he had grown to love.

There was deep joy in a plantation. It came in the

touch of the earth, rich, sweet-smelling, as it crumbled in a man's strong hands. It came with a swelling heart when the corn grew tall and the tobacco leaves spread wide. It came in the songs of harvest. There was music in the thump of kegs and casks on wooden wharfs; a breath of freedom in the sails that filled your harbour.

Lawrence Caswell had reached out feebly and taken Hillary's hand. "I send you out to do all my business in this world, Hillary. You'll do it well, won't you, son?"

"I promise I will."

And again Lawrence Caswell seemed to fall suddenly asleep—but he did not waken as before. Hillary had leaned forward and kissed his father's cheek. Then he was alone.

They had spoken of many things in those final days: of Richard Caswell—the man who now rode beside Hillary along the stately rows of cedars toward Manor House. Outwardly, Lawrence had said, Richard would seem like any other gentleman of the East: well-educated, polished and obedient to the obligations of his class. But he was different from the other gentlemen in that he was a leader, with greater abilities and strength than they. "Nay," Lawrence had said, "there is one other virtue: he has the power to mediate among men. It is a rare power."

Richard Caswell's voice cut through his memories. "One more turn and we'll be in sight of Manor House."

"And that will be a pleasure to me," Hillary said. "The day's been too long already. Then, of course, sir, I'm eager to meet my relatives."

"Just don't let the number of them appal you," Richard warned good-naturedly.

From the path ahead the sound of hoofs, and a moment later Richard's body servant, Puti, and a groom, Mombassa, who had crossed Albemarle Sound before the Caswells, rode out to greet them.

"Sar, they knows you arrivin'." Puti spoke with a magnificent bass richness. His grin was broad in anticipation of Richard's next command.

"Ride on to the house, Puti. If the folk know they're to have us as visitors we shan't rob them of a moment."

"No, sar!" The two slaves wheeled their mounts and spurred them back down the avenue.

Richard's eyes twinkled as he turned to Hillary. "Puti has a full sense of the dramatic. There's nothing better in the world than to arrange the grand entrance for me. Any separation of more than a day calls for ceremony."

"And you'd rather not disappoint him?"

"I couldn't," Richard said, "even though the introductions were to my enemies."

"I've heard that you have none of those."

"None yet," Richard said wearily, "but I may have. I may have."

Then they made the final turn along the cedar path and the large two-story house was in view. Lower wings stretched on either side, and the structure was in a setting of towering, moss-covered oaks. Hillary could not help feeling a slight tinge of disappointment. He had expected to see a large brick home like the manor houses of Maryland. The one before him was wooden—clapboard painted white. It couldn't be called a great house; it wasn't even so large as his own at Sedgefield. Well enough, his friends had warned him! They had taken great pains to explain that North Carolina was provincial. The people, they had said, were backward—if not bordering on a savage state. Hillary glanced toward the fine figure of Richard Caswell and smiled at the thought. No, one could hardly call the people of North Carolina backward or savage.

He had little time for contemplation. The slaves had met Squire Matthew Caswell at the entrance of the avenue, and the Squire galloped his bay down the broad, tree-lined path to meet them.

Matthew Caswell sat tall and straight in the saddle, an impressive man with a well-set head and erect figure. His slender bay danced nervously, hoofs pressing the rich earth. Richard and Matthew both dismounted swiftly and clasped hands in a hearty greeting.

"You're looking well," Richard said. "It's good to see you again." He beckoned to Hillary, who swung down from his saddle. "Come and meet your uncle, Hillary. A true kinsman. This is Matthew, chief of the clan of Caswell."

Hillary felt his hand in a firm, strong grip, and he looked into flashing blue eyes which were proud, yet kind and understanding.

"Welcome, Hillary. Welcome for your dear father's sake—and welcome for your own. Our young folk have been impatient for your arrival. They're curious about you outlanders—you Marylanders."

Richard had motioned for the grooms who had followed Matthew. They led the horses while the three men walked toward Manor House.

"And where are the lads now?" Richard asked.

Matthew chuckled. "They're out shooting geese—" he corrected himself—"rather, they're shooting *at* geese."

"Come now, Matthew," Richard chided, "that Robin Chapman's not a bad shot. I'd like to pit him against Hillary. We'd have a good match."

"You're a good shot?" Matthew asked Hillary.

"No, not at all," Hillary said.

"He means that he doesn't like guns," Richard explained, "but, I assure you, we ate well on our journey. He has one of those disturbing talents—accuracy."

"Then we really *should* have a match, but now—" Matthew turned to Hillary—"the lassies are here. Might they be of interest to you?"

"Uncle Matthew, I'm afraid women are always of interest."

"Now that surprises me," Richard said. "I think he pretends for you. The only talk I can get from him concerns the relative state of policies and politics in North Carolina and Maryland."

"I've heard you have a position in the Governor's household. You're to be assistant to Edwards—Isaac Edwards, isn't it?"

"Yes, sir."

"Does that mean you plan to travel soon to New Bern?"

"As soon as possible, Uncle Matthew. First I'd like the blessing of Cousin Richard; otherwise I might find some of the doors shut against me."

"Palace doors, I take it you mean," Matthew said dryly.

Richard laughed. "You can see, Hillary, that Matthew's tone indicates he doesn't quite approve of the Palace Governor Tryon is having built."

"Not when I'm paying for it, Cousin," Matthew said testily.

"We all pay for it."

"We pay enough for ten palaces—none of which I'd want. Tell me, Richard, where *does* all the money go? Just to Tryon? Or to his sheriffs?"

"Now, Matthew, don't give your nephew *that* opinion of the Governor. If he's to work for His Excellency, he should be allowed to have respect for him."

"You'll learn, my boy," Matthew said wisely. "You'll learn."

Hillary admitted reluctantly to himself that he had much to learn about the workings of the government of North Carolina.

On approach, it could be seen clearly how Manor House had been constructed in the center of a wide circle of tall trees—ancient oaks, cedars and pines. To the west of the house were the dependencies, barns and stables. Beyond lay the meadows and the fields of corn—the brown stalks broken with the autumn. The land, still green, was dotted with grazing cattle.

Partially behind the east wing of Manor House was the kitchen, and, farther back, separated from it by a row of young cedars, was the dormitory and a series of small buildings used for storage.

The warmth of Matthew Caswell's greeting had changed Hillary's opinion of Manor House. It's a goodly estate, he thought, and then asked himself how he could have been so mean as to think otherwise. He remembered, too, that there were other Caswell estates in Tyrrell County.

"Crops are fair this year," Matthew was saying to Richard. "We've especially good corn." Then he turned to Hillary. "Politics!" There was disapproval in his tone. "I'd wager that was the life Lawrence imagined he longed for." Matthew chuckled. "But he could never tear himself away from the land. Instinct kept him where he belonged. Now you take Richard—he has the same instinct, but won't recognize it. His only happy feeling comes from working his estates, while the poor man mistakes it for just an occasional relief from the politics of New Bern. Isn't that so, Richard?"

Richard smiled. His contentment at his return to Manor House would not admit him to be drawn into an argument. He adroitly changed the subject by saying, quite casually, "I've heard that the Governor is laying a new tax on the exportation of corn."

Hillary noted the look of concern which came immediately to Matthew's face. "I've heard nothing of *that* one! I've two ships loading now over at Joseph Chapman's yards bound for Nassau and Antigua. You don't mean it, Richard?"

"Best send them out as soon as possible, Matt. Remember, you've had no official notification, so get them sailing at once."

Matthew hesitated on the steps leading to the main entrance of the house. With a look of annoyance he turned toward Hillary and Richard. "By gad, this *is* too much! A man can't hope to make any money these days. Do you spend all your time with Tryon inventing new taxes?"

"We've been considering one on air," Richard said pleasantly.

"I don't doubt it for a moment."

"It seems you have the same problems we have in Maryland with Governor Sharpe," Hillary suggested. "So I'd think the taxes were more the work of London than of our Governors."

"Perhaps," Matthew said, looking down at the steps. "But I'd swear that Tryon needs no urging from London on that score. In any case, we've got the taxes and we can't make money. . . ." He called to a small Negro boy who was watching them timidly from the side of the house. The lad came scurrying forward. "Tell Puti to give the gentlemen's horses an extra eight ears of corn —but to let them cool off first. And mind you say to Puti he's to give them a mighty good currying before he puts on the blankets."

"Yes, sar." The boy turned and ran toward the barn. Matthew led the way up the broad stoop. A smiling old Negro with grey hair opened the front door for them ceremoniously. "Mister Richard, it does us proud to welcome you to Manor House and dis young gemman. Is he Master Lawrence's son? A fine young gemman."

"Ebenezer, I'll swear you look younger each time I see you," Richard joked.

Ebenezer grinned, caught the cape which Richard tossed to him and laid it carefully on a bench near the front door as the men entered the hall.

The hall extended the depth of the house. At the far end, opposite the front door, was a large fire-place which held six-foot logs. The doors on either side of the fire-place led to a small back room and to a covered passage-way to the kitchen. The stairway to the second story was just to the right of the main hall. This central room—for it was room rather than hall—was comfortably furnished in massive English design. The tall, wide-bottomed chairs were covered with crewel-work. Mirrors in carved gold frames hung on the side walls, pitched to reflect the long Elizabethan table and ornately carved benches. One could tell at a glance that it was a countryman's home. Huge antlers nailed to the wall near the door were crowded with hunting caps and three-cornered hats. Brightly lined capes and leather jackets were piled on a bench braced against the stairwell; hunting boots were piled carelessly beneath. Richly coloured Turkey carpets lay on the floor, and the wide boards were polished and gleaming. The doors to either wing, the drawing-room and the dining-room, were closed, but through the glass Hillary could see soft fires burning in the grates at the ends of both. Ahead of him in the main hall, in front of the long brass fender, two old hounds lay sleeping. As the men approached, the dogs had both raised their heads, gazed, then rested forward again on their outstretched paws. Now and then an eye was opened to view the newcomers.

A series of old hunting prints decorated the walls. Hillary remembered seeing many such living-halls in England when he had visited in Devon and Hertfordshire. Before him was a comfortable, lived-in room.

Ebenezer, having disposed of all travelling capes and hats, left the room to fetch a hot posset for the gentlemen. Matthew took a clay pipe from the rack beside the fire-place and tamped it. "Sit down, sit down. Elizabeth and the girls will be in presently."

Richard, following his host's example, took a fresh church-warden pipe from the rack. He put a quill into the fire-place and lighted it. Matthew, having adjusted himself in his chair, said, "I hope you're going to stay long enough to get in a little shooting. We've hundreds of geese on our lake and myriads of ducks. And, too, we've had some luck with our deer drives this year. Say you'll stay for a week or two at least." He looked toward Hillary for a response.

"Thank you, Uncle Matthew, I should like to very much, but I think the length of my stay rather depends on Richard."

"Well, Richard's going to be here for several weeks, certainly."

Richard laughed. "Ah, Matthew, it's good of you. You know how I love this country and the contentment I find here. But I couldn't stay for more than a few days. You know the Palace is being finished, and the Governor should be coming from New Brunswick."

"That's no excuse, Richard."

"Let me ask you a similar question, then. Why don't you come and visit me for a while at New Bern?"

"Impossible!" Matthew said. "I'm a planter, and you know there is scarcely time enough in the winter to prepare for spring planting."

Ebenezer returned with the hot possets and served the men. The drink relaxed them, and Matthew continued the conversation. "Anyway, Richard, even if there weren't business to keep me here, I couldn't tear myself away from this land. My first love is here."

"You always were a stubborn man, Matthew," Richard said. He turned to Hillary. "Since you've got your mind on government, you probably won't have much to say to your Uncle Matthew—" he smiled—"unless, of course, you choose to speak of the Governors themselves. That's Matthew's special field of study in our government."

"Aye," Matthew said, "and they've sent us some sorry Royal Governors . . . except, perhaps, Gabriel Johnston. He loved the Colony—wanted it to prosper and to grow. Dobbs might have been all right, but he had no health. Now Tryon?" He pitched his voice higher in question, then continued, having settled the problem in his mind. "Tryon likes his palaces and nurses his pride. And that reminds me, Richard—one of our kin, Spruill, in the Assembly, told me that even *you* had come to grips with the Governor on several occasions."

Richard flushed slightly. "We've had our difficulties, I'll grant that, but I agree with him on this dispute between the East and the West. Those Regulators in Orange and beyond have to be crushed. We can't have a hand of fanatics forcing our hand. It's anarchy!"

Matthew shook his head. "It's bad—bad when two parts of the Colony start fighting each other. We've enough troubles across the sea without wasting our energy on each other."

Richard stood up impatiently. "But you're not going to hold with those fanatics around Hillsborough, are you?"

"I'm just a planter," Matthew interrupted. "I told you I don't understand these matters. I *do* know that your man Fanning is having trouble with the people up there. And when an officer of the Crown has trouble with its subjects, well, it seems likely to me that something may be said on both sides—mind you, Richard, I'm only guessing."

"First of all, let's clear one thing: Fanning's not *my* man. If he's anybody's, he's the Governor's." Richard turned to Hillary. "If you knew the reports we've received on the Regulators! I tell you they are utterly lawless. Fanning has sent in a dozen accounts of riots in the village." Richard sat down wearily.

"Perhaps those reports may have slighted some of the facts," Matthew suggested.

"Lord, Matt! I'm not saying our government's perfect, but I say we've got to take pains to preserve the good that we have. In any case, the Crown must maintain its authority and a decent order. Husband, Howell,

Butler—they'll break the Colony's back if they're left free to their own designs."

Richard would have gone on, but Matthew interrupted with a hint of relief in his voice. "Ah, here comes Elizabeth with the lassies." He rose as he spoke.

3

Manor House

Stately Elizabeth Caswell moved gracefully down the stairs and into the hall where the men awaited her. She was a tall woman with brownish-red hair, rich colour that was almost auburn. She had an erect carriage, a regal bearing: that manner of confidence which Hillary had noted in all the Caswells of North Carolina. Elizabeth was smiling, and her face had a warm, pleasant beauty.

Behind Elizabeth, hesitant, waiting for introduction, were three young women. The younger daughter, Hillary had been told, was Angela. She was only fifteen. Her hair was a pale, ash blond, and her figure was small and compact. Ann, the elder, was rather sedate. Her complexion was dark; her expression serious—quite different from Angela's. But Hillary's eyes and thoughts went to the third young woman, a red-head with quick movement and a roguish gleam in her light-green eyes. She stood slightly apart from the two sisters.

Richard had come forward to greet Madam Caswell. He kissed her cheek and held both of her hands in his. "My dear Elizabeth. More enchanting, more beautiful than ever!" he exclaimed.

Elizabeth Caswell blushed and shook her head. "Positively lawless to say such untruth. I can see why you're a successful politician."

Richard laughed. "With you, Elizabeth, there's no need for flattery. I speak only the fact."

"Ah, begone with you, Richard. How you would teach the lassies to exaggerate!"

But Hillary observed as she approached him that Richard's words had pleased her. "And this is Hillary," she said as she took his hand and kissed him lightly. She drew back to survey him. "You're Lawrence's own son and a true Caswell. I hope you will stay with us for a long, long time." She turned slightly. "But here, you must meet my girls. This is Ann; and this, Angela." She motioned with her hand. "And this red-headed lass is Cecelia Chapman, our dear cousin."

The girls curtsied solemnly, but their eyes were sparkling.

"Off with you, young people! Take your new cousin into the drawing-room." She explained to Hillary, "They've been looking for your coming ever since we received Richard's letter telling us he was bringing you to North Carolina."

The girls had made no move, but were looking at him shyly. "Go on with you!" Madam Caswell urged. "Hillary, you're in for a trial and you'd as well get it over with. They're dying to ask you about the latest Eastern Shore fashions. Are the ladies wearing powdered hair? And are farthingales still in fashion?"

"Mother!" Ann's face was bright red. "How can Cousin Hillary know anything about Maryland fashions?"

Cecelia could not help laughing at that, a low rippling laugh that was contagious. Hillary glanced at her quickly, then he, too, joined in the laughter. "But really," he said, "I don't know much about Eastern Shore fashions. I've been away in England and on the Continent."

The girls crowded about him then. "Ah, London! Do tell us."

They opened the drawing-room doors and entered. Hillary sat down on a long bench near the window. Ann and Angela seated themselves on either side of him, while Cecelia placed herself in the chair before him.

"I've braced myself," he said. "Begin."

"Yes, this is much better," Cecelia said. "Let's get down to serious affairs. What were the ladies wearing in London? Are they putting their hair high in the French

manner any longer? And are the skirts wide?
Yes . . . that's the real problem, are the skirts wide?"

Angela said, "Cecelia's father buys her anything she
likes—lutestrings, calabash hats. His ships go right up to
Tilbury dock. . . ." Her voice trailed off as if she were
aware that she had given too much praise to another
woman. Angela smoothed her full, blue taffeta skirt in
sudden disinterest.

"Do young ladies powder their hair of an evening?"
Ann asked.

"But your hair is beautiful now," Hillary said. "Why
should you worry about the fashions?"

Ann blushed again; Hillary was certain she had practised that art for a long time.

"Oh, he's worse than Cousin Richard," Cecelia said,
leaning back in the chair. "I should never trust him."

"Girls, give me some time. Let me answer before my
character's torn apart." He counted on his fingers.
"One: skirts were full, very full when I left London;
they rustled a lot—but I haven't any idea what made
that swishing sound."

The girls laughed. "We know—taffeta petticoats."

"Second question: powder?"

"Yes."

"Young girls do *not* powder their hair; some older
women leave it off, too. Third: as for tall hair—I've
seen it mounting to the stars with a ship in full sail on
the top. But that was an old woman, and naturally I
didn't observe her too closely."

"I presume that was to attract attention to the ship
and not to the face—which was probably old and wrinkled," Angela said. Her wide blue eyes were looking
into his in perfect innocence.

"A pleasant thought," Hillary said and then, glancing
toward Cecelia, added, "but the young girls wear no
such folderols in their hair. Sometimes a long, soft curl
is permitted to fall over one shoulder."

Ann knit her brows. "I really do suspect men when
they're experts on these affairs."

"No. I've changed my mind," Cecelia said, placing a
finger thoughtfully to her lips. "He's really an innocent
lamb."

"Thank you, at last."

"Good heavens," Cecelia said, "don't take it as a compliment, Cousin! Now tell us about the hunting clothes. Do the ladies wear velvet? In colours? Hats with plumes? Hunting pink?"

"That *does* interest you?" Hillary asked.

"Hunting always interests Cecelia," Angela said. "No matter what the game."

Cecelia glanced at Angela, a look of amusement in her bright eyes.

Hillary took note of the exchange but went on to answer the question put to him. "Well, it all seems a matter of preference. I noticed that the best riders wore not too long skirts, and pink coats cut almost like a man's. Their hair was smooth and trim under a net. . . . I say, I'm not really a fashion authority."

"You're doing very well," Cecelia said brightly. "Aren't you paying court to some London lady or a girl of the Eastern Shore? Come now, confess, Cousin."

"Miss Cecelia, I assure you I court no one but myself."

"Such a pity!" she said. "A young man going completely to waste. Cousins, we must do something about this."

Hillary looked at the laughing lips of Cecelia Chapman. Fashions, he thought—he should know better than to talk of things of which he was ignorant. The sisters' interest seemed sincere—but not Cecelia's. In each remark she made he noted a hint of laughter. In each movement of her hands, the tilt of her head, in the way her lips moved, he felt a slight mockery that matched the mockery in her eyes.

He was trying to think of words to say to Cecelia Chapman when Ann interrupted his thoughts. "Do you like to hunt, Cousin Hillary? We'll be having a hunt before Boxing Day."

"Very much," he answered, his thoughts still on Cecelia Chapman.

Angela's soft voice broke in. "I think people who hunt all the time and are so distracted over horses, get to look like horses."

"Angela is afraid of them," Ann explained.

"And you?" Hillary asked Cecelia.

"Of course not."

Angela pouted. "I always fall off, Hillary. They all make fun of me. And I think they're very cruel."

Ann smiled and said, "Angela has bad luck. Even our little piebald pony runs away when Angela gets on his back. Cecelia, remember when Gyps got into the pocosin by the Scuppernong? What a sight Angela was then!"

"I think you're horrid, Ann. Hillary will think me a goose." Her round blue eyes clouded over. For a moment Hillary felt sorry for his little blond cousin. She could appear so fragile and defenceless.

"I won't think you a goose, Angela," he said. "Plenty of people don't like to ride, and I'm sure they wouldn't get near a horse if there were any other means of transportation." Angela raised her eyes to him gratefully, and then she turned toward Cecelia with a triumphant flash.

"You *will* be here for the hunt, won't you?" Ann asked. She brushed back her dark hair. "You're not going to ride off to New Bern with Cousin Richard?"

"I'm not certain about that yet. We'll probably decide to-night."

Cecelia Chapman appeared surprised. "To New Bern? Have you affairs to take you there?"

"I shall have," Hillary said. "I'll be assistant to the Governor's secretary."

"But I thought Squire Matthew told us you had a plantation in Maryland, and some land here in North Carolina?"

"That's true."

"And you have no intention of being a planter?" she asked incredulously. "I don't understand."

"No. For the present I'm interested in government." He knew he could not explain the promise he had made to his father.

Cecelia Chapman was openly disappointed, as if he had not come up to her expecations. When she spoke to him after that, there seemed to be a different tone in her voice. The teasing, the touch of light mockery, was gone. For the moment the matter was dismissed, and they began to speak about their various cousins.

"You'll never remember all their names," Angela said.

"There are Meredith, John and Robin," Cecelia said; "we're all Chapmans. And there are Gregory and Matthew—they're Caswells."

Ann broke in: "Then there's a mess of cousins like the Spruills, Davenports, Phelpses, Blounts and a host of others, but you won't have to meet all of them to-day."

They continued giving names of the near and the distant, and Hillary was on the verge of throwing up his hands to bring the lists to a close when Elizabeth Caswell opened the door to the drawing-room. "You're surviving?" she asked in mild surprise.

"Barely."

"Your Cousin Richard has gone up to rest," she said. "He told me to ask you to come up after your ordeal. Eb will show you to your room. You must be exhausted after your journey."

Hillary thanked Madam Caswell and excused himself from the young women. Ebenezer was waiting for him in the hall and Hillary followed him up the broad stairway to the second floor and along the hallway to his room.

Richard Caswell had already undressed and wrapped himself in a heavy robe. He was lying on one of the great canopied beds, and when Hillary entered he rolled on his side and asked, "Did you prove yourself an expert on the latest fashions?"

"Cousin Richard, there'll never be a way to satisfy women."

Richard laughed, and rolled on his back again. "No. But it's the curse of man that he must continually try. I called for you only out of my merciful heart. Now if you'd rather . . ."

"Thank you, but no. I feel as tired as you after to-day. Believe me when I say that your gesture was truly noble."

Richard Caswell shrugged. "Humane perhaps. I wouldn't dignify it by calling it noble. And on the subject of the humane, Eb's going to bring us a bite to eat and something to drink. We can rest until supper-time."

Hillary had slipped off his high boots, jacket and

breeches and lay down on the bed. He was hardly settled down when Ebenezer knocked at the door and entered at their request. He carried a large bowl of fresh oysters and a tankard of ale for each man.

"Sar, the oysters he come from Pamlico Sound. He is as fresh as to-mororw. Mighty fine big fellow, they are." He pulled a table between the two beds. " 'Twill last your stummick till supper-time."

Hillary and Richard sat up on the edges of their beds. Ebenezer, grinning, left the room and the two men dipped into the oysters. "Sweet and good," Hillary commented, "but not up to Chesapeake Bay standard."

"Spoken like a true Marylander." Richard wiped his mouth with a napkin. "And that reminds me, you'll find you make more friends down here if you don't make unflattering comparisons with Maryland."

"Ah, but I feel sure a good half would be flattering comparisons," he answered. But certainly, he thought, Richard was right: it would be best to close his mind to the past and to accept things as they were. That had been part of his father's teaching. "The most civilized person is the one most readily adaptable." He must remember that. Or must he? Was it really honest to adapt, adapt, adapt?

Richard interrupted his thoughts. "I was speaking with Matthew again while you were out, and the more we talked the more I've noticed the difference between our views."

Hillary leaned back on one elbow. "And how is that, sir?"

"He is hot against the Ministry in London over taxes and trade. Of course we all objected to the Stamp Act, as internal taxation, but that was repealed more than two years ago. Now he is just as angry about the Townshend Act and the new customs arrangements and the vice-admiralty courts that were passed at the same time. In Matthew's eyes, our trade is intolerably swaddled in regulations and port duties and import taxes. It galls him beyond measure."

"Does it amount to so much, Cousin Richard?"

"It's as a man sees it, I suppose, Hillary. For many years we were pretty much let alone to work out our destiny. About five years ago there was a change. The Ministry and Parliament decided to manage us and to tax us. If one device was too strongly resisted, they resorted to another, and another. It comes down to a matter of principle. Parliament flatly declares its right to tax us. We claim that no free-born man should pay a tax he has not levied on himself through his representatives. Our view is that the power to tax rests in our own assemblies. There is the tug."

"What would Matthew do about all these duties and restrictions on trade?"

"What he does is mostly swearing and sputtering. You know there are non-importation agreements in many of the Colonies. New York and Philadelphia came in last summer. By this means we hope to bring the English merchants to petition Parliament for relief—theirs and ours."

"How is it all to end?"

"God knows, Hillary. Parliament is resolved to master us; we are determined to resist. We have friends in Parliament—Chatham, Pownall, Barré and Burke, to name a few—but too few and too weak, just now. I tell Matthew we must have patience."

"But, Cousin Richard, you seem worried yourself. Is this where you differ from Matthew?"

"Yes, Hillary. He sees trouble and danger from across the sea. I see it here within the Colony. We have our government here, established and easy, and we know how to live with it. But the Western counties have been filling up with a new kind of men. They fear and hate our sheriffs, our lawyers, our justices of the peace. They claim they suffer from unequal representation in our Assembly. They claim they are charged exorbitant fees by the sheriffs and sub-sheriffs, and they are bitter against the poll tax as a particular injustice.

"Tryon's Palace at New Bern has brought it to a head. They say not a twentieth of them will ever so much as see it, since their trade in large part goes to South Carolina and they refuse to pay a tax to help meet its cost. They band together in associations and threaten the peace of the Colony. Governor Tryon holds them no better than rebels."

"Is there no colour of right on their side?"

"A colour of right? Yes, of course. Our government is not perfect. It is true the West has fewer men in the Assembly. And there are always some abuses among the sheriffs. Tryon said last year that perhaps as much as half of the taxes they collected never reached the treasury—call them embezzled if you wish. But on the whole the thing works, and we live easily under it. These Western men would destroy it all in the name of reform. They aren't solid men. Give them their way and all government would break down. If we don't contrive to stop them it will come to bloodshed, for they have no sense of order."

He paused and shook his head sadly. "They are our own people, men of the Colony of North Carolina, and they have to be restrained. Matthew does not think as I do. He has no use for Tryon's Palace. He listens to their complaints of injustice. He is deceived by the colour of right we mentioned. For all that, these Western rebels must be held in check if we are to have peace and a prosperous growth."

"Are there so many of them?"

"Enough. The reports I receive . . ." He let his voice trail off. Abruptly he began again. "How can one be sure of gossip?"

Richard shut his eyes, signalling that he had had enough of the talk and enough of the worry. He lay back on the bed and fell asleep almost immediately. But it was a troubled sleep. He dreamed that he was planting a field with indigo. His motions were incredibly slow, weak and unsure, as often happens in a dream. At the edge of his field lapped the broad ocean, and every time he put a plant into the earth, a veiled woman who followed him yanked it from the ground and threw it with incredible strength into the darkening sea.

Hillary Caswell watched the restless movements of his cousin; he himself could find no sleep. He lay wide awake, going over and over the conversation between Richard and Matthew. He thought: whatever happens, I shall be on the side of the Royal Governor. Like it or not, I shall be there. Eventually his mind turned ruefully to Cecelia Chapman and to her look of disappointment when he had said he had no intention of becoming a planter. What a foolish thing to say! Why hadn't he told her of his promise? Restlessly he went back to the problem between the East and the West. He rolled uneasily on the bed. He would side with Richard and the Governor. Of course he would. Fate could not cast him on the wrong side; surely it could not.

4

Taxes and Troubles

The lads had come in from shooting and the hall was filled with their hearty, vibrant voices: Manor House was a place of happiness. Richard Caswell stood by the fire in the great hall. The worried look on his face had given way to pleasure, but still he wondered in his heart how long it would be before the angry days, the days of fire. Matthew's talk was enough to give any man alarm.

The Caswell and Chapman boys took off their shooting jackets and their scarlet hunting caps and carelessly threw them on benches and chairs. Two small Negro boys struggled with boot-jacks, pulling off hunting boots. The girls came in with a great flutter and rustling of silken skirts. They had changed for supper.

Angela claimed this was only to impress their new cousin. "It's all very well for you, Ann," she said. "You can look superior. You've already got Tommy Blount mad about you. He told me he was bound to marry you as soon as you finish at the Sisters' school."

Ann turned severely on her younger sister. "Keep your hush!" she said quickly. "I'm not through with school yet, and you know what Father says: that we're not even to think about marriage until we're educated."

"I'm only repeating what Tommy told me himself. And what about Cecelia? She's got half the lads in Charleston after her!"

Cecelia laughed. "Good for me! Keep them dangling, I say. I'm not going to settle down for years and years. I've a whole world to see, and then, after I've seen it,

perhaps I'll take a man. But not before. And not one of
your city macaronis, Cousins. I want a man who has a
plantation."

"A farmer," Angela teased.

Cecelia looked serious for a moment. "Yes, even that.
But he'll be the grandest one in the world, I promise
you!"

"Then you'll let me have Cousin Hillary?" Angela
asked.

Cecelia Chapman brushed back her auburn hair.
"Yes, Cousin. You may have him. He hasn't any place
in my world with that talk about government. I shall be
married before he comes to his senses."

Hillary Caswell stood at the first landing of the stairs,
looking down to the corner of the hall below. It was a
gay, pleasant scene, young lads and maidens rushing
about with those most important affairs of living.

He glanced at himself. He was glad that he had
changed from his leather riding-breeks and jacket. He
wore a dark-blue coat over his tan knee-breeches. His
lace stock and ruffles were fashionable and his square-
toed shoes with steel buckles quite in the mode. His
brown hair, freshly combed into a club by his servant
Andrew, was just right. He could not help smiling as he
realized that he, Hillary Caswell, rather fancied himself.

Uncle Matthew joined him. As they stood looking at
the merry scene below, Matthew said, "The Caswell
clan is not too bad, Hillary. They make quite a showing.
Aye, the lads are fine and tall, and the lassies—well, you
see for yourself."

Cecelia Chapman was standing by the door next to a
tall, angular young man who still held his hunting cap in
his hand. She was blushing; her cheeks were a delicate
tinge of pink. Her skin was a lovely creamy white and
the blush became her.

"Greg, you're a horrid tease. But maybe I *shall* go to
Court someday! Father or even Robin could take me to
England on one of their sea voyages. And what would
be so strange about that?"

"Nothing. Nothing at all. But I'd advise you to get
there soon, or you may not be able to go at all."

"Now what do you mean by that, Gregory?"

Gregory shrugged his lean shoulders. He aimed, and threw his hunting cap to the farthest bench. "Why? Because we'll all be at war, my girl."

"Oh, Greg, don't be so dramatic," his sister Angela cried. "What is there possibly to fight about?"

"All right. Let's bury our heads in the sand like so many ostriches. But remember that I told you."

Madam Caswell entered the great hall clapping her hands sharply. "Boys! Boys!" she cried over the din of laughter. "Hurry and change. Supper will be served in fifteen minutes. You know your father doesn't like dallying before mealtime. Elisha, John, Gregory, make haste!"

The boys grabbed up their garments and ran out of the hall, bumping and pushing as they opened the door which led to the rear quarters. They sprinted across the open space and disappeared into the long building of the coach-house.

The dining-room was almost as large as the great hall. Hillary Caswell again reflected on his original impression of Manor House, of its meanness in comparison with the great Maryland mansions. How could he have forgotten that it was only the inside of a home that could give the majesty of happiness? Unaccountably, as he approached the doors, he found himself searching for Cecelia Chapman.

In the dining-room was a large sideboard with twin pedestals; the corner cupboards held a multitude of plates and china. Almost covering the end of the room was a great fire-place, the one which had gleamed so softly through the door-windows on his arrival. The great mahogany table, made up of several sections, was stretched down the middle of the room. Hillary remembered having seen a similar one in the Harmon-Harwood house in Annapolis. It had been banquet-size, seating thirty people.

Elizabeth Caswell was directing each person to his place, and Hillary was to sit between Angela and Ann Caswell. Looking directly across the table he found himself gazing into the eyes of Cecelia Chapman. It was a rather pleasant sensation. She was smiling, and her bright-green dress was like a blaze of fire.

Matthew Caswell bowed his head, and in a rich, resonant voice he gave the grace: "Come, Lord Jesus, our guest to be. Bless this food bestowed by Thee." He paused a long time before saying, "Amen."

The guests looked up, and the dinner meal was begun. Ebenezer acted as butler. He watched his young assistants with an eagle eye as they carried in the platters laden with ham and wild turkey, as they brought the bowls of rice and greens, the corn pudding, golden-brown on top.

There was a babble of voices about the table, and Hillary was struck with the rich colour of it all. Now and then he glanced at Cecelia, but she seemed completely occupied with young Gregory Caswell. Most of the time he spent parrying the remarks of young Angela, who seemed determined not to let him have a bite to eat. Often he heard the voice of Madam Elizabeth Caswell urging the guests to savour her Indian relish on the ham, or to taste her brandied plums. Matthew and Richard, Hillary noted, were again involved in discussing colonial affairs. Hillary strained to hear their words, but Angela was busy questioning him on the proper age for girls to marry. Fifteen? That didn't seem too young, did it?

"You really aren't courting a young lady? I mean you've no one you're particularly fond of in Maryland, have you?" Angela asked.

Hillary smiled. "No. No one at all."

He heard Cecelia say, "Now, he's a little like you, Gregory dear. He's terribly fond of himself; there's no place in his heart for anyone else."

"You're sure you have no one?"

"Did you try the brandied plums?" Ann asked.

He would have said that he didn't have time to—but there wasn't time. Angela was pressing him. "Some girls are married very young, aren't they?"

Ebenezer himself brought in the dessert, delicious sillabub. He carried it like a crown for a king. Hillary had already heard the stories about Eb before the dinner began. Angela had told them to him in detail. He noticed a certain old-fashioned elegance about Ebenezer.

He had been the body servant to the first Matthew and had travelled with him from Virginia in 1720. He had helped to train all the young sons of the house in manners and good behaviour. Though they were nearly all full grown, he still felt it his duty to instruct them in some fine points of etiquette. The phrase "Mind your manners, Massa," was often on his tongue.

Angela had said that there were many strange things about Eb. He had come from the east coast of Africa, from a tribe called the Yaos, a Mohammedan tribe. He still practised his religion. He said his morning, noon and evening prayers kneeling on a little prayer-rug and facing the East. The lads, when they were younger, used to hide the small, red rug and would only disclose its hiding place at the last moment when the sun was about to set.

Ebenezer stood back from the table, his eyes skimming over everything. A strange being, Hillary thought. Somewhere in his ancestry an Arab had given him his thin, straight nose and curved lips so unlike the Negro. Then Hillary wondered idly what Matthew and Richard were talking about and—damn, there he was, looking again at the smiling lips, the dancing eyes of Cecelia Chapman!

The young folk had eaten with zest. Usually they were eager to be off to games and dancing, but tonight they longed for bed; the long day's shooting had begun at daybreak.

Elizabeth Caswell rose, and with a scraping of chairs the young folk followed, leaving their elders to their port and pipes. A rotund Negro woman in a flowered calico gown and bright-coloured turban came to tell her mistress that Callie's baby was crouping. Madam Elizabeth immediately told Ann to fetch her medicine case, and the women hurried quickly to the Quarters line. The lads exchanged a few pleasantries with Hillary, made excuses for their abrupt departure to bed—and were gone.

Cecelia and Hillary were left standing alone together

for the moment in the great hall. He started to speak to her but was interrupted when the main door was opened. Cecelia's father, Joseph Chapman, and his son Robin entered the hall.

"Robin! When did you come?" Cecelia cried as she ran to her brother's arms.

Hillary observed the two men carefully. Joseph Chapman was tall and lean with a long face and heavy brows over large dark eyes. Robin was slightly taller than his father, but he had the same narrow face, straight nose and dark eyes. His face had been weather-roughened by the sea, and it gave him the appearance of complete maturity although he was not much older than Hillary. His hair was neatly clubbed and had a reddish tinge in its brownness.

Joseph Chapman embraced his daughter in turn, saying, "We came to take you back to Red Bank. Your mother would like to have you home, and Robin will be here for only a few days since he must take the *Laughing Girl* to Nassau on Thursday."

Matthew Caswell had come in from the dining-room. "Joseph, good to see you. And Robin, too. You just got in, I suppose?" Matthew turned to introduce Hillary. "This is Lawrence's boy Hillary. Come in, come in, gentlemen. Don't stand there by the door. Richard is here and he's been asking about you."

"We shouldn't stay, really, Matthew."

"Nonsense! I won't hear of it. Neither would Richard, since he wants to talk to you and Robin about the situation in Boston. You'll have to tell us what you've learned on your northern voyage. Hillary, won't you join us?"

The men began moving toward the drawing-room where Richard was waiting. Cecelia had called to Angela on the stairs, "You'll help me pack my clothes, won't you?" Then she glanced at Hillary. "Well, my cousin, am I going to see you again? If you go immediately to New Bern I'm afraid I shan't."

"I *do* hope to see you before I leave," Hillary said with more seriousness in his tone than he had wished.

Immediately her manner was light. "But if you're to be a politician, you'd be a terrible waste of time."

"It's not exactly that I . . ."

"You're not fickle, too! Do you change so easily? No. Don't answer me. I can see for myself." She turned, smiling, and hurried up the stairs after Angela. There was that peculiar swishing noise—what was it they called it?—yes, taffeta petticoats.

Hillary left the hall and entered the drawing-room, found a place by the fire and sat down. Robin was sitting in the chair across from him. He had just lighted a pipe which Ebenezer had brought for him.

"Uneasy. Very uneasy, sir," Robin was saying in answer to a question which Richard had posed. "There has been a succession of incidents, some of which you doubtless know. The new customs commissioners set up headquarters there some time back. No doubt at their request, the fifty-gun *Romney* put into Boston in early June. Within a week some of the *Romney's* men seized Hancock's ship *Liberty,* on the allegation she had dutiable goods aboard. In no time the Boston mob was in a frenzy and three of the customs men barely saved their lives by taking refuge on the *Romney*. The fury of the mob was such that Governor Bernard was ready to wilt with fear.

"So much for that. Governor Bernard kept insisting he had not asked for troops, but somebody must have. In September, General Gage wrote that four regiments of Regulars were on the way, two from England and two from Halifax. Before the end of the month the Halifax regiments arrived and, in spite of bitter protest, have been quartered on the town.

"Of course Otis and Dr. Warren and Sam Adams and the others have had much to say. But when I left nothing more had happened. The town is a powder keg, and I must confess I breathed a sigh of relief when we were safely at sea again."

"Did Bernard fear they would rebel against the King?" Richard Caswell asked incredulously.

Robin Chapman paused thoughtfully. "Governor Bernard has some cause to be frightened, sir, but I don't think it is a question of rebellion against the Crown. Massachusetts is an old Colony, and for many years it pretty much governed itself. It grew set in its ways.

Then when the Ministry and Parliament sought to impose their rule, it incensed the people of Boston. They've nothing but loyalty to the King, but they'll fight every inch of the way to preserve the ancient liberties at least tacitly granted them by the Crown. The swarms of customs collectors, judges, inspectors and now soldiers sent to master them have put them in a rage, and they in turn have put Governor Bernard in a sweat."

Joseph Chapman leaned forward, looking first at Matthew and then at Richard. "The people in Charleston are more docile, but it is as bad with its vice-admiralty court and its customs men. It isn't so much the taxes. The old molasses tax was higher but of course nobody thought of paying it. Now it is down to a penny a gallon but the customs men want it paid. They are touchy about an occasional cargo from the French islands, too, and they can't abide our running a cargo of tobacco into a Spanish port as we used to. They swarm everywhere with their damnable rules and regulations and port duties and customs and so forth and so forth. It's enough to drive a man mad."

Hillary thought he noted a flicker of a smile on Robin Chapman's lips when his father launched into the subject which struck him most sorely. Then Robin winked at Hillary, obviously in amusement at his father's sudden concern over his personal plight, not over the state of the Colonies themselves.

"Arbitrary rules," Matthew Caswell was saying slowly, "completely arbitrary . . ."

Joseph's long face was lined with wrinkles. "Arbitrary! They're damned unfair, I say. Why, a man may just as well sink his ships in mid-Atlantic as try to sail them for a profit. Tell them about the new rules on naval stores, Robin." Then without waiting for his son to speak, he continued: "They've got us in an iron vise." He waggled a finger. "This will affect you, too, Matthew, with all your tar and pitch and turpentine. Damme, what do they think they're trying to do? Do they plan to buy all their naval stores in Scandinavia after they've strangled us?" He dug into his coat pocket angrily. "Here, read this!"

Richard Caswell had been standing near the fire-place. He took the paper from Joseph's hand and scanned it. Then he sat down and read more closely. Chapman continued to speak. "You're in the Assembly. My Lord, you're Speaker of the thing! You ought to be able to do something to stop this."

Richard Caswell said, "This first part seems to be a memorandum to the Earl of Hillsborough, Secretary of State for the Colonies, from two firms of London merchants. It's not new rules, only suggestions for new rules."

"The Assembly's so subservient to Hillsborough and Tryon it might as well be law," Chapman grumbled.

"Bridges & Wallis and Hundlet & Needham," Richard went on patiently, "trading in North Carolina . . . handlers of naval stores. . . ." He began reading aloud: " 'Whence it is necessary for better making of good tar and pitch for cordage in all the British Plantations, that the last half of every kiln of tar, when drawn shall be made into pitch, free of drops and the whole kiln of tar, unless made into pitch as aforesaid, be forfeit.' "

Matthew Caswell shook his head. "Arbitrary and very expensive for us if we try to follow their pattern. Read some more to me. I'd like to see just how far these honourable merchants of London *will* go."

"Just wait. Just wait and hear," Joseph Chapman warned.

" 'The manner the planters have constantly pursued in burning the tar kilns, has been to run it off into open drains cut into the ground, exposed to the weather; rain water often intermixed with the tar while it is hot, and when they take up the tar out of the drains to fill the barrels, sand, dirt and water are taken with it—which should be prevented.' "

Richard glanced up. "That's true enough, gentlemen. I know myself about that matter. I've seen it happen."

"At least *we* attempt to clean the tar," Matthew said.

Richard began reading again: " 'By sinking a large cistern or cask into the ground to receive the tar as it runs from the kiln, with a cover to prevent rain from getting into the cistern, when the tar is hot, so the water will not impregnate; later on it will be impossible to entirely separate the one from the other. And as for the barrels—they are abominable.' " Richard smiled. "As is this writing," he added.

Joseph Chapman sat up suddenly. He had been slouching in his chair, rubbing a thumb over his chin, and his eyes had held a faraway look.

"Barrels!" he exclaimed. "By Gad, that was the part that choked me! There's nothing wrong with the barrels made in *my* shipyard annex." He turned to Hillary, hoping to find a sympathetic listener. "The staves are strong. Three-quarter-inch oak, sir! We make them out of oak just as they do in Devon. Not out of pine, sir!"

Hillary nodded, but could think of nothing to say. Matthew held up his hand. "Now don't go off the handle, Joseph. Let *us* hear the letter out. We'll get mad with you when we know all of their complaints."

Richard went on reading in a flat tone, constantly interrupted by Joseph Chapman. Hillary's attention wavered as he watched these unfamiliar North Carolina relatives of his. He saw Robin Chapman raise his glass of port to his lips to keep from smiling openly at one of his father's outbursts. Then Richard's determined voice broke in momentarily: " 'We ask for an Act of the Assembly to oblige the planters to put all tar into well-hooped casks of thirty-two gallons each; made of well-seasoned pine staves, three-quarters inch thick to each stave, the casks to be properly bunged at the kiln when the tar is burnt, the bung to be made of cork or wood.' "

As Joseph Chapman began another tirade, Robin motioned to Hillary, signalling that they should leave the room together. Richard was skimming through the next few pages. Joseph Chapman was on his feet, and Matthew was holding up his hands in a vain effort to stop his flow of words. In the midst of the confusion, Hillary and Robin made good their escape.

The great hall was empty. Robin shook his head and turned toward Hillary, smiling. "You see how it is, Cousin? People are apathetic until something touches them directly. My father will not countenance any criticism of his barrels or the slightest thing that could interfere with his shipping."

"This doesn't sound so slight to me."

"No, it is not slight."

The two young men sat down near the fire and stretched out their legs before them. "What a lot of taxes and troubles we've talked about to-night!" Robin exclaimed. "It was Richard's presence that encouraged us, I suppose. Cousin Matthew and Father never succeed in changing his mind but they are continually making the attempt."

"Richard starts much of the talk himself. Riding down here, he must have discussed the same sort of thing six or seven times. No doubt he is measuring people's views and the heat of their tempers."

Robin took a leisurely pull on his pipe. "Well, let's have no more taxes to-night. Let me ask you one more question, and then no more. How do *you* stand on this business between the East and the West?"

Hillary paused to arrange his thoughts. "It seems to me—now remember," he hastened to add, "I don't know much about this—if these Regulators are true frontiersmen, the kind about whom my father has spoken, they aren't going to stop with anything less than what they believe are their full rights. They won't give up because of a rebuff from the Governor."

"They won't. You're quite right."

"And it bothers me, Robin. I've already put myself on the Governor's side by accepting a position with his secretary. Well, I *should* be for settled government and the upholding of law. There's no getting around that. But if it's true the Regulators are getting more than their share of taxes without being equally represented in our Assembly . . . and if . . ." Hillary's voice trailed off.

Robin was smiling. "You mean you don't like to believe that the government of even one county might be corrupt, and Tryon might wink at what his friends do there?"

"No. It may be so; and if it is, the breach will widen. I don't like the thought of a battle among our own people."

"What's this? You're talking like a true North Carolinian."

"I'll have to discover all this for myself."

"You will," Robin said. "You will."

There was an odd tone in his voice, as if he had already made up his own mind on the subject, as if he could see the future with clear eyes. "And it will be worse before it's better," he said with finality. "Anyway, Cousin, I have a feeling that we shall both be on the same side if there are arms to bear."

"You're so certain of it," Hillary mused.

The men were just leaving the drawing-room when Madam Elizabeth Caswell and Ann entered the front door. Madam looked exhausted, lines of despair about her face. Ann was as white as paper and she looked nervously about the great hall.

Madam Elizabeth approached Joseph Chapman, and, taking his hand, she asked, "Joseph, would you have one of your men make a small casket tomorrow? Callie's infant has passed away. There was nothing we could do." Her voice was low, discouraged, as if an infinitely heavy weight pressed down on her heart. "It was membranous croup," she said. Then she turned and walked into the hall where she sank down into a chair. Matthew Caswell followed her, took her cape and placed it on a bench. He said, "You musn't take it so hard, my dear. It is Nature, and there's nothing can be done for it all."

Elizabeth looked up with a faint smile. "That's what you always say, Matthew, but Nature can be very cruel." She clasped her long, slim fingers together. "Poor Callie! It was her first child, Matthew." The tears gathered in her eyes. Joseph Chapman stood uneasily by the door. Richard Caswell waited at the entrance to the drawing-room, his eyes showing his deep sympathy.

Matthew laid his hand on his wife's shoulder. "I know, my dear, I know."

Hillary thought he had never seen more tenderness in a gesture, but he wondered if possibly they had lost a first child themselves, and this was the bitter reliving of an old sorrow.

It was much later in the evening. Robin reminded Hillary that he was getting the *Laughing Girl* ready for a voyage to Nassau. "Would you like to come over tomorrow and watch us load her? Gregory could show you the way since he's bound to come."

"I'd like to very much," Hillary answered.

"You would like to what, Cousin?" Cecelia's voice came from the stairway. A moment later she appeared, followed by a stout Negress who was carrying her portmanteau.

"To visit us to-morrow," Robin said.

"Good," she said. "I'm going to convert him to plantation life," she explained to Robin. Then to Hillary she added: "Did you know, Cousin, that you're also coming over to visit us next week and to stay for part of the holidays! I have to go back to school at Charleston directly after Christmas."

"Charleston?"

"You needn't sound so happy."

"I wasn't happy, I assure you. But as for the invitation—I haven't spoken to Richard yet."

"But you don't have to do that. I've already talked to him," Cecelia said. "It's all settled. Uncle Richard is going to Kings Town for a week and after that to New Bern. At least there's a little time you can spend with us. Father said he would show you the entire yards."

"And when does all of this begin?" Hillary laughed.

"Just after the deer drive."

"You see," Robin said as he stood up, "Cecelia is the best arranger in the world, and I'll wager you don't reach New Bern until after Christmas. A man has absolutely nothing to say about his actions. Everything is settled in advance for him."

Ebenezer stood by the entrance to the hall and addressed Robin. "The horses, they are ready now, Massa Robin."

"Thank you, Eb. Come along, Cecelia. We've given Father enough head start for him to be home by now."

The three young people, who must bear the brunt of their fathers' battles, walked to the porch, chatting happily.

The horses had been brought from the stables. They lifted their heads impatiently, tightening the reins held by the young Negro boys. Eb had hurried down the stoop with the lanthorns. Matthew, Elizabeth and Richard stood waving at the front door.

Robin gave his sister a hand up, and Cecelia sprang into the saddle with a grace that caught Hillary's eye.

The last farewells were called and the riders were off down the long avenue of cedars.

Hillary stood for a moment in the evening after the others had turned and re-entered the house. He watched until the riders had disappeared at the turn of the road, and he found himself wishing suddenly that there were no such place in the world as New Bern. And since the half-moon was high in the night it seemed impossible that there should be a group of men called the Regulators, and that a barrel of tar filled with chips and dross could flame into a war. The air was crisp and dry, and the hoofbeats faded into the distance.

The dome of the heavens was indigo blue and the stars shone palely. The evening star, Venus, was disappearing, sinking behind the dark trees that cut the sky.

From the kitchen behind Manor House came the sound of gay laughter, the murmur of soft voices and the clatter of dishes as the house slaves finished their labours.

Hillary walked slowly down the avenue to the verge of dark grass. A brick path led to the late-autumn garden. Nightbirds were chirping softly, and in the woods beyond, an owl hooted.

A horse neighed in the stable; pigs grunted; a cow lowed; a hound bayed—each sound giving a colour to the night, painting the night in deeper pastels. Each sound mixed into the air with the heavy odour of burned leaves and the sharp tang of apples rotting.

Hillary Caswell stood motionless as the solitude bore down on him. He watched the moon moving across the night sky, and the immensity of the heavens and the universal quiet gave him a moment's sense of peace. Then he walked toward the house, away from the night scene, thinking that if there were a time for war, then surely there must be an hour for peace.

5

A Deer Drive

The morning was crisp and clear—one of those brilliant days when every branch, every crisp leaf not fallen, seems to stand out, to be etched against the vivid blue of the early morning sky. When Hillary mounted his roan that morning for the deer drive it was with a sense of regret that he had only a few days before his journey to New Bern and the entanglements of a world which did not promise to please him.

A heavy jack-frost lay over the stubble of brown fields and sprinkled the long streamers of grey moss hanging from the limbs of the oak trees. The cocks were crowing as the young men of the household rode out; behind them followed the servants and the pack of hounds. The horses were turned toward the great swamp on the verge of the wild desert that lay between the bend of the Alligator River and Pamlico Sound. Deer abounded there, and bear, wild turkey and quail.

Gregory and Elisha, mounted on swift, strong banker ponies, were in the fore; then Gregory broke ahead to lead the way down a narrow path that crossed the turpentine woods.

Hillary preferred his own mount to those which had been offered him. For the time, nothing, it seemed, could be more pleasant than the hunt. The air smelled crisp and clean, and the feel of his horse's rippling muscles between his thighs was good to him. His well-worn leather brocks and jacket kept out the chill. The tabs of his hunting cap kept his ears warm although his breath vapourized as it issued from his nostrils and mouth.

Hillary felt the same strong exhilaration that had always come to him at home in Maryland when he mounted a horse for the hunt. He glanced forward to his companions, the newly found cousins Elisha and Gregory, who rode ahead of him. They had turned out to be agreeable fellows—young, but pleasant. At the last moment Robin Chapman joined the party. He reined his horse near Hillary's and explained, "One last shoot before I go to sea. This is the one thing that the land can offer."

They rode in silence for some distance. Hillary held the reins loosely in his hand. The file of riders was passing under tall turpentine pines. The sunlight broke over the horizon, slanted through the trees, spread a geometry of light on the earth. The beauty of the woods finally put the night's conversation out of his mind.

Later, when the trail had widened, Elisha held his banker pony in check until Hillary had reached his side. Elisha grinned and waved his riding crop, showing the deep wood.

"Have you woods like those in Maryland, Cousin? Or have you sweet black water like that yonder?" He indicated the Scuppernong River which threaded its way through the forest.

Hillary smiled, remembering Richard's warning not to be constantly comparing Maryland with North Carolina. He recalled his father's advice—that he must adapt himself to the ways of others. Idly he wondered what the perfect gentleman would be like. Would he be an opinionated man who would not dare to voice an opinion? Sometimes, he thought, even a gentleman must take a stand. "No," he said to Elisha, "we don't have magnificent pines like these in Maryland."

"They bring us a mint of money, these trees," Elisha continued. "See the ones that are boxed? The sap will run into those boxes. Father's sending a whole shipload of naval stores out this week. Captain Chapman carries them to Nassau and trans-ships them to England for us." He sighed. "I wish I were going out with them." He babbled on youthfully and somewhat disconnectedly.

"Captain Joseph let me go with him to Antigua one year. He'll 'most always bring back a cargo of rum and sugar for Philadelphia. It's wonderful at Nassau with the houses built of a kind of coral and painted pretty colours. . . . I think I'll have ships to sail the western ocean when I get old enough—though I'm almost ready now. Robin Chapman's already got a ship of his own and he's scarce twenty." A touch of envy appeared in his tone.

The other riders had spread along the trail and were lost to the view of Hillary and Elisha. After about ten minutes they came to the old tar pits and the two huts where the charcoal burners lived. Elisha spurred his mount and cantered from the trail toward the huts. He returned shortly with a look of disappointment on his face. "Nobody home," he said. "A nice mulatto gal lives there." He looked at Hillary out of the corner of his eye. "Do you like girls?"

"Why, yes, of course, some girls," Hillary answered.

"Oh, I don't mean regular girls like one's sisters. I mean girls who let you take liberties."

Hillary had no intention of talking about his private affairs with this new and young kinsman. Moreover, the way in which Elisha had spoken made the entire subject distasteful to him. But he did volunteer, "You ought to be careful of the French disease, you know."

"Yes, but that's what everyone says. I don't think there's much chance of it anyway. She's a clever girl and knows how to take care of things. She's lived in the islands." He said this as if the bare fact would settle the whole matter of worry. He gave Hillary a knowing smile.

The smile alone was enough to make Hillary want to answer. He had a feeling that the young man didn't quite understand the horrors of the French disease, and that it was time he should know. Hillary did not get the chance to explain, however, for at the next turn of the road they overtook the other riders. Including himself, Hillary counted twelve. There were some introductions, and Hillary was immediately lost in the maze of his cousins' names.

The deer drive near Scuppernong Lake was ready to

begin. The Negro boys had the hounds on leash—impatient hounds, barking, pulling, tugging, eager to be off.

Robin Chapman was at the centre of the group, for he was to take charge. "Hillary and I will go in toward the north end of the lake, and the rest of you should find your stations along toward the south. Don't leave your stations—you know that. Old Metephele—" he motioned to the smiling Negro—"says that there are plenty of deer not too far from the shore. Hillary and I will need about half an hour; then you can have the hounds on the scent. Is everything all right?"

There was a general assent. Robin glanced toward the Negro again. "Metephele, take over the hounds!"

The young men dismounted and tied their horses to the bushes and small trees in the grove. Then they paired off and began walking, guns under their arms, toward their stations. Their red coats and caps blazed brightly against the dark young pines and bay bushes. Robin motioned to Hillary and then led the way through the brush and vines and thorns at the verge of the lake.

As Robin had predicted, they walked for nearly thirty minutes before they came to a small clearing—the place he had chosen for their station. A little stream ran into the lake, and there were animal tracks along the bank. Larger animals, bear and deer, had been there, each leaving his mark of pad or hoof. The smaller animals which had come to drink had made tunnels in the tangle of vines and berry brushes.

It grew warmer as the sun climbed higher in the sky. Robin stripped off his jacket and spread it on a log. "We can thank the Lord that there won't be any ticks or red bugs at this season. Burrow right into your flesh and fester there. They love old logs—and I love to sit on old logs—but it's in the summer when they're devilish." Robin seated himself on his coat and rested his gun on his knees. Hillary was glad to follow his example. He was slightly winded from the fast walk, the quick scramble through the thorn bushes and the stumbling march over the grape-vines.

Robin yawned. "Metephele ought to be unleashing the hounds now. If we have any luck they'll be springing a deer before long. Most drives have been good this year."

They waited quietly in the forest. The stillness of the deep wood seemed to magnify the few solitary sounds that reached them: a small bird chirped as it hopped along the bough of a near-by tree a hawk screamed as it knifed through the crisp air after its prey; a waterfowl cried from the lake. A rabbit ran along the narrow path before them, stopped to drink at the stream's edge and then ran on. A partridge scudded out from under a bush, paused to gaze curiously at the two motionless figures on the log, and then, satisfied, began to feed. The stream flashed and sparkled as a small fish leaped and fell back again with a splash.

The sound of a larger animal moving on the far side of the creek put the two young men instantly on the alert. Robin stood up cautiously; Hillary moved slightly to his left. A moment later a deer came slowly through the opening in the brush. Robin raised his gun to his shoulder very slowly; he frowned, lowered his arms and held his gun in one hand. "A doc." His lips formed the words.

The doe stood quietly, lifting her head from side to side, sniffing the air. Robin and Hillary were downwind, so she did not detect their presence. She walked boldly to the edge of the stream, drank her fill and moved away without fear.

The forest world settled to its own peculiar silence again, and after a few moments Robin began to speak in a low tone. "You know, I'm sorry I talked so much about Massachusetts that first night. The situation *is* bad there, but the elders didn't really believe me. They don't want to think that our present cross purposes with Parliament might come to an open break. It's strange. Consider my father: he talks of a break, but in his heart he always hopes and believes that a friendlier attitude toward America will prevail in the Ministry and in Parliament. Then consider Richard Caswell: he swears that there'll never be a break with the Crown, but I'll wager he's prepared for it if it comes. Sometimes I think he lets Tryon's voice lull him to sleep, and other times I think——"

"What kind of a man *is* Tryon?" Hillary asked softly.

"Neither so good nor so bad as he is painted. Anyway, he talks about developing the Colony. Some of our best men are for him. Then there are others like the Ashes, Maurice Moore and Colonel Waddell who think he's only a clever, prideful man busy feathering his own nest —trying to make himself appear brilliant to the home Government."

"But I thought they were the very men who are on the Governor's side in this argument with the West."

Robin looked gloomy. "They *are* the same men, and there are others almost like them. They fight Tryon on all other scores; but they stand behind him when he lets citizens of North Carolina suffer more grievous wrongs than people in any other Colony!"

For a moment Hillary sat in silence. Then hesitantly, as if embarrassed, he spoke. "Robin, Matthew and Richard and your father have argued heatedly about the troubles in the West. You feel deeply about them, I can tell. But I've just come from Maryland and these things are strange to me. Tell me, Robin, just who are the Regulators and what are they complaining about?"

Robin smiled. "I suppose we never reached down to first principles. There are many issues but I'll try to gather them into as brief a compass as I can manage. The coastal counties settled first. Most of us are Church of England. Then came many newcomers; Scots, Irish and men from the north. Many of them are Dissenters, a good number are poor men with little education. Finding the coast counties full, they moved on to the hill country. There you have the people.

"In the upland counties they found the government in the hands of Eastern men. The Governor appoints the justices of the peace. They in turn choose most of the other officers. The conservative planters say this puts substantial men in office. The Westerners say it puts them under the rule of Easterners who tyrannize over them. It's a fact none of their own people are chosen."

"That doesn't seem fair," Hillary said.

"There's more, Cousin. About half the inhabitants of the Colony live in the hill counties but they have only seventeen members in the Assembly against sixty-one from the Eastern counties. This they brand an intolerable injustice."

Hillary nodded emphatic agreement.

Robin went on. "They complain of taxes as you've heard, especially the levy for Tryon's Palace, and have banded together to refuse to pay. They complain, too, that the sheriff and the registrar—often the same man —charge them outrageous fees and cheat them. If they hire a lawyer he is hand in glove with the Courthouse Ring and only helps to cheat them. There's more, but here you have their principal grounds for discontent."

"Are they really cheated, Robin, to your knowledge?"

"Last year Tryon wrote the Earl of Shelburne that not half the taxes the sheriffs collected ever reached the Treasury, and not one in twenty sheriffs can make up his accounts."

Hillary nodded. "Richard mentioned that. But I shouldn't think the Governor would favour them. I should think he would put down corruption."

"No, Hillary." Robin shook his head. "The sheriffs are mostly planters, mostly his friends. He favours them above the rude men of the hills. And—this he can't stomach and neither can the conservative Eastern gentlemen—the Westerners have formed an association. Fanning and Tryon call them a pack of rebels, tell them to give up their name of Regulators and petition as private men."

"What's wrong with all this?"

Robin shrugged. "Ask Richard, Cousin. I put the case as I see it. Richard thinks they're rebels, thinks they threaten stable government. It's true they've grown ugly and are in a mood to fight for what they call their rights. I think they've been goaded into it. So does Matthew. It seems to us almost as if Tryon would welcome an outbreak, though that's scarce within reason. Well, make what you will of it; you'll have ample opportunity, working with Edwards." Suddenly he tensed and rose to his feet, his head bent forward, listening.

"I hear it," Hillary said. "Baying . . . yonder to the south."

Robin smiled. "Thank the Lord. No more politics for a while. Sounds as if they're in full cry." He took up his gun as Hillary did. "We'd as well get in position now," he said.

Robin moved behind a giant pine tree and leaned against it. Hillary took his station at a near-by ironwood which had a low limb that could be used as a gun rest. Robin nodded approval, for the long English deer gun which Hillary was carrying had a heavy recoil, especially when both barrels were fired.

The baying of the hounds had grown louder, but it had become more difficult to place its exact direction. Barriers of trees and shrubs either dissipated or reflected the sounds until noise seemed to converge from all points.

Hillary glanced at Robin—his body was motionless; he had not yet raised his gun. A single shot broke above the jumble of noise, and the hounds, after one great burst of baying, fell silent.

Robin turned to Hillary. "They've either got a buck or the hounds have lost the scent."

The silence continued. Then a hound's voice was raised; a long, low cry penetrated the forest and echoed and rocked across the lake.

"That's Prideful Bess. I'd know her voice anywhere She's laid on the scent again, but I don't hear the rest of the pack."

"Maybe off in the wrong direction?"

"Possible. Not for Bess, though. She's got a nose. She's never long lost."

Her baying was much closer now and Robin said quickly, "I'll take the first shot, Hillary. You the second."

Almost immediately after he had spoken there was a loud crashing in the brush ahead and to their right. A buck, panting, with lolling tongue and great, frightened eyes, broke through the underbrush on the opposite side of the creek. It hesitated, exhausted, quivering a moment before it would leap the creek. It dropped to Robin's fire.

Hillary held his gun in readiness as he again heard the snapping of the underbrush. He glanced beyond the thicket, and in astonishment he caught a glimpse of a red-coated hunter moving clumsily through a thorn patch. A second buck came bursting into the clearing.

The stumbling red-coated hunter raised his gun. From Hillary's station he could see that Robin was directly in the line of fire. He dropped his deer gun, at the same moment hurling himself sideways with a driving force that knocked Robin sprawling to the ground.

His warning shout came at the same instant as the blast. It seemed to explode next to his ear. He felt a scalding pain burn across his shoulder. He stumbled, gripped at a tree limb for support. He heard Robin's voice dimly, then felt himself sinking to the ground.

Robin Chapman had been thrown clear of the shot. He rolled over once and jumped to his feet, realizing what had happened. A frightened face, paper-white, appeared through the tangle of vines and hanging moss on the opposite side of the stream.

"My God! Have I killed him?" Elisha Caswell came splashing through the stream.

"You fool! You blasted, stupid fool! Why didn't you stay at your station?" Robin was bending over the unconscious Hillary, cutting away his jacket with his hunting knife. The shot had struck him high in the shoulder, and the blood from the wound had already spread out, staining his shirt in an ugly splotch of red.

"What can I do? Is there anything I can——"

"Sound the horn," Robin said angrily.

The long call broke steadily and urgently, and in a short time the first of the hunters had gathered from their stations. Young Elisha was quivering like an aspen in the wind. His face was still white and his fingers worked together nervously. "Is he dead?" he asked. "I didn't mean to do it. I didn't even see him. I didn't think you were near, and the buck was going to——"

"Cousin, you didn't think at all. No, he's not dead, but I can't tell how badly he's hurt."

Gregory arrived on the south side of the stream, saw the fallen figure and called even as he forded, "Dr. Armitage is at Buncombe Hall. He came last night."

"Metephele!" Robin called to the Negro who had arrived at the same time as Gregory. "Metephele, take my horse. Ride to Buncombe Hall and fetch Dr. Armitage to Manor House. Ride like the devil and don't come back without the doctor. Understand?"

"Yes, sar." Metephele turned and sprinted off toward the horses. Robin knelt again beside Hillary and tried to stop the flow of blood from Hillary's shoulder. He had slashed loose the tail of his shirt, wadded the cloth into a swab and made it firm against the wound.

"How'd it happen?" John asked.

"Never mind that now. You fellows cut two strong saplings. Make them seven feet long. And, lads," he called, "I want four jackets for this litter."

Elisha quickly offered his jacket and then, not knowing what to do, stepped to the edge of the crowd, the anxiety deepening on his young face. He remembered he had dropped his gun on the far side of the stream, and he splashed numbly back through the water to find it.

Gregory was giving instructions to the Negroes. "Get some horses and drag the deer out to the road." Young Spruill was slashing the second sapling down at the bank of the stream.

Robin called to Puti. "I want you to ride home and tell the master what has happened. Just say there's been an accident, that Hillary's hurt—we don't know how badly. We're bringing him in. Tell him we've already sent for Dr. Armitage."

"Yes, sar."

"You go *kanirira*."

"Yes, sar. Puti go very fast."

Tom Blount and Robin fashioned the litter, thrusting the poles through the buttoned jackets and testing it for strength. They lifted Hillary gently onto it.

"Four men and two to change," Robin ordered. "The lad's no light weight. David, you and Tom can be the first relief."

Gregory grunted as he lifted his share of the pole. "You meant it when you said he wasn't light."

"Easy now," Robin said. "We don't want to start the blood flowing again. Elisha!"

"Yes, Robin?"

"You call in the hounds."

As the procession moved through the splashing sunlight of the forest, Elisha Caswell put the hunting horn to his lips and blew long blasts. Many had answered at the first call; Prideful Bess was already padding along beside Robin. Now others answered from a distance.

Hillary Caswell was still unconscious as they moved along the trail of shadow and light. Robin half turned toward Gregory and John. "By the way, lads, Elisha told me you had a discussion a few days ago about your new cousin—you weren't ready to make up your minds about him."

"That's true."

"Now I wouldn't want to affect your free judgement of him, but I should tell you that I owe him my own life. That shot would have caught me square."

"I guess it's time to make up our minds, isn't it?" Gregory said.

"I'd think so."

And the procession moved on through the tall turpentine pines, toward the place where the horses were tethered and then toward Manor House.

6

Angry Men

Nothing is more common than for persons who consider themselves injured to resent and complain. The loudness of these grievances is usually proportionate to the apprehension, rather than the reality, of the injury. Our fearfulness frequently augments our real as well as apparent dangers. Let us adjust our apprehensions to the reality of the injury received."

Harmon Husband's voice was strong and vibrant as he read those words. The crowd of sturdy frontiersmen had gathered from the wide boundaries of the Western counties to meet in Maddock's Mill and hear their leaders. They filled the room: some were sitting cross-legged on the floor; others rested on grain sacks; some perched on barrels; a group of five stood by the partly opened mill door.

Rednap Howell, a quick-moving man with bright eyes and a wide mouth that bespoke humour, sat by himself on the floor, slightly to the left of Harmon Husband. He held a sickle in his hand and methodically, in a rhythm that denoted impatience, dug the point of it into the wooden floor. Thomas Person sat on Husband's right. He was surveyor of Granville County and a member of the Assembly. He nodded in agreement as the words rolled forth from Husband. Directly in front of those three leaders were scouts, men of the trails, men of the backwoods, rough farmers, who sprawled on the mill floor, their rifles within easy reach.

Rednap Howell jammed the sickle into the floor harder than usual when he heard the word "adjust."

"Oh, for God's sake, Harmon," he called out without raising his eyes. "You're not dealing with a bunch of churchgoers. They're thieves! Make it tougher. Let 'em know we mean it!" He leaned forward again and once more began pounding the sickle point into the floor.

A square-jawed woodsman sitting by a coil of rope leaned to his friend and whispered, "Give you a guess where I'd like to have this." He patted the rope. "By God, it'd pleasure me to see Fanning do a stretch of dancing from one end of it."

From the left and behind Howell came other words: "Where's all this fine talk gettin' us?"

"Harmon, air you scared of them fellers?"

"Fanning let you off pretty easy back there at Hillsborough. Sure you ain't still sweatin'?"

"What about them promises you made to Fanning?" shouted a round-faced young man. "Air that why you're so easy?"

Rednap Howell looked up quickly. "Now hold on a minute. Wait a minute! He was under duress, Henry." Howell had turned about to face the speaker. "You may not know so much 'bout law as you think. A man can lie his fool head off when he's under duress and it don't mean a thing. You go easy on that point."

Thomas Person had stood and walked over to Rednap, sat down, and began speaking to him in low tones.

Harmon Husband had lowered the paper to his side. He surveyed the crowd of angry men who had gathered at the mill to decide some way of breaking the power of Colonel Edmund Fanning, the leader of the Courthouse Ring at Hillsborough. Husband listened first to one man and then to another, as each shouted his complaint. On hearing some of them, he wondered if they had understood a single word of what he had told them: a *peaceful* settling of their grievances . . . an ear to *reason* and their own shortcomings.

Outside, through the partially opened mill door he could see the waving grass in the summer wind. He could see the flutter of coloured skirts and hear the vague, light laughter and voices of women: women who had travelled the roads with their husbands to the meeting at Maddock's Mill. And the angry voices which assailed him in the room made the peace and hope of the world beyond the mill door, made the waving grass, the fluttering dresses, the light laughter seem like useless dreams of beauty.

"Ah got a question! Listen to me, Husband."

The strident voice came from the far corner of the room, from the centre of a group of men who had been banded together in anger and loud protests since their entrance to the meeting.

"Quiet! Quiet!" Harmon called. "Let's hear everybody's mind. Stand out so we can see you," he called to the voice in the corner. Person and Rednap Howell seemed worried. They continued to speak in low tones together, now and then glancing up to the faces of the crowd.

A short, stocky man, his head angled and broad, stepped forward from the group in the corner. His short, thick arms were crossed in front of him. "My name's Hamber," he said belligerently, and he waited, as if there were some reply to be made. Then he continued: "I farm north of Hillsborough."

Harmon Husband nodded for him to go on.

"Tell you, Mr. Husband, you may be a mighty fine man with words and all of that, but it ain't doing me no good. I been cheated out of my land deed. I been cheated on my court fees. I been cheated on my taxes. I got a brother 'bout ten miles from you on Sandy Creek, Mr. Husband. And he ain't got nothing left. He's lost everything. Most of my kin, we kind of feel we better start doing something instead of talking."

Husband nodded. "Yes, yes, I knew your brother."

"Now I'm just telling you these things so you'll know why I stand where I do. Might be hard for you to see with the amount of land you own."

There was an angry muttering through the mill. "Go on, tell him, Hamber."

"Mr. Husband, I figure I got cause to start me a fight. I say if you talk to Fanning with all these fine words, he ain't gonna pay no 'tention to you, to me or to nobody. Husband, he doesn't give a damn for the likes of us. He doesn't care what happens. Did you ever hear what he's done to old Few's wife? Hell, he ought to be horse-whipped for that!"

"You're right, Hamber! Tell him."

The stocky farmer took another step forward, as if his intent was to gain the centre of the floor. "Now I say that there ain't much talk Fanning's gonna understand. But I'll tell you there's *one* way I know to make him listen."

Harmon's deep-set eyes were focused directly on the bull-shouldered farmer. He wondered how long he could afford to let the man speak, how long he could risk Hamber's inciting the men.

"You know, Mr. Husband—" Hamber let his arms drop to his side; he was beginning to feel at ease in front of the sympathetic crowd—"there's one way, like I said, to make Fanning listen to us." He paused. "It's about the same way he made *you* listen to him last year!"

Rednap Howell tried to catch Harmon's eye, tried to warn him that the meeting would soon be out of hand. Rednap was a man of action, but he had his moderations, too, and Husband had convinced him that for the time violence was not the solution of their problems.

Hamber had the crowd's complete attention. "Now what *I* say you ought to do with our great and good Assemblyman Fanning, is to take him and strap him to a skittery little colt. And I say you run that colt under a good stout oak. And I say you whip a rope around Fanning's neck and then you slip it over a limb. *Then* you can talk to him. And if, by God, he so much as raises his rotten voice over a whisper, that skittery little colt's liable to slip right out from under him! That's the way to talk to Fanning!"

"Aye!" A roar from the crowd.

"You've got it straight, Hamber!"

"How about it, Husband? Better 'n words, ain't it?"

"We got time to ride there tonight."

Harmon Husband raised his voice. "Men . . . gentlemen! Give me a chance to speak. You can't take this in your own——"

A tumult of angry voices swept the room. The woodsmen in front of Harmon had shifted their positions uneasily; those lying down had begun to sit up, their hands reaching unconsciously for their guns. Harmon Husband was shouting to be heard. Hamber's voice cut above his.

Then it was Rednap Howell who jumped to his feet, and his booming voice carried above all. His genial, smiling face had taken on a look of iron. His eyes glared. "Shut up!" he roared. "God damn it, shut up!"

The violence of his outburst, his booming voice, shocked the room into silence.

"Hamber—" he continued, pointing his finger at the man—"you get off the centre of the floor and sit down."

Hamber eyed Rednap Howell for a moment, hesitated, then turned slowly, and walked back to his place and sat down with his group of farmers.

"Now you listen to me for a while," Howell said. "I want to have my say before you go on any cheap hanging party." The room was still; all were curious to hear what Howell would say.

He began easily, half-smiling. "Now, neighbours, have any of you ever known me for a peaceful, God-fearing man? Have I ever been accused of that?"

They could not help smiling with him.

"Now you know I write . . . well . . . verses—you sing my songs. You know I'm a schoolmaster, among other things. Some of you might call me an educated gentleman. But by the good Lord I defy any man here to say I've ever gone along with an unjust law when I could get around it or fight it. You all know my temper's quick and I'll stand up to any man."

There were scattered cries of "Yes."

"Then I've as much right as neighbour Hamber to raise my hand. And I've been accused of slapping the rumps of a few ponies in my day, just as Hamber wants us to do. But I'm denying myself that pleasure today. I'm denying it to some of you, too." His voice had quieted. "Now you got a man called Harmon Husband here. He's been doing some of the writing that you men can't do. You can plow straight furrows, and you, Hamber, I reckon you're one of the best men with a scythe in the whole country—but you can't write. You can't talk to the men of the Tidewater."

"I could talk to Fanning," somebody shouted.

"No," Howell said without looking at the man, "you couldn't. Not even Harmon—or I—could do that. We're writing these complaints to the *Assembly* in their language, not to Fanning. And Harmon will do it better than any of us here. It seems to me and Mr. Person that the Assembly's where we'll get our satisfaction. Seems to me and Mr. Person that if we elected an educated pair of men to represent us, we might get a new sheriff. Let them speak loud for us to right our wrongs. We might even get a few more men to represent us in the Assembly. We might even have a fair representation for the number of people we got. We've got about half the people in the whole Colony, but in the Assembly they outnumber us more than three to one."

The men were quiet now, listening to their poet-leader Rednap Howell. He rubbed the back of his hand against his forehead. Things looked better to him. He went on: "You got an election for new Assemblymen coming in July. Do you want Fanning again?"

There was a full chorus of "No!"

"Do you want Judge Lloyd to be elected again?"

"No!"

"Then get a pair of men who *can* speak for you. Get two men those people from the tidewater will listen to. Get two who can catch that Speaker Caswell's ear and bring over some Easterners with us. We aren't going anywhere by hanging one little colonel. But if you can get this Colony in one piece, if you can get it working for its entire self, if you can get equal justice East and West—then we'll be safe and sound."

Rednap Howell could almost see his words building up a restraining barrier in the men's minds, overcoming their natural bent toward violence. And violence, he considered, might be the only satisfactory expedient. Still, he felt with almost mystic certainty that Harmon Husband had a better way.

"Person!" Howell called. "Tell them what we've been talking about."

Thomas Person, who had been sitting during the entire conflict, now stood up. His vest was open. He hooked a thumb in his watch pocket.

John Pryor had been about to ask a question, and he

put it to Person. "Do you really think a pair of honest Assemblymen might help us?"

"Come on out here where the men can see you, John. I been looking about for you."

John Pryor advanced reluctantly. "A little farther," Person said, "Move over there beside Harmon. That's it."

The eyes of the mill crowd were focused on the two men.

Person cleared his throat for attention. "Look at them well, men. Look at them, because they're the two men I'd like to see elected to the Assembly this July."

There was a flurry of voices in the room.

"When we came here, we sort of planned on picking ourselves a couple of Assemblymen. Well, what's wrong with these? I don't think you'll find two abler men to speak for us. Vote for them and you'll be rid of Fanning. You'll be rid of that Courthouse muck. What do you say to it?"

Another murmur of voices whispered through the room, a hesitation, then a cheer, shouts—one great roar of enthusiasm. It was the excitement of a unified action, of each man helping the other, a forgetting of the deep troubles that had beset them a moment ago, a forgetting of their hatred of Fanning.

For a fleeting instant, Harmon Husband was thinking, they had caught glimpses of a dream which arched outward from the mill, which curved in grace between the seacoast and the hills of North Carolina. Perhaps some dreamed a greater dream.

Rednap Howell was on his feet again. "Before you read some more of that paper of yours, Harmon, I got one last thing to say."

Harmon nodded. Person drew slightly back from the floor's centre.

"I don't want any of you men to go away from here thinking you've lost the Rednap you used to know. I'm for peace if peace will rid us of the damn sheriffs, but if this legal way doesn't work, then I'm going to search out Mr. Hamber, and we're going to get ourselves some deer guns. And we, and anybody who wants to come with us, are going down to New Bern. And we're going to have our rights, or we'll have ourselves a Royal Governor, and his pretty Palace, and his whole bunch of thieves— and, men, if need be, we'll even have us a piece of the King of England."

There was a second's awed silence in the mill, then half of the crowd broke into cheering. Harmon Husband looked dubiously at the man who at one moment advocated peace and at the next blew dreams of it apart like a powder blast and threatened war.

Harmon lifted his paper quickly. He was ready to read.

Rednap Howell stepped out of the mill into the fresh air of May, into the freedom of grass and sky. Outside the women waited nervously for their men. Beads of perspiration were running down Howell's forehead. He walked along the stream that passed the mill, and he leaned on a wagon which was far from the crowd of waiting women.

Strange, he was thinking to himself: it was not long ago that he was all for Hamber's idea of riding to Hillsborough, beating Fanning into submission, hanging him, taking Lloyd's neck and wringing it. Then suddenly he had changed, and in an hour had begun to look to Harmon Husband for approval.

Rednap picked a piece of straw from the wagon-bed and began to chew on it thoughtfully. It was a shame, he thought, that a fine man like Husband didn't have a little war in him. He'd be a real leader then. Well, he didn't, so that's why God put the Rednap Howells in the world.

But could he himself have a little peace in him? he mused. Not for long. He'd said as much at the end. Of course not! If nothing came from the election, then let the scythe swing! If the fields were full of rank grass, then harvest the rot: there'd be nothing else to do.

He was smiling to himself when he heard the voice of Charity Allen beside him. "Mr. Howell, thee has done a good thing today."

"Ah, Charity. Well, you heard my downfall. In my heart, Miss, I'm a battle poet and a fighting man. Now you've heard me use namby prose and peace-talk."

She smiled. The summer wind whipped her skirt. "Be

what thee may, thee is still a poet. Let me see . . ." She put her finger to her chin. "Last night I heard one of the men chanting:

> " 'When Fanning first to Orange came
> He looked both pale and wan . . .' "

"You learned that?" Howell asked in surprise. "I thought you Quakers had no sense of humour?"

"Truly, not much," she answered. "But I've been known to laugh in my life."

"Proper," Howell said. "Lord, it was hot in there!"

"Does thee believe Harmon will go to the Assembly?"

"Hope for it, lass. For if he doesn't, and Fanning does, then you'll have little to say to me in the future; because I'll start a fire that will burn from the hills down to the Palace. I swear that to you."

"Then I shall pray he is elected."

"Aye, if it will help, do so by all means."

"Thee has no belief?"

"Very little, lass. Very little."

She looked at him pensively as they stood by the wagon in the mill yard.

"You save souls, don't you, Miss?"

"I speak when the spirit moves me," she answered simply.

Rednap tossed to the ground the straw he had been chewing. "Will you be going with Harmon toward New Bern?"

"Perhaps. I don't know yet. I must spend more time about Hillsborough. They are like all people—in need of God and the Inner Light."

"*A* god, Miss."

"*The* God, Mr. Howell."

"Well, if you pray for damned souls, I suggest you breathe a whit for Fanning, for Tryon. You might even give a whisper for the secretary, Edwards—he's got a house for himself in Hillsborough."

"No doubt I shall. Listen!" She cocked her head, turned to the wind. Then she added, "You're still a poet first, Mr. Howell."

From the interior of the mill came the chant of Rednap Howell's latest poem:

"When Fanning first to Orange came
He looked both pale and wan.
An old patched coat was on his back,
An old mare he was on.

"Both man and mare warn't worth five pounds,
As I have oft been told;
But by his civil robberies
He's laced his coat with gold."

"I must make my bows, Miss," Howell said good-naturedly. "They're lifting a tune that's more to my knowing than peace. You'll excuse me, but my last talk got me so I hardly trust myself."

"I excuse thee," she said. "And I shall pray for Harmon's election. And if that is not the Lord's will, then I shall pray thy mind still turns to peace."

Rednap Howell hesitated a moment longer before going back to the mill, and he said, curiously, "You're a strange one, Charity. You Quakers ever marry?"

"Some of us."

"Can you ride a horse good?"

"A bit," she said, and smiled. The wind whipped her skirt again.

Rednap Howell nodded pensively, then turned and made his way toward the mill.

7

Richard Buncombe

For a while Hillary Caswell lay in delirum from the fever that followed his gunshot wound. There had been an infection which at first caused Dr. Armitage great concern, but as the days passed, a constant, gentle cleansing of the wound began to effect a healing.

At the beginning he remembered hearing the voices of Cecelia, Richard and Matthew; but, somehow, he did not care to open his eyes to see. It was easier to rest in a world of dreams. On the third day he felt an intense restlessness, a dark energy that forced him into consciousness. It was a painful awakening, an act for which his body was loath but to which it was driven. It was as if his mind suddenly realized the danger of resting too long in quiet shadows.

When Hillary opened his eyes, blinked, and smiled weakly, Richard Caswell dabbed the young man's forehead with a handkerchief. "Well, we can thank the Lord and you, Dr. Armitage. It seems he's out of danger."

Dr. Armitage smiled. "Give more thanks to the Lord than to me that the fever broke. You'll be going home now?"

"First, and then to New Bern."

"For the Governor, I suppose?"

"No, for once it's about my own affairs. After all, Armitage, you know I'm still a planter even though I may appear to be anything else."

"Nay, sir, everything else, for all of us, and your lands are clear and prosperous as well."

Richard Caswell did not start his journey until the noon meal. The short December daylight made it reasonable, he told himself, to stop for the night at Kendrick Creek, the home of Colonel Richard Buncombe.

He found that gentleman sitting in his library, a letter-board propped on his lap, and his bandaged foot resting on the stool before him.

"Whatever you do," Buncombe counselled. "Don't allow yourself to get the gout from too much eating. I can tell you it's a damnable disease, and the cures for it are ridiculous, man, ridiculous! Would you care for some wine?"

Richard smiled and said, "No, thank you." He had seated himself comfortably in the great arm-chair by the fire. Buncombe held out his glass, and a servant who had been hovering near the library door entered quickly and filled the glass with Canary wine. He left the room immediately, his sole duty having been performed.

"Perfectly ridiculous," Buncombe repeated. "Armitage tells me that I must give up my port and Madeira." His tone was that of a man who had been informed he was to have both arms and legs removed from his body. He brightened a few moments later and added, "So you see I have to drink Canary instead. There's no point in having a doctor unless you obey him, wouldn't you say so, Richard?"

"Oh, certainly."

"My ship just brought in a dozen pipes of Canary," Buncombe explained. "Frankly, for my health's sake, it couldn't have come at a better time."

Richard could not help smiling. He stroked his chin. "Take a *little* care of yourself. We'd like to have you at New Bern before the session is over."

"Oh, I'll be there. You can count on that. I'll take my coach—are you sure you wouldn't like a touch of Canary?—and I'll keep my foot high on a pillow. Couldn't miss this session with the stir of things."

"You're expecting more than the usual commotion?"

"After the rumours I heard? What else can I expect?"

Richard did not bother to ask *what* rumours; he knew he would be told in the next sentence.

"They tell me that Harmon Husband and a man

called Pryor—John Pryor, I believe—were elected to
the Assembly. Elected in place of Fanning and Lloyd."

Richard Caswell showed no surprise, but he leaned
slightly forward in his chair, nodding his head thoughtfully. "How reliable was that rumour?"

"Oh, you know how rumours are! A kernel of truth
with the chaff of lying. I can't be certain."

Not certain, Richard thought: Rather it was *absolutely sure*. Buncombe had an uncanny knack for knowing
the affairs of the Colony quickly and accurately. His
easy, laughing manner was perfectly sincere, and it was
also a perfect disguise. Buncombe was a large, hearty
man with a proud bearing. His features were full, his
face—especially his cheeks—tinted with red. He wore a
white wig.

He had come to North Carolina from the West Indies, bringing household goods, slaves, and, it was said,
a ship load of gold. After he had built his large brick
house on Kendrick Creek he had put a sign over the
gate entrance: "Welcome All to Buncombe Hall." The
sign had been written in earnest and was accepted in the
same manner. Since the hall was near the ferry from the
northern shore of Albemarle Sound and the Boston Post
Road to Charleston, he had a multitude of visitors, all of
whom he entertained in a lavish way.

Buncombe changed the subject abruptly. "I'm afraid
you'll have to put up with a bachelor establishment, Richard. Madam Buncombe has gone to St. Kitts for a visit and won't be home until spring. I told her she'd have
to return for the opening of the Palace, though." He
chuckled as he took the letter-board from his lap and
placed it on the floor against his chair. "My wife, sir, is
not too enamoured of Governor Tryon's wife. She feels
the lady goes a bit beyond herself in wanting to be
called *Lady* Tryon."

Richard Caswell was letting his mind run along two
channels: overtly following the conversation with interest, but to himself considering the explosion which Husband's presence in the Assembly might cause. The
Governor, of course, would be angry, feeling that
his will was being thwarted by the people. Fanning
would be desperate. Well, so much for their troubles! If

the election was fair, nothing could or should be done to stay those men from their rightful seats.

"I must agree with your good lady," Richard Caswell said. "I understand there are to be *two* gilt elbow-chairs on the dais in the Assembly room: one for the Governor and the other for Lady Tryon."

Buncombe's hearty laugh rang through the hall. "Wonderful, sir! I'll be delighted to tell her." His servant, who stood inconspicuously by the door, looked up and grinned. "I can hear her saying, 'I told you so.' Now, for myself, I find Lady Tryon quite stimulating, though my wife says I'm dull about women. She's hardly the one to speak about that, but I don't like to remind her of it too often." He held out his glass, and his servant hastened to fill it. "A toast to the ladies! God bless them!" he said, and drank.

After dinner the two men talked more seriously about the problems of the Colony.

"I've sent out three full-laden ships to the Indies," Buncombe said. "Thought I might as well escape that new export tax. Damn taxes, anyway! Caswell, sometimes I think we did better under the old government of the Lords Proprietors. At least it paid them to have the country prosper—particularly Lord Salisbury." He puffed his pipe and sent out a cloud of smoke about his head. "How's that young cousin of yours coming along? Armitage told me he received a nasty shot."

"As well as can be expected. Do you happen to know the number of deer they brought in that day?"

"Two, wasn't it?"

"I should have known better than to ask."

"Well, it's good he'll survive. We'll have to save the young people for our battles."

"And which battle are *you* speaking of?"

"First things first, Richard," Buncombe said. "A battle in the West. This Colony has to be united even if it takes a civil war—otherwise we'll be nothing."

Buncombe leaned forward on his cane as he spoke. He eased his weight and tapped the cane on the floor to call his servant's attention. "Bring me my portfolio," he said. He pointed with his stick to the tall mahogany desk. "Yes, that's it."

From the case he extracted a stack of papers, riffled through them and finally found what he was looking for. He held it out for Richard to see. "Here, read this."

The paper was headed quite simply: "Advertisement."

"I suppose you've seen it already?"

"No." Richard shook his head.

"Read it aloud. It rather amuses me," Buncombe said.

Richard Caswell glanced at the paper for a second and began reading: " 'And being conscious of our loyalty to King George the Third, on the present throne, and our firm attachment to the present establishment and form of government, which we sincerely believe all our grievances are quite opposite and contrary to, by downright roguish practices of men who have crept into posts of office, and have practiced upon our ignorance and new settled situation.

" 'We therefore order the above committee to implore the governor's pardon and forgiveness, in the most submissive manner, for any errors that we may have committed, that it is or may be construed to derogate from the honour of his Majesty's Crown and dignity, or tending to obstruct the peace and good order of government.' "

Richard lowered the paper and Buncombe said, "A very mild document, don't you think? Very mild."

"I've heard of this," Richard said. "A very mild document put out by the Regulators—also a very old one. It's been nearly two years, hasn't it?"

"Yes, they've gone those two years without redress," Buncombe said. He was pawing through the papers again. "Ah! Now here's a letter Fanning wrote to Governor Tryon. Don't ask me how I got this copy, because I don't remember—and if I did, I might not tell you. It was written after seventy Regulators rode into Hillsborough and retrieved a member's horse which had been distrained for non-payment of taxes. They took it away from some offices and fired a few shots over Fanning's house. They were saying then that they considered him responsible for the thievery of their land titles. Perhaps you recall the incident."

"Quite well." Richard was glad that Buncombe had not asked *his* opinion on the subject of those riots.

"Let me read it," Buncombe said. "I can catch the spirit of Fanning's grandiloquence. I've had practice. I'll skip a little, too."

Richard Buncombe adjusted himself more comfortably in his chair and began with gusto:

" 'The late orderly and well-regulated County of Orange, is now—oh, my favourite County and people, how they are fallen—the very nest and bosom of rioting and rebellion. The people are now in every part and corner of the County, meeting and complaining and confederating by solemn oath and open violence to refuse the payment of taxes and to prevent the execution of the Law, threatening death and destruction to myself; requiring settlement of Public, Parish and County taxes to be made before *their* leaders; clerks, sheriffs, registers, attorneys and all officers to be arraigned at the Bar—of their shallow understanding—and to be punished according to *their* will: in a word, for *them* to become Sovereign Arbitrators of right and wrong.' "

Buncombe finished reading and said, "I do it rather well, don't I? But truly you see, Caswell, that Fanning hasn't said a word about the abuses of the law by the officers of the court, nor has he so much as mentioned that the raising of fees has gone to the point where the rich farmer can't pay the excess—let alone the poor one."

"Would you expect him to say that?"

"You'd have mentioned it, wouldn't you have?"

"I'd not have had the fees so high in the first place. Good Lord, Buncombe, are you like the rest of them? Do you feel that I approve of the stealing of deeds, the insane fees and the poll tax?"

"Frankly, Richard, I *was* of that opinion for a while. Why do you think I took the trouble to read this to you?"

"I'm afraid to guess. But as I've said before: one can't right an abuse by violence; one can't find law through anarchy."

"What if that were the only way?"

"Then we would have had no law in the first place. I have some faith in Governor Tryon, you know. He knows of the abuses. He told me himself that he'd written Lord Shelburne that the abuses 'cry aloud for, and shall receive, attention and correction.' "

"I know," Buncombe said. "I saw the letter. Let me quote the next line to you: '. . . nor shall embezzlement and irregularities committed by the officers who collect the public revenue escape the most exact inquiry.' That was the way it went."

Richard nodded, curious as to how Buncombe managed to learn the contents of so many private papers.

"So Tryon's said that there are abuses. Now tell me honestly, Richard, what has he done to relieve them? It's fine to talk and talk and talk, but I'll believe a man's good will when I see him act, and not before."

"Damn him if you wish, but he has to uphold the law."

"What law?"

"The same law that you and I stand for. Myself, I hope the Regulators are crushed quickly—the sooner the better for all of us. Then we can set about righting their wrongs. If they didn't keep up this stir and move so quickly, I believe I could get enough of the Assembly behind me to bring about the just changes they demand. As it is, Fanning can cry out on all their storms, and I haven't a chance of holding the powerful men together. Don't underrate Fanning. He's greedy of his power; he never moves backwards; and he always stops short of his own disaster."

"And why, pray tell, does the Governor put up with him?"

"We see the raw side of Fanning, Buncombe. But he's a cultured gentleman. No, don't laugh. He's a little flash of New York, of Boston, of London, a slight decoration, but real—and the Governor has his vanity. Most of us, Buncombe, are striving to build this Colony— and we haven't too much time to cater to that little streak of brilliance in the Governor. Fanning has the time. Perhaps we should find it—we'd get more done. Odd, isn't it?"

"My God, Caswell, don't tell me *you're* not a match for Fanning!"

"Sir, I may be a match. I hope so. But I seek nothing more than North Carolina and her plaudits—not the whole world's. But that's not enough for Governor Tryon."

Buncombe suddenly exploded in anger. "Damn it, Richard, when it comes to the final scene with the Regulators you'll have hammered me to your side! But I won't like it. I'll probably have only half my heart in it. Don't you ever get mad, Richard? Don't you get fighting mad?"

"Sometimes. But I try to keep it bottled up."

"You'll burst, mark me, you'll burst. Or worse, you'll get the gout. By God, that'd serve you right! By the way, don't you have any qualms about letting your cousin get into all this mess? I'm told he's bound for the Governor's household—assistant to Edwards."

"I think he should stick to being a planter."

"Well, make him stick," Buncombe said with a wave of the hand.

"Just after I make you King, sir. To get a taste of government is his idea."

Their talk was interrupted by the housekeeper, a plump Scotswoman, whom Buncombe had accused of being "incorrigibly tidy." A wisp of grey hair hung over her forehead; it seemed out of place, but likely she had placed it there with delicate care. She carried a tray on which were three glasses and a bottle of Madeira. The first glass was filled to the brim with a dull brown liquid; the second with a dash of port that barely covered the bottom of the glass; the third was empty.

She smiled at Richard Caswell, made a short and precise bow, and said to Buncombe, "Sir, 'tis time for your dosage."

Buncombe screwed up his face. "Go away, Martha. I won't take the bitter stuff."

Martha did not move.

He waggled a finger at the port. "What's that in the bottom of the glass?"

"Sir," she said seriously, "I've brought ye a wee bit of

port to ease off the bitter taste. I know 'tis against orders . . . but . . . anyway the medicine's for making ye well so ye can mount your mare and ride over the plantation."

"There's more port than that in pure air." He continued to grumble, but eventually took the bitter dose—having swallowed the meagre amount of port first—only to show his contempt. He reached for the bottle of Madeira but she drew away saying, "No, sir. That was for your choice. Now you've made it, and it's done with. Ye took the port, and ye must be off to bed. To-morrow is Parson Earle's day here and you want to be strong to argue."

"Woman, woman! You're a martinet."

"Whatever that be, I'm not it. It's looking after your interest I am, just as the Madam instructed me before you let her sail to those far islands."

"All right, all right. Run along now. I'll go to bed."

At the door Martha turned, her hand on the doorknob, and added, "Squire Adam Rutledge will be by on the morrow too. His man Herk came to inform you. I've ordered a shoulder of pork with greens and a fine apple pudding."

"Good Lord, woman, if you can't be kind, it's no cause to be brutal!"

"Mr. Rutledge likes his food," she explained to Richard Caswell, and then turning back to Buncombe she said, "You'll have your gruel as the doctor ordered."

Buncombe waited until he was certain that Martha was out of earshot. "That woman will drive me crazy." He took a key from his pocket. "Caswell, open that liquor table and get out some whisky. If I must die of thirst or gout, I'll choose gout."

8

Pine Barrens Hunt

It was the last hunt before Christmas—a Christmas of calm and joy before the gathering storm. Word had drifted back by the circuitous routes of travel that Governor William Tryon had prorogued the Assembly at New Bern; but this word had not been confirmed until Adam Rutledge returned from his brief sojourn at the capital. Isaac Edwards arrived at the Caswell Manor House a few days later and explained the cause of the Governor's action: the Assemblymen of North Carolina had argued against the sending of colonial citizens to England for trial. The Governor's reaction to that was quite simple, Edwards explained—he was infuriated.

Yet, in spite of the double threats of doubt and hate within and without the Colony, there was happiness at Manor House, a happiness which impending conflicts could not impair.

The week before, the weather had been cold, but now the air was crisp and clear. There was a slight wind from the south, but it would not be enough to cause the hounds to lose the scent when the hunt started.

The men had been at Matthew Caswell's hunting camp on Lake Mattamuskeet for almost a week, for the geese were heavy in the waters of the lake. Matthew's sons, John, Elisha and Gregory, were up before dawn lighted the eastern sky and flamed the scant clouds; but old Eb and the grooms who were doubling as cooks had tea ready before any of the hunters were out of bed.

Robin Chapman and his brother Meredith rode over

from their camp which had been made farther down the
shore, and they were in time for the breakfast sausage,
grits and eggs. They were all seated at the rough pine table when Hillary, sleepy-eyed but almost fully recovered, joined them.

"Why didn't someone waken me?" he asked after he
had seated himself and taken a gulp of hot tea.

"He can talk," Robin said.

"I slept like seven sleepers last night," Hillary continued, "and I dreamed we were hunting a brace of foxes
with two packs. I missed the kill, naturally, because I
couldn't make up my mind which pack to follow."

"Don't tell a dream before breakfast or it'll come
true," John said, his mouth full of sausage. He motioned
with his fork. "Eb'll tell you that."

Eb rolled his eyes. "Yes, sar, Mas' John he speak the
truth. Dreams are queer folks: they tell you what's gonna happen—things like you ain't never thought of yourself."

Hillary helped himself to corn pone and gooseberry
jam. "Elisha, I thought there was a lady in a pink coat
riding hell-for-leather right in front of me. She zigzagged
all over the landscape; first after one pack, then after
the other. She was in on both kills and finally rode off
into the woods laughing at me for trying to follow her."

"Miss Celia!" Elisha laughed. "That's Miss Celia
Davenport sure as anything."

Gregory looked up, smiling. "Or *Cecelia,* maybe.
You've got to remember whose dream it was."

Matthew Caswell opened the door to the lodge and
called, "Up and away, lads! The horses are ready and
waiting. We've some riding to do if we want to get to the
charcoal huts before the meet starts off."

He began to sing in stentorian tones:

> "Pleasure that most enchants us
>   Seems the soonest done.
> What is life, with all it grants us,
>   But a hunting run?"

Hillary stood up and rubbed his bad shoulder gently.
He followed the men outdoors and mounted nimbly
enough in spite of the pain which occasionally stabbed

at his shoulder. Dr. Armitage claimed he had mended quickly; to Hillary the time had seemed years. He drew his horse alongside Matthew's.

"We're likely to have a good run," Matthew explained. "The wind is low. Given a good scent, the riding will be hard with the hounds to show us the way." The old gentleman's eyes were bright and sparkling. "You're certain that shoulder's good enough?"

"It has no choice."

Matthew Caswell nodded. This was the way things should be for a hunt. Nothing interfered. In his pink coat, velvet cap, leathern breeks and half-boots he looked the perfect country squire. "We've many coverts in this wild desert country. Even though the foxes are thick, they won't leave their burrows unless properly found by the hounds."

John and Elisha Caswell passed them riding hard down the trail.

"Leave be! You'll wear out your——" Matthew turned to Hillary. "Do the young ones ever learn? They'll wear out their mounts before the hunt begins."

A moment later Gregory too spurred by them. "Now I thought *he* knew better." Then he went back to what he'd been saying. "One difficulty here in the pine barrens is that the foxes can see so far in front of them. They'll come to a little rise; they'll see someone on the ridge a mile away—and they'll turn back. They may run either left or right through a hedge—and what happens? The hounds come in full cry over the hedge and flash on half-way down the slope. The field can't see the hounds check, and, the first thing you know, you're beyond where the fox turned." Matthew smacked his lips. "It's hard to kill your fox in galloping country. Ah well, that's as it should be, too! I love it all."

"You must have been on some great hunts in your day, sir."

"Great hunts?" He smiled, thinking back. "Yes, yes indeed, I have, Hillary. Perhaps not like my father. He used to regale us with stories of the great old hunts in the Midlands of England.

"There's one I can't forget. He'd heard about a hunting party that passed between the encamped armies of

Charles the First and Oliver Cromwell before the battle of Naseby. The cry of the hounds and the sound of the hunting horn were lost in the first blast of the Roundheads' guns. Several of the party were so annoyed that they immediately took side with Charles the First. You know, Old Ol' would have no truck with such frivolous doing, and in *his* time England and Virginia both suffered in good sportsmanship."

The dusk of early morn had given way to light. The two riders had come to the verge of the pine barrens where the trees were sparse and curiously dwarfed with tufts of green boughs on slim trunks.

The flush of a fiery sunrise had spread outward from the first low clouds; the green of the pines was accentuated. Matthew reined his horse; his eyes were twinkling as he turned toward Hillary. "I know a secret path through the pocosin, Hillary. We can outwit the lads and arrive at the huts before them."

He turned his horse from the main trail and plunged along a faint track that led through a thicket of yapon bushes to the heavier wood of the pocosin. Soon they were travelling along a narrow ridge of solid earth; on either side the swamp water was black and fearsome. The knees of the cypress roots thrust up grotesquely from the heavy, slimy waters like prehistoric creatures, dim in the eternal morass, lost in the infinity of time. The only light through the blackness of the pocosin came from the dull reflection of the bare trunks and branches of an occasional beech tree. A heavy terrifying silence infused the land, to be penetrated at strange secluded intervals by the fall of a rotted limb and its dead splash into the swamp water.

Hillary shivered under his well-padded hunting coat. He hoped Matthew was sure of his way along this narrow ridge of firm land. One wrong step on either side would pitch a rider headlong into the dark, cold water. Hillary's mount was restless, uneasy. He stepped gingerly along the faint trail.

For some time they rode through the gloom of the heavy trees and the bare cypress. Now and then the sound of birds' wings beat on the silence. There was a flash of white against the darkness as two egrets flew past; a moment later followed the shrill caw of a crow. High in the air was a burst of colour, a chattering, an arc, and a flock of parakeets flew from one tree to another.

Light began to penetrate the gloom. The shapes of the tall trees stood out against the sky which was now enveloped in the morning red of full sunrise.

Matthew called back over his shoulder, "Not far now. We'll soon be through the swamp."

When they emerged it was into a small clearing beyond the camp of the charcoal burners, amid the heavy growth of the turpentine pines. As their horses moved side by side across the clearing, Matthew chuckled. "We saved at least three miles. Ha! The boys still can't outfox their old father." Matthew pointed with his riding crop. "There's the M.F.H., Rutledge, on the path. Good horseman, that fellow. That's Miss Celia Davenport—the tall woman in the pink coat. I suppose you recognize the young woman with her?"

Hillary had glanced ahead to see Cecelia Chapman; yes, he recognized her, he said. There was not one chance in a thousand that he would mistake the young woman who had visited him so often while he lay with his shoulder healing.

Matthew had turned to Hillary, his eyes sparkling. "Methinks you have an eye for that beauty, Master Hillary."

Hillary felt himself turn red. He did not answer, for at that moment he was wondering if it were possible Robin Chapman might have insisted that his sister visit him. No, surely that could not be the case. But then, on the other hand, had she ever shown any real interest in him before that business at the deer drive?

Matthew had not appeared to notice Hillary's discomfiture. He was saying, "I was Master for twenty years." They jogged their horses across the clearing. "Twenty years," he repeated. "Yes, I've seen some good hunts in my time. I wonder," he mused, "if the hunts haven't been the best of my life. Transient, ephemeral joys, I suppose, not good solid things such as getting great acts passed by the Assembly. No. A hunt is like last year's crop, my lad. It is no more; but it has been and it has left a fond memory. You see, I'm getting old; I talk to myself."

"No, sir. I believe you're talking to me."

Matthew looked at him curiously. "Yes, you're right. I *do* speak to you." He smiled, and when a few moments later he introduced Hillary to a tall, distinguished-looking man with straight, sharp features, he made the introduction with a peculiar pride. "Adam Rutledge," he said, "may I present my nephew, Hillary Caswell?"

Adam Rutledge was dressed in a pink coat, tan breeks and a black velvet cap with a visor. When he shook hands with Hillary, his grip was firm, warm and friendly.

"I knew your father, Hillary, and I loved him well," Adam said. "We're all happy that you're among us. You must come visit us at Rutledge Riding—soon."

Hillary thanked him. There was no doubt in his mind that someday he would find a firm friend in Adam Rutledge. Then he recalled, too, the Rutledge his father had described as a "complete man." This Adam Rutledge was surely the same man.

Elisha, Gregory and John came bolting across the clearing, their horses breathing hard. Gregory reined his horse short when he saw his father and Hillary. The smile on his father's face completed his mortification.

Adam had turned to Matthew. "We're running two packs today: Mary Warden's bitch pack of ten and my own of twelve and a half couples. We ought to do well since there's not enough wind to bother."

"If the foxes don't take to the pocosin," Matthew said. "These pine barrens foxes are getting wily; we have to be sure to keep them in the open."

They had come up to the main group, and Hillary was thinking that it made a good show even though the men wore scratch clothes. Many had Oxford coats with different-coloured collars. A few were dressed in scarlet or hunter's pink—including the Master, Parson Earle and Matthew Caswell. Of the women, Miss Celia Davenport was dressed in pink; Mary Warden, a small, charming woman who sat her horse with surprising grace, was wearing a habit of Lincoln green.

Matthew was explaining that she was the wife of William Warden and that they lived across the sound in Chowan County. "Queen's Gift," he added. "It belonged to her grandfather, Roger Mainwaring—a great character. The people of the County used to call him the Duke, or Duke Roger. The title was always there."

Hillary was only half listening to Matthew as his eyes searched among the gaily dressed hunters to find Cecelia Chapman again. Once he was certain he caught a glimpse of her—she was speaking to Gregory Caswell —but then another rider moved before his view, and Matthew had begun talking once more.

Mary Warden spurred her horse gently forward and rode to greet Matthew. "It's been too long, Matthew," she said as they clasped hands. "And where is Elizabeth?"

"She said she was going to make Christmas cookies this morning, but you know that old Belinda won't let her in the kitchen."

Mary Warden laughed a light and lovely laugh that was a delight to the listeners. She held out her hand to Hillary. "And you are Lawrence's son, I'm certain. It's good to have you down here in the Carolinas." When she had turned again to Matthew, Hillary was caught by the grace of her movements. She was a small woman, but exquisitely formed, and her face seemed almost heart-shaped. Her little three-cornered hat fitted closely to her head, and her trim hair, done in a bun at the nape of her neck, was unpowdered.

It was a few moments before Hillary saw her husband, William Warden. He was years older than she. His face was thin and cadaverous, and his dark burning eyes were those of a fanatic. For some unknown reason Hillary glanced toward Adam Rutledge, and Adam met his eyes with a strange look, as though he felt Hillary had discovered something.

Others were assembling, until it seemed to Hillary that there were not less than thirty riders in all.

"Will you start both of the packs?" Matthew asked Adam.

"Just mine, first. Later if we have luck and the scent is easy, I'll throw in Mary's bitch pack. She wants to try out Crossie."

"Crossie?"

Adam laughed. "I know, I know. She finally inveigled me into letting her have Crossie."

"For breeding purposes only," Mary said with a smile.

"Of course I know very well she wants to run her," Adam continued.

Matthew turned to Hillary. "There's your new employer." He nodded toward a thin, rather short man with cold, hawk-like features. "That's Isaac Edwards. You've never met him, have you?"

"No," Hillary said as he surveyed the gentleman, "I haven't."

"Well, there'll be time after the hunt."

It was a pleasant scene as the riders prepared for the signal, a scene dear to the eye of a true sportsman: the pack moving restlessly about, eager to be off; the wide-smiling Negro grooms holding the taut leashes; the horses trampling the earth, tossing their heads as their riders tried to quiet them by voice and rein; the vivid, short pine trees; and, beyond, the deep greens and black of the pocosin.

Robin Chapman was acting as whipper-in. He was in lively conversation with Adam Rutledge even as the huntsman started to lift his horn.

The full, clear notes rose on the air, then fell to the distance of swamp and pines. The grooms unleashed the hounds, and they were off, running, scampering, tails wagging, across the open logged land, their noses close to the earth.

A hundred yards away was a narrow creek. The women were following Adam Rutledge, and one by one their horses took the stream in stride—first Miss Celia, then Mary Warden and the others. To their right, Hillary saw Cecelia Chapman riding beside Gregory, and then the field spread. No scent had been picked up.

Hillary waited until the hounds were well away before he joined the field. He caught himself humming an old English hunting song which his father had loved to sing. He felt the south breeze blow gently on his face.

The sun was now well up, and the light sparkled on

the waters of the narrow creeks which the field of riders were taking in graceful stride.

Matthew, who had lingered behind to give orders to the Negroes, passed Hillary, driving his great bay stallion hard. He shouted, "Crossie's got the scent. I think that's her voice. See, Mary Warden's turned to follow."

Hillary followed the point of Matthew's crop. He could see Mistress Warden on the west side of a narrow creek. Ahead of her was a lone hound, nose to the ground. It veered suddenly, taking to a patch of burned-off timber; disappeared into that peculiarly desolate realm of blackened stumps, of occasional tall trees charred to the tip.

Hillary felt the exhilaration of the crisp air. He began to sing a song of Quorn Hunt that he had learned in England:

"Who is that trumpeter blowing his horn?
That is the trumpeter coming from Quorn.
The very worst huntsman that ever was born."

Adam Rutledge's horn sounded. Now Robin Chapman had turned. Half a dozen hounds had taken up the scent and ran yapping after Crossie. Soon the entire field had turned and was running a good pace to the west. For half an hour they gave chase through the open country, and then they came to a stretch of land where the yapon bushes were five and six feet high. The hounds scattered, running in different directions.

Robin Chapman was laughing. He held up an opossum that had diverted half the pack. Crossie kept on, followed by four others, noses to the ground.

Hillary saw an opening and spurred his mount across the charred ground to intercept the dogs. Then the bushes thickened again, and he could not see far ahead. The hounds were silent and he was certain they had lost the scent. He pressed on through the brush to the eastern side of the charred wood until he came on an open space where five hounds were moving about in circles.

Hillary reined his horse and glanced about. He laughed when he saw it. The tail of the fox stuck out from the leaves near the top of a tall, sturdy yapon bush.

He watched as the fox moved slightly, peering down at the circling hounds with a seemingly dispassionate interest. A moment later the hounds were in full cry across the field; Crossie had picked up another scent.

Hillary heard the thudding of hoofs and turned to see Isaac Edwards riding toward him. Hillary pointed with his crop, and Edwards glanced at the yapon bush.

"I suppose that I should have knocked him out of that bush. But since he was too clever for them, I had to let him alone."

"Perfectly right," Edwards said.

"Look at him," Hillary continued, "trying to pretend his tail's just another yapon leaf."

They turned their mounts slightly. "I'm Isaac Edwards," the hawk-faced man said with a smile. "I don't think I've had the chance to meet you."

"I was looking forward to the privilege of an introduction at a quieter moment," Hillary answered. "My name is Hillary Caswell." He offered his hand.

Edwards' clasp was less firm than the spirit of his words. "My assistant! Truly a pleasure, Hillary. It's more than I'd hoped—to be working with a sportsman."

Their attention was diverted for a moment. The wily fox had decided it was time to make his parting. He was absolutely unafraid of the two men, as if he divined their sentiments. He came out from the yapon bush with great deliberation, looked about and then trotted quietly off in the opposite direction from the hounds.

"Quite business-like, isn't he?"

"It's a fair chance that he's an old one at the game," Hillary said.

"Like an old politician," Edwards commented.

"Or a planter at the market."

The hounds were making a great cry in the distance. "Come on," Edwards said, spurring his mount. "We can be in at the kill if we hurry." His mare splashed through a shallow stream and started through the pine barrens. Hillary followed apace. They came on in time to see Mary Warden holding up the brush.

They had been out a little over half an hour, and had raised two foxes. By noon, two more had been added to the first kill.

Hillary arrived at the meeting-place late; many of the younger hunters were already riding away. Robin, the whipper-in, was gathering the hounds, and the slaves were putting them into a wagon which was drawn by two white mules.

"Hillary! Hillary!" Robin called. "Want to stand by? Three hounds haven't come in yet, and I've got to send men out after them."

"Surely," he answered. He dismounted and led his horse toward Robin Chapman.

"Shoulder's better, isn't it?"

"Barely feel it now, but I'm using it as a lame excuse to stay through Christmas. I met Isaac Edwards out in the pine barrens. Strange fellow, but rather agreeable."

Robin was stooping to gather two leashes which had been left on the ground. "Most men are agreeable when you meet them out of their own bailiwick." Robin added without looking at him, "Damn it, Hillary, do you really know what you're getting into?"

"Honestly? No, I don't."

"I thought as much. Listen. We've got to have a long talk—soon. I found——"

He broke off as Miss Celia Davenport and his sister Cecelia rode up. Hillary could not help remembering Angela's comment that women who had a fondness for hunting horses eventually grew to look like horses. The maiden lady, Celia Davenport, *did* have a long, narrow horselike face, but in spite of that she was an impressive person. She was tall and broad shouldered, with a flat, tapering waist, and she sat her horse superbly. She leaned over her mount's neck and shook hands with Hillary.

"Well, my lad, I'm happy to see you. Though you're not a lad now; you're a man. Oh well, time," she explained with a wave of her riding crop. "Do you know that I might have been your mother?" She laughed. "Yes, Lawrence and I were engaged at one time, but we were always quarrelling, mostly about horses. So, of course, we finally gave it up. A good thing, too—" she laughed heartily, her eyes twinkling—"for we weren't the least suited. I was cut out of spinster cloth, and I must say that I don't mind the material at all."

She laid her crop on Cecelia's shoulder. "My niece, here, is a different story, I'm afraid. She's bound to marry one of those young jackanapes who are always at her feet. You're not one of them, are you, Master Hillary?"

Cecelia Chapman was blushing violently.

"Miserably in love," Robin called jokingly from the wagon.

Hillary compounded her embarrassment by adding, "I've already proposed twice, Miss Davenport, but she'll have none of me."

"You're wretches—the pack of you!" Cecelia said.

"Don't speak that way, Niece. I dare say he'll be like all the others—following you around like a puppy." She glanced at Hillary shrewdly. "Not too bad," Celia Davenport went on: "An alliance between Lawrence's son and my niece." She paused. "I must give it some thought. Cecelia is my heir, you know. It really wouldn't be too bad a match."

"But I've already tried," Hillary protested in mock hopelessness.

Cecelia's face was still scarlet.

"Be bold, my lad. Be bold. A woman likes a romantic lover." She walked her mount toward the wagon where Robin was standing.

Hillary looked to Cecelia. Her eyes were flashing, as if she were between speechless rage and tears. He walked to her mount, took the reins and looked up at her. "But why be so angry?" he asked.

She could not control herself to answer him. She gripped her riding crop tight.

"Honestly, Cecelia, ever since the first time I saw you at Manor House, I've thought you the loveliest creature I've ever known."

"I don't believe a word of your blarney."

"Must I insist?"

"No. There's no need to." Her voice softened. "But you're going to New Bern. And you'll be gone a long time. . . ."

"Not for long, I hope."

She looked at him curiously. Her eyes were shining and bright. At that moment Hillary wanted to reach up and take her in his arms. He thought she leaned toward him, but even as he moved to touch her hand he heard the voice of Isaac Edwards. "Hillary, Hillary Caswell! Ah, I've found you. We have much to talk about this evening. . . ."

9

Christmas at
Manor House

As Christmas approached, a great excitement pervaded Manor House, an excitement compounded of more than the Christmas spirit. If the summons "To arms!" was not shouted in the hill country, it was muttered loud enough to be heard near and far. Couriers dashed about with plans and counterplans. All this made a different world of the holiday season.

Hillary received a message from Isaac Edwards, urging him to travel to New Bern as soon as possible after the holidays. The Governor's dismissal of the Assembly had brought up a maze of new matters and also Edwards had much to do to prepare for the Governor's move in early spring from New Brunswick to the Palace in New Bern, which was being given its finishing touches.

Packets had come from New Bern: messages for Richard Caswell, information for the ailing Colonel Richard Buncombe. Adam Rutledge, of course, received more than one man's share of communications—but all did not come from New Bern. Many came by word of mouth from men dressed as backwoodsmen and scouts who stayed on briefly at Rutledge Riding and then melted back into the forests whence they had come.

But Christmas was a time for rememberance.

The slaves at Manor House came in from the woods and swamps, bringing the high-wheeled Devon carts loaded with holly, mistletoe and great stacks of cedar boughs.

The rooms were fragrant with the sweet odour of evergreens. Christmas cakes, spiced and sugared, were in the serving pantry, laid out on tables until the icing hardened. The tang of those rich spices was in the air from the kitchen to the house, trailing down the passageways. Slave girls were preparing apples stuck with cloves to be hung on the giant Christmas tree which would stand at the end of the hall. Corn had been popped and strung. Popcorn was dipped in molasses and made into balls to be hung on the tree.

The house had been swept and polished from the attic downward. Windows shone, brass gleamed. Manor House had taken on the Christmas spirit of gaiety, welcome and joy.

Hillary caught the spirit and went into the swamp with the lads to cut the Christmas tree. It was a matter of moment, for the finest tree must be had for the great occasion. The young men scouted for nearly two hours before Elisha and John could decide which tree was to be cut. In the end, Hillary's vote gave the favour to Elisha's choice.

Two slaves cut the tree and with the aid of the young men they carried it to the wood road. Then they moved through the forest singing, "God Rest Ye Merry, Gentlemen" at the top of their lungs, half-dragging, half-carrying the tree behind John's horse. The rich, rhythmic voices of the slaves joined in the song, and they beat time on tin pans and buckets.

Gregory, who had arrived after the tree was cut, kept saying that it was a shame the girls couldn't be with them.

"My dear brother," Elisha countered, "if you're thinking of Miss Cecelia, you ought to remember your relationship."

"I wasn't thinking of her. I just think it would be nice if they were here."

Unperturbed, Elisha continued: "And the only member of this group distant enough to court her is Cousin Hillary." He glanced at Hillary for confirmation.

"Now, Elisha, do I look like a courting man?"

"Frankly, you do. But you're rather clever about it, and I wish you'd be more in the open so we'd have something to talk about."

Hillary smiled. "All right. Where *did* the girls go?"

"There! At last he asks. To St. David's Chapel to decorate the altar. The curate's going to hold a midnight service on Christmas Eve, and then he's having a choir rehearsal too—with our ten thousand cousins."

They set the tree in the great hall and spread piles of evergreens near the fire-place. The pungent odour filled the room where Hillary sat with Madam Elizabeth as she made wreaths and garlands. Hesitantly he tried winding a garland.

"The Negroes love Christmas," Madam Caswell was saying as she wound some bright-red holly berries into a wreath. "They have a two-day holiday and Matthew allows them plenty of cider. Some of it's a little hard, I'm afraid."

"Made so on purpose?"

"I suspect Matthew of seeing to that, but he always claims that it happens by accident." Madam smiled. "Oh, and tomorrow you'll see one of the customs of the Negroes called 'John Kooner.' I'm sure they brought it with them from Africa. It might have come from Guinea —some of our oldest slaves are from there. A lot of them still have love for their native land and seem to re-member it quite well. Sometimes I wonder——" She broke off, and then began again. "There are some fear-some stories about the journey along the Great Slave Road, and then the passage across the Atlantic when they were packed between the decks. Old Eb could tell you some of those tales."

She held the wreath before her with an appraising eye, put it down, and began another. "The ships sailed into Albemarle, and most of the Guinea slaves were sold to the planters in Tyrrell County. Colonel Buncombe bought some, and the Collinses at Lake Scuppernong acquired a number. Ours were bought by Matthew's father, the first Matthew Caswell."

"They seem to have worked out well."

"Oh, they're very good, but they're still ruled by an

incredible number of superstitions, charms, philtres and such-like. I guess Matthew could tell you more about that than I can. But truly, it's strange what they've done to Christmas. They've made it something of their own by adding their weird tribal rites."

"And what are those?"

"Well, I've never seen any myself, but Matthew has, and he tells me that some of them are horrible. He mentions only the mild things to me. They take gizzards of chickens, heads of snakes, livers of dogs, lizzard tails and offal and make a concoction of it all to cure their ailments. It's really terrible to speak about it, but one accustoms oneself to the facts when one must deal with savage folk."

Again she wove a wreath with the brilliant red berries of the holly. "We try to teach them. I'll wager that old Eb can repeat the prayer-book through and through—" she paused—"repeat the prayer-book, and walk right down from the balcony at St. David's and go into the swamp to his own tribal rites. You see, he has two religions. I doubt if he's nearly so bad as the others. We teach them!" She shook her head. "We teach them and they sacrifice a pig or a chicken in place of a human being."

"That's some progress, isn't it?"

"Is it? If we weren't here, they'd go back to their old ways."

"I'd like to see some of these rites," Hillary said. "How should I go about it? Should I ask Eb?"

Madam's face became serious. "No. No, don't do that. It's better that you don't try. It would only cause trouble." There was something akin to fear in her bright eyes.

"We've had no trouble on our plantation," she continued, "but others have. A few years ago they found a white man crucified. There are other stories—much more terrible—and I shan't tell you those. Take my word that it's best to let the rites stay in the swamps—unknown. Anyway, you'll see a mild form of their superstitions in 'John Kooner.' "

"I can't seem to get this garland right," Hillary said.

"Then let me help you." Both Hillary and Madam

Caswell turned at the sound of Angela's voice. She stood in the doorway, her cheeks still red from the nipping wind. She drew off her knitted cap and mittens and unhooked her fur-lined cape.

"Angela!" Madam Caswell said. "I thought you'd gone to the Chapel."

"I started, but it was too cold."

"I've never known you to complain of the cold," Madam Caswell replied.

"Well, there weren't any boys—just a pack of girls." She looked from under her long dark lashes at Hillary and said candidly, "I thought that at least Cousin Hillary would be there."

Elizabeth Caswell could not repress a smile.

"And I'm flattered," Hillary said, "unless, of course, just any man would have done as well as I."

Angela sat down on the floor at Hillary's feet and began to wind a garland with swift fingers. "No," she said. "Not *any* would have done so well."

"You're quick with those garlands," Hillary exclaimed, purposely ignoring her flattery. "I'm all thumbs at it."

"My mother will tell you that I can do many house-wifely things," Angela said pointedly.

"This is *my* daughter speaking?" Madam Caswell said in astonishment. "My dear, you're indeed a helper. You're clever with your hands. You can sew and cook. But I haven't thought of you as quite ready to become a wife, not yet."

Angela drew herself up. "I'm quite grown-up now." She glanced at Hillary, her eyes shining, "Quite grown-up."

Angela's manner had left Hillary and Elizabeth self-conscious. Neither knew quite what to say in front of the girl, but at that moment John rescued them by entering the room and asking what he could do to help. He added, "Elisha's followed the girls over to St. David's. He heard the Swain girls would be there."

The holiday spirit was beginning to wear on Madam Caswell. She stood up, saying, "My back's broken bending over those wreaths. John, why don't you and Hillary loop the garlands over the mirrors? You can hang the wreaths at each of the windows in the drawing-room and the dining-room."

"It should look nice that way," Hillary commented. He thrust a number of wreaths under his arm. "Let's be at it, John."

John groaned. "But that's not what I meant by 'help.' Every year I have to string garlands and hang wreaths. I want something only a man can do. And, Mother, how does it happen that Elisha is always somewhere else when there's work to be done?"

Angela brushed her full skirts free of needles. "Because Elisha uses his head, John."

Madam Elizabeth turned from the mirror which she was draping with a string of cedar. She looked at her younger daughter who was now standing with both arms raised, brushing back her blond hair. Madam Elizabeth started to speak, thought better of it. She observed the full figure of her daughter, the way she placed her hands on her hips. Hillary was thinking this was perhaps the first time Madam Caswell had noticed that her daughter was growing into a woman, and he could not help smiling at her consternation.

By noon all of the work was finished. The slaves had finished sweeping the floor clear of cedar when the young men and girls burst into Manor House, red-cheeked and bright-eyed. Caps, mittens, capes and cloaks flew through the air, some to land on benches, some on the floor, while the owners crowded to the fire-place, warming their hands and all talking at once. Each tried to impart the miscellaneous news he had gleaned at St. David's.

"The curate said that we sang very well. . . . Colonel Buncombe has had another spell of the gout . . . the Swains have another baby . . . and Elizabeth Swain is angry at her mother for having it right at Christmas . . . the Blounts are going to have a suckling pig with a red apple in its mouth and a great haunch of venison . . . the Blounts are going to have a masque ball on Twelfth Night . . . and . . ."

Hillary was standing in the hallway near Madam Caswell, his hands to his hips as he listened to the bedlam about the fire-place. Much of the news and gossip had been directed to Madam Elizabeth, but most of it to those who had already heard it three times.

The door of the study opened and Matthew Caswell appeared in the doorway, smiling. "What *is* the cause of all this?"

Angela ran to him and threw her arms about him. "Christmas! That's reason enough. The spirit and everything. Come on, Daddy, play your fiddle so we may dance!"

"At this time of day, chick? Dancing is for the evening."

"Then you promise to play after supper? Please say you will. It's practically Christmas this moment and we ought to be gay."

"And we are gay," Matthew said.

"Oh, yes, some—but not so gay as I want to be."

Hillary turned from the crowd of young people gathered about the fire-place and walked to the stairway. His mind was filled with a multitude of thoughts: Christmas —and we ought to be gay, New Bern, his own last Christmas. . . .

He was three or four steps up when he heard the voice of Cecelia Chapman. She had been sitting on the stairs, listening to the gaiety in the hall below. He had been so involved in his own thoughts that he had not seen her.

"So serious, Hillary. Is the world coming to an end?" she asked.

"You're lucky that you spoke. I was so absent-minded I'd have walked right over you—honestly."

He sat down on the step beside her. It seemed to him that he had never seen her looking more beautiful. Her eyes were dancing with a merriment that made fun of his sombre feelings. "But I've been looking for you," he said.

"Why?"

He stammered for a moment, then managed to say, "Oh, I was tired of too much noise, too much happiness over nothing. . . ."

"So you looked for me. That's flattering. But I've never known happiness to be for nothing."

"Perhaps, perhaps," he said, unable to think of anything else. How many things, he was wondering, joined to make that impulse of emotion which welled in him? The closeness of this lovely girl brought all memories together: the tang in winter air, the rich sweet odour of the pine, the laughter from the hall, his own peculiar loneliness in this Christmas. He took her hands in his. He leaned forward and pressed his lips against hers.

When they broke away, Cecelia's eyes were enormous, and she did not speak.

Hillary, surprised at himself, at his impetuous feeling, said softly, "I'm sorry, Cecelia. But you looked so lovely, and I . . ."

Then a smile came to her lips. "You're sorry! You kiss as if you've kissed many women before. Do you always tell them you're sorry?" There was that slight mocking tone in her voice.

The voices from the hall seemed to have grown louder. Cecelia raised her eyes to the turn in the stairway and stood up. "You're honestly sorry?" she asked.

"No."

"Come out of sight then," she said.

Hillary looked about, not understanding. He saw her skirt swirl about her as she ran up the stairs, caught a flash of her slim legs before she reached the landing and disappeared around the turn. Then he followed her, wondering if she were angry, wishing for the moment again.

As he gained the landing and stepped toward her, she turned to face him. She looked at him wide-eyed, with almost the same astonishment that she had shown when he kissed her. Wisps of her auburn hair fell across her forehead; her cheeks were flushed, and she leaned toward him.

"If you were not sorry, then . . ." Her voice was low. In a moment she was in his arms, her body lightly against his. Her head was back, her lips slightly parted. Hillary pressed his lips against her smooth, warm mouth. For a long time they clung together. She was sweet and yielding, and Hillary felt his heart racing, the blood pounding through his veins.

Cecelia released herself, gently pushing away from

him. She was breathing quickly, her lips still parted, her eyes betraying her surprise at herself.

"Cecelia," he whispered, "give me your lips again."

"For the farewell to New Bern?" she asked quietly.

"Don't speak of that."

"But it's true, isn't it?"

He held her shoulders in his strong hands, and she had begun to yield when a door slammed in the upper hall. They drew apart. "Better go downstairs," she said softly and took his hand. Decorously they sat down on the steps where he had found her. Cecelia's face was flushed. She had folded her hands in her lap, and when he reached to touch her, she moved away.

"Not here," she said. "Besides, you're supposed to be sorry about such things."

"Don't talk such nonsense."

"Then let us find some peace—" she looked at him inquisitively—"somewhere away from the noise and a thousand people."

"But there's no place to be alone here," he said.

"Dear Cousin Hillary, either you're not very inventive, or you don't want to be alone with me." The mocking tone had come back to her voice.

"I'd rather be alone with you than anything else in the world, and yet . . ."

"Yet what?"

"Yet I'm afraid of it."

"Afraid? That's nonsense. I think it's fun!"

"Cecelia," he asked hesitantly, "do you kiss others as you did me?" He had asked it, remembering the gentle press of her body against him, the searching of her lips.

She laughed then, a slow rippling laugh, which affected him strangely. "Of course, silly. Do you see any harm in that? Surely it doesn't bother you?"

He was too astonished to answer, and she continued roguishly, her finger to her cheek, "So you object to kissing! You refuse to think of a place where we could be alone. Hillary Caswell, how could you ever be my lover?"

"I wish you wouldn't say things like that," he said. "When I think you might say them to someone else . . ."

"But, dear," she said, "I promise I'll never say them in exactly the same way."

He was embarrassed. He was quietly and efficiently making a fool of himself—and she was paying him back in kind for the talk at the pine barrens hunt. "And you act this way with all the boys here?"

"Of course not! I know them far too well. Now the young gentlemen of Charleston—that's another matter. They're very gallant fellows." She laughed. "And if a young lady should ask to be alone with one of them, I'm quite certain he'd find a way to arrange it."

She had stood up and now looked down at him in amusement.

"I'd rather not hear about the Charleston gentlemen," he said.

"Ah, possessive, as all men are." She walked slowly down the steps toward the noise of the great hall. She turned once and continued, "I shall tell you, Cousin Hillary. If you're worried, I promise never to let you be alone with me. I'll never give you that chance to worry again."

"Cecelia, you don't know what you're saying."

"Cousin Hillary, you don't know what you said."

Then she left him, turning at the bottom of the stairs into the hall, leaving him confused and somewhat disconsolate.

Thoughts of Cecelia bothered him for restless hours. It was the first time he had not spent the interval before sleep considering the problems of the Colony of North Carolina, the voices and thoughts of Richard and Matthew Caswell. Now he could think only of Cecelia, the softness of her body, the way her lips had clung to his.

She had kissed him at first as though she had never been kissed before. On the stairs it had been different. She had talked as though she knew the world too well to suit him.

At last he fell into fitful sleep. And when he woke in the morning at cock's crow he first quietly damned the gallant gentlemen of Charleston, and then himself.

Hillary Caswell hurried to the window and looked down toward the quarters line. The Negroes were stir-

ring as the first streaks of dawn lined the eastern horizon. By full sunrise they would be on their way to Man-
or House on this, their day of celebration. Hillary could
hear them already, warming up for John Kooner's Day
by crying, "Chris'mus gif'! Chris'mus gif'!"

Hillary hurried to put on his clothes, not waiting for
the morning tea. He was whistling as he walked down
the stairs. Matthew Caswell was waiting for him at the
bottom of the steps. "Christmas gift!" Matthew called.
"I got you first."

Laughing, Hillary reached into his pocket and took
out a tuppence which he placed in Matthew's hand.
"You caught me while I was whistling."

"Well, I'm glad you're prepared to pay the price of
happiness."

"Adam Rutledge warned me. He bought enough
tuppences for me from goldsmith Coletrain when he was
in Edenton."

"Wise thing. You'll need them," Matthew said, taking
Hillary by the arm. "Come out on the gallery and watch
the show."

In about ten minutes the entire family had gathered at
the far end of the gallery where a large table, covered
with glass cups, had been placed. Hillary looked for Cecelia and then realized that she had returned to Red
Bank last night. It took something of the joy out of the
morning, for he knew there would be little time left to
see her. Doggedly he tried to concentrate on the rites of
John Kooner.

Near-by was a smaller table than the first on which
had been placed a large, glass punch-bowl filled with
rum punch. Two house-servants dressed in white stood
by it, ready to serve. Piles of presents were on the long,
low benches at the gallery's edge where Madam Elizabeth stood, waiting to pass the gifts out to the slaves.

During the night the pinch of cold weather had eased,
and now a gentle wind from the south moved the long
streamers of moss that hung from the oaks. It was a soft,
salubrious wind that already smelled of spring and the
warming earth.

John and Elisha appeared in the doorway bearing another hamper full of gifts which they added to those on

the benches. Angela, looking coquettish, and Ann, trying to appear serious, stood by their mother to help pass out the presents. There were gloves and comforters, shawls, gay handkerchiefs for turbans, and innumerable bright-coloured cloths.

John had edged over to Hillary and pointed toward the road. "They're coming. Do you see them? Look down the quarters line."

In the distance was the beat of a drum.

Another pounding sounded close at hand, a quick, heavy rhythm. The beat was echoed back and forth between the two drums. A long line of men and women had formed by the quarters line and now began to move forward slowly.

The music began: a weird, chanted, broken-rhythmed song. The drums beat louder. Now a *shansi*, an instrument like the lyre, took up the song of lost Africa. The two-stringed native violins began, and the pan pipes cut in sharply. The younger children wandered in and out of the moving procession, playing the pipes loudly, wildly.

Hillary moved forward to the edge of the gallery, beside Matthew, to watch. Even in the midst of the drumming and noise of the boisterous procession, they heard the sound of a galloping horse. In a moment the rider was dismounting from his foam-flecked grey. It was Isaac Edwards, looking tense and hurried.

Hastily coming up to Matthew, he grasped his arm and said, "I regret breaking in on your Christmas celebration, Mr. Caswell, but it is imperative I leave for New Bern at once and I must speak to Hillary before I leave." Without giving Matthew a chance to answer, he turned to Hillary. "Come, my boy, where can we get out of this din? I can't waste a minute."

Half dazed by the man's importunity, half angry at being taken away from the excitement of the John Kooner celebration, Hillary led him into the house. Edwards began to explain the emergency taking him to New Bern—something about paying the men working on the Palace mainly, it seemed, though there were other matters as troublesome and as pressing. Then Edwards was going over his arrangements with him, arrangements already made. Through the walls, somewhat muffled, came the highly accented John Kooner's song. He was missing everything. Edwards was only being fussy; his whole visit was for nothing. Now the slaves were singing a song each line of which ended with an emphatic "Juba."

Edwards was asking if he had everything clear. When Hillary said it was, he was as much in a hurry to be off as he had been to start the interview. Suddenly he was gone.

When Hillary at last came out and rejoined the family on the gallery, the exuberant troop of slaves, once more in ragged procession, was moving back toward the quarters, marshalled by a noisy beating of drums.

"Now they go down to 'draw Christmas,' " Matthew explained to Hillary. "We give them an extra allowance of rice, molasses, coffee, sugar and corn-meal. But come along—we've more to do."

The house slaves brought in the Yule Log which John and Elisha had cut a week before. It was Gregory, however, who took charge of the ceremony—with old Eb on hand to see that affairs were handled properly.

The fire-place was measured for the hundredth time, and the log was carried into the hall. Gregory ordered the brass andirons pulled back, and a young Negro boy made a bed of wet ashes on which the great log was placed. The lightwood and seasoned oak were laid against it.

The entire Caswell family had gathered around the fireplace, and when the flames leaped high up the blackened throat of the chimney it was time to cast away the sins of the year.

Angela presided over a silver tray on which were piled bunches of mistletoe. Hillary moved forward to the table with the others. He was thinking of Angela, and how the green leaves and the waxen-white berries matched her gown as if they had been torn from the cloth.

She put a sprig of mistletoe into Hillary's hand. "I'm sure you haven't any sins to burn up, Cousin Hillary."

He smiled at her. "None that I know of."

"Perhaps you should have some," she said. "Perhaps

you should. I suppose we should wait to do this until after the dance tonight."

"To do what?" he asked, not suspecting her meaning.

"Why, to burn our sins, Cousin," she answered. "Surely you'll have some small sins after the dance."

The fire was flaming high, for the Christmas log of cypress was dry. One by one the sprigs of mistletoe were thrown into the fire; they crackled and sputtered, and the waxen white balls were caught in flame.

Hillary cast his sprig, watched it burst into flames, and turned a second later to see Angela. She had been watching him intently, and when his eyes met hers she smiled and said, "At last. One year's sins are gone, Cousin. Think of it! We have a whole new year before us."

10

Christmas Night

The Christmas dinner was a grand affair, an occasion of joy, of peace and calm. It was as if the sins of the year truly had been cast into the fire and the white seeds of their wrath consumed.

Hillary Caswell stood in the group of gay chattering guests who waited by the open doors to the dining-room for Matthew Caswell and Madam Elizabeth to lead the way. Hillary smiled, musing as he thought of all the others who, along the far-flung coast of the colonies, prepared for this respite from the year. Candles gleaming in every home, laughter from many lips, made fragile, sparkling links between the peoples.

Matthew Caswell moved forward, escorting Madam Elizabeth into the dining-hall, leading the procession of neighbours and kinsmen. Hillary searched for Cecelia, but could not find her; and then at the last minute she appeared, radiantly beautiful, holding the arm of Gregory Caswell. He turned from the pair quickly, a pang of disappointment in his heart. He heard Angela's voice beside him: "Cousin Hillary, you look so forlorn. Why, sir? Aren't you delighted at the prospect of escorting me to dinner?"

He smiled at her, though he was not in a mood to smile, and held out his arm. "I'm delighted at the prospect," he said, certain that he had not put the proper enthusiasm into his tone.

"Well," she said, "you hardly sound as if you mean it." She took his arm, turning a moment to speak to

Elisha who was behind her, and pressing against Hillary as she did. The firmness of her movement, of her body and of the pressure of her hand, made him look at her in surprise. She smiled at him.

"Hillary, Hillary," she chided softly, "must you always be thinking of Cecelia? I'm certain I could be as nice as she."

"But I wasn't thinking of Cecelia," he protested, though from the corner of his eye he could see the auburn of Cecelia's hair, and he could hear her light laughter as she talked with Gregory.

Angela was holding tightly to him. "Sometimes I don't think you're very clever when it comes to the proper treatment of a woman," she said as they entered the dining-room. "I could practically throw myself at you, and you wouldn't even notice."

"Hush, Angela. That's no way for a young girl to speak."

"I thought we settled the fact that I'm not a young girl."

"Well, Angela, the only proper treatment for older women is to beat them constantly. You wouldn't like that."

"Do you mean it, Cousin Hillary?" she asked half seriously, relaxing her grip on his arm.

"It's the only way to teach them."

"I *don't* think I'd like that," she said. "Should men be beaten, too? I'm sure I shouldn't want to beat you, Hillary. Let's sit over here." A moment later she added, "But if it would help to teach you about women, I might try."

The Christmas dinner proceeded with cheer and a goodly share of noise—loud enough for Andrew, Hillary's servant, to hear the laughter from below as he cleaned up his master's room. He picked up the discarded clothes, brushed them and hung them in the wardrobe. He worked rapidly: mended the fire, straightened the bed, brushed a pair of boots lightly, then gave the room a cursory glance before he hurried out, humming a little tune.

Andrew was courting a "yellow gal" who helped him

in the pantry. She often had a slice of pie or cake, or even a dish of pudding waiting for him at tea-time. He walked down the stairs. Outside, he found a window through which he could survey the kitchen. It was, unhappily, a beehive of activity. He rubbed a finger thoughtfully across his chin. He could see Mammy Tulli, the chief cook, seated on a high stool against the west wall where she had a commanding view of the entire room and the entrance to the buttery. She was old, but her eyes were as sharp as her tongue, and the young servants flew to do her bidding.

Whispering the words to the tune he had been humming, Andrew inched around to the back of the kitchen and climbed into the buttery by a partly opened window.

The girl was waiting for him. "You late," she said, pushing a dish of hasty pudding toward him. "Old Tulli won't let me get my hands on Christmas cookin' till after the white folk finish the supper." She smiled. "I put plenty of blackstrap in the puddin'. It sure ought to hold you."

Andrew caught the girl around the waist. "Give us a kiss," he said. "I'm honeying for a taste—better than all the blackstrap in the world."

"Oh, go on! You jest talkin'. I bet you off with some of them gals down the quarters line, minute you go from here."

Andrew sighed. It was a sigh fraught with pain for the little faith of women. And momentarily he turned his thoughts to a handsome slim-hipped girl he had held the night before—at the quarters line. "Me! *Me,* taking up with a gal from the quarters line? Honey—" his tone was unforgiving— "I'se a houseboy, I is. I don't have no truck with them field hands."

She giggled, now docile as he held one arm about her. "You know, boy, that's what you always say about eatin'-time."

Andrew put both arms about her. "Come here, you. You speakin' mighty silly talk."

"Andrew! Someone's comin'."

Andrew was prepared for all situations. He let go of the girl, pushed the pudding behind a crock of flour and quickly picked up a tray of dirty dishes. When Tulli hobbled to the door Andrew was just putting the tray back on the table and saying, "You thank that Mammy Tulli, 'cause my master, he sure do love this cookin'. He say the tea and cakes—why they is the best he ever——"

Andrew turned in surprise, leaving the sentence unfinished.

Tulli, whose single joy and only pride was her cooking, smiled at him. "What you doing here, Maryland boy? Don't you go making no flatterin' words like that!"

"Mammy Tulli! I didn't hear you come up. How long you be listenin' to me? Flatterin' words? Master Hillary, he always saying Carolina cookin' is sure good. Why, he eats like a starving mule, he does."

When Tulli had gone off in peace, Andrew smiled, drew the pudding from behind the flour crock with one hand and with the other took the girl's hand.

"Andrew, you learn that talk in Maryland? Boy, you sure am a honey-tongue. I wouldn't trust you nowhere at all."

"To-night?" Andrew asked casually.

"Where?"

Once Andrew had settled his evening affairs, he strolled to the stables to rub down his master's horse. He sang as he worked, content that the night was his.

> "My hen is a white one;
> It loves me,
> Scraping away at the grain, Master,
> With its little leg.
> My child come back to-morrow
> And you will see it."

He paused. He sniffed at the air as a dog sniffs. The pungent odour of burning tobacco drifted in the night air. He dropped the brush he held, took up a lanthorn and walked slowly down among the stalls, examining each. It was in the last stall that he found a small boy, all alone, puffing vigorously on a roll of tobacco.

"Hey there! You get yourself gone from here!" He caught the astonished boy by the shoulder and pulled him to his feet. "Your master ought to use the kiboko on you. You tryin' to set fire to this-here barn?"

The boy's eyes rolled in terror, and Andrew loosened his grip on his shirt. He wriggled free, stumbled, scrambled to his feet and darted from the stable. Andrew watched him go. He shook his head, suspecting that the young folk just weren't being raised right. . . . Ah, well, he thought, perhaps it was just a North Carolina weakness.

Before returning to his work and then the pleasures of the night, he leaned at a stable window. The moon was rising above the trees. From the hall he could hear the sound of the young people singing. Dinner must be over. He began singing quietly in harmony with the voices from the hall. His spirits rose even higher. The words sounded deep and full from his throat and from his heart:

> "While shepherds watched their flocks by night,
>   All seated on the ground,
> The Angel of the Lord came down,
>   And glory shone around."

"It would seem like Christmas, but . . ." Robin Chapman left the sentence unfinished. He was listening to the rich, deep voice which sang from the stable.

"Andrew, I think," Hillary said, and then, returning to Robin's conversation: "It would seem like Christmas, but one keeps looking at the future, is never content with the present? Is that what you meant?"

"In a way. I keep thinking of war. That was my real thought. I don't see any way out of it."

"If there's a time for it, it will come. Is there any need to hurry it in your mind?"

"It will be either with England or among ourselves," Robin continued. He looked up at the sky. "I'm not even sure where my own father stands. Can you imagine anything worse than to find your own father drawn up in battle against you?"

"He won't be, Robin."

"Are you so sure? I'm not."

"The sides haven't been chosen yet. Come, stop worrying."

"But they have for many people."

"You?"

"Perhaps."

Hillary hesitated. "It's strange how often one sees sides in war and sides in the heart as different things. Oh, I mean, I never choose to do what I *would*. Let's go inside. I'm getting cold and talking nonsense. I'm not sure what I mean myself."

The two young men walked about Manor House once more and then strolled onto the gallery. They could hear the sound of the fiddles being tuned inside the house. A banjo strummed a trial chord, was adjusted and strummed again. Then came the tapping of a small drum, calling the dancers to their places. It was the beginning of an end: the season of the Christ was passing and the red star of the new year was in ascendance.

The door to the gallery was opened. Noise drifted outward and the two young men turned to see Ann and Cecelia. "Here's Robin," Ann said. "And Cousin Hillary —I didn't see you at first."

Cecelia stood hesitantly in the doorway. Ann stepped forward and slipped her hand under Robin's arm. "Come along, Robin. They're starting a contra-dance and I want you to be my partner."

"Haven't I anything to say about this?"

She pulled him toward the door. "Of course you have. You can say yes."

"But I can't leave Hillary out there to freeze alone," he said.

"And what do you think sisters were made for?" Ann asked. "Cecelia can take care of him," she added glibly. She and Robin disappeared through the doorway, leaving Hillary and Cecelia alone.

Cecelia spoke first. "I would come farther, but then I'm afraid we'd have to be considered alone together, and you've told me that you wouldn't want that."

"No," he answered with a touch of anger in his voice. "No, I wouldn't want that." He did not bother to correct her—that he had said merely he was *afraid* to be alone with her. As he spoke, he had walked across the gallery to her. He took her hand lightly and wondered if she could guess the feeling in his heart. It was a strange sensation: a mixture of love and anger—anger that she had suddenly come to occupy so much of his thought. He had wanted to hold her in his arms and never let her go; to bid a fond farewell to all the politicians of New Bern and be done with them forever. But his promise held him, and he did no more than ask her if she would care to dance with him.

She said she would be happy to. "There's always safety in numbers, don't you think, Cousin?" Her silken skirt rustled as they passed through the doorway into the well-lighted hall. "I see Aunt Elizabeth is making the set."

"Cecelia," he said, turning to face her, "I'm sorry about the other night."

"About what? There's nothing to be sorry for."

"I can't explain it," he said. "I never seem to know how to explain to you exactly what I mean."

"You must try, though. Other men speak their minds to me. Must I guess yours?"

"It might be better," Hillary said. "At least you'd have some idea how I feel. These men at Charleston, do you really . . ." Damn it, he thought, must a man who begins to love a girl always make a fool of himself?

"Dear Hillary," she said, leaning toward him, pressing her shoulder against his, "it's not polite for you to ask questions about my friends. And furthermore, Madam Elizabeth is looking this way. Do you want me for a partner or not?"

"I do," he said, and they stepped out on the floor together to the gay music of the dance. Never before, Hillary thought, had he felt so happy, so annoyed, so comfortable and yet so pained when he was with a girl.

He spent most of the evening dancing with Cecelia. Once, when Gregory had asked her for a minuet she had answered that she was sorry, "but I *did* promise this dance to Hillary." It was not true, but Gregory did not know it, and while they danced the minuet together she asked Hillary, "Are you feeling more at ease, Cousin?"

"Much more," he answered truthfully, "but it seems that if I'm not unhappy about one thing, then it's another. Now I think about New Bern—and you will be at Charleston."

"With all the Charleston men," she added.

"With all the Charleston men," he repeated.

"And New Bern? Is it only a man's town?"

"For me it will be."

"Will it really? Such commitments, Cousin. I don't believe you."

"Can girls always be so light when a man is serious? Would you believe me if I told you that I loved you?"

A delicate touch of crimson came to her cheeks. She was serious for a second, then the lightness of her manner returned. "If you said it, Hillary—no. I don't think I'd believe you. But it's an idea."

She might have answered yes, he thought. Then at least her seriousness would have shocked him into some sense. As it was, he felt desire sink deeper into him, and with it the pleasant fright of knowing he was caught. But she was free.

At midnight the dancing stopped, the oldsters joined the younger men and women, and all began to sing carols. Even Joseph Chapman, usually reticent in any group, entered into it with a strong, vigorous baritone.

But as his wife, who sat in the corner of the main hall looking on, seemed tired and indisposed, Joseph was forced to leave early. It was agreed, of course, that Cecelia and Robin should stay the night with the Caswells. Hillary helped them see their parents to the chaise.

"You really must come visit us, Hillary. There'll be no excuse to delay now that your shoulder's better," Mrs. Chapman said as they waited on the gallery. "It won't be so exciting as Manor House, but we'll have sailing on the Sound, and perhaps a journey in the sloop to the outer banks." Then with a rather distracted air, she added, "I shall be awfully lonely when Cecelia goes back to school."

"Some good fishing on the banks, my boy," Joseph Chapman put in. "Surely you won't be long at New Bern?"

"After Manor House and your invitation, I can say only that I hope not."

The chaise drew away down the avenue of splendid cedars, Robin returned to the house, and Hillary and Cecelia were left standing alone on the gallary, hesitantly, but not wishing to return to the crowded hall.

Without speaking, but knowing each other's thoughts,

they walked down from the gallery together, hand in hand, along the path in the frozen moonlight. When Cecelia spoke, her voice was low and disturbed. "I didn't want to go back into the hall," she admitted.

"Nor I," he answered. "There seems so little time, and I longed to be alone with you."

He put his arm about her and they strolled slowly away from the gleaming candles of Manor House; the sounds of laughter fell far behind. The moon made a broken light through the tall cedars.

She turned to face him, her hand gently touching his shoulder. "We could walk to the summer-house," she said. "We would be alone there. We wouldn't have to talk to people."

Her tone, the trembling of her voice, Hillary thought, was that of a young girl afraid—without fear of him, with fear only of her emotions. He took her hand again, and they turned past the cedars, strolled down the footpath until the dark summer-house was outlined before them in the moonlight. By the side entrance was a lattice which arched over the doorway, a fragile netting of wood on either side. They stood there for a long moment together, not speaking, until finally Hillary drew her into his arms.

Someone—it sounded like Robin's voice—began calling "Hillary!" The sound came from the general direction of the house. Cecelia put her fingers to his lips, waited until the calls had stopped, then put her arms about him. He kissed her gently, feeling the softness of her yielding lips and the touch of her body against him.

"Cecelia, I love you. Don't ever tell me of your Charleston men. Promise you won't."

He felt her moist lips against his cheek. Then she drew back a little though her arms were still about his neck. Her cape had fallen slightly open. The delicate curve of her breast caught the lustre of the moonlight.

"But you're going to New Bern," she said, her voice low and full of emotion.

"And I swear I'll return," Hillary answered, "If you'll only wait for me. When I think of others with you——"

She started to draw her cape back about her, but her hands faltered as he pulled her to him again and kissed her shoulder. He felt the gentle but urgent pressure, the touch of her hands to his cheek. She whispered, "Hillary, Hillary—" her voice almost a sob —"take me inside the summer-house. Take me with you."

"Dearest, you don't know what you're saying."

"I do," she murmured. "I do know."

"God knows I want to . . ." He kissed her again, holding her tight, but trying to keep himself in check.

And again she whispered, "Don't you love me?"

"Too much for that."

Again the caress of her finger-tips on his cheeks. Lord, he thought, surely she must know what she's doing to me! He turned slightly, put his hand on the door latch and slowly lifted it. In vain he fought against the burning desire to possess the girl before him, to claim her once and for all as his own. He yielded to the moist pressure of her lips against his cheek. The door to the summer-house swung slowly open to the dark, cool interior. But when he stepped forward she seemed to draw back. Tears welled in her eyes.

"I . . . I don't believe I can . . . now," she stammered. "But, Hillary, I love you so. . . . I want you now . . . because we'll be apart for months and months, you in New Bern, I in Charleston."

"I know." Hillary sighed. "It'll seem forever."

Her limbs seemed frozen, unable to move, unable to take her across that dark threshhold. Hillary started to speak, but stopped. He glanced through the lattice. By the slant reflection of the moon the window glass seemed to be dancing with light.

Still Cecelia stood at the door, arms to her sides, and she was crying softly. "I can't do it, Hillary. I can't go in. I can't. What can you think of me now?"

"Only that I love you."

"And that I've ruined it all."

"Stop! You don't know what you're talking about. Nothing's ruined."

"But it is," she said, "for me."

She took several faltering steps away from him, as he stood in the doorway. She turned so that he saw her in profile, hands now to her bosom, her lips parted. She glanced toward the cedars, toward Manor House, across the narrow footpath by which they had come, and finally toward the barn.

Hillary let the door to the summer-house close. He heard the latch click heavily as it fell back in place. When he turned again to Cecelia she was staring at the barn with a look of terror on her face.

"The barn!" she whispered. "The barn's aflame!"

Through the barn window they could see leaping flames, framed like a picture of Fire incarnadine.

"Run quickly!" Cecelia ordered. "Ring the plantation bell. Hurry! I'll tell them at the house." She ran from him even as she spoke, holding her full skirt in both hands, her cape flying behind her.

Hillary dashed from the summer-house, leaped a low hedge that bordered the path, darted across the grass plot in front of the kitchen building. Right behind it was the plantation bell.

He grabbed the heavy rope and pulled, ringing the great bell three times, then three more—the signal of fire. Then he let go the rope and ran back toward the barn lot. He guessed that the stables could not be more than twenty yards from the barn.

Already pungent smoke from burning hay had drifted toward the stables on the light wind. He heard the whinnying and stamping of the horses trapped inside. He pulled open the wide end doors of the stable. From the lane he heard slaves shout as they ran toward him, roused by the giant bell. He heard the Negro women scream to their men to hurry.

He blocked the doors open. He threw off his fine coat —its tightness bound him—unwound his stock. At the opposite end of the stable he saw a small, frightened boy trying to lead out Matthew's great stallion. For a moment he wondered how the boy had got there so quickly.

"He don' want to come," the boy cried with tears in his voice. "I cain't bring he." He yanked desperately on the halter rope.

"Put a toe sack over his eyes," Hillary shouted. "He'll come."

He cast a lightning glance toward Manor House. Dark figures were running toward them, lanthorns bobbing. As he entered the stable he kept thinking one foolish thought: They don't need lanthorns, the moon is as bright as day . . . and if not the moon, the fire will be.

Hillary's own horse was in the first stall. Talking to him, patting him on the neck, he led the quivering animal into the open. He threw the halter rope to the first slave who arrived on the run, and called as the horse was led away, "Tie him to the fence! Keep him far away!" Then he rushed back into the stable. The giant stallion was rearing. Its mad plunges had thrown the small Negro boy against the stall sides and knocked him senseless. Hillary ran, grabbed the rope the boy had been holding, pulled the horse out and away from the inert body on the floor. His voice was calm and reassuring as he talked to the stallion.

"Robin," he called to the young man who had just appeared in the passage-way, "will you take this brute?"

Robin grabbed the lead rope, and, speaking in the same even tones Hillary had used, guided the big horse into the open barn-yard.

Hillary rushed back into the stall, knelt, gathered the young boy in his arms and raced back down the dirt corridor to the open.

"Is he all right?" Robin demanded.

"I don't think he was trampled. But it was close," Hillary answered.

"The others are over at the barn. They're trying to control the fire, but I doubt if they'll save it."

One of the Negro women who had been crouched near a great tulip poplar east of the stables, came up with fear in her eyes and took the child from Hillary's arms. She hastened back to the tree with her burden.

In the silhouettes made by the flames Hillary could distinguish the men of the house ringing the barn. He heard Matthew Caswell's deep voice booming out commands. Robin had gone back into the stables. Sparks now rose from the roof of the flaming barn. They drifted across on the light wind, yet fell short of the stable. Hillary noted a subtle change in heat.

As he turned back to the stable he heard Elizabeth Caswell's voice break through the wailing of the Negro women who huddled near the tulip poplar. "Stop that crying. Mandy, you wind up the well bucket. Tulli, get the women formed in a line; send all the girls to the well back of the stable. Quick now, start hauling water. Get to work!"

The power of her voice dominated the woman's fear. Then the whiplash calls of old Tulli came singing in and redoubled their hurry.

Hillary plunged back into the stable. A moment later he was helping Robin lead out the last horse, a powerful gelding that kicked and jerked frantically.

"Work horses for the most part are in the far barn. We're lucky," Robin said. "Can you get a ladder to the roof? We've got to start wetting it down before the sparks set it ablaze."

"You can handle this?"

"I think so."

Hillary worked his way around the gelding, was knocked once against the stable wall, caught his balance and moved clear. He found the ladder at the end of the corridor of stalls, grabbed it at the centre and returned to the yard.

The wind had grown stronger but had shifted slightly to the east. Sparks rose from the barn. Some found their way to the roof of the stable, and others sailed beyond before dying out in the night.

Hillary kicked off his slick, silver-buckled shoes. A slave ran to help him place the ladder to the roof and brace it against a rickety fence which angled from the side of the stable. Hillary scrambled up the ladder even as a tremendous spray of sparks burst from one end of the barn roof upward to the sky. The two smaller buildings for tools and storage were in the windward path and came under this shower of fire. A dark figure standing on one of the roofs let out a scream of pain as the wind blew the sparks down on him. His shirt caught fire. He flailed his hands frantically against himself. Another figure on the roof rushed to him and smothered the flames with his arms.

Robin Chapman climbed the ladder a moment after Hillary. The two young men crouched apprehensively, waiting for the first buckets of water to be passed to them.

In a few moments the line of women, directed by Tulli and Madam Elizabeth, began bringing water. Gregory Caswell stationed himself at the half-way point on the ladder and swung the buckets upward. Madam Elizabeth ordered two water-soaked blankets passed to the men on the roof.

They sloshed the water across the cypress shingles. They whipped the sodden blankets against the falling sparks. They pressed the blankets often to the charred spots which already showed at the end of the stable nearest the flaming barn.

"Pour this bucketful on yourself," Hillary shouted. "The heat's getting worse." He had already doused himself.

The figures had retreated from the small tool and storage buildings. Ten minutes later the first shed, the one closer to the barn, exploded in flame—the heat too fierce for the dry wood to withstand. Moments later the second was ablaze.

It seemed to Hillary that they had worked a hundred nights. At times when he swung the heavy blanket, or dashed the buckets of water on the roof, he pulled muscles which had not yet healed and felt a sharp stab of pain in his shoulder.

People came and went in a dream. Someone brought grog and sandwiches. Still the fire blazed, lighting the sky, throwing weird shadows on the pine trees behind the quarters. The men who had circled the barn had drawn back. They had tried only to control the blaze, for it was impossible to extinguish it.

Gradually the heat lessened. The bursts of sparks grew fewer. The east and the centre of the barn had collapsed in a rage of fire and slowly burned out. Some men left the fire at the barn and took places in the bucket brigade.

"Anyway, the wind didn't shift. It would have been worse the other way," Gregory said.

"I know," Hillary answered. "We might have lost the slave quarters. How fares it with you, Gregory?"

"Tired."

Hillary lifted a dipper to his lips; he drank and pushed the bucket to Robin who was wiping his sooty face with his sleeve. After that moment's pause, and in spite of the pain in his shoulder, Hillary went back to work. Suffering showed in his face. Robin started to say something to him about it but caught himself. If a man wanted to work himself to exhaustion it was his own affair, his own right.

It was nearly daybreak when Matthew Caswell shouted to them from the ground, "You can call quits, boys. I'll send some of the slaves up. I believe we've got it all under control now."

"Control" was a euphemism. The barn and the nearby storage sheds had been reduced to heaps of smouldering embers. The final upright on the end of the barn had collapsed and sparks had burst upward in a final solitary flash.

Hillary and Robin climbed down the ladder wearily and joined Matthew and Gregory. "Come into the house, lads. The cook will have some breakfast for us. God, what an ending for a Christmas!" Matthew's sleeves were torn, his shirt in tatters. Soot covered his face. He had lost his queue ribbon, and his grey hair tumbled down his back. He examined his left hand curiously—a welter of blisters had risen where he had been burned. "Pitching out hay," he explained. "Thought we might get enough out to ease the heat."

Madam Elizabeth and the house slaves had set the table, loaded it with food and drink. Many had gathered already: the neighbour boys who had worked valiantly; Elisha and John, who had tried to save the storage sheds; the Spruill lads, their faces still covered with soot. The girls moved quietly about the room, white-faced with dark circles under their eyes.

The cups in front of the men were filled with rum and water, and they drank thirstily. Matthew had slumped into a chair at the head of the table. He motioned Hillary and Robin to either side of him. Madam Elizabeth wanted to put a salve on his hand, but he waved her away. "Time for that later, my dear. I'm too damn jerky to hold still for anything."

He surveyed the crowd of tired young men, looked at his cup of rum and then straightened in his chair.

"Gentlemen—" he raised his cup—"to you! I've been most fortunate. I lost only a hay barn and two sheds—it might have been the stable, the quarters, or Manor House itself. No doubt the wind played a part, but my heartfelt thanks go to every one of you for this night's work."

That said, he leaned back in his chair again. He examined his hand again. "Elizabeth," he said, "would you bring me some of that salve now? I'm not so jerky as I thought I was."

Breakfast was over and the guests were going wearily to their rooms before Hillary found a chance to speak to Cecelia. He had paused in the hall for a moment when she approached him almost timidly and touched her hand to his sleeve. "I want to say something about last night."

"There's nothing to say, is there? Nothing was done —and nothing we said can be taken back."

"Perhaps it can be taken back. But . . . but I'm happy you're safe. All the night I worried and prayed for you."

He took her hand. "Then all's well."

"No." She shook her head slowly. "I think of what we almost did, and I hate myself for it. I wanted things to be good between us, and I ruined it all." Her voice broke with emotion.

"Cecelia," he said, "you're only tired. Nothing's ruined; nothing's changed."

"No. You don't understand what I am or how I feel. Hillary, believe me when I say that I love you—but I don't want to see you again."

"I can't believe both."

"Then you can't know me." She turned from him, tears in her eyes, and ran to the door.

"Cecelia!"

"You don't understand at all," she said, and then was gone.

His first impulse was to follow her, but he stopped himself, trying to comprehend her words. Surely she didn't mean it. Then a ponderous weariness spread through his body; the pain in his shoulder was like the sharp stabs of a dozen needles. He climbed the stairs to his room discouraged, confused and with the lonely prospect of New Bern before him. But he refused to believe he would not hold Cecelia in his arms again.

11

Journey to the Capital

Hillary Caswell departed for New Bern on a day when the sky was overcast and the clouds were heavy with rain. He leaned forward and patted his roan on the neck, guiding it along the narrow path through the woods. Behind him he could hear the quiet chatter of Andrew, his servant, as he talked to his horse. Andrew's monologue touched on a variety of subjects: a medley of Andrew's excursions down the quarters line, a series of twisted proverbs, a digression on the merits of hasty pudding, praise for his own heroic part in the fire and a lengthy prayer for the lusty potential of New Bern women.

Hillary was trying to keep his own mind blank, barren of thought, as bleak as the desert of scrub pines which they crossed after passing through the forest. The effort was useless.

He had not seen Cecelia after the night of the fire, though he had sent two notes by Robin Chapman. She had answered the second, but it had been nothing to cheer his heart. She had said that she would be returning to Charleston on the same day that he left for New Bern. There would be no point in seeing each other again, for there were too many affairs to keep them separate. "My father and my brothers love the sea, dear Hillary. I love that element no more than the world which you must fashion for yourself in statecraft. Both go against me. I feel as though I belong only to the land, and the man whom I shall marry someday must have that same attachment. Perhaps it is too much to ask for myself . . . it makes no difference—I still ask it. We shall forget each other in a short time; the holidays were made for brief romances, loves that could never last a season's change.

"Were all that not enough, there is more. I need not write to you of that, for I told you my feelings after the fire."

Then had come the portion of the letter which had shocked Hillary. He slapped his roan on the flank. Or had it truly surprised him? Had he not guessed it when he spoke to Robin in those days at the Manor House? Robin had intimated that his own house was divided.

"I talk with my brothers often," she had written. "I'm not always the foolish girl you saw laughing at the Manor House. I take their ideas—perhaps too much. As do they, I believe there will be a war in our Colony. Strange for me to say this. And when it comes, you will be on the side of the Governor and all the people of the Eastern counties. You'll have no choice. You'll defend what Tryon thinks right.

"Yet my brothers will not be on that side. Nor shall I. Hillary, it seems so useless. Everything would go against the two of us. Can you understand why I don't want to see you again? I don't want to be any more deeply in love with you than I am. Women have a way of being practical, Hillary, and I have made up my mind.

"I shall be on board the *Laughing Girl* by the time the groom brings this letter to you, and you will be prepared for New Bern. Is it not for the best?"

She had signed her full name: Cecelia Chapman.

Hillary spurred his mount along the narrow track which cut through the wild desert. Matthew Caswell had told him he would save miles if he used that path instead of the wagon trail. He had taken Matthew's advice, though he had not cared to save time or spare himself the labour of the miles.

By noon the rains came: heavy, beating rains. Though the season was early for an electrical storm, the sky was branched with lightning and low thunder rolled across the heavens.

Hillary buttoned his cape so the rain wouldn't run down his neck, and pressed on, for there was no shelter but the scrub trees along the path. Andrew cantered to catch up with him. "Massa, don't we hab no place to light?" He was wet and miserable. The rain dripped from the brim of his broad hat, and his coat and breeks were soaked.

"Why don't you throw a blanket over your shoulders?"

"Massa, you done ride so fast I cain't do nothin' but hurry 'long behin' you."

Hillary reined his horse impatiently. "I'll wait for you," he said. "Get off and unstrap the blanket now."

Andrew dismounted and unrolled a blanket from his pack. He put his head through a slit in the middle of the woollen square and mounted again, smiling broadly. The truth of the matter was that he had not thought of any means to keep himself dry. In a few minutes Hillary could hear Andrew speaking again to his horse in agreeable, contented tones. Yes, he was saying, he'd certainly seen worse rains than this before. This was merely a sprinkling of dew.

But the thunderstorm continued for more than an hour. They made slow time as the trail became a mass of mud. Then at last they came to dry country, a place where the rain had broken off, almost as if a jagged line had been stick-drawn across the land. It seemed as though it would be brief respite, for ahead the clouds were dark and low. The horsemen stirred up a covey of partridges; the birds rose with a whirr and settled again in distant bushes. Waterfowl flew past: heron, white crane and goose. A cormorant perched on a dead tree trunk. It turned its ugly head toward them but did not move as they rode by.

"Massa, I'se sure tired. You reckon we stop soon?"

"We should come to an inn with another three or four hours' ride."

"It'll be dark, and I'se pretty sore of this horse, sar. We musta rid thirty mile or more."

"Not yet we haven't," Hillary said. "Would you rather camp early and sleep under a tree?"

Andrew's eyes rolled white. "No, sir. I don' want to sleep under no tree. Don' want to push out de tree spirits."

"Oh, there may not be any tree spirits near here." Hillary glanced about at the dead landscape. "I don't think they'd like it here any better than we do."

"Sar, my mammy, she tell me they is everywhere. They cut your haid right off you neck."

"Then we ride on?"

"Yes, sar. I guess we rides on."

Hillary said nothing more, but he felt a certain pity for the boy with all his fears and superstitions. He knew the belief in evil spirits was deeply imbedded in the African mind. *A fiti mankawalla,* as they called it, was an integral part of their lives. Hillary smiled to himself as he trotted along the faint trail. Well, hadn't he enough of his *own* fears not to laugh at another's—no matter how foolish they seemed? Weren't some of his trials as ridiculous as Andrew's?

It was another two hours and long past sunset before the path crossed a wide road, rutted and cut by wagon and chaise travel.

"We'll find an inn somewhere about, Andrew. I'll wager we come to one before long."

"No wager, sar." Andrew pointed ahead, and Hillary saw the twinkling lights of an inn ahead of them on the road. Their horses seemed to know that they were at the end of their day's journey. They quickened their pace. A slight wind had risen, and the sign which swung over the inn door, marking it as the Pamlico, squeaked on rusty hinges.

Andrew led the horses to the stable behind the inn. Hillary pushed open the oak door to the entrance hall to find the proprietor and arrange for lodging. The innkeeper, who sat at a small table by the door to the ordinary, was listening to the noise from that room with satisfaction. He turned and smiled a broken-toothed grin. He listened to Hillary's request, then very slowly, as if the labour were almost more than he could perform, he wrote Hillary's name in a ledger. The innkeeper was a thin, wiry man with leathery brown skin. His hair was stringy and black. When he straightened up frcm the book he grinned again. "Crowded tonight," he said, "very crowded. You're lucky. You get the last room." He stood up, moved around the narrow table. "Yesterday not a traveller stopped here, and to-night we have twelve. Ah," he added wistfully, "if they'd only learn to space themselves! Truly hard for a man to make a living." He still carried his quill in his hand. "Oh, and your man will sleep in the hayloft."

"I'll need feed for the horses," Hillary said.

"Yes," the taverner replied thoughtfully, "I suppose you'll have to have that." He glared at the pen in his hand, returned to the table and the ledger and opened the book again. He thumbed the pages slowly and wrote a series of figures under Hillary's name with effort. "Now—" he clapped the book shut once more and looked suspiciously at Hillary—"there isn't anything else, is there?"

"No."

A look of relief came to his lean face now that he would not have to use the pen again. "Then I'll show you to your quarters. Mind you, it's the last room—not our best, but sufficient, sir. Sufficient! Better than spending the night in rain." He led the way up a rickety staircase to an attic chamber. The room was hardly more than a cubbyhole. A pine table with a bowl and ewer stood beside a single cot. Hillary went to the single window and discovered that the house stood on the shore of a stream of some size. A ferry was tied up at the bank. It must be the Pamlico River. More than half the journey had been put behind him.

Hillary washed, and unpacked dry clothes from his saddlebags, and after dressing he walked down the steps to the ordinary for a mug of ale and some hot food.

He ordered the stout from a heavy-jowled potman and then went to a small unoccupied table in the corner from which he could best view the room. It was crowded with travellers, many more than the inn could accommodate with sleeping rooms. Three gentlemen, elegantly dressed in spite of the fact that they must have been on the road, sat at a table three paces to his left. Their conversation ran the gamut from crops to politics. On the basis of what Hillary could overhear, their attitude was that the Ministry could do no wrong. Most of the other men in the ordinary were, from their dress, farmers or woodsmen.

The broad table nearest the bar seated the most interesting men in the room, though they seemed well on their way to getting drunk. The leader of that crew managed himself better than the others, but he was free with his talk, and his voice had a booming quality that carried above all others'. His face seemed slightly flushed, perhaps from ale, though perhaps his natural complexion was ruddy. His eyebrows were a contrasting blond, his hair a soft red. His arms were big, clublike. In general, his features looked rather refined. As for speech, his phrases had a peculiar, fanciful turn, quite out of keeping with the company.

Suddenly one of the group stood up. He was a big hulking fellow with a broad, beefy face. Tottering slightly, he raised his mug of ale. "Gentlemen," he said, spilling some of the ale over his hand and onto the table, "a toast!"

The wizened little drunkard on his left shook himself awake. "Good! Damn good! A toast."

The elegantly dressed gentlemen stopped their conversation and glanced toward the front with obvious distaste.

At the front table the red-haired man had become quiet. He sat with his chair pushed slightly back from the table, his legs crossed, smiling absent-mindedly at the man who was about to propose a toast.

The man raised his mug higher and began a drunken chant:

"To hell with old Fanning, the Hillsborough King
    With the taxes that nourish the Ring!
To hell with the East, the Palace, the nobs!
    To hell with all rascally snobs!"

A united shout of approval went up from the men at the table. The red-haired leader tilted his chair back and smiled more broadly. The farmers who stood at the bar or sat in little groups about the room grinned, but they were in some perplexity.

"Ho! Big Burke from Orange!"

The big man lowered his ale mug, obviously pleased with the success of his toast. "Aye, what is it?" he said to the slim farmer who stood at the bar.

"I hear talk you Orangemen are going to have Fanning for an Assemblyman again. Now what's the truth in that? You elected Mr. Husband last year. Are you going to throw him out now and take Fanning back?"

"Friend," Burke answered, "we'll not elect a thief, but if our good English Governor wants to make a separate borough out of Hillsborough, I don't know how we can stop him."

The farmer hitched up his trousers and directed his attention to the red-head. "Your taxes any lighter this year, Rednap?" he asked.

Rednap Howell let his chair fall forward and uncrossed his legs. "No, friend, not lighter, but at least we've an idea where the money goes. Not all of it gets to Fanning."

The wizened drunkard piped up: "Down here you don't know what taxes are. By God, you coast folk ain't felt nothing. We get taxes for taking a leetle extra breath of air. They take us to court and charge us triple —ten times if we gulp more air on our way."

Rednap interrupted. "He means we have to hold our breath when we get into court because of the dreadful stench there."

The slim farmer laughed, waved a hand at Rednap and turned back to his mug of ale. The room quieted. But the conversation seemed to have revitalized Rednap, and he engaged four or five people around the room in sharp interchanges, shrewdly probing for their political sympathies. But there was a gaiety in the man, a good humour that kept the crowd laughing, and no one took even his sharpest shafts amiss.

After a time Hillary felt the man's gaze light on him, deliberately, appraisingly, taking in his clothes, his build, his manner. Their eyes engaged. There was no antogonism in the collision of looks, Hillary was aware, but a kind of friendly recognition. He knew Rednap would speak to him and he had no idea how he would reply.

"You there in the corner! You, sir!" Rednap called. "What's your trade?"

"Thief, I suppose you'd say," Hillary found himself responding.

"By the Lord, an honest thief! You go to New Bern?"

"Aye."

"Do you stand for the Crown?"

"Aye."

"For the Governor?"

"Aye again."

"For the East?"

"Nay, for the Colony."

Rednap looked surprised, then grinned. He turned. "Potman, take a mug of ale to that gentleman," he ordered. A moment later the heavy-jowled potman placed the ale in front of Hillary.

Hillary raised the mug in salute as Rednap sat down once more. He noticed that one of the elegantly dressed gentlemen at the next table was evidently singling him out for comment to his fellows, occasionally nodding in his direction.

Presently the nearest of them, a man wearing a small, sharp beard and dressed in a handsome red-velvet jacket, leaned close to Hillary and said in a confidential tone, "You should watch the company you keep, lad. You'll excuse the advice, I trust. By your dress you appear a gentleman, but your tongue and your friends might not suggest it."

Hillary answered sharply, "I have no friends here." The anger in his voice made it clear he did not relish criticism from a stranger.

"But you seem to get along well enough with Rednap Howell," the man persisted. "Do you know who he is?"

The other gentlemen at the table had swivelled in their chairs to hear his answer. The name was familiar to Hillary: it had come up often in his conversations with Richard and Matthew.

"I've heard his name."

"A leader of the Regulators, sir," the man in the velvet coat said quietly.

"And you're advising me not to speak to him?"

"I would advise just that, sir, although I don't presume to manage your affairs. It appears, however, that you are young, a gentleman, and excusably ignorant of Mr. Howell. I'm saying this only in friendship."

"You're quite right," added the man on the left. His face was flat and vacant; his manner was arrogant. After he had spoken he looked away with disinterest. The third member of the group pursed his lips, nodded his agreement, then turned his back to Hillary.

"You're not from the Tidewater?" the first gentleman asked.

"Yes. My name is Caswell."

"Caswell?" The arrogant man turned again to look at Hillary. He pinched his lips together. "Related to Richard?"

"Yes, a cousin."

"Aha! I thought as much." The arrogant one tapped his friend on the shoulder. "You see, Delbert, you've saved no one. The lad should know where he's going if he's Richard's cousin. Richard doesn't trust the rabble." He spoke even lower when he said the word "rabble," as if to make doubly sure Rednap did not hear him.

The man in the green coat and white breeks addressed only his friends. He remained with his back to Hillary. "Richard Caswell has his sympathies, too. You might remember that."

The man called Delbert stroked his beard and said, "No, I agree. Richard Caswell doesn't trust the rabble, no matter how good their ideas."

"How good?" the arrogant one exclaimed.

Green Jacket eased himself about in his chair. His heavy black eyebrows drew together. "I suppose you know Adam Rutledge?" His lips turned down as he said this to Hillary.

"Gentlemen, I didn't come here to answer your questions, I beg to remind you of that. As it happens, I *do* know Mr. Rutledge."

"Very well," said Green Jacket, shifting again toward his friends. "You can see why he sits alone."

The elegantly dressed gentlemen did not attempt to continue their conversation with Hillary.

It was just as well that it had ended, Hillary thought. He wanted time to consider his own behaviour. He gripped the handle of the ale mug. Why had he answered Rednap Howell so quickly and called himself a thief in jest? To Howell a man on Tryon's staff might seem a thief in earnest. Had he spoken so only to please a genial red-faced fellow who was a bit drunk? Certainly there had been no harm in speaking to a man in a tavern—it would never go farther than that. None of the coarsely dressed men at the front table were the sort invited to Manor House. Perhaps it was wrong that he had not answered the man differently. He might have called himself a planter, a shipman, a merchant—any of them would have served.

Yet, all in all, Howell's rabble had been no more unpleasant than the gentleman of elegance. And he could have brought *those* men to Manor House.

Merely because of his speaking to Howell, the gentlemen had made him feel a traitor to his own people—but who were his people? No, they had made him feel a traitor to both sides—a traitor to his class, and a traitor perhaps to his convictions and natural sympathies.

Hillary drummed his fingers lightly on the table. He muttered to himself in disgust; he was too tired to think. He rose and took a candle from the table to see his way to his room.

He stopped at the innkeeper's table, borrowed pen and ink and purchased some paper.

"A lively place, don't you think?" the man asked.

Hillary nodded agreement and started for the stairs, From the ordinary came the booming voice of Rednap Howell: "Mr. Lloyd, Mr. Lloyd! Were you planning on returning to the Assembly again?"

"Mr. Howell—" Hillary recognized the voice of the man in the green jacket and white breeks—"I do not discuss my affairs in taverns—nor with rebels."

Hillary climbed the stairs to his room. There would be time for arguments in New Bern, time for reconsideration.

He threw the bolt on the door to his room, seated

himself at the pine table. He was prepared to write a short letter to Cecelia, but he did not finish until the candle had burned low. When he finally lay down on the uncomfortable cot, it was only a matter of seconds before he was asleep.

In the morning at sun-up he and Andrew boarded the ferry across the swollen, muddy waters of the Pamlico River and proceeded on their way to New Bern.

12

New Bern

It was three o'clock in the afternoon when Hillary Caswell arrived at the Swan Inn where he had planned to stay in New Bern until affairs were arranged so that he might move into the boarding-house near the Palace.

He changed from his splashed and muddy riding clothes quickly, for the pulse, the movement of the capital had given him fresh energy. Had he been permitted, he would have thrown himself into his work that very night. He walked to the attic window and pushed the shutters wide. He stood, hands to the sill, looking down into the streets of the spreading city. Somewhere, he felt, in that bustling New Bern he would find the answers to the vague questions which his heart asked. It would be well to be at it—be at the seeking of his life.

Men on horseback were riding up and down the muddy streets. Country-men driving high-wheeled mule carts were moving slowly: shouting, swinging whips over the flanks of their mules. More often than not, the carts were filled with brick and lumber. Directly below Hillary on the board walk in front of the Swan stood several gentlemen, brilliantly dressed, in lively discussion.

Beyond and above the roofs of the buildings of New Bern, along the road to the river, Hillary could see the east façade of the nearly completed Palace. In comparison with the buildings near it, the Palace was enormous. Tryon's Palace, the Western men called it, not the Palace of the Governor of North Carolina, but only Tryon's Palace. It was now, Hillary decided, the symbol of only half a Colony—the eastern half. There was no reason, though, why it could not be accepted as an emblem of both halves, of a single united Colony, rapidly rising in the orbit of trade and power.

It stood stately and handsome, like a giant English countryhouse. Perhaps it lacked the sweep of a greensward and formal gardens which he had seen in the English shires, but it was a dignified building and certainly a credit to the Colony of North Carolina. Beyond, Hillary saw the flow of the River Trent, which added to the beauty of the Palace. There was no doubt that John Hawkes, the architect, had accomplished his masterpiece.

Hillary stretched, yawned, then reached out to close the shutters, for the sky was still full of rain. He walked to the mirror and was straightening his coat when he heard a rap at the door. On opening it, he saw a young Negro servant who asked, "Massa Caswell?"

"Yes, I'm he."

"Massa Edwards he say I give you this." The boy handed a folded note to Hillary, who thanked him and then opened the message. The boy waited, drawing slightly back from the door. "He, Massa Edwards, say I to wait for your answer."

Hillary nodded as he read.

My dear Hillary, I asked that the keeper of the Swan inform me on your arrival—which he has done. Would you do me the pleasure of joining me for dinner at six? The servants will direct you to my table.

ISAAC EDWARDS

"Tell your master that I shall be happy to join him."

"Yes, sar," the boy said, evidently happy to receive an affirmative reply for his master.

Hillary had over an hour to wait until dinner, and he spent most of that time at his window surveying the city. Even at sunset the bustle in the streets did not flag. At exactly six o'clock he started down the stairs to meet Isaac Edwards.

The secretary to Governor Tryon was resting on a settle beside the fire-place. A serving-boy was just placing a larger table in front of him so as to make room for two people. Edwards glanced up, saw Hillary and beckoned him to come forward.

Edwards stood up, holding out his hand. "I'm glad to see you again, Hillary. Was the journey a pleasant one, or did the rains hold you back too much?"

"The journey was pleasant enough," Hillary answered, "though I've had my fill of water for a time."

"I too. It's been abominable here." He raised one finger. "Boy, bring us two mugs of stout!" Then he turned again to Hillary, "It's the best cure for an overdosage of water. But I should warn you, this is one of my rare celebrations. I'm so short of help that I've denied myself the normal pleasures of life. Now you've an idea what you're getting into."

While Edwards spoke, Hillary took the opportunity to observe the man carefully, more carefully than he had done on the pine barrens hunt or at Manor House, for then he had been pushing away the thought of going to New Bern.

Edwards was thinner than Hillary had supposed. His face was more hawklike, more bony, his nose more aquiline. He reminded Hillary slightly of the man called Lloyd whom he had seen so briefly at the inn on the Pamlico. His hands, which he clasped on the table before him like a man in prayer, were delicate, the fingers long but the knuckles slightly swollen.

Edwards' back was slightly hunched, but it was possibly more from the habit of leaning over his writing-desk than from a physical affliction. He wore a black suit, well-tailored and evidently quite new. The singular lack of colour in his dress served to accentuate the blue of his eyes.

"I suppose," Edwards said, glancing down and studying his long fingers, "that you've spoken enough with Richard Caswell to understand the general situation in the Colony—wait, don't stop me." He raised one hand slightly. "I don't mean that I expect you to have a thorough working knowledge of the affairs of North Carolina; just a nodding acquaintance will suffice at first." He had a quick, nervous, almost fussy way of speaking.

"Frankly, Mr. Edwards, I can't pretend to much in

the way of information. I *have* spoken with Richard, however."

"That should do well enough," Edwards said smiling. "You'll probably have much the same idea when you've gone through some of our correspondence. I imagine you've heard of the Regulators?"

"It would be difficult not to have heard of them."

"True. You have formed an opinion of them?"

"No."

The slight raising of his eyebrows gave Edwards away. He considered it impossible not to hold an opinion on the Regulators. He knew his surprise had shown and therefore he asked, "You really do not have an opinion, and yet you've talked with Richard Caswell?" He laughed. "You'll pardon me for asking twice. It struck me as strange."

"Oh, I suppose that I have opinions, but they're not considered. I doubt if you'd care to have me parrot Richard's words."

"True enough." Edwards dismissed the Regulators for the moment and said, "I expect the Governor to be here within the next week or ten days. You'll be busy, I promise you."

The dinner hour passed easily enough with the two men exchanging light remarks on the Caswell clan and old acquaintances. It seemed fairly obvious to Hillary that the questions about his relatives, friendly as they might seem, were part of a calculated interrogation of his own thoughts and feelings. Edwards was fairly adroit, and fairly unsuccessful, in discovering what he sought. It was when they had finished eating and Edwards had called for his pipe that the gentleman finally began to volunteer some information about himself. Perhaps, Hillary thought, it was only because he felt a need to balance the conversation, and yet it seemed as though Edwards were actually hungry to talk about himself. It might be a pleasure which he was often denied, for he had few inferiors and many superiors in New Bern.

"I live here at the Swan when I'm not in Hillsborough or about the Colony. I have my family in England, you know, and this work keeps me separated from them."

He checked himself, almost asking to be told to continue.

"You live in Hillsborough?" Hillary asked.

"I have a home there." At the mention of home his features seemed to lengthen, the bony structure of his face was accentuated, giving him the look of a small tragic figure in a minor play.

"In any case, it's not a permanent home. I'll be returning to England someday. My son is fourteen now."

Edwards pushed back his chair from the table, signalling that he was ready to leave. He must have felt that too much of a luxury took the edge off one's pleasure. "You'll meet me here in the morning?"

"At whatever hour you wish."

"Good. That's the proper spirit. Then shall we set the time at seven-thirty?"

"Fine."

With that Edwards departed for his room. Hillary lingered for a while on the board walk of the Swan, observing the passers-by and reflecting on the character of Isaac Edwards. An hour in that unknown town sufficed to drive him to his room. He told himself that he should brace himself for work on the morrow by gaining one good night's sleep.

But his sleep was not so profound as he had wished it to be. His mind whirled with a multitude of thoughts— thoughts and apprehensions. He tossed and turned, as again and again the idea recurred to him that he was being drawn irrevocably to one side in a divided Colony. It was a side which he had not chosen and which his judgement when fully informed might not favour. Already he was allied with a group of men whom he might respect, but few of whom he could love.

When Andrew wakened him in the morning and had thrown open the shutters of the attic window, Hillary felt inordinately depressed. Somehow the very shouts in the street, the early bustle of the citizens of New Bern made his long indenture to a promise seem pointless: pointless, and already moving toward a collapse. Why that particular feeling should strike him, he did not know. There was no reason to look for anything but success from the Palace and the government.

Andrew was laying his coat and his ruffled shirt on the bed, having pressed them early that morning. He was delighted with New Bern. "Sar, we eats good at this place and have a room right over de kitchen for sleepin'. All de fine gentlemen brings dey man wid 'em, so we has a good time."

"Don't get yourself into any card games, Andrew, or you'll lose all your pennies."

"No, sar!" He was emphatic. "I don' do that. Dese Cahlina folk am a card-playin' pack o' fools. Dey's worser than us Marylanders by a long way. Why, just an hour ago I was watchin' a boy pull three cards off de bottom of——" He stopped, realizing he had said too much.

"How much did you lose?" Hillary asked wearily.

Andrew broke into a grin. "I won me a tuppence," he said.

"And I'll wager you've lost it back by to-night."

"No, sar. Them fellows always let a new man win a little. But I always quits after de first day. It makes 'em mighty sad-like."

When Hillary sat down to breakfast at seven-thirty, Mr. Isaac Edwards had preceded him by a full half-hour. "You mustn't let my habits disturb you too much," he explained. "I enjoy my work and have enough of it to do, so I rise a bit early and go to bed a bit late. I wouldn't expect you to keep the same hours." Edwards smiled genially, but his tone had intimated that he would expect Hillary to keep precisely the same hours as he.

"We'll have more regular time later on, Caswell," he explained. "For the present, however, I'm eager to get matters settled over at the Palace. The papers are in a fair state of confusion." He waved to a splendidly dressed man who was sitting alone on the far side of the ordinary. "Mr. Willie Davenport, representative from Tyrrell County. Fine man, a close friend of Governor Tryon."

Edwards waited with polite impatience while Hillary hurried through his breakfast. "We'll be having two offices," he was saying: "one will be in the Palace, and the other off the main grounds. The latter is where we'll probably get most of our work accomplished."

When they left the Swan for the Palace Edwards explained, "I prefer to walk the distance. A certain amount of habit keeps a man on an even keel. Good work is the fruit of system and habit."

The road from the Swan was muddy and full of potholes. A surprising number of folk were early abroad: working-men with their tool-boxes, drivers urging their sheep and cows through the streets to market, fine gentlemen on horseback early pursuing their affairs in the capital, women with empty market baskets and with children clinging to their skirts.

The road passed near the bank of the River Trent, which was swollen from the rains and swirling with muddy water. Hillary noted the large warehouses and the stores by the docks, where there was great activity.

"Whole business belongs to Mr. Cornell," Edwards said, noting Hillary's interest. "I'd say he's far and away the richest merchant in New Bern. You might be interested in the fact that his daughter Sukey is the reigning belle—that is, when Esther Wake isn't about. Of course she's already being courted by Willie Jones."

"The one with the giant plantations up-country?"

"The same."

"I've heard of him. I believe he's a friend of Richard."

"Quite possibly. Offhand, I don't know anyone of importance who isn't a friend of Richard Caswell. He has a peculiar art of not making enemies in the wrong places."

"It might be his honesty. . . ."

"Lord no, not that! Oh, I don't mean to say that he isn't honest—above all, he's that. But I assure you it isn't just his well-known integrity that keeps him in good company." Edwards hesitated, trying to decide precisely what it was that made Richard Caswell so acceptable to the powerful men of the Colony. "Perhaps," he said tentatively, "it's his ability to think and talk calmly. Men listen to him without wanting to chop his head off, no

matter if they disagree. That's not the case with the——
Well, no matter. Ah! You get a splendid view of the
Palace from here." Edwards stopped. It was the first
time he had been willing to slow his pace since they left
the Swan.

Hillary rested his hands on his hips and gazed at the
edifice. Its beauty now was overwhelming—much more
powerful than his distant view had promised. It was
stately in the true English tradition of the century. The
main building was flanked by curved colonnades, with
two-story wings at either side.

"I think the other aspect is even better," Edwards
said. "It is the main entrance. As a matter of fact, the
ground is rather muddy for us to go on this way. Let's
turn up to the next road and go in the front gate."

The Palace was built of pink brick with stone cornices.
There were seven large windows across the front, and
the entrance was in Doric simplicity.

"The Dorian mode," Edwards said, smiling, "rather
fits a military man such as the Governor."

An iron fence had already been erected about the
grounds, but the carriage gate stood open. A sentry-box
for the Palace guard stood a little to the left of the gate,
but the sentry himself was thirty paces away, chatting
with a workman who was gathering scrap lumber.

"Things seem informal," Hillary remarked.

"Yes—and probably will stay that way until Governor Tryon arrives. After that you'll notice a change—quite
a change."

They picked their way across the uneven ground
which one day would be lawn and garden, entered the
shell of the Palace and climbed the stairs to Edwards'
office.

The secretary had spoken the truth when he had said
that there was work to be done. Boxes and crates of papers had been dumped in the middle of the floor. Stacks
of books were piled in front of the fire-place. Several tall
desks had been pushed against the wall, and a long table
covered with more unsorted documents had been drawn
into a corner. Three chairs partially blocked the entrance door.

They spent the morning unpacking and arranging papers in order, putting them into files or piling them on shelves as neatly as possible.

Luncheon was disposed of quickly. Edwards had sandwiches and ale sent up from the kitchen, and Hillary noted that he was allowing himself a second celebration while he kept working. After luncheon was finished—an affair that could not properly be said to have begun—Edwards handed Hillary a large, leather-bound ledger.

"This is the Governor's letter-book," he said. "Frankly, I'm so far behind with entering his correspondence that I'd rather not look at it. The letters to be copied are in that box on the end of the table." He strode to it, riffled through the papers, and drew one out. He smiled as he handed it to Hillary. "It is simple wisdom to start you off with something interesting. Here is a copy of the Governor's own description of the hurricane of September seventh which he has promised to send to General Gage in Boston. Take the desk by the window. You'll find the quills, ink and sand-box all there."

The thought occurred to Hillary, as Edwards left the room with his peculiar hump-backed walk, that the secretary was either very far behind in his work, or preferred to wait until he had more reason to trust him before delivering into his hands any matter of importance. He shrugged, seated himself at the desk, tried two different quills and found neither to his liking. He cut a new one, and then set about copying the letter to the Earl of Hillsborough, Secretary of State for the Colonies.

Brunswick
15 September, 1769

My Lord:
On Thursday the seventh we had a tremendous gale of wind here. It began about ten in the morning at northeast and blew and rained hard 'til the close of the evening, when both wind and rain increased.

The wind shifted before midnight to northwest. The gale became a perfect hurricane between twelve and two on Friday morning the eighth. The fury of its influence was so violent as to throw down thousands and, I believe from reports, hundreds of thousands of the most vigorous trees in the country, tearing some up by the roots, snapping others short in the middle.

Many houses were blown down, all the Indian corn and rice levelled to the ground and the fences destroyed. Add to this more than twenty sawmill dams carried away with many timbers, works of the mills.

Scarcely a ship in the river that was not driven from her anchor and many received damage.

This, my Lord, is in relation to what happened within fifty miles of Brunswick.

We are in hourly expectation of receiving melancholy accounts from other parts of the Province.

It is imagined that the corn was within six weeks of its maturity. The planters may save about half a crop, but they have no hope of recovering the rice, lying at this period under water from the freshets this gust occasioned.

The country will, I fear, be greatly distressed this winter for provisions as far as the gale extended, for the people will not only be short of food, but the hogs, which are the support of many families, will lose the acorns and the nuts in the woods which used to fatten them for market, the wind having stripped every acorn from the trees before they were ripe.

In short, my Lord, the inhabitants never knew so violent a storm: All the herbage in the gardens was stripped of leaves.

This hurricane is attributed to a blazing planet or star that was seen both from New Bern and here, rising in the east for several nights between the twenty-sixth and the thirty-first of August. Its stream was very long and stretched upward towards the southwest.

Hillary yawned. He was annoyed that he had not been able to sleep well at night since he had left Manor House. He shook his hand, then rubbed it. He surveyed the work he had done: a fair page with no blots, it was a reasonably good job.

Isaac Edwards entered the room again while he was studying the letter, checking to see that he had left out no words. He stood with his hands clasped behind him and peered over Hillary's shoulder. "Not too bad, not too bad," he remarked. "You've a firm, clear hand." He turned away and began shuffling through papers on the long table. "My last helper wrote abominably, so, of course, I dismissed him." He touched a finger to his high-boned cheek. "Talked too much, also. Impossible to have a man like that about. Oh, his sympathies were all right. I'm sure he was loyal to the Governor and the Colony down to the marrow of his bones, but he liked gossip. That doesn't seem to me the proper way to serve one's master. Does it to you, Caswell?"

"No. I wouldn't think so."

Edwards rephrased the point that nagged at his mind. "You don't gossip do you, Caswell? So much of our work is confidential."

"No, sir," Hillary answered shortly. "I've never considered myself a gossip."

"No, no, I suppose not. None of us do," Edwards added. "But one has to be guarded, doesn't one?"

"Yes," Hillary said, returning to his work again. He did not consider it the most pleasant task to answer a series of rhetorical questions.

They worked until supper, and then returned in the evening. Edwards lighted the candles and then settled himself at the desk next to Hillary. They worked steadily from supper-time until midnight, and Hillary began to believe that Isaac Edwards was indefatigable. Hillary's back ached, the muscles of his legs pulled, his fingers were cramped, but he kept working, driving his pen across the paper slightly faster than Edwards. It did not occur to him until later that it might have been he, rather than the secretary, who had set the night's pace. He resolved to be more careful in the future.

When the little French clock on the mantel chimed twelve, Edwards looked up from the papers spread before him. "I suppose we must stop," he said regretfully. "If we can keep these hours for the next few days I think we'll have things in order by the time the Governor arrives."

"I suppose so," Hillary said.

"His Excellency doesn't like it when papers aren't in order."

"He appreciates what you do?"

Edwards lowered his eyes. It was as much as if he had been caught in a lie. After a few moments he answered thoughtfully, "No, I'd think not. But then, should that make any difference to me? He trusts me, and I have a duty to do. I would imagine that a man could not ask for much more from life than that: to be trusted and to have a duty."

Hillary nodded, but in his heart he felt that those were only the necessities of life. A man might be allowed to expect much more: for instance, a family which was not in England.

As the days passed in New Bern, Hillary felt no closer to Edwards than he had on the first day. Their relationship was at all times cordial. On occasion—but rarely and sparingly—Edwards would speak about himself. Gradually he came to trust Hillary with more important documents.

Hillary had transferred his residence from the Swan to quarters near the Palace. His room was pleasant enough, and from the windows he had a fine view of the River Trent. In the few hours which he could steal for himself late at night he managed to write letters to Robin Chapman, to Matthew Caswell, to the uncle who managed his plantation in Maryland, and to Cecelia. The only word of her came in one of Robin's letters: she was well, as beautiful as a sister could appear to a brother, and she had asked after Hillary. No encouragement in that, Hillary lamented: she would have shown as much interest in a casual acquaintance.

William Tryon, Governor of the Royal Colony of North Carolina, arrived at his Palace in New Bern at exactly five o'clock in the afternoon. The small French clock opposite Hillary's desk rang out the hours. Edwards had been waiting nervously at the main doors for nearly forty-five minutes.

Hillary left his desk, put his quill behind his ear and strolled to the window to watch the Governor descend from his chaise. Somehow, Hillary had not expected to see a man of such stature. Governor Tryon was broad of shoulder and slim of girth. His bearing was erect, soldierly and severe. He wore a long, blue military cloak. His hat was cocked over his carefully queued hair.

Tryon exchanged a few words with Edwards, who said yes to every question. Then the Governor turned to assist his wife from the chaise.

The impression made by Lady Tryon was that of an energetic, quick-moving woman, of great poise and assurance but certainly of no great beauty.

She glanced back at the chaise. "Hurry up, Esther." There was no reply. "You know how difficult it will be to dress with the rooms in such disorder and our clothes all higgledy-piggledy."

"My dear sister," came the rich voice from the chaise, "two minutes either way will make no great difference in our beauty."

Lady Tryon glanced to the Governor for support, but he merely shook his head, implying that there was no way on earth to hurry Miss Esther Wake.

Dainty foot first, a flutter of flounced skirts, and Esther Wake appeared. She did not have Lady Tryon's energy and bustle. She moved deliberately with a languid grace, perfectly aware that the Governor and her sister would wait for her.

It was a sight, Hillary thought, to please the eye of a Western man—even an Easterner for that matter. He turned abruptly away from the window and took the red quill pen from behind his ear. He smiled to himself, thinking that beauty is a lovely sight that does not always make one covetous. Esther Wake would indeed be a handsome piece of art to have about one's house, but he felt neither inclination nor energy to acquire it. As he walked from the partially opened window he decided it was rather a pleasant sensation to turn away from beauty before it could capture you. He started to seat himself at his desk, laughed at himself, and returned to the window. He might at least compare Cecelia's charms to hers. The lovely Miss Wake now had her back to him.

Servants in livery appeared at the bidding of Edwards, who had set the scene so that they must wait his command. The great doors were thrown open, and Governor William Tryon entered his Palace. The ladies followed, then Edwards, and finally the servants carrying bags and bandboxes from the chaise. Hillary smiled. Tryon appeared to know full well the honour due to His Majesty's Royal Governor.

Edwards and Hillary had finished their part in putting the offices in order, and soon half their materials were transferred to a small building just off the Palace grounds. That secondary office was suitable for work. The room was less lavish than the one in the Palace, but free from disturbing interruptions.

After the move to the new building and in the days immediately following the Governor's arrival Hillary saw less and less of Isaac Edwards.

The secretary would appear in the early morning to lay out the day's work and then disappear. Hillary's speed in copying letters gradually improved, enough so to cause Edwards mild surprise on several occasions. For the infrequent occasions when a decision was necessary, he found his assistant more than competent.

Hillary had time to go through the files and arrange the diverse documents and papers in perfect order. He found moments to read the memoranda and notes to the Governor from the far reaches of the Colony and England on all sorts of subjects, but his interest was centred in the case of the Regulators and their futile protests.

He read carefully those complaints in which William Butler and Harmon Husband declared:

We are determined not to pay the tax for the next three years for the edifice of the Governor's house. We want no such house, nor will we pay for it.

A cutting from the *Maryland Gazette* showed that his home Colony scoffed at "the enormous sum for building a house for a Governor." One from the *Boston Chronicle* stated: "A man that is worth 10,000 pounds, pays no more tax than a poor back-country settler who has nothing but the labour of his hands."

He came upon an envelope which held only a single, small slip of paper which was evidently part of a petition.

*We humbly beg of Your Worships to take into serious
consideration the sums given to erect a public edifice. It
is a pitiful consideration to us poor wretches to think
where or how we shall raise our part of the sums designed for that purpose. Good God! Gentlemen, what
will become of us when the demands come against us?
Paper money we have none. Gold and silver we can pur-
chase none.*

Hillary shook his head in consternation. Were these
the men branded fanatics and rebels? Were these the
men whom Edmund Fanning damned in each of his
ponderous letters to his friend the Governor? Howell,
Husband, Butler and a few others—these names were
repeated over and over again in the letters Edmund
Fanning had been writing to the Governor over the past
three or four years. Surely there must be something
more on Fanning's side than Hillary had yet discovered.
He read everything he could find. One day he came on a
new pamphlet titled *An Impartial Relation*. He turned it
over in his hands. It was dated 1770, evidently fresh
from the press. The compiler of it had not identified
himself in print, but someone had written in a bold,
strong hand on the cover the name Harmon Husband.

Hillary opened the pamphlet and leafed through it. It
rehearsed the troubles in the Western counties, especially Orange, over several years, with many copies of letters, petitions, court records and so forth. He began to
read, starting with a passage describing the harsh treatment citizens of Granville County received at the hands
of their officials. The author of the unsigned tract assured his readers that conditions in Granville County
had been appallingly similar to those of Orange County
a little later. He proceeded to quote from a Granville
paper:

*Well, gentlemen, it is not our form or mode of gov-
ernment, not yet the body of our laws that we are quarrelling with, but with the malpractices of the officers of
our county court, and the abuses that we suffer by those
that are impowered to manage our public affairs; This is
the grievance, gentlemen, that demands our serious attention. And I shall show the notorious and intolerable*

*abuses that have crept into the practice of the law in this
county, and I doubt not but into other counties also;
though that does not concern us.*

*In the first place, there is a law that provides that a
lawyer shall take no more than fifteen shillings for his
fee in the county court. Well, gentlemen, which of you
has had your business done for fifteen shillings? They
exact thirty for every cause: and three, four and five
pounds for every cause attended with the least difficulty
(and their fees in our superior courts are almost as
many hundreds); and laugh at us for our stupidity and
tame submission to these damned, etc.*

*A poor man is supposed to have given his judgement
bond for five pounds; and this bond is by his creditor
thrown into court. The clerk of the county has to enter it
on the docket, and issue execution, the work of one long
minute, for which the poor man has to pay him the
trifling sum of forty-one shillings and five pence. The
clerk, in consideration he is a poor man, takes it out in
work, at eighteen pence a day. The poor man works
some more than twenty-seven days to pay for this one
minute's writing.*

*Well, a poor man reflects thus: At this rate when shall
I get to labour for my family? I have a wife and a parcel
of small children suffering at home, and here I have lost
a whole month, and I don't know for what; for my creditor is as far from being paid yet as ever. However, I will
go home now, and try to do what I can. Stay, neighbour,
you have not half done yet; there is a damned lawyer's
mouth to stop yet; for you impowered him to confess
that you owed this five pounds, and you have thirty
shillings to pay him for that, or go and work nineteen
days more; and then you must work as long to pay the
sheriff for his trouble; and then you may go home and
see your horses and cows sold, and all your personal estate, for one-tenth of the value. . . .*

*I believe there are few of you who have not felt the
weight of those iron fists . . .*

The door to the office opened suddenly and Edwards
came in hurriedly, a worried look on his face. Hillary
closed the pamphlet, placed it on the corner of his desk
and asked, "Are you troubled, Mr. Edwards?"

"A letter from Colonel Fanning," he answered crisp-

ly. "Arrived by messenger a little while ago." He sat
down at his desk, folded the letter and sealed it. He
drummed his fingers on the desk for a moment and then
asked, "Did you finish with the correspondence?"

"Yes, except that I still have a note for Richard Buncombe."

"Oh that." Edwards dismissed it with a wave of his
hand. "You can do it later. It seems he knows everything we have to tell him anyway." He handed the message from Fanning to Hillary. "Take this over to His
Excellency's office. Give it to the Governor personally.
Well, if you can't see him, find Mr. Emory. You'll recognize him, he has a face like a hatchet. He'll see it gets
to His Excellency."

Hillary put on his coat, tucked the letter into the inside pocket, and left the room. He felt a certain amount
of bitterness that he, of all people, should be forced to
carry the messages of Colonel Fanning. He told himself
that it was merely part of his job and that he had no
control over such affairs.

In the past few weeks the Palace grounds had improved greatly. Greenery had begun to appear; a look of
finished elegance enveloped the grounds. The guard at
the sentry-box rarely strayed from his post now. His
manner was officious; he would have nothing to do with
the common workers. Although he knew Hillary well he
explained in detail how he should find the Governor's
office. Hillary listened, and found himself mildly curious
whether the guard had ever been inside the Palace.

As he was walking down the central hall Hillary met
Miss Esther Wake. She had just descended the main
staircase, and it seemed to Hillary that he had never
seen a more beautiful creature—perhaps too languid,
but he was willing to pass over that possible fault. Her
eyes were hazel, deep and almost sparkling. Her skin
was amazingly white, and her mouth warm and generous. She walked with the same easy air that he had noted on the day of her arrival, a slow, liquid grace implying there was time for everything. She seemed a woman
completely comfortable with herself and her beauty. Her
dress was yellow and wide-flaring and was cut low, ex-
posing the curves of her voluptuous bosom.

She turned right at the base of the stairs and started down the hall. She had nearly passed Hillary when she stopped and cocked her head curiously to one side, as if trying to remember something.

"I know!" she said aloud. "The man in the window!"

"I beg your pardon?"

"You." She put one finger to her lips and then smiled. "I was only remembering where I had seen you before. Now I know."

"And that was?"

"You were framed in the window on the day of our grand arrival."

Hillary nodded. "I'm surprised you should have seen me, much less remembered."

"Truly?"

"You have an air," Hillary said, "an attitude that makes one feel you neither observe nor care for anything that goes on about you."

She laughed. "You're absolutely correct—except in one instance, Mr. . . ."

"Hillary Caswell."

"Then, Hillary, you're right in your observation except when I find that a man isn't looking at me. I detest that. When he stands at a window, watches a carriage, observes a Governor—whom he can see whenever he pleases—Lady Tryon, Edwards . . . and then when I finally arrive, he turns away. Of course I'll notice *that* man. Otherwise you would have passed into oblivion. I can't stand being ignored by a man. It shows a lack of taste on his part or a lack of beauty on mine. Oh, and I can't stand a man who waits on me either."

"A plight. Believe me, you have my sympathy," Hillary said. "Do you know if the Governor's in his office now?"

She looked at him curiously. "Follow me, sire," she said with a sweep of her hand a mock curtsy.

She led him down a corridor, stopped in front of a heavy oak door and tapped lightly. A moment later, without waiting for a response, she opened it. "A young gentleman to see you," she said. "I found him wandering and bewildered in the corridor."

Hillary stepped forward with the letter in his hand.

"A message from Colonel Fanning, Your Excellency. Mr. Edwards says that it's urgent."

The Governor was seated at his table desk which was piled high with papers. "All messages seem urgent," he said wearily, holding out his hand to receive it. Esther Wake had turned to the door when he added, "Oh, Esther, stay a minute, would you? There are some things I've meant to tell you."

"Important, I hope."

"Lady Tryon," he answered, unfolding the note.

Hillary had stepped back, waiting to be dismissed by the Governor. When he glanced to Esther Wake he saw that her eyes were sparkling, her lips teasing. She smoothed her dress about her waist.

The Governor merely skimmed the letter and then placed it on the pile to his left. When he looked up at Hillary, he said, "I don't seem to recollect your face, young man. Who are you?"

"Hillary Caswell, sir."

"Of course. Richard's cousin," the Governor stated.

"Yes, Your Excellency."

"Do you intend to follow the same course as he?"

"I had hoped to."

"Then get yourself a plantation. That's the first step."

"I have that, sir."

"Then farm it," the Governor said. "Or if you must, go into the military. Both are better lives than this. That's my advice. You may take it or leave it as you please."

"Thank you, sir."

"Let me see, you are from Maryland, aren't you?"

"Now from North Carolina."

"That rather surprises me. You have changed allegiance?" The Governor looked down at his desk, and spoke to it rather than to Hillary. "I suppose you're getting enough work to keep your satisfied?"

"More than enough."

"True, true." The Governor nodded.

Hillary remembered that he had failed to say "sir" after his last words. Well enough, he thought if a title did not come quickly to his lips, it was not worth the giving.

"Esther, you like to go riding. Why don't you show Mr. Caswell the country one of these afternoons?" the Governor said.

"I'd be delighted, William. I just didn't think it was decorous for the lady to propose it." She turned to Hillary, smiled, and asked, "Shall we?"

It seemed a foolish question. He had been requested by the Governor to go riding with the most beautiful woman in New Bern. He smiled. "I'd enjoy it very much."

Hillary spent many of the following afternoons with Esther Wake riding into the country about New Bern. Edwards considered it a duty of great importance—more important even than copying the Governor's correspondence. Since a part of his duty was to keep the Governor's household content, he begrudged not a minute of the time.

On the third afternoon Esther Wake dismissed the groom who had been accompanying them. "I like a little informality now and then," she had said.

13

A Storm and a Journey

Hillary watched as Isaac Edwards shifted his position on the high chair at his desk. Through the whole morning the secretary had appeared uncomfortable, as if something were preying on his mind, something he wanted to mention to Hillary but couldn't quite bring himself to do.

Outside, the late summer was unbearably hot and humid; the River Trent was sluggish; the sounds of the carts in the road beyond were heavy and slow. Hillary yawned, stretched, bent to his writing. He heard Edwards turn on his chair again, heard the little cough that called for attention, and was aware, without stopping his work, that the secretary was looking at him.

The slight cough came again. Finally Edwards said, "I spoke with Adam Rutledge today. I suppose you've seen him since he's been here?"

"I had dinner with him," Hillary answered without glancing up.

"He's riding to Hillsborough on the morrow."

Hillary straightened and nodded, feeling that the prelude to Edward's complaint was nearly finished. "Yes, so he told me."

The stifling summer heat settled again in the room. Quiet continued for another twenty minutes. then Edwards spoke again, it was to continue the conversation as though there had been no break in time.

"I took the liberty of asking him . . ."

"Whom?"

"Of asking Adam Rutledge to let you ride with him to Hillsborough. I've always considered that a long journey can be accomplished best by two men. It's safer, you know."

"I'm to go to Hillsborough?"

Isaac Edwards nodded. He took a packet of letters from the table and brought it to Hillary. He aligned the letters meticulously on the edge of his desk. "These are for Colonel Fanning," he explained. "I want you to see that he gets them personally."

Hillary put down his quill pen and turned to face the secretary, smiling slightly. "Perhaps I don't understand. If it is only a matter of delivering letters, I think Mr. Rutledge would be happy to do it for you."

"Some of these might not please him too much. But that's neither here nor there. You'll have to stay in Hillsborough for a few days doing some copy work for the Colonel. I don't think Mr. Rutledge would have the time for that." His tone was patronizing.

"No," Hillary said, "I doubt if he would. Is that all I'm to know about my journey?"

Edwards frowned. He walked away from Hillary's desk and slumped down into a chair by the long mahogany table. He thumbed desultorily through a sheaf of papers, and finally said, "Yes, I suppose there are some other things that you should know—but in the main they don't concern your work in Hillsborough." He paused, trying to find another approach to what was clearly a painful subject. He began more directly than he had intended. "It's a matter of attitude, Hillary. Now don't mistake me! You've done excellent work for me. I'm not criticizing your work. It's just that . . . well, your approach to certain subjects seems a little off the mark."

"Go ahead. What subjects?" Hillary spoke in a level voice, trying to conceal his anger. He could take criticism of his work, but as to his personal opinions—that was a different affair.

Edwards had caught the tone of voice. "No. Forget it. Perhaps I shouldn't say anything."

Hillary was in no mood to press him. "If I'm to be leaving in the morning, there are some matters I should arrange. I'll have to speak to Adam Rutledge myself."

"Yes, yes, go on," Edwards agreed. "I certainly intended to give you time." He was observing Hillary's shoes.

"You might tell Miss Wake that I shan't be able to ride with her to-morrow—but never mind; I'll send her a note."

Perhaps, Hillary thought, it was the oppressive heat that made him short-tempered. There had been no wind. The streets were full of dust. The rains had not come to cool the land.

He put on his light coat, went back to his desk to straighten his papers and picked up the packet of letters which Edwards had placed before him. "I left the two letters to Hillsborough in the file book if you should want them," Hillary said. "There's another message to Iredell in with them." He turned toward the door. He would be glad to be gone and avoid an open clash with Edwards should the secretary decide to speak his mind —or whosoever's mind he happened to be speaking that day.

From the open window came the trill of a warbler. "Caswell."

Damn it, Hillary thought, he was going to broach the subject after all. Hillary turned from the door. He pulled a chair from beside the long table and sat down. All summer had been like that: a nagging summer without point or meaning. Summer had been a time of waiting.

"I might as well say it," Edwards continued. "Your work has been excellent. I'm highly pleased with the way you've . . ."

"Pass over that part, please." Hillary made a motion with his hand.

"Very well. Have it your way. I shall." Edwards straightened in his chair and began speaking rapidly. "For the last two months, whenever the subject of the West or the Regulators has come up, you've seemed to take an almost . . . well . . . belligerent stand. You give the impression you actually believe the right is on their side! Can you imagine how that looks?"

"Can you imagine that I don't care?"

"Wait till I've finished. You seem even to applaud

when they defy the Government. And you can see why I think that's a disturbing attitude for my assistant to take —one who's known to be in the employ of the Royal Governor.

"You're not like your cousin Richard. He feels . . . Now listen to me, Hillary." Edwards leaned forward, his blue eyes intent. "I don't mean to be harsh. It's possible that I might feel the same as you. I realize that some of the Western people are being cheated and overcharged in their courts. Certainly I know it. That's something for us to try to correct. I know the Regulators are supposed to stand for certain ideals—freedom, justice, honour, equality—all those fuzzy-headed words. Maybe, God knows, maybe they think they're really the ones to protect the Colony. But I'll tell you this, Hillary: they're *not* the men who can do it.

"You take ninety-nine per cent of those men and you'll find that they're drunkards, butchers, idlers, thieves, criminals, fanatics. They wouldn't know an ideal from a good day's work. They just follow the shout in the street, follow the hell-raisers to raise their own hell."

Hillary started to speak, but Edwards raised his hand, motioned with one slender finger. Suddenly it struck Hillary that in spite of the expletives, which were unusual for Edwards, there was no feeling behind his words. He spoke for another.

"You take the other one per cent of those Regulators, take the one per cent that doesn't fall into the class of low life—what are they? Nothing but dreamers. One of them gets hold of a Bible, another reads a poem, a third hears a speech—and they're inspired. Inspired to what? Inspired to tear up the earth, knock out the cornerstones of our Colony. And they do it all under the aegis of self-protection and noble ideals. By the good Lord, Hillary, building a government and a body of law and forging a colony out of a raw country aren't things you can trust to dreamers. It takes work.

"The madman may be able to say the right words, and he may lay out the course of true justice by accident, but good Lord, man, you're surely not going to trust him to bring all those dreams to pass. No! You'll listen and learn. Then you'll give the task of straightening affairs to a man who's solid, steady and a worker."

He hesitated a long time before he spoke again. "Most men can dream, Hillary. Dreams are cheap. But find me a rare man like Richard Caswell, and he'll put your dreams into solid, lawful action. Find a leader like William Tryon, and you'll get the work done."

"Have you finished?" Hillary asked.

Edwards paused, then answered: "Yes, I suppose so."

"As to the Regulators, I haven't really formed any opinions as yet. I'm surprised you can tell me what my opinions are."

"I'm not saying what they are! I'm only telling you what they appear to be. . . ." Edwards broke off in a short spell of coughing; his eyes were watery when he finished.

"You ought to take something for that cough."

"Thank you, I do."

"I've seen the Governor's letters saying that he was going to clear up excessive fees and corruption among the Courthouse officials in the West." Hillary said. "Some go back three years to 1767, others two. Now tell me, what has he actually done?"

"Many things. To give some examples, he ordered lists of legal fees published and posted, warned lawyers and officials against overcharging and instructed the attorney general to prosecute cases of extortion. That was two years ago. He went to Hillsborough himself to lend his influence."

"But most of the officials were his own men. Was that the time Colonel Fanning was fined one penny?"

"There were extenuating circumstances. Damn it, there you go again. When you take the Governor's wages he expects full support. He has been paying for your loyalty."

"I wasn't aware, Mr. Edwards, that I had put my loyalty up for hire or sale."

"No, perhaps not, perhaps not," Edwards answered, his voice drained and tired. He knit his brows and studied the flat surface of the table. Finally he looked up. "Well, now I've said it. You may as well go along and get ready. It's a long journey."

Hillary stood up and moved to the door. At the last

moment he turned and asked, "Have you seen my cousin Richard lately?"

The barbed question caught Edwards unawares. He flushed, the crimson giving a touch of life to his pale face. "Yes, now that you ask me, I have."

"Perhaps I should have been more careful in expressing my feeling to my cousin—yes?"

"Hillary, it was only for your own good, believe me. He knows you're impressionable and . . . well . . . young."

"And now I'm to be allowed to see the rebels at first hand? Was that his idea too?"

"No," Edwards said wearily, "as a matter of fact, it was mine."

Hillary felt a certain sorrow for Isaac Edwards. He wanted to say something friendly to the man, something which might bring a bond between them, but it was impossible. Instead he said, "I'll promise you this much: I'll never let my personal feelings interfere with any work you assign me."

The picture of Edwards nodding his head slowly in understanding, in recognition of his failure and personal defeat, came back to Hillary as he rode along the trail to Hillsborough with Adam Rutledge. Herk and Andrew were trailing far behind.

Hillary had seen Edwards again on the morning of his departure, and the secretary had seemed anxious to patch up their argument. He had insisted that Hillary use the facilities of his house as long as he remained in Hillsborough. He seemed honestly pleased when Hillary accepted.

Adam Rutledge was good company, and Hillary respected him. During the long journey to Hillsborough he took the opportunity to ask Adam's opinion on many subjects, but not on the Regulators. For the time being, this had become a personal issue, one he wished to settle for himself without relying on Adam Rutledge or anyone else.

More than once along the trail he thought of a letter he had seen which Governor Tryon had sent to the Earl of Shelbourne. He remembered the words well: "The sheriffs have embezzled more than one-half of the public money ordered to be raised and collected by them."

Then why had the Governor not acted against them?

Hillary recalled that on another occasion the Governor had agreed with the Assemblymen and said: "The abuses in the sheriffs' office cry loud for, and shall receive the strictest attention and correction, nor shall the embezzlement and irregularities committed by other collectors of public revenue escape the most exact inquiry."

And again Hillary asked himself why the Governor had not acted. What possible motive could he have for delay?

On the fifth day as they were riding under a lowering sky, hoping to reach Hillsborough by nightfall, Hillary asked, "Mr. Rutledge, if you had to give a character of the Governor in a few words, how would you describe him?"

Adam looked at him quizzically, gave him a slow, friendly smile. "He's a difficult man to put in a few words, Hillary." He guided his Saladin around a pool of water in the road and, going slightly ahead, called back over his shoulder. "A proud man, a vain man, and an extremely competent leader when he lets neither pride nor vanity blind him."

Hillary nodded, once more plunged into his worries.

"It's a storm sun," Adam said. "We should move faster." He put his horse into a trot, motioning at the same time for Herk and Andrew to follow.

When they had approached within a few miles of Hillsborough, the carts, wagons, riders and foot travellers became more frequent.

"Are there always so many on the road?"

"I'm surprised myself, Hillary. No, there aren't usually."

Ahead of them they could see a lightning-blasted tree. It marked a fork in the road. Near it was a small wagon that had been drawn off onto the grass. An old man was sitting beside the wagon. As soon as Adam saw him he spurred forward and then reined in. "Hiram, it's good to see you!" he cried. He reached to shake the hand of the old man who had risen spryly to his feet. "What are you doing here? I thought you were in the Illinois country."

Hiram's hair was as white as a fluff of cotton and tied in an old-fashioned queue. His horse looked as old as he, a bony grey that munched the lush grass contentedly.

Hiram grinned. "Aye, it's good to see you again, Mr. Rutledge. I was in the west, but I've come back to lead another party out there. This will be the third that's gone from Hillsborough in the last year." He nodded to Hillary to emphasize his words.

"The third!" Adam said. "You surprise me. Hillary, this is my good friend Hiram Whitlock. He lives out on the banks of the Mississippi—just at the confluence with the Missouri, isn't it?"

Hillary was astonished that an aristocrat like Adam Rutledge would show such genuine feeling for a man of lower station. It was a thing rarely done. If a man like Rutledge would break the barrier—— He left the thought unfinished. No, they both seemed unaware of a difference in station. There was nothing false between them they were obviously friends.

"Why are so many going west?" Adam was asking.

Whitlock glanced suspiciouly at Hillary, but Adam signalled that it was safe to speak. "Various reasons, I'd say, Mr. Rutledge. Perhaps the most of 'em now don't like the folks who run this Government." Again he glanced toward Hillary. "I'm not saying that'll be the case later—but for right now that's it."

"Don't worry about Hillary. I can trust him to keep words to himself."

"Mr. Rutledge, it's *bad* here. You know I don't complain unless I got something to sink my teeth into. Round here a poor man has little chance, what with the skunks running the Courthouse and throwing those fees at us." He shrugged his shoulders, but his thin, lined face was serious. "I'm a little different from the rest of 'em. I've got you to thank for pointin' the Northwest Territory to me. I don't have to stay and take it. But, by the good Lord, some of 'em do! And it ain't nice, Mr. Rutledge."

"We'll have to do some talking to-morrow. I take it we'll see you in Hillsborough. Where do you stay?"

"At the Star, sir, behind the Courthouse."

"Good. We'll be staying there too. Perhaps we can have dinner together."

"If I'm there in time, I'd like it, sir."

Adam glanced at the sky. "We should be getting on if we're going to beat the rain." He turned his mount back to the road.

After they were on the path to the town again, Adam commented, "There's one of the finest men God ever let live."

"Whitlock? Does he do any farming?"

"He used to," Adam said. "But now with his guiding wagon trains for the folks going west, he doesn't have much time for it. I imagine one would call him a scout. His wife, Miranda, is as good a soul as Hiram. She keeps the farm going while he takes the settlers over the mountains. Strange, but I've often thought God must have a special place for those men who brave dangers of a new country—brave them for a purpose that's beyond gold or power or prestige. Lord knows they get little enough acclaim on earth."

"He didn't want to talk in front of me," Hillary said.

"But he did. Many of my friends wouldn't have."

"What is it, Adam? Do I have the air of the Palace about me?"

Adam laughed. "No, but your mannerisms place you in the East. By the way, you heard me tell Whitlock that it was all right for him to speak his mind in front of you?"

"Yes."

"In effect, that meant I gave him my word you wouldn't repeat anything you heard. I don't misjudge you, I'm sure—even though I failed to ask you in advance."

"No, sir, you do not."

"Good. We've not much farther. This trail bends north for another half-mile and then we'll be at the edge of the village."

They rode on in silence until Adam spoke again. "As long as you're with me, Hillary, you'll be hearing of affairs that are probably foreign to you—at least the sentiments will be foreign. I realize you've a duty to perform,

a service, for you're in the employ of the Governor—
but, of course, they didn't buy your honour."

"No. They haven't quite managed that. But I think
they'd try."

Adam smiled at Hillary. "And I hear you've been
doing more than merely keep your eyes on Miss Esther
Wake."

"She's a thing to catch the eye, isn't she?"

"A striking woman," Adam said; "a very peculiar
woman, too. At times when I've heard her speaking, I've
been certain that she mocks the Governor. One can never be sure about women."

"I'll agree to that," Hillary said. In their brief summer
he had suspected that Miss Esther Wake, perhaps with a
relative's licence, held the Governor lightly. He reflected
on the various statements Adam had made about Tryon
and the intimations to be drawn from them. There had
been a certain barb in all he'd said. Hillary fancied that
even in their most casual talk he had been receiving a
lecture, and education given in the most painless manner.
He could not be sure. Adam Rutledge was much wiser
than an Edwards.

The clouds were still full, and the sun had disappeared
behind the mountains. A dull red infused the skies; the
ponderous quiet of a summer evening spread over the
land, a quiet broken only by the sounds of their horses'
hoofs along the trail.

"I owe my first insight into the grievances of the
Western man to Whitlock," Adam said. "Until I knew
him, I had only the sketchy reports one normally receives in the East. Whitlock was the man who showed
me the first Advertisement put out by the Regulators. It
seemed to me you were often about to mention them
along the trail—but you always held back."

"I was about to—but I felt I ought to discover a few
things for myself," Hillary said.

"I don't suppose you hear too many good things
about the Regulators in your position," Adam said dryly.

"No, I don't. But there are pamphlets to read. As for
the spoken word, I've been impressed with the fact that I'm

to show unceasing devotion to the Governor and all his works—" he hesitated—"which I suppose is as it should be. But sometimes I can't help feeling I'm going to be called on to do things that go against every belief I hold dear."

"Then it's best not to have beliefs?"

"No. Of course you're right, Adam. One *must* have them, no matter how impoverished they may seem."

"There's the village ahead. Do you see the lights? We're lucky to be so close with the sun down."

They trotted the final short distance to the village and the Star Tavern. The last words Hillary heard Adam say before their arrival were "You won't be alone in fighting against some of the things you believe, Hillary. There may be many of us." He did not carry that remark further.

At the inn an old, white-haired Negro in a green coat and yellow breeches came out with a lanthorn. "Cassius will carry your horses around to the stable, sirs. Let Cassius take——"

The massive figure of Herk, Adam's body servant, came between Cassius and his master. "I will do," he said shortly, and he stepped forward to assist Adam to dismount.

Hillary remained on his roan. "I think I ought to go to Edwards' house to-night. He was kind enough to give me the invitation."

"Nonsense!" Adam said. "Keep me company this evening. I'm sure we'll find room."

Hillary gave in to his friend; Adam Rutledge *was* good company.

The inn was crowded, but the host, a plump, short, jovial man, greeted Adam with enthusiasm. "Ah, Mr. Rutledge, it's good to see you again! I have one room left . . . sort of held it back . . . must have guessed you were coming." He added, somewhat apologetically, "It's the corner room west. The tariff——"

"Is always too high, Pitkin," Adam said. "We'll take it."

When he had signed the ledger-book he turned to glance in the ordinary. The room was full and noisy. He stood surveying the men in the room from the doorway, then went back to the innkeeper. He asked in a low voice just loud enough for Hillary to hear, "Doesn't Fanning have a warrant for the arrest of Rednap Howell and William Butler?"

"And Harmon Husband, sir." Pitkin nodded.

"Husband's a member of the Assembly."

"Well then, maybe not for him, but I'm sure about the others."

"I haven't met Husband yet."

"He's here, too, sir," Pitkin said.

After a moment's thought Adam turned to Hillary. "Well, come along. We might as well get to our room and clean up. Then we can have some dinner."

"You look thoughtful," Hillary said.

"I am," Adam said gravely. "I was thinking we might have some trouble tonight. You may get a close-up view of the Western problem, Hillary. It might be even closer than either of us wish."

14

Letters

Three letters awaited Robin Chapman on his return from Nassau. He moved his straight-backed chair to the window, from which point he could see the harbour and the masts of the *Laughing Girl*. That good ship was far more his home than his father's house; he knew no greater pleasure than to see her riding gracefully in the water—unless, of course, it was to feel her alive beneath his feet.

Hadn't he told Cynthia Martin, "A sailor is the greatest homebody in the world"?

"Then why in the world are you sailing to Antigua?" she asked, laughing.

"I bring my home with me. I can't bear the thought of leaving her."

"And what of your wife to be, Robin? Would you expect her to fall in love with the *Laughing Girl,* too?"

"As much as with me. I'm not the jealous type."

"But I prefer my gentlemen jealous," she said. She had leaned back in her chair then, her lips in a half-smile, and added musingly, "Still, I'm very fond of the *Laughing Girl.*"

Of the three letters in his lap, one was from Cynthia, brought from Antigua by the *Heart of Oak*. He put it to one side, deciding to save it for last. The others were from Meredith and Cecelia. He opened his sister's letter first, breaking the amber seal and unfolding the pages on his lap.

June 18, 1770

My dear Robin,

Have you any idea how unearthly boring our fair town of Charleston can be? One might as well be placed back in time, say for instance, to the Roundhead days. Those Puritan hours must have been gay and flippant compared with this last month. Could Manor House have spoiled me for the entire year? If so, I long to be spoiled again and wish these months would pass quickly.

Twice I received letters from Hillary Caswell, and twice I have put him out of my mind. I didn't want to fall in love with a "politician," dear brother, I would as soon marry a sea captain, and you know where my heart stands on that subject. Hillary tells me of New Bern, of the Governor, of Isaac Edwards, of Lady Tryon—and I should never forgive him for this—of Miss Esther Wake. A charming woman, he says, with a trail of suitors that would stretch from Boston to Antigua. I don't think it's very fair to tell me such things. And if I should ever be so foolish as to write to him, I shall tell him so.

A lesson for you, my brother: No woman enjoys being told of her rivals, even if she has no designs on the man. Or maybe I should make the statement more general: No woman enjoys being told of another woman. After all, we're rivals for every man, whether we will or no. Surely God has made us this way, for I had no intention of being a jealous, selfish woman—even as I know Miss Wake must be.

As small news, I pass this on to you: I have received a proposal in marriage. Are you surprised, dear Robin? I was, honestly I was. He is a young gentleman of Charleston, Emory Little, and quite handsome—far more handsome than Hillary. Of course, I dare not tell Father or he will be curious how I've spent the days of my education. Sometimes Emory is quite clever, and at other times unbearably dull. He has, he claims, prepared himself to be a plantation owner. That is to say, he has prepared himself for nothing. He dances excellently, dresses as most proper gentleman and is the perfect escort. He knows nothing of books, ledgers and figures, and does not care a whit for politics—his saving grace. I have one question, though. How can a man propose to a girl when she has not even let him kiss her?

As for Master Emory Little, I have refused him. I did not make it definite and forever—I fear one should be very silly to do such a thing as that. But when I consider Mr. Rutledge, Uncle Matthew, Colonel Buncombe and the planters of our beautiful country—oh, Robin, they make me laugh at Emory Little! They want something beyond a dance and to-morrow's tea. And I want a husband like that.

I have forced you to read this far because you're expecting more important news. You know that I always end my notes with affairs that interest you. I'm afraid you've taken to reading them from the end backward.

Emory's father does a lively trade with England and is more English than Lord North himself. He has heard serious rumours—which he foolishly imparted to his son —that Governor Tryon is to receive a promotion to a Colony in the North. He did not specify the Colony, and I did not ask. Anyway, it may not be true, since one can't be promoted from our Colony of North Carolina.

Emory is very glib and foolish, but I don't think he talks to anyone save me. He has the undying urge of a young man to impress a woman. Ah well, he will learn. If our gentlemen of Tyrrell talked as much as he, I'm sure I'd be a veritable royal report on colonial affairs.

I can think of nothing else to say, unless it be to ask you to bring me something bizarre from the Indies on your next voyage. Do they have monkeys there? If I had the courage, I'd lead one about on a leash through the streets of Charleston. At least it would liven things in the fall season, even though you might not care to call me sister.

> *My love, dear Robin.*
> *Cecelia*

Robin folded the letter carefully, carried it to his desk, where he tucked it among his other papers. If the rumour were true, perhaps the whole situation in the West would change. With Tryon would surely go Edmund Fanning; but the question was: could the removal of a man or two straighten things out at this late date?

Robin sat down again by the window and gazed out at the *Laughing Girl*. And yet . . . Tryon was a man with pride. It would be hard to imagine that he would wish to leave North Carolina in an obvious state of unrest—a state of rebellion. When he heard of his promotion, might he not precipitate a crisis, only to show that he was master of his house, a man fit for great things?

Robin tore open the letter from Meredith with more eagerness than he had opened his sister's.

July 8, 1770

My dear brother,

It's good fortune that you haven't been in the West. Your temper would be as short as mine. Affairs have grown worse instead of better as I had hoped. If you have been on a voyage, this may come as fresh news to you: Edmund Fanning is certain to be returned to the Assembly. After he had been defeated in Orange County the Governor created a borough for him in Hillsborough. Whether the main of the Orange people like it or not makes no difference to our haughty and—I hope— damned Governor.

We shall have Fanning, and Tryon will have—what? I should like to know. What possible good can he see in Fanning?

I find it difficult to write coherently. Since the March test case of the Colonel, my ire has been high. You know of it? Let me tell you. Mr. James Hunter of Orange, feeling he had been outraged by Fanning, at last brought his case to our most excellent courts, and proved (at least to my mind) that Fanning had extorted fees from him as well as from the populace at large.

Judges Maurice More and Richard Henderson and Chief Justice Martin graced the bench and listened to those pleas for redress. In God's name, how those gentlemen could swallow their consciences I do not know! The test case failed. I have no doubt the good Colonel and his hired judges had a merry time toasting one another that night.

That same panel of judges (Oh, how they have fallen!—to use the Colonel's own bloody words for his people) found Harmon Husband on the left side of the law. He was forced to pay the most vicious fees and to placate several grubbing lawyers for something that happened two years ago.

Were I a judge with conscience—discovered late, of course—I would sentence myself to be hanged. I would pray that my bailiffs jerked me from the bench I had

*disgraced and put an end to my evil days. It would be
small recompense to a people I had betrayed.*

*My dear brother, the angry humours are in my heart.
I need words from you to tame me or my talk about the
gallows may bounce back on me. It does not do a man's
body grace to play the pendulum from a tree, and I
think, were my heart known, the Colonel would be happy to see me swing.*

*If there were an outright battle it might not be so
frightful. But there is no battle; there is no army to fight.
One might take his sword and pistol and run into the
streets shouting that he'd fight for liberty. Excellent!
Well and good! But with whom would he fight? Colonel
Fanning? He wouldn't fight. No issue is clearly drawn.
There is nothing but oppression from all sides. When the
people raise a strong head against it, it withdraws a little. When they disperse to their homes, it closes in once
more.*

*I have considered the quality of Governor Tryon. I
have placed his image before me and studied it to find
what makes it move, what turns the mainspring. I have
pondered long on what could wind him up. Pride? Ambition? Hate? Love misguided? I cannot tell. To me he
is inscrutable and running an inscrutable course. His
very virtues portend dangers to the Colony. It seems his
moderation, his readiness to pardon, his reluctance to
apply harsh remedies to our troubles leads us ever closer to a contest of arms. He not only permits men's passions to boil high but stokes the fire.*

*Will he let the poor men push themselves to the point
of fanaticism, and then rush down, the avenging arm of
the crown, and in one sweep of his sword dismember
our hopes—and our bodies? Will he let a Fanning build
us up to anger until in desperation we go against all
principles of law? Will he strike then, with the shield of
the law and of the Crown before him?*

*Tryon is a military man, and, therefore, I suspect
him. It is on the field he knows he can win glory. Would
it not be natural for him to wait only till he finds his
suitable battleground, only till our feeble forces are
gathered for one fight in one encampment—and then to
cut us down?*

I'm sure such action would find great favour in the

House of Hanover. It would be the stairway to Tryon's greatness, and our bodies would be the steps.

The far west is the place to be. There a man could be free of the curse of another's ambition. There are many who feel as I.

James Robertson has already left. A strange man, he. Always talking of a place called Watauga, saying that he will make his home there. Perhaps I should not count him as one of those who leaves because of the oppression: he is a wanderer. It may be he will not even stop in the Watauga country, but will push on.

I, too, am tempted. Yet I am not like the judges of our courts, and I cannot desert our Colony and turn traitor to our dreams.

I await news from you, and from our family. May your latest voyage have been successful! May the next Christmas see us together again! May the new year see an end to folly! But, God knows, and my heart knows, it will not.

Meredith

Robin Chapman sat quietly for a long time in the straight-backed chair. When he looked out to the *Laughing Girl* he smiled, thinking how natural it was for each man to seek a home away from trouble.

Then he frowned. For all his talk he knew that his birthplace was this land. When the time came, he would not be able to seek another home.

He held the letter from Cynthia Martin in his hand, but he would not open it until he had made a decision in his heart.

15

Night at the Tavern

Herk was unpacking the saddle-bags, shaking the clothes free of wrinkles and hanging them on the wall-pegs when Adam stopped him. "Herk, take your horse and ride down the road until you meet Hiram Whitlock. Tell him I've room for him here with me."

"Yes, sar," Herk answered. He stepped quickly to the door.

Hillary, who had just unpacked a ruffled shirt, straightened with a look of mild surprise on his face.

Adam smiled at his consternation, "What's the matter, Hillary?"

"Nothing." He hung his shirt on a peg, examined it longer than was necessary and finally said, "Oh, perhaps I was a bit surprised that you were asking Whitlock to stay here."

"Do you object?"

"No, certainly not."

"But you wouldn't have done it in my place?"

Hillary turned from the wall. "No, probably not. But I confess you're a new experience for me, Adam. I see the difference in social class between you and Whitlock."

Adam began combing his hair. "True, there is a difference. In the great houses on the Tidewater here or in Virginia it might be thought a gulf between us. It is so in most old, settled places."

Hillary nodded thoughtfully.

"But Hiram and I," Adam continued, "have lived and travelled in the western wilderness. I have land in Illinois. He, as I told you, is a scout. It's a country of vast promise, a challenge to men of spirit. It has no customs, no settled manners. Out there you do not judge a man by the clothes he wears nor by his manners, but by what he can do in a pinch; not by his forefathers but by what he is. Put Hiram and me in Illinois, Hiram is not improbably the better man. I've learned the western way of looking at my fellows. He is my friend, and I'm glad to have him as a friend wherever we are."

Hillary laid aside his unpacking and sat down on the side of his bed to wrestle with the unfamiliar view Adam was painting for him. His forehead wrinkled. "I suppose Colonel Fanning would say this western way would break down the orderly structure of society."

Adam smiled. "Fanning, like most of the Governor's friends, looks back across the sea to the old world of England. Others of us look to the west and the new world of America. Not all poor men, either. Even Fanning's arch-enemy Husband is a man of substance. He must have two thousand acres on Sandy Creek and extensive lands on Deep River. As more men look to the west and its promise, I think the old classes among men will disappear, but not without a struggle."

Hillary knitted his brows. "All this is strange to me. It isn't the way I was brought up. Coming from you, it is not so hard for me to accept." He paused, staring at the wall. "Now I think of it, my sympathies have gone to the men of Orange from the beginning, though Fanning and his friends are more of my class. Perhaps without knowing it I've already come around to your point of view."

Adam had finished dressing. "If you have, it is no wonder you are uneasy as part of Tryon's official household. Well, you may be uneasy to-night."

"Why, Adam?"

"We'll be going down to the ordinary in a few minutes to get something to eat. I may be talking to several people." He turned to face Hillary, his eyes steady. "Officially, you'll have to forget everything you hear."

"Of course."

"I'm sorry to keep repeating it, but I *must* make that point clear. After all, you're in daily contact with Edwards and the Governor's other people, and although Edwards is an old friend of mine, I don't always agree with his opinions. His heart, even his soul, is in his work: that often leads a man to strange extremes. Are you nearly ready?" Adam turned again to the window.

"One thing left," Hillary said, rising from the bed and shaking out a pair of breeks which were in his saddle-bag: "I hope the food for the servants is good. If not, I'll be hearing from Andrew for the next week."

"Pitkin sees they're treated well."

In a few moments the two men descended the stair-case together.

The ordinary was crowded, and Hillary could barely hear Adam's voice above the noise and laughter. "They've delicious spare-ribs here. Can you see the ta-ble by the fireplace? Let's take it."

They made their way around the tables where men sat in buckskin and rough homespun clothes: frontiers-men and farmers of Hillsborough. Ale flowed and tongues wagged freely. Many were beginning their meal of spare-ribs, cracking the ribs with their teeth to taste the juicy morsels within the bones. Some were laughing; some singing; a few were serious. A small group of bronzed men at a table not far from the one Adam had chosen were leaning forward in earnest discussion.

Adam had been greeted by several persons, and his back was turned when a voice broke over the hubbub calling to Hillary.

"It's the thief! My sainted aunt, what do you do in Hillsborough?"

Hillary looked quickly toward the table of earnest men. One face in the group was grinning, and he recog-nized the genial man with the red hair who had spoken to him months before at the Pamlico inn. "My old occu-pation," Hillary answered.

"Profitable?"

"Like a lame horse."

Rednap Howell shook his head as if to say it was a great pity, and then he turned back to his more serious companions. Adam had stopped short, hearing that brief conversation, and after they had sat down to their table he said, "I'm astonished you should know that man."

"I met him by chance at the Pamlico a while back."

"You haven't spoken of it to Edwards?"

"No."

"It's just as well you don't."

They were served their spare-ribs and had barely begun to eat when they saw their host, Pitkin, push his way through the packed ordinary toward the table of Rednap Howell and his friends.

Adam was saying, "Those are the chief Regulators. The man to Howell's left is William Butler. I don't recognize the others, but Pitkin told me that Harmon Husband is one of them."

"Which one would you say?" Hillary asked.

"The gentleman opposite Butler. Notice when he speaks how the others listen to him. He never seems to raise his voice. From what I've heard that would be most like Husband."

"I'd guess the same," Hillary said, "but for different reasons. Look at his hair, the way he turns his mouth, and his eyes—they're the eyes of a dreamer."

"Perhaps," Adam said. "But don't let appearance deceive you. I think Husband's a divided man. In some of his tracts I find very little of the dreamer. He's more practical than one is given to think. And, after all, it's difficult to read a man's character from his eyes. Colonel Fanning's glance seems quite frank and open at times, and yet I think sincerity is foreign to him."

Mr. Pitkin, his black, clubbed hair in disarray, had reached Howell's table. The rebels fell silent as they listened to him. His face was lined and anxious. When he had finished what he had to say they rose quickly, and at the same time Pitkin signalled a potman to clear the table. The men left hurriedly, up the side stairway which led directly from the ordinary. Hillary guessed that for some reason they did not wish to make a slow passage through the crowded room, or perhaps to risk being stopped at the main door.

Hillary looked inquiringly at Adam, but Adam shook his head. "I don't know. I imagine we'll find out presently."

The potman had cleared the dishes, and a waiter had

spread a clean, checkered table-cloth and was laying out silver and glasses when the main door was flung open. Four men wearing the tawny uniform of the local militia pushed their way into the room. The noise in the ordinary died down as the people craned to see the militiamen. The stares were hostile and were returned in kind.

The sergeant in charge quickly surveyed the room. Then he turned to his men and made a comment that Hillary could not hear. From the sergeant's expression he could tell he was displeased.

The soldiers seemed in some hesitation. Then the sergeant strode to the empty table by the fire-place which had been recently occupied by the Regulator leaders. He took a chair and beckoned the corporal to sit beside him. The two privates stood at attention behind them.

"Pitkin!" the sergeant shouted.

The host, who had busied himself near the casks of ale after he had spoken to these new arrivals, hurried to their table, bowed obsequiously and asked for their orders.

"Let your boy bring ale for us." Pitkin started to move away. "No. You stay here for a while, Pitkin. We've questions for you."

"Anything at all," Pitkin said. "Anything you wish."

"I can imagine," the sergeant said wearily. "Has Howell or Butler been here today . . . or Harmon Husband?"

Pitkin shook his head, a slight look of dismay on his round face. "Not today, Sergeant. None of 'em today." At the sergeant's scowl, Pitkin repeated, "Believe me, sir, I haven't seen them. You know I'd tell you. I've no reason to hide them."

Adam glanced at Hillary. "He doth protest too much." And in a lower tone he added, "It's nice to find a man who doesn't lie too well."

"Now, he *was* here about a week ago," Pitkin said. "Who was?"

"Howell, sir. Rednap Howell."

The corporal, a fellow with a thin face and blond hair, spoke up. "Which way was he goin' then, Pitkin?"

Pitkin hesitated. "Why, I don't rightly know, Corporal. So many people come and go that I've no idea . . ."

"But he put up here for the night?"

"Yes, sir."

"You have your ledgers to prove it?"

Pitkin was obviously flustered. "Why . . . why . . . yes. I suppose I do."

The sergeant interrupted the interrogation. He rubbed his hand over his unshaved cheeks. "Bring us the books. I wouldn't want to think you'd lied to us, Pitkin. I want to see his name in the books. If I didn't see it I'd have to guess you were being just *too* accommodating to us."

"Sure, he's accommodating to everybody," the corporal said, pleased with himself.

"The books—yes, of course. I'll fetch them now. Mind you, I'm not certain which day it was. It may take me a moment."

"We'll wait."

"And you better show us," the corporal added, feeling mightily important.

Pitkin hurried from the ordinary back to his stall in the entrance-way where he kept his ledgers. Noise began to fill the ordinary again as if nothing had happened, but the glances toward the militiamen were still hostile. A few guests made it a point to leave the room in obvious disapproval.

"You see what comes of talking too much," Adam said to Hillary. "I think our host will be doing some fast registering of Mr. Howell in his book. Shall we hope he hasn't saved too much paper and crowded the names in? He must have room to insert Howell's?"

Hillary bit into one of the spare-ribs. "These are things I'm busy forgetting."

"By all means," Adam said.

The corporal, whose chair was nearest their table, rested one arm over its back and surveyed the room. To the private behind him he said in lowered tones, but loud enough for Hillary and Adam to hear from their vantage point, "Strangers, most of 'em. Farmers. You'll get to know 'em when you've been around a while. There's Mr. Rutledge of Albermarle. He looks out of place here."

"Where's Pitkin?" the sergeant asked, though the

question seemed directed to no one. It was merely a sign of his impatience.

Adam, noting this restlessness, excused himself from Hillary, rose and stepped across to the sergeant. "A bad night for riding, Sergeant. Which way are you going?"

"Mr. Rutledge, sir, we're riding down to Mecklenberg County—Colonel Fanning's orders."

"I've come from there—fairly recently. The rivers are high, particularly the Haw. If it rains to-night it should make the fords all but impassable, and one can't be sure it hasn't rained already."

"Thank you, Mr. Rutledge. I couldn't trust these farmers around here for the time of day."

"Don't mention it, Sergeant."

"And say, Mr. Rutledge—" the sergeant glanced again toward the door—"you haven't seen Husband or any of those Regulators around here, have you? If I threatened to close their houses I couldn't expect these innkeepers to tell me the truth."

Hillary was curious how Adam would reply. He leaned forward slightly.

Adam paused thoughtfully. "Sergeant, I don't know whether I'd recognize Husband if I walked into the man. I've never met him."

"Just wondered. Thank you, anyway, Mr. Rutledge." Adam returned to his table and heard the sergeant say to his men. "That settles that. They haven't been here."

"Do you think you gave Pitkin enough time?" Hillary asked.

"I don't know."

The sergeant had just slammed the flat of his hand on the table when Pitkin hurried back into the ordinary, carrying with him a heavy, bound ledger. He placed it on the table in front of the sergeant and thumbed through the pages.

"You took your time about it. Is the ink dry?"

"Sir, I wouldn't try to deceive you."

"I hope not, Pitkin. I truly hope not. Boy," he called, turning from the table, "more ale!" He looked back at the ledger and followed the host's finger as he pointed to the name.

"There it is! Exactly a week ago, as I said."

"That his name?"

"Read it for yourself, sir."

"Damn it! I asked you the question."

"Yes, sir."

"Fred, how's it look to you?" the sergeant said.

The young private leaned over the book, trying to spell out the letters. After a moment he said, "I think so, Sergeant."

"If he returns, Pitkin, I'll expect you to tell me. That's clear, isn't it?"

"Yes, sir."

The sergeant looked again to the writing in the book and rubbed his hand across his chin.

Hillary and Adam rose from their seats, left the ordinary and climbed the stairs to their room. Neither spoke. Herk had found Whitlock and the two of them were waiting.

"Glad you're here," Adam said. "You can see we've a big room with plenty of beds."

Whitlock smiled. "You're very kind, as always, Mr. Rutledge. I might have had to sleep in my wagon since the town's so full of folk to-night."

"I was noticing that. Why is it? Market day to-morrow?"

"I'm not rightly sure, sir. It might be market day. I know court day begins at eleven."

"There seems to be more people on hand than could be heard in one day's court," Hillary commented.

"You're right, Mr. Caswell, in one sense," Whitlock said. "In another way, though, you're wrong."

"How's that?"

"One man alone—or even ten men—won't be heard in a Hillsborough court. It takes more, many more, to secure a hearing."

"We just saw four militiamen down in the ordinary," Adam said. "They claimed they were going to ride to Mecklenberg County. I told them the rivers would be high."

"They will be," Whitlock agreed. "Course, they may not ride that way. For me, I'll wager they stay in the village to-night."

"To-morrow will be as serious as that?"

"Aye, sir, I think it will be." Whitlock walked to the door. "I'm going down to catch a bite to eat, sir. I may go outside for a spell. Then I'll be able to tell you better."

"I'll expect you when I see you," Adam said. To Herk he added, "Take a blanket off one of the beds. It might be best if you slept outside the door to-night."

"Yes, sar. There's a mess of folk 'bout to-night."

Hillary stood up and put on his coat.

"And where are you off to?" Adam asked good-naturedly. "Aren't the streets full enough for you?"

"Too full, but I thought I'd better drop these messages at Colonel Fanning's house. They might be important to him. I suppose the innkeeper could tell me the way to his house, but it might not be wise to ask with the climate as it is."

"No. By all means don't ask him. I don't know myself, though I should. Herk!" A moment later the giant body servant appeared in the doorway.

"Go into the streets and find where Colonel Fanning's house is. It shouldn't be too difficult. Don't act as if your master's a friend. Do it in a nice angry fashion. Then tell Mr. Caswell. He'll follow you."

After the two had left, Adam Rutledge sat at the table for a long while trying to solve the riddle which had come to his mind: the appearance of the Regulator leaders, the crowds in the street, the opening of the court—and Fanning's obvious desire to have the Regulator leaders arrested.

Eventually, unable to satisfy himself, he walked from the room down to the ordinary again, determined to question Mr. Pitkin.

The room was much less crowded. Adam went to the bar and ordered a brandy. He took a table on the opposite side of the room from the militiamen who had yet to leave in search of their prey.

Pitkin himself brought the brandy. Adam said in a conversational tone, "I see that most of your guests have left. I suppose that's a relief to you after a busy day."

"Yes, sir. I like to have a busy house, but then it's nice to have it quiet, too."

It was another ten minutes before the militiamen took their capes and went to the door.

"We'll remember what you said about the fords, Mr. Rutledge," the sergeant said. "We may have to see the Colonel before we leave."

"A wise idea," Adam agreed. "The ride might be hard."

The innkeeper stood at the door and watched them ride off into the mist and the darkness before he returned to Adam's table.

"Sit down, Mr. Pitkin. Will you have a brandy with me?"

"Thanks, Mr. Rutledge. I'll take the chair, but not the drink. They buried old Tom Scanley just last month. 'Twas enough for me." He pulled out a chair, sat down in a relaxed manner, but kept one eye on the door. "They got away all right. It's good I have a back stairway. That man with the thin face was Husband. I heard you tell 'em you hadn't met him, just as you told me. Was that the truth? You'll pardon me for askin'."

"It was."

"Lindsey," the innkeeper called to the boy who was cleaning the tables, "you mind what the guests want. I'll be busy for a while."

"Yes, sar." Lindsey grinned; he enjoyed playing host.

Turning back to Adam, Pitkin said, "Would you be curious to know what's been going on around here, Mr. Rutledge?"

"I'm very curious."

Pitkin leaned forward in a confidential manner, but one which seemed to hold an element of fear. "I'll tell you, sir. Plenty's been going on. First of all, that Fanning's been getting himself thicker and thicker with the Governor. He's been sending a lot of messages saying that we . . . well, I mean the Regulators—I'm not one of them, please understand—but we've found nothing but lies in all those letters. All lies. And the Governor's just letting him have his head. Fanning's got the people up here so damn mad they're liable to take him out and tar and feather him, then ride him a spell on a rail—and if that's all he's lucky."

"And he's been elected to another session in the Assembly, hasn't he?"

"Aye, by his friends. That-there Governor made Hillsborough into a borough for him, one so small you couldn't see it with spectacles."

"I've heard about that," Adam said. "I'm sorry it's true. Any fresh grievances?"

Pitkin pulled his chair closer to the table. He took his eyes away from the door and looked soberly at Adam. "Mostly the same old sores, Mr. Rutledge, but galled raw and bloody a thousand times. Oh, to be sure, they have some different ways to put the old abuses on us. The new seat for Fanning I just mentioned is one. Then the regular juries weren't harsh enough on the Regulators last year so lately they've had hand-picked panels ready with guilty verdicts before they heard the cases. Then James Hunter says there's proof the county justices are in league with the sheriffs to fleece the poor farmers. It was common knowledge they were hand in glove with the sheriffs, registry clerks and lawyers, but maybe the proof is new."

Adam sat back in his chair while the innkeeper gave his wry account of the state of things in Orange County. When Pitkin came to an end, Adam shook his head soberly. Then abruptly he turned to another subject. "Tell me, Pitkin, how scarce is hard money up here? Can a farmer come by enough to pay his poll tax?"

"It's scarce, sir, and no mistake. If a man was disposed to pay, he'd not find much coined money at hand. But who's so disposed? Most of the Western men can't abide Tryon's Palace and have sworn not to pay a penny toward it. William Butler says there'll be no taxes paid in Orange while the Palace levy stands. Tell me, do you blame them?"

"I don't blame them. I don't say it's right either. Hillsborough's full of farmers to-night. Why are they all here?"

"The court," Pitkin said abruptly.

"They're looking for trouble?"

"No, sir. That's easy enough to find without hunting."

"Special cases to-morrow?"

"Quite frankly, Mr. Rutledge, there's a rumour about

that James Hunter offered a petition to the judge yesterday. It takes up the items I've just been telling you, and a few more. These men in town to-night want to make sure Judge Henderson reads it all through."

"That's a difficult thing to do in a quiet, peaceable way," Adam said seriously. He had been looking at the door, and now he saw Hillary enter the main hall. "There's my friend. You'll excuse me, won't you? I appreciate what you've told me."

"I'm the one to thank you for listening, Mr. Rutledge. You're one of the few men who could help us, if you've a mind to."

"I've a mind to, certainly, but I'm not sure if I have the means." Adam bade his host good-night.

"And I wish you a good night's sleep, sir."

Adam strode to the door, then up the stairs to the room. Herk, sitting cross-legged by the door, said, "The young Caswell, sar, he just come back."

When Adam entered the room he found Hillary already partly undressed. His boots were on the floor before him.

"Tired? You've met the Colonel?" Adam asked.

"Yes, I've met him."

"And you've no opinion to volunteer?"

Hillary moved from the edge of the bed and picked up his boots. He grinned and said, "I suppose I shouldn't pass judgement on one of my employers after only five minutes' acquaintance."

"No, that's a little rapid for sound judgement."

"He wants me to meet him at ten to-morrow at his office."

"By ten I hope to be on my way to Cross Creek," Adam said. He took off his jacket and hung it on an empty peg.

An hour later neither man had fallen asleep. Whitlock had not returned. Hillary said wearily, "I am working for Colonel Fanning."

"And?"

"And I trust him no farther than I could throw the Governor's Palace. By the way, Adam, you were right about his eyes."

16

Adam Pays a Visit

The first rains swept over the country during the night, but with morning came a let-up. The clouds were still low, in washed pastels. The men and women who walked in the streets of Hillsborough talked in subdued tones; but there was a tension in the morning quiet that the storm had not relaxed. A tautness was in the faces of the outlanders, a biting at lips, a rubbing of hands at their sides, when they glanced up at the Courthouse clock and waited for eleven.

Adam and Hillary rose early. Whitlock was already up, had been to breakfast and returned. "A quiet day in the streets," he observed.

"Too much noise to suit you yesterday?" Hillary asked as he tucked in his shirt.

"Nothing happens when there's noise." Whitlock walked impatiently to the window. "I enjoy a quiet day."

Hillary said to Adam, "I'm going over to Edwards' house to let his servants know I'm here. Shall I see you again before you leave?"

Adam stretched his arms above his head. "If we shouldn't meet each other at Fanning's office, then I think not. I've only one bit of business to conclude with that gentleman, and it shouldn't take long." He rose and shook hands. "I'll probably see you next at New Bern." He paused for a moment. "I'd thought about stopping off at Husband's plantation at Sandy Creek before going to Cross Creek. If by any chance Fanning would give you a day or two of leisure, you might ride along with me that far."

"I'd like to, but it would be too much to hope for. I'm sure Colonel Fanning will keep me busy for a few days."

"But if you should get free . . . you're welcome."

After Hillary had bidden the two men good-bye, Adam sent Herk down to the innkeeper to order breakfast.

"Seems a good lad," Whitlock remarked.

"Yes, a good man," Adam agreed. "Only he's in a rather unfortunate spot."

"How's that?"

"By birth and occupation he's squarely for the Eastern people. By heart and by youth, he's for the West. That's a dilemma for a young man."

"And you, Mr. Rutledge? Is your own position any different?"

Adam smiled. "No, Hiram, not a bit different in sentiments, but my path is easier. I'm a little older than he; I have a wife; my plantations are settled; my friendships are secure—these things give a man stability. It would be hard for one struggle to break me, to embitter me. But a young man has to put all his heart and all his soul into his battles."

"I know what you mean," Whitlock said. "But I've never noticed you holding back on what you believed, and I've never felt myself a laggard."

Adam grinned. "True, but we've both survived the age of twenty."

"A good man has to keep the spirit of twenty forever."

"Perhaps." Pulling a chair to the table, Adam sat down and invited Whitlock to do the same. "I've got to be at Fanning's office within the hour, Hiram. There are some things you could clarify for me, if you would."

"Surely, Mr. Rutledge." He took a chair on the other side of the table and listened carefully as Adam explained his conversation of the previous night.

"You see," Adam said, "Mr. Pitkin gave me quite an earful. I trust him as far as I know him—but I'd like to hear you confirm or deny what he said."

Whitlock considered the problem for a moment.

"From what I know, it's the truth. Pitkin gets a little excited now and then, but he keeps his stories straight. He might have added a bit more."

"And that?"

"There was another meeting of the Regulators, and they wrote another Advertisement. In part it had to do with a letter Fanning had sent to Tryon, most of which was lies and can be skipped. But the gist of the Advertisement was that we in Orange have to pay larger fees for recording deeds than the people near us. You just cross a little way into the Eastern counties and things are cheaper. We've petitioned the Assembly through our representatives but nothing's happened. You know that's true. We've appealed all right."

"I know. I know it," Adam said with a note of depression in his voice.

"Most of what we wrote was pretty mild—course, that's due to Husband. He's just not a fighting man, Mr. Rutledge. Anyway, after we'd made our complaints, we said the growing anger of the people endangers the peace. We were telling the simple truth—that's what's going to happen if they keep on ignoring us."

"And this was addressed to the Governor, or to the Assembly?"

"To the Assembly first. But of course it gets to the Governor."

"It sounds like a threat."

"It's the truth."

"Good Lord, Hiram, the truth is always a threat to some people!"

"And you think the Governor will take it as one?"

"It depends on several things: how he likes his eggs the morning he receives the Advertisement, and how it fits into his own plans. Wait, hear me out. I don't mean Tryon's so flighty that a botched egg would send him storming out with the militia. It wouldn't. But it might lead him to give Fanning more rein in Hillsborough."

"More! By God, that's impossible, Mr. Rutledge!"

"Then there are his own plans. I don't know what they are, yet."

"He's Governor—what else could he want?"

Adam could not restrain a smile. "Who knows? Maybe he looks for a title to run in the family."

Herk came in then with the breakfast and placed it on the table.

"Have you eaten yet, Herk?" Adam asked.

"Yes, sar. That Mr. Pitkin made 'em take care of me fine."

"Good!" Adam turned again to Whitlock. "I hope the Advertisement doesn't get changed between now and the time it reaches New Bern. I'll support it, of course; but I want it in as mild a form as possible. My friends are difficult to deal with when they think they're being pushed."

"So are mine, Mr. Rutledge. I don't know how long Husband can keep them in check."

"Some toast?"

"No, thank you. Pitkin did well by me, too."

"I wish," Adam said deliberately, "that you could get a man like Richard Caswell to take up your cause. He's the one person who could push a redress of your grievances through the Assembly."

"How could we get him?"

"It's probably too late now. He's heard of too much violence, and he knows some of your leaders. They're not the sort of men Richard Caswell takes to."

"Send him up here to see for himself."

"Are you sure it would be to your interest?"

"No. The morning is too quiet."

After breakfast Adam prepared to pay a call on Colonel Edmund Fanning, Register of Deeds.

He took care with his dress, knowing that the more elegant he appeared to Fanning, the more he would accomplish. Over a brass-buttoned waistcoat he wore a blue coat of broadcloth. His white scarf was ruffled, the ruffles on his sleeves freshly pressed. He had selected the new chamois-coloured breeches and seen that his high riding boots gleamed.

He mounted his horse in front of the Star, noting with some concern the growing crowds in the street. A few of the men he recognized, and they greeted him cordially.

A tipsy reveler shouted, "There's the only Easterner who gives a damn for us!"

Adam took his Saladin at a trot through the streets of Hillsborough. He stopped once to ask directions to Fanning's office and was told its location with a sneer.

Adam had put himself in an uncompromising frame of mind before he left the Star Tavern. He knew he might have sharp differences with Colonel Fanning. Enos Dye, an employee of his, had been dispossessed of his property on the Deep River, presumably for nonpayment of taxes. Dye had had a crop each year, so his title could not have lapsed on the grounds of non-use. As for taxes, Dye swore he had paid the sheriff what was demanded and could bring forward neighbours to attest the fact. The sheriff claimed that nothing had been paid for several years. Adam suspected that the sheriff had simply pocketed the money and made no entry of it. Today he was determined to find out what sort of story had been brought forward as a pretext for dispossessing Enos Dye.

It was exactly nine o'clock when he reached Fanning's office. He had his doubts that Fanning would be there.

The junior clerk who sat outside the door glanced up when Adam entered. "What can I do for you, sir?" he inquired.

"I want to see Colonel Fanning."

"Sorry, sir. He's not in."

"My main purpose was to check the record of some Deep River land belonging to one of my men, Enos Dye. I'm informed he was recently dispossessed."

The clerk hesitated. "And your name, sir?"

"Adam Rutledge."

"From the Albemarle, sir?" The clerk was surprised. "Yes."

"Ah, Mr. Rutledge, I've heard about you, sir. It's a pleasure to meet you. Ordinarily we're not allowed to open the records to the public. Those are the Colonel's orders. But I'm certain he would make an exception in the case of an Assemblyman. I'm quite certain."

Adam laughed. "Well, I'm not sure of it, but if you are, it would help me to have a look at them." He had not thought it likely that Fanning's clerk would welcome him, but this well-scrubbed young fellow seemed delighted to serve him. Adam looked carefully at the young man, and at the same moment he had a thought of the copies of Fanning's letters that seemed always to be finding their way into the pockets of Richard Buncombe.

The clerk had opened a large drawer in the oak highboy standing in the corner. He leafed through papers and finally said, "Here it is." He glanced over several sheets of paper. "Just what was it you wanted to find out?"

"Dye was dispossessed recently. I can't believe he let his title lapse through non-use. I'm sure he put in a crop each spring. Was it taxes?"

"Yes, sir."

"I suppose there's no record that Dye paid taxes recently?" Adam asked smoothly. "It's a peculiar thing. The present sheriff tells me that his predecessor, Tyree Harris, was sometimes careless about entering tax payments. Did he ever get his books in order after he resigned, a year or two back?"

"Confidentially, I'd say no."

"Dye swears he paid what was asked, even in '68 when so few farmers did. It's a pity he should suffer only because Harris was absent-minded about keeping his receipt books. It's a nuisance for Dye—and embarrassing for Harris if it came out." He looked disconsolate, then brightened. "It might be a little informal, but it occurs to me that we might make up for Harris' forgetfulness. Why don't we just enter the payments for '67 and '68 now?"

The clerk smiled. "Why not? Harris was, as you say, absent-minded, especially about payments. So is the present sheriff. I may as well mark in '69 at the same time." He busied himself with quill and ink.

A half-hour later Colonel Fanning came in and saw Adam. "Mr. Rutledge!" he exclaimed, and held out his hand. "Won't you come into my office? In this barbarian country it's always a pleasure to encounter a gentleman."

Somewhat stiffly, Adam followed him into his office.

"One of my men, Enos Dye, has informed me he was dispossessed of some land he held on Deep River. I've been inquiring into the matter with your clerk."

"Dye . . . Enos Dye . . ." Fanning repeated the name, apparently trying to remember the case. "I don't think I recall anything about him."

"It's rather extraordinary," Adam said. "He lost his land because of non-payment of taxes, yet there's record of payment through last year. How could it be?"

"No doubt there's been some mistake. These accursed Regulators have raised such a pother in Orange that much of the orderly business of government is confused and marred."

Adam looked at him coldly. "A mistake is a charitable explanation, sir. I must confess that my first thought was that the sheriffs had simply pocketed the payments. Dye is a good man in my employ and I value him. If he was deprived of his land by mistake, I desire that you take immediate steps to correct the mistake, sir. I'll not have my people imposed on."

"Nor would I ever want a gentleman such as you to suffer any inconvenience through any act of mine, deliberate or accidental, Mr. Rutledge. I conjecture the fault lay with the sheriffs who are always late with their papers. No doubt the seizure of Dye's land was put in motion before the sheriff entered the payments and it appeared he was in arrears."

"It is Dye's inconvenience, not mine, that I'm thinking of." Adam's voice was impatient. "See that he is put in possession of his lands at once. You don't court the good opinion of the small farmers, do you?"

Fanning's face hardened. "They hate me. They have reason to, for I hate them, the ignorant, unwashed, rebellious dogs! I'd like to harry them over the mountains."

As Adam made his way back to the Star Tavern he remembered the venom in Fanning's eyes. This is the man, Adam reflected, who manages affairs in Hillsborough. This is Tryon's friend on whom the Governor relies for news of Orange. No wonder there is trouble brewing.

17

Day in Court

Hold on, boy. I don't reckon I know you!"

"No, I guess you don't." Hillary started to move past the lanky frontiersman who blocked his entrance to the Hillsborough Courthouse.

"I said I didn't know you, boy. This-here court ain't openin' till eleven. Lot o' people waitin' to git in. What makes you think you're goin' in ahead of them?"

"Are you a court officer?" Hillary asked.

A mob had gathered before the Courthouse. They carried whips and heavy clubs. They milled about the yard impatiently, waiting for the clerk of the court to open the doors. Their talk was angry. Their faces were severe. From the edge of the wide-spreading crowd Hillary had seen the tall frontiersman allow Judge Richard Henderson to pass. Hillary had hesitated before climbing the steps; he carried a message to the Judge from Colonel Fanning.

"I don't dare see him myself," Fanning had said. "The mob might not let me pass. You could get through, though."

"I'm willing to try, sir."

"No," Fanning had said as he placed his seal on the message. "Trying isn't enough." He leaned forward. "Give this only to Judge Henderson. If you should be stopped, I'll expect you to destroy the note. Do you understand?"

"You git yourself down there in the yard, boy. I ain't never seen you in these parts. Maybe you're one o' Fanning's men."

The buckskinned guard was using a heavy walking-stick to bar the way. Now he pressed his cudgel into Hillary's midriff. "Go on, boy! You heard me. Air you daft? Git on back down."

A slender, well-dressed man moved from the crowd and up the steps to Hillary and the guard. "What's the trouble, Richie?"

"This fella, Mr. Hunter. He thinks he's a-goin' into the court afore it opens. You said to let nobody in 'cept the clerks and the judges. That right?" The Regulator's tone was self-righteous.

Hunter nodded, then turned to face Hillary. "Is your business official, sir? Do you have anything to do with the opening of court?"

"I've a message for the Judge, Mr. Hunter."

James Hunter pursed his lips and scrutinized Hillary. "Will you tell me who it's from?"

"I'm sorry, sir, but I'm not at liberty to say."

Hunter shook his head. "Do you see those people, sir?" Hunter waved his hand to the press of people in the courtyard. "They, too, have a message for the Judge. Can you give me any reason why your affairs should come before theirs? They've been waiting a long time. They've come a long way."

"Boy, I told you to git back and wait your turn. Now Mr. Hunter tells you, so I reckon that's 'bout enough." Again Richie made a threatening gesture with the stick.

James Hunter had turned away and walked down the steps into the crowd. Hillary hesitated a moment longer trying to think of a way to bluff past the guard.

"I said git!" The lanky frontiersman threw his weight behind the cudgel, sending Hillary spinning, tripping and then tumbling down the courthouse steps, to sprawl in the yard. He scrambled to his fee, started dizzily for the steps and the Regulator who waited for him at the top with cudgel raised. The two men nearest Hillary grabbed and held him.

"That's no way, lad," one said. "You'll just get yer brains beat out with that-there cudgel."

"Calm down, boy," said the other. "You weren't hurt. Them doors'll be open soon enough. We all got complaints."

"And I've got one more now," Hillary said, brushing the dirt from the shoulder of his jacket.

"Richie up there," the first said, "Don't make no distinction between people—" he lowered his voice—"unless it's against gentlemen . . . and you're too well dressed to be one of us. Maybe you better get back in the crowd a ways. Richie's got a bad temper."

"Quarter to!" A shout went up from the crowd. The voices ceased for a second as the tired faces turned toward the Courthouse clock, then back to the doors. The noise began again.

"Why don't we go get Fanning? We got some cases against him!"

"You'd never find him. He ain't going to show up here."

Richie, the tall Regulator, remained standing at the top of the Courthouse steps. He held the cudgel like a gun at port arms. He grinned. He wiped his hand across his mouth and called down to Hillary, "Boy, you figger you know where to stay now? *I'll* tell you when you can come."

Hillary held his temper, trying to think of a way to gain entrance: perhaps there was a side door or a window.

A burly-shouldered, square-jawed man had elbowed his way to Hillary's side. "Your name's Caswell?" he said.

"That's right."

The crowd shouted again.

"Ten minutes. Ten minutes to go!"

"They tell me you're one of Fanning's men, lad. That right, too?"

"If I am, it's none of your concern." He wondered how they could have found out about him. Then, on glancing in the direction from which the burly man had come, he thought he saw the face of Fanning's clerk. That would be the only person who knew his affairs. He was certain he was right when he heard the next words of the big-shouldered farmer.

"You've got kind of a smart mouth for a boy. Folks tell me you've got a note for Judge Henderson. You gimme that note and I'll see it gets past Richie up there."

"I told Mr. Hunter I had a message," Hillary said. "If I tell it to you, how do I know you'll remember it right?"

The farmer motioned to Richie, then turned to Hillary again. "What are you waiting here for?"

"To hear what goes on in court."

"Oh, so you got a case coming up like the rest of us? We got a case and a petition for a new jury. What's yours?"

"Business in court is my own affair."

"Why don't you gimme that letter?"

A voice cried: "Five minutes! Five more."

Shouts went up from the crowd as they began to press closer to the steps and the doors.

"Look here," the burly man said, "let's move out of the way so's we can talk." He took Hillary's arm and started pulling him to the edge of the crowd and around to the right of the Courthouse. There they would be hidden from the crowd in front of the main steps, and the rutted street was empty of people. "You don't mind talking, do you?"

Hillary glanced at the hostile faces of the crowd, and he realized the hopelessness of trying to enter the court before eleven. He allowed himself to be led along by the farmer.

Richie had moved down from the Courthouse steps. His place had been taken by James Hunter. Richie forced his way through the crowd and fell into step on the other side of Hillary. The three men had reached the corner of the building. The street was empty.

"Three! Three!" The crowd chanted the minutes away.

"Saw you motion. You be needin' some help, Brother Hibber?"

"Don't know yet, Richie. But I thank you for walking a spell with us. 'Pears the lad has some respect for you, and I was about to ask him a favour."

They were nearly at the rear of the building now.

"Lad here has a letter for Henderson. Guess it's from Fanning the way folks talk."

They had dropped Hillary's arms. He waited for their next move with body tense. Hibber suddenly spun Hillary around to face him. His eyes were small and angry. Richie stood behind Hillary with his cudgel.

"Now, Caswell. The letter. We'll have it."

"You'll have it in hell."

He felt the prod of the cudgel in his back.

"Boy, didn't you hear him say he wanted the letter? You got awful bad ears."

"Two minutes!" the crowd shouted.

The cudgel smashed across his shoulders. Hillary jerked in pain. Damn that clerk! He alone could have told them about the letter. And these were the excellent Regulators—these men who took the law into their own hands.

He expected another blow, braced himself for it. He saw an old man, bent, white-haired, walking slowly down the street. The old man paused and looked at them, then turned abruptly into a narrow rutted walk beside the Courthouse.

Someone yelled, "Tell 'em to open up them doors!"

"It ain't time" came another shout.

"Clock's wrong like everything else. One minute to go."

Hillary had decided to wait until the very moment the Courthouse doors opened; then he would try to break from the men—or else fight them. In the rush of the crowd there might be no others to help them.

"I'm waiting," Hibber said. "But I'm getting impatient."

The cudgel slammed across his shoulders again, then across his side. Hillary doubled in pain. Hibber's rough hands seized his collar, jerked him upright.

"Tear the damned coat off his back," Richie drawled.

"I got a mind to. Lad, you ain't got no sense a-tall." Hibber let go of Hillary's collar suddenly and brought the back of his hand sharply across his face. "None a-tall. Gimme that letter!"

"It's open. By God, she's openin' up!" The clock on the Courthouse tower began to chime the hour in heavy clangs. A tremendous shout of triumph went up from the farmers, the woodsmen, the villagers, as they pressed forward to crowd toward the court-room of Judge Richard Henderson.

Hibber drew back his hand to strike again, but a moment later, with a look of complete astonishment on his face, the burly man went spinning backward to the ground. Hillary had lashed out with his fist, and caught the man squarely on the cheek-bone. Hillary threw himself to one side. The cudgel cracked down where he had been standing.

"Get him; Get him!" Hibber muttered dazedly, trying to rise from the ground.

Richie whirled the cudgel sharply, smashing it on Hillary's left arm. He wheeled it for the cross-blow, but again Hillary stepped clear. He could feel nothing in his arm; it had gone numb.

Richie came on, thinking the quarry finished. Hillary felt a certain sense of pleasure as he drove his right fist into the lanky man's stomach. Richie bent, grabbing at his middle in pain.

Then Hillary felt the blow across his neck. There was no pain, but he knew he was falling, knew when he struck the ground. He lay semi-conscious. Hibber stood over him, his face red with anger.

Richie had straightened up. His thin lips were pressed in anger. He raised the cudgel, ready to bring it down full force on Hillary's head. Hillary tried to move, tried to roll to one side out of the path of the blow, but his muscles would not respond.

The blow did not fall.

He heard angry voices, confusion. He shook his head to clear it, and risked looking up. There stood Rednap Howell with Richie's cudgel in his hand. As Hillary took in what was happening, he saw Rednap toss the heavy club contemptuously away. Beside him was the white-haired old man, still out of breath.

"Boys," Howell said, "I thought we'd settled it once and for all that we weren't going to have any of this. Hibber, if I catch you at it again. I'm likely to break you in half."

"Hell you say, Rednap. That cheap bastard's got a letter from Fanning to the Judge."

"Just because you can't write, Hibber, you shouldn't take it out on those who can. Why don't you get into the court for your case before I lose my temper?"

"Mr. Howell——" The lanky frontiersman was cut short.

"I'd keep my mouth shut if I were you, Richie. You'd better get moving, too, before I teach you how to use your cudgel proper."

Hillary had got unsteadily to his feet. He watched his two attackers shuffle around the corner of the Courthouse toward the doors. He turned to Rednap. "I thank you, Mr. Howell, and you, sir—" he bowed to the old man— "But I did have a letter from Fanning."

"I know it."

Hillary, still dazed from the blow on his neck, had to sit down by the roadside. "I don't understand."

"The letter's not going to make any difference with what happens to-day. The only thing he could tell the Judge would be to leave Hillsborough."

"Still dizzy?" the old man asked.

"Better, thanks."

Rednap Howell said, "Let me give you a word of advice. I've seen you with Mr. Rutledge. He's a good man to be with. I've heard you've been with Fanning. He isn't. Let your duties keep you down in New Bern. That's where you're from, isn't it? Stay there where you know the people. Help the people you know how to help. Don't come up here to do your work against the folk who've been lied to and cheated. You won't do any good for anybody up here. You won't understand."

Rednap did not wait for a reply, but walked away toward the crowded Courthouse.

Hillary turned to the old man. "I guess I owe you more than a little for bringing him here."

"Did you listen to what he was telling ye?" the old man asked.

"Yes."

" 'Twas good advice if ye mind it, lad."

"I don't know if I have a choice."

"But, lad, it's *your* life. Its *always* your choice." He bobbed his head in agreement with himself.

Hillary took the message back to Fanning's office immediately. The clerk was away from his desk. Hillary knocked at the inner door.

"Who is it?"

"Hillary Caswell, Colonel."

"Come in. Come in."

Fanning was seated at his desk, but had turned his back to the door. He was looking out the window which opened on the north of the village, away from the riots, away from the Courthouse. Beyond the roofs of Hillsborough he could see the quiet stretch of mountains. He did not change his position, but asked, "You delivered the message, Caswell?"

"No, sir. I was unable to reach the Judge. Someone warned the Regulators that I had it."

Fanning turned slowly in his chair. His proud handsome, face was lined with concern. "You were stopped! What sort of messenger are you? Did they take the note?"

"No, sir." Hillary put the sealed message on the desk.

Fanning surveyed him with obvious distaste. He noted the smears of mud on his clothes, his ripped jacket, the slight cut on his lip. He made no comment on them. "Did you get inside the court building?"

"No, sir. They had it blocked and guarded. It was only opened a few moments before I got here."

"You didn't even get inside?"

"No, sir," Hillary said shortly. "You might look into your clerk's affairs, Colonel Fanning. He might know something about my failure."

"My dear sir, I trust my clerk. I've had proof of his loyalty. It seems to me, though, that I've not had proof of yours. The whole crowd stopped you from entering?"

"Two men stopped me."

"Only two? And the others?"

"Either did nothing, or weren't needed."

Fanning rose from his chair, straightened his waistcoat. "I suppose I shall have to deliver my own messages," he said wearily.

"I wouldn't advise that, sir."

"*You* wouldn't advise it! You! Who *are* you, lad? You had a duty to perform, and you couldn't or you wouldn't see it through. Now you object to my performing the very mission at which you failed."

"I'm only telling you for your own safety, Colonel." Hillary felt a tinge of red rush over his face.

"Mr. Caswell, I know your cousin Richard. He doesn't approve of me—and I can't say that I approve of him—but we have one thing in common. When we set ourselves to a certain task, we complete it. As long as you wish to pretend to be on the side of the law, as long as you wish to pretend to the honour of a position with the Governor—or with Edwards—then you might consider your small tasks worthy of completion. Am I clear?"

"It's becoming clearer, Colonel."

Fanning started to put on his jacket. "You needn't keep up the pretence, young man, that you feel any loyalty toward me. I suppose I shouldn't expect it of you." He paused, looked down at the floor. "I shouldn't expect it of anyone. This is a long cry from New Bern." He looked squarely at Hillary. "Well, since there is no one on whom I can depend, I must do everything myself. I know one thing: It will do no good to go out there and talk to them as if they were rational beings. What sort of response would I get? What sort of response *will* I get?"

"I'd rather that you didn't go out there, Colonel."

"Only two men stopped you. I should think you might have held your own."

"Only two were needed. There were more."

"Have some pride."

"Have some sense, Colonel . . . I'm sorry that I said that. I speak only for your safety. Believe me. Where are your militia now?"

"You have the audacity to tell me to have sense. I tell you to have honour."

Fanning stepped to the door, opened it. "Would you care to learn how to reach Judge Henderson—or are you afraid to be seen in the streets again?"

"You're going to the Courthouse, sir?"

"Yes."

"Let's be gone then." Hillary's voice was edged with anger from Fanning's steady flow of insults; his conscience was pricked by only one of them—the slur on the honour of his position. The Colonel's bravery had obviously increased when Hillary had stressed that only two men had stopped him. There was nothing to do now but give him his loyalty.

The farmers who were still in the streets near the Courthouse jeered as Hillary and Colonel Edmund Fanning rode their mounts steadily toward them.

"You're doing well," the Colonel said. "You hold your head high. You keep your eyes raised."

"I have nothing to be ashamed of."

"Your opinion, sir."

Hillary guessed that the building was full, the large court-room more than full. The overflow of farmers spilled haphazardly down the steps. Some few were waiting impatiently in the yard.

Hillary and the Colonel dismounted, tied their horses to the store rail opposite the building and then proceeded on foot. They had no trouble until they reached the base of the Courthouse steps. There the crowd seemed unyielding, but Fanning pushed his way ahead, shouting, "Make way! Give me room!"

"Aye! Give way for the fine Colonel."

"Give him room. Give him a little room under his feet."

"And a tree over him."

"He's got a muddy gentleman with him. Let him in, too. Get 'em both inside."

"Give him *lots* of room."

A narrow path was opened for them, and Fanning had gained the hallway before Hillary. As Fanning brushed by the farmers, he wore a contemptuous look, as if to touch them made him dirty. Hillary tried to follow close, but the press of human beings shut in behind the Colonel as he passed, and suddenly Hillary felt strong hands seize him. He tried at first to jerk free, then realized the absurdity of his position and waited.

Fanning turned momentarily and saw that he had been cut off from Hillary. He moved quickly, threading his way through the crowd standing in the aisle near the back. A heavy riding crop lashed out and struck him on the shoulder. Fanning gave a cry of pain, wheeled to face his tormentor, but even as he did so, gripping his shoulder in pain, he backed away, backed toward the judge's bench.

"Let's take him outside," a voice cried. "I'm sick of this playing around."

"Henderson ain't goin' to do nothing."

The man standing near reached out to grab Fanning. He shook free of the hands and raced down the aisle to the protection of the bench. Hillary tried to break loose from the hands that held him, but in vain.

"Order! Order!" Henderson was shouting.

Two men got up from their seats in the court-room and tried to block Fanning's way just before he reached the judge's bench. Jacket ripped, ruffled shirt torn, he burst between them. He screamed at them in a high-pitched voice, drew in his shoulders like a frightened child. His haughty composure, his arrogance had vanished. His high cheek-bones, his carved lips, his flashing eyes, all reflected his terror.

"Let go! Let go! Don't touch me!" He danced, skittered, and then in violent, short, angular movements pitched himself beyond his tormentors, gained the platform, and stood tense and frightened behind Judge Henderson. He was babbling like a man taken of the devil, completely unable to control himself.

"Fanning's got himself an old woman to hide behind!"

Judge Henderson pounded his gavel futilely. He shouted for order in the court. The farmers seemed unwilling to throw off all respect for the court and drag Fanning from the bench.

"Get him and take him outside."

"Take his old woman, too."

Hillary's arms were locked behind him by two weather-worn frontiersmen. When he saw Fanning's sudden cowardice, he ceased his struggles. Then the grips of the two men noticeably relaxed.

"Yer usin' some sense now, laddie. Wouldn't get you nothin' but trouble if'n you got up thar."

Hillary scarcely heard them; he was studying Colonel Fanning. Pitted against reality, thrown against the actual mob, he had broken completely. That angular, aristocratic face was a mask of terror.

A voice near the centre of the court-room kept shouting for quiet.

As deep as was Hillary's disgust for Fanning, he realized a still more profound depression and discouragement: the sight of the Regulators shaking their fists, brawling, cursing, a howling mob setting themselves like a pack on one man, trying to vent the hate of years in a violent orgy. Reason was dead. It would be as easy to argue with half-starved dogs.

"Come on! What you waiting for? Get him outside!"

James Hunter was now standing on a bench in the centre of the court-room. His black coat was wrinkled, his hair tousled. He had extended his arms as if for a benediction over the shouting mass of men. Finally his voice rose above the yammering noise, and gradually, reluctantly, the crowd obeyed him. The shouting died away. Calls for order and quiet broke here and there as the strident voices fell silent.

"Honourable Judge," James Hunter called in loud, firm tones. "We citizens submitted a petition to you. We ask you, sir, what is your decision? Will you act on our requests? Will we get new juries to hear our cases?"

Henderson, flushed and angry, answered, "There'll be no reply from this court until there's order. If there's another sign of violence, I'll *close* this court for the term!"

"Hell you say! Take him out with Fanning" came a voice from the crowd. The muttering began again.

"I warned you!" Henderson called as be banged his gavel.

Hunter was shouting for quiet. "Listen to the Judge. Listen to him!"

"What's he going to tell us? Same as always?"

"Quiet!"

Fanning, sensing that for the moment his danger was past, took advantage of the interruption to whisper to the Judge. Henderson nodded.

A shout: "Let Fanning bring his case to court like the rest of us."

"Your Honour," Hunter cried again, "I should like to present another petition for your consideration before the cases of the day are brought. Will it please your honour to listen?"

Henderson paused before giving his answer. He glanced nervously over the press of men in the courtroom.

The same voice: "It damn well better please him."

The Judge ignored this. He leaned toward Fanning, asking him some question, and Fanning responded with a nod.

"Don't let the two of 'em talk. They're plannin' something."

"For God's sake, men, hold your peace!" Hunter cried.

Henderson spoke at last, slowly, his voice halting. "The . . . the Court will . . . take pleasure in . . . in hearing your petition, Mr. Hunter. However, you understand that it . . . it is in no way *binding* on this Court to take action . . . if it does not so please."

"I understand that, Your Honour. Since there are several cases against Colonel Fanning, I feel that this petition is particularly appropriate."

Hillary guessed at the moment what would happen. He knew that Fanning would never allow a session of the court, in the face of this threatening mob. It would be stopped—how, he did not know. And by surprise or guile Fanning would make a break for freedom.

The frontiersman on his left had let go of Hillary's arm; the man on his right held him loosely.

"You see, laddie, tryin' to save that-thar Fanning ain't no good. He ain't worth the trouble."

No, Hillary thought, he was *not* worth the trouble. But he was one man against a mob—there would be nothing to do but help him.

James Hunter adjusted his glasses. He drew the petition from his pocket, unfolded the papers, and raised them before his eyes. He had just begun; "We, the people of the County of Orange, respectfully submit . . ." when Edmund Fanning made his bolt for freedom. He leaped from the judge's bench and rushed straight down the centre aisle. Hunter lowered his paper.

Shouts: "Grab him!" . . . "Don't let him get away."

Only five men remained to block his exit from the court-room, but Hillary realized that Fanning's rush would not carry him through them. Hillary shook loose from the frontiersmen and plunged toward the main door. The force of his drive broke an opening through the astonished men. Hands clawed at him, blows rained on him as he pushed on, clearing the way for Edmund Fanning, who darted past him, leaped down the front steps and darted through the sparse gathering in front of the court building.

"Catch him!" . . . "Stop him."

Hillary stood dizzily in the courtyard. Blood was running from a cut on his cheek. He could see Fanning far ahead.

In the grand clamour of the escape no one noticed Judge Henderson, who had slipped quietly from the bench and hurried toward his private chambers. He had thrown off his splendid robe of red and black. While Fanning distracted attention in front of the court-house, the Judge made good his escape out of the side entrance to his chambers. He was on his horse and away before the Regulators realized they had been cheated. He was off to summon the militia.

Fanning had raced across the street into a clothier's, where he tried to hide. It looked like short peace for him. The crowd had poured out of the court building.

Hillary wiped his hand across his face. He leaned against the steps. He heard the voice of James Hunter, who was standing near him. Hunter was calling to a tall, lean, red-haired farmer in faded blue breeches, who stood at the top of the courthouse steps. Hunter's voice was tense. "For God's sake, Rafer, get 'em quiet. They'll kill the man sure as God made green apples."

"Now, James," Rafer drawled, "don't get yourself in a fret. I'm going to have to give 'em something for their money."

"Do that. Do that. But don't let them kill him. Run him out. Do anything you like except——"

"I'll try."

Hillary shook his head. He was dizzy. He dabbed a

handkerchief to his cheek to stop the flow of blood. What *was* it worth? he wondered. The rank and file of rebels were men of violence; it was the leaders who kept trying to slow them down. What would Richard think of this? The leaders whom he feared were the only men to trust. And the people themselves—the persecuted commoners—were the ones who sought violence.

Four men armed with clubs approached the clothier's. They were followed by a young boy, about sixteen years old, who carried a long coil of rope.

The man called Hibber whipped up a group to march down the street toward Fanning's house.

"Burn the damn thing down!" someone shouted.

"Just chop the supports. Burn his clothes."

"How about that other place?"

"Sure, take Edwards' place, too."

Another group formed to march on Edwards' home.

"They've got him!"

"We got lot's o' trees."

Three men appeared in the clothier's doorway, roughly tugging and dragging Fanning along. At the foot of the steps a swarm of men joined them and formed a square about him. His face was white as milk. His eyes stared straight ahead as if paralyzed by the spectre of death. He stumbled in the rutted road.

"Give the Devil his due. Let's have a judge for him," someone yelled.

Hunter cupped his hands at his mouth. "Rafer Panky will do the judging," he shouted.

"Give him hell, Rafer!"

"How about that tree?" the boy with the rope wanted to know. He pointed to a wide-spreading oak at the edge of the courthouse yard.

"Wait for the judging."

The oak was the obvious destination of the men who escorted Fanning, but the drawling voice of Rafer Panky halted them in front of the courthouse steps. He mounted them part way and stationed himself where he could look down on them.

"You the judge, Rafer?" one of them asked.

Rafer looked quickly at Hunter and then said with a

grin on his face, "Why sure, Mr. Hibber. You and Clarkson ain't got no objections, have you? Now if'n you don't want me, why, I'll——"

"Rafer's good enough!"

"Sure."

"Ought to give him a trial just like he gives us," Rafer said.

"Get on with it."

Hillary saw James Hunter dab a handkerchief to his forehead. He seemed greatly relieved—Hillary could not imagine why. The mobsmen were not in a jovial mood. They were ready to hang Fanning.

Rafer Panky stood at ease, his fingers hooked into the top of his breeches, a long blade of grass dangling from his mouth. "Well, now there, Mr. Fanning, you look like you ain't got no colour in your cheeks."

Fanning made no reply. His eyes seemed focused on the farmer's mud-stained shoes.

"Mr. Fanning ain't talking," Rafer explained to the crowd. "Cat's got his tongue."

"Thought you wuz goin' to judge him and hang him," shouted a man near Hibber.

"Now, Andy, I *am* a-goin' to. But these things take a little time. I had a case in this court for two years, so I figure five minutes one way or t'other ain't much to ask."

His slow, drawling voice seemed to ease the tension. It was a lazy voice, the voice of a summer afternoon.

"Now, Mr. Fanning, afore this court sentences you to hang, I guess it'd be fair to hear your side of the story." He waited for Fanning to speak, heard no reply, and went on: "I mean, Fanning, do you really think it's worth a rope to hang you? Ain't it sort of a waste?"

"He'll rot it," Hunter cried. Then he mopped his brow again with his handkerchief.

"Rot it plumb in two," chuckled an old man, the joke now his.

Fanning still did not answer. He was immobile at the base of the steps.

"He's all tuckered out," Rafer said. "Tuckered out from running. Well, answer me, Fanning. Is it worth the rope?"

Again no reply.

"You know, Colonel, I jest can't make myself believe you're worth the trouble." Rafer looked out over the crowd. "I'll tell you men truthfully, I got a feeling it'd be a disgrace to go touching a man like that. Hibber, you all move back a stretch, some of that-there smell might rub off on you."

The men who formed the square about Fanning all moved slightly away, as if Rafer's words were true.

"No, sir. I figure a man gits jest so rotten, and then he ain't a man no more. He ain't human—he ain't even animal. A dog's got pride. Even a pig's got pride compared to this-here thing. Lemme show you somethin'."

Rafer directed his eyes toward Fanning again. He rolled the blade of grass with his tongue. He unhooked one hand from the band of his breeches and pointed a slim finger at the Colonel. "Fanning, I asked you a question a moment ago, and you never answered it. I'm tired o' gettin' no answer. I said you wasn't worth the rope to hang. You tell me if'n I'm right."

The voice was scarcely a whisper. "You're right."

"What's that? Louder! Speak up so the *men* can hear you."

"I said you were right."

"Aw hell, spit it out. Gimme the whole thing. You want me to hold you in contempt o' this honest court?"

Someone in the crowd laughed; again the tension eased. Hillary listened as Fanning began to degrade himself.

"Answer me!" Rafer's voice lashed out.

"I'm not worth the rope it would take to hang me," Fanning said.

"Now that's better. Tell the boys you've cheated 'em and lied to 'em."

Fanning hesitated.

"Tell 'em!"

"I've cheated you and . . . lied to you."

"You steal their deeds. You're hungry for land."

"I steal your deeds. I'm hungry for land."

"Not land—dirt. You're like a pig in dirt, in mud. Say it so the men can hear you. Speak up."

Fanning's answer was mechanical. "I'm like a pig in mud."

"In slop!"

"Like a pig in slop."

"You're Tryon's lickspittle."

"I'm Tryon's lickspittle."

The shaming went on, and Fanning echoed every debasing word. A hush had fallen over the crowd. They seemed to draw away from the man who abased himself endlessly before the red-haired farmer with the blade of grass.

"You really love North Carolina dirt, don't you?"

"I love it."

"Show the boys how much you love it. Get down on your knees, Fanning."

He looked about, perplexed, and then slowly sank to his knees in the mud before the courthouse steps.

"Git yourself a handful o' mud there. Go on. Jest grab yerself some."

Fanning, his eyes never leaving the lanky farmer, grubbed blindly before him, catching up a handful of mud.

"That's it," Rafer said. "You've wanted our land so damn much, jest have yerself a mouthful of it now. Go on. Put it in your mouth. Hurry up! Don't you want to make a favourable impression on this-here court?"

Colonel Edmund Fanning clapped his hand to his mouth, forcing in the mud; he dropped his hands before him.

Fanning's jaws were moving; there were tears in his eyes. Rafer glanced at James Hunter. Hunter nodded almost imperceptibly. Now Rafer's tone changed. It was no longer one of contempt, but one of pity.

"Is this the fellow you want to hang, men? This man on his knees afore you? This man with a mouthful of mud? Don't touch him. Don't soil your hands on him. A man who's so afraid to die ain't worth the killin'. Pity him. Look at him, all of you. Look at him and have pity. Thank the good Lord you're not like him. Fanning!" The word cracked like a shot through the silence. "Get on your damned feet and run! Nobody here's a-goin' to touch you. *Run!* Keep running till we can't see you no more! You make us sick. By God, don't let us see you no more! Run. Git going!"

At the final injunction Fanning stumbled to his feet. His glance circled the silent figures about him. None raised his arm to stop him. He ran from the court-yard, ran down the street, ran out of sight beyond Brek's crossroads.

Rafer Panky came down from the top of the steps to join James Hunter. His dialect was notably less. "We should have hanged him, James. The man's got no soul, I swear it. It must be I don't have any, either. How could I do that to a man?"

James Hunter placed a hand on the lanky red-head's shoulder. "You did right, Rafer. The Lord says not to kill—and you saved his life."

"Saved him? No, I damned him forever. I might have saved him if I'd let them take him."

"No. You only brought up what was in him. You found nothing new."

"I wish I hadn't done it."

The crowd had begun to break up. Hillary was starting to move away from the base of the steps when James Hunter and Rafer Panky passed by him. Rafer stopped for a moment and looked him over, like a man appraising a horse. "Did you like the way your master acted?"

"Not particularly."

"If I'd had you out there, would you have done the same?"

"No," Hillary said dully.

"I'd have hanged you then."

"Probably."

"Might still . . . sometime," Rafer said as he moved on, rolling the blade of grass in his mouth.

18

Charity

The farmers and frontiersmen were withdrawing from Hillsborough, taking their separate paths into the hills. The village people came timidly from their homes to see the damage caused by the rioters, to explain their own actions, to exercise their newly recovered courage, to be out and on the streets before their neighbours. The tawny uniforms of the local militiamen were more frequently seen. The forces of the Government and Colonel Fanning made their appearance with obvious hesitation, but by two o'clock their occupation of the village was complete.

After meeting Hunter and Panky, Hillary had gone back to the Courthouse steps and sat down. He watched the rioters pass toward the hills, heard the rattle of carts, the thud of horses' hoofs, the coarse shouts of the farmers as they vacated the village.

He tried to imagine the result of the day's struggle but could not see the end. He realized only that Fanning had escaped and would never forgive the men who had insulted him—nay, who had discovered him! And as for the Assemblymen of the East, they would never hear the grievances of the Western men—never, short of war. Letters from Fanning would be going shortly to New Bern stating the results of the riot, not the cause.

Tryon would back Fanning, believing whatever he was told, subtracting nothing from Fanning's heroic description of himself.

Hillary stood up slowly and walked to the store opposite the Courthouse where he had tethered his roan. Someone had loosened the hitch on Fanning's mare and led it away. Hillary swung onto his horse and turned it in the direction of Isaac Edwards' house. He was curious to see how badly it had been damaged.

A few of the villagers looked at him oddly as he rode past them. They saw his torn jacket and the scar of blood across his cheek. The faces of the Hillsborough people were neither angry nor sympathetic. Theirs was the curiosity of men coming out of a cave after a hurricane has passed. They had had no part in it and now wanted to find out what had been done in their absence.

Well, Hillary wondered, just what had been done? The oppression of the farmers would be doubled, and there would be no ear to hear their grievances. The leaders—Howell, Butler, Hunter, Husband, even the lanky red-head, Rafer Panky—would be blamed for everything. Strange, Hillary thought: If an excuse were sought to destroy the leaders of the Regulators, a better one could not have been offered.

Edwards' house was in the centre of the block. A few men and women were gathered in front of it when Hillary rode up, but on seeing him they withdrew quietly to watch from the other side of the street and talk among themselves.

He dismounted and hitched his roan to the black post before the house. He strode up the narrow path to the stoop and pounded on the door. There was no answer. He knocked again, waited, and at last heard footsteps, approach hesitantly.

Very slowly, very cautiously, the door was opened, but only a few inches.

"Come, come," Hillary chided. "It's all over. You can let me in. You remember, I was the visitor, Hillary Caswell."

Finally the door was opened wide enough to admit him, then pushed shut and the bar slid into place again.

"Massa Caswell, sho' am glad to see you, sar!"

Hillary glanced about the main hall; everything seemed in order except that the glass of the window farthest from the door had been shattered.

"You air hurt, sar." The old Negro turned from Hillary and called up the stairs, "Mandy, you come 'n fetch some water. You bring me some clean rags, too. Massa Caswell done come and he got hisself cut."

"None of the mob came inside, did they?" Hillary asked.

"No, sar. They don' come in. They jest stand thar and throw de rocks at de windows and break 'em all to pieces, mostwise upstairs, but they don' come in."

Mandy, a portly Negro woman, hurried down the stairs and into the kitchen. She rattled the basins and then slipped outside to the well. Hillary sank down in a chair in the front hall.

"You haven't heard anything about Colonel Fanning's house?"

"No, sar. We done bar us-selves in here. You tell Massa Edwards, sar, that Scipio and Mandy let nobody come in here."

"I'll tell him that, Scipio."

"Thank you, sar."

Mandy entered the room with the basin of water and a clean piece of cotton cloth. She placed the basin beside Hillary, and bent over to examine the cut expertly.

As she dabbed the cloth into the water and pressed it gently to Hillary's cheek she said, "That cut, she not so bad, Massa Hillary. But there am a little dirt in her. Best we get that out and clean 'cause it don' make a young gentleman look so fine."

"All right, Mandy. But go gently. I've got a fierce headache."

"And you tell Massa Edwards he not to come here for a spell," Scipio said gravely. "These folk, they lose all de sense de Lord gave 'em."

"You needn't worry now," Hillary said. "I've seen enough militiamen in the village. The outlanders are leaving and everything should be quiet to-night."

Mandy had finished cleansing the wound. "She not bleed any more."

"Good!" Hillary said. "I want to see what's happened over at Colonel Fanning's house."

"That Andrew, your man, sar, he come here 'bout an hour ago lookin' for you."

"Where did he go?"

"He say he goin' back to de Star an' wait for you."

Hillary eased himself out of the chair and walked to the door.

"Them men sure done tore up your fine clothes," Mandy said.

"I'm lucky they didn't tear me up." Hillary's lips spread in a grin. It pulled the cut on his cheek. He found a frown more comfortable. As he stepped onto the narrow porch he said, "I'm sure all's safe for the night, but I'd keep the bar up if I were you, and admit no one unless you know him."

"Yes, sar."

Hillary walked down the steps, and again the men and women opposite the house surveyed him intently.

As Hillary rode on, his eyes went first of all to Fanning's house. It looked as though it might collapse at any moment. The supports of the house had been hacked with axes, the windows all smashed, and the front door splintered wide. Out in front were the smouldering remains of a fire. A fine coat, partially burned; a ruined boot with a wisp of smoke still trailing from the heel; a boxful of papers reduced to black ash —these were the last remnants of Fanning's personal possessions in Hillsborough.

Engrossed in assessing the damage, Hillary had paid little attention to four militiamen teasing a girl just beyond the gate into Fanning's yard. As he tied his roan to an intact section of the broken fence and walked toward the gate, he studied them more closely. They appeared to be drunk and he wondered idly whether they had spent the hours of the riot hidden away in the Star's taproom quietly drinking. They were treating the girl rather unceremoniously. He noticed she wore Quaker grey, and he thought it odd that a Quaker would associate with soldiers in such condition.

As he came closer, he realized she was not with them willingly. With what dignity she could maintain as they crowded in on her and touched her, she was asking them to leave her alone and let her pass. Still several yards away, he heard her say, "Sirs, I'm searching for my uncle. Will thee let me pass?"

"Will thee let me pass?" the sergeant mimicked. The elder of the two privates reached out and yanked the Quaker bonnet from her head, releasing a cascade of blond hair which fell over her back and shoulders. Hillary hastened his step, wondering how to deal with four men in their cups.

The corporal, who was standing behind her, put his hands on her hips, then put his arms fairly around her waist. The defenceless girl tried to twist free, but he held her. With a drunken laugh he said, "You men want me to show you how to tame one o' these touch-me-not Quaker lasses?" He spun her around and was about to pull her to him when he felt himself rudely jerked back by his collar.

"What the hell——"

Hillary shoved him roughly to one side and stepped up to the girl. "At last," he said. "I've been searching the village for you. Your uncle wants you immediately."

For a brief moment the girl thanked him with her eyes. Unobtrusively she retrieved her bonnet and began to gather up her hair.

The corporal recovered his balance. "Who in the hell do you think you are?"

"I'm on Governor Tryon's staff, Corporal, up here on a mission to Colonel Fanning." He wasn't sure how far Fanning would back him after the morning's happenings, but he needed the best connections he could give himself.

"He don't look like anybody the Governor would have around. Look at his clothes," the corporal said, appealing to the others for support.

"Corporal, I was caught in the mob together with Colonel Fanning. Where were you then?" He took the girl's hand and drew her a little away from the militiamen.

"Where do you think you're taking her?"

"I'm taking her to her uncle. I don't think it would be wise for you to try to stop me."

The sergeant and one of the privates had had enough. They shambled off. The corporal and the other private truculently stood their ground. Fifty feet off, the sergeant turned and shouted at Hillary. "I remember you now. You were at the Star last night with Mr. Adam Rutledge."

This was too much for the corporal. All at once he was obsequious. "Pass on, sir. Sorry about the young lady, sir. We was just having a little fun. You know how it is." He and the other man stood aside.

In silence he took the girl's arm and led her to his horse. They were safe enough now; the danger was past. There had been too many crises on this long day and he felt drained. Moving slowly, he untied the roan and slipped the reins over his arm to lead the horse.

"How did thee know where to find me?" the girl asked.

"To find you? I don't understand," Hillary said. "I don't know you at all."

"Surely my uncle sent thee?" she persisted.

"I don't know your uncle either. I heard you say you were looking for him and made use of it with the militiamen; that's all."

For a moment they walked in silence. "All things come from the Lord. He sent thee in my need," she said. "What is thy name?"

"Hillary Caswell."

"Caswell," she repeated. "There are Caswells in Maryland."

"That is where I come from." It occurred to him that he must find out who her uncle was so that he could put her in safety.

To his question she answered, "He is Harmon Husband. He has a place on Sandy Creek southwest of here where I live with him and my Aunt Amy. He was in the village today and I was to ride home with him." She gave her name simply: "I am Charity Allen."

"Husband? But he's already gone. I heard someone calling for him at the Courthouse hours ago."

Rain began to spatter from the low-hanging clouds. As it increased he tried to hurry her to the Star Tavern, which was not far ahead, but she held back.

"Come on," he urged. "There's shelter just ahead."

She followed him into the hall of the Star. She turned to a window and stood watching the rain. "Friend, I thank thee, and now I must bid thee farewell."

"Where will you go now? Look at the rain outside."

"Why, to Sandy Creek. The trail is still there, is it not?"

"Surely, but you can't go alone."

"And why not?" she asked, her blue eyes wide and ingenuous.

"Well . . . it just isn't . . . after all, Charity, you're a woman. Those trails aren't safe. There are still militiamen and rioters on the paths . . . and . . ."

"Do you mean Regulators?"

"Yes."

"I shall be safe enough among them."

"And you insist on going alone."

"I insist on going."

Mr. Pitkin, the host, had been standing by his table desk, taking in the conversation. He interrupted: "Believe me, Mr. Caswell, I've given her the same arguments as you on other occasions. But our young Friend is quite a stubborn girl."

"Friend Pitkin," she chided, turning from the window, "you know I'm a minister and that my calling takes me the breadth of this country—safely."

"I know, Miss Allen," Pitkin said, "but to-night you'd do well to take some company with you in this storm— and considering everything."

She laughed. "I might do well, but I have no need, Friend. The Lord is with me."

"Sometimes," Pitkin muttered, "the Lord needs servants to do His will." He called to a hostler. "Bring the young lady's mare out front." Then to a servant who lounged on a bench near the ordinary he shouted, "You follow Mistress Allen to her room and carry down her saddle-bags."

Charity Allen thanked the innkeeper and went up the steps to her room.

"She always stays here," Pitkin said proudly. "I keep a good house."

"Is she truly all right on this journey?" Hillary asked. "I don't know the path to Sandy Creek, though I had thoughts of travelling that way to catch up with Mr. Rutledge."

"You'll be leaving?"

"I have no business after to-day."

Pitkin laid down his pen. "Path's not too hard," he said.

"Then she'll be safe?"

"Now that's another matter. Depends on how you look at it. If you figure God's keeping an eye on you, I guess you're safe enough. Me, Mr. Caswell, I carry a gun."

"The same with me," Hillary said.

Pitkin smacked his lips and looked up at the ceiling for a second as if he expected to see the Deity. "Not that I don't trust Him . . . but I'm damned if He doesn't 'pear a bit lax now and then."

"I've had that feeling, too."

Pitkin rambled on: "Course, you needn't mention to the young lass how I feel. Charity takes Him a mite more serious than we do." He smacked his lips again. "Trail's pretty bad," he said shrewdly.

"She chooses a very bad time to make for Sandy Creek," Hillary said angrily.

"You worry?"

"A little."

"I suppose you'll be telling me in another minute to make out your bill, since it seems you'll be riding with her. You just owe for your man and the stall. Mr. Rutledge took care of the rest."

Hillary hesitated, smiled. "Oh, go ahead. Might as well do it," he said wearily.

"I'll send a boy out to find your servant," Pitkin volunteered. "I'll let you tell Mistress Allen."

In twenty minutes Hillary and Charity Allen, followed by Andrew, were on the trail for Sandy Creek in the driving rain.

19

Harmon Husband

L ate in the afternoon, as Adam was riding toward Cross Creek, he was overtaken by a heavy rain storm. The rain beat down the bushes, and the wind whipped the white backs of the leaves. Though it was not yet sunset, the storm was bringing darkness under the dripping trees. Adam was wet and miserable and tired of listening to the monotonous squelching noise of his horse's hoofs in the mud of the trail.

He had hoped to reach Harmon Husband's place for the night. Because of the storm and the early darkness he did not know whether it was near at hand or ten miles ahead. Beaten by the rain, he was ready to stop off and seek shelter at the first house he came to.

For some time Herk, his gigantic Zulu servant, had been urging him to stop at the nearest dry haven. Adam, still intent on getting acquainted with Harmon Husband, had not listened to him. They had passed a few tumbled-down barns, a weather-beaten shed, and a lean-to. None had been inviting enough to change Adam's mind, in spite of the rain. But the darkness and the relentless rain were more persuasive than Herk. Just when Adam was ready to turn back to the last ramshackle barn that they had passed, he made out the farmhouse through the murk. It was at the end of a lane of tulip poplars, a dwelling that spoke of comfort and well-being.

"Herk!" he called. "There's a house." The servant, who had been trailing some yards behind, spurred his mount to draw even with Adam.

"Let's put our beasts to a gallop, Herk. By Gad, the rain is well down my neck, and my arms are wet above the elbow!"

Herk smiled broadly. "Sar, we will gallop, *'ndi-Kamla-'ndi-Nzaru*. Shake the water off, sar, and empty your sleeves. We'll be there soon."

When they had reached the wide yard before the house, Herk dismounted in haste and ran to the shelter of the porch. He knocked at the door, then looked back to Adam to signify that he heard someone coming. After a few moments the door was opened by a woman who held a candle in one hand. Her eyes were large and dark; smooth bands of hair were braided about her head.

Herk gripped his rain-soaked hat in his hands. "Ma'm, my master, he asks shelter from the storm. May he enter?"

The woman protected the candle from the wind. "Aye. Ask him in. Thee may take the horses to the stable. Thee will find a boy there who'll rub them down and feed them."

Herk thanked her and ran back into the rain to tell Adam; then he took the reins of the horses and led them out toward the barn. The woman held the door wide for Adam to enter.

"Thank you, madam," he said as he approached. "I was about to be completely drowned." He left his rain-soaked cape on the porch and entered the hall. There was a cheery fire crackling in the grate at the north end of the wide room.

She had shut the door and was saying, "I think thee will find the fire to your liking, sir. The rain seems cold."

"Even the sight of it is cheering," he admitted. "I'm Adam Rutledge from Chowan County. Whom do I have to thank for this hospitality?"

"This is the home of Harmon Husband, Mr. Rutledge. I'm his wife, Amy. Perhaps thee knows of Harmon?" She looked at Adam intently, as if trying to discern his feeling about her husband.

"Indeed I *do* know of him, though I've never met

him. This is the very home I had hoped to find this night. I'd wanted to speak with him."

"Thee was not at the Assembly, then?"

"I was—but only after it was dismissed this last year."

"Come, won't thee move closer to the fire, Mr. Rutledge?" She touched her finger to her cheek. "I was thinking thee might put on some of Harmon's clothes . . . but I'm afraid thee is too tall."

Adam walked to the fire-place. "Oh, thank you just the same, Mrs. Husband. It's kind of you, but the fire will dry me quickly."

Amy Husband walked to the door that led to the kitchen. "Lucius, bring a hot posset for our guest, Mr. Rutledge." She returned and took a seat near the fire. "I don't know when Harmon will get home," she said. "He had to be in Hillsborough early this morning. He expected to leave early but he had to make a short side journey. It is a bad day for travel."

Amy Husband seemed a gentle creature, but Adam noted the quick movements of her hands, a gesture now and then as she spoke, that seemed born of fire. Strangely, these were mannerisms that reminded him of Mary Warden. He felt a tenderness for the woman who sat before him.

"I wouldn't worry too much about Harmon Husband," he said. "From all I've heard about him, he's a man who can handle himself."

"I thank thee for thy words, Mr. Rutledge."

Lucius appeared in the doorway carrying a steaming mixture in a small bowl. Amy took a cup from the cupboard in the hall. She returned and ladled out a draught from the bowl and handed it to Adam. "This should warm thee, Mr. Rutledge. Shall I send a portion to thy man?"

Adam glanced at the woman curiously. "Why, yes, that would be very kind of you," he said. "The rain *has* been a cold one."

She gave orders to Lucius, then took the chair by the fire again.

"It really must be good fortune that holds me now,"

Adam said. "I'd been wanting to speak to Harmon for some time, but gave it up when the rains began."

"I'm sure the feeling will be the same with Harmon. He's spoken of thee often, Mr. Rutledge, and he's spoken well. That's enough to make me more than pleased to have thee for our guest. Would thee care for another cup?"

"No, thank you. This has already warmed me so that I've forgotten about the weather."

They passed a few minutes in conversation, and then Amy stood up. "Let me show thee to thy chamber. After thy long ride thee will want a rest."

"It really wasn't so long a journey, but I confess I'm tired. To begin the day I had a not very cordial . . . discussion with Colonel Fanning."

She nodded. "I've nothing but pity for him. I can't have any hate . . . It seems so clear what he is."

She led Adam to the spare room. Lucius had just finished lighting the fire. In the room were a comfortable chair, a small table, a wash-stand and a low, oak desk. At the centre was a great four-poster with a tester. The valance was of calico and the bed was covered with a quilt made in a cheerful rose pattern.

Amy smiled. "Thee looks weary, Mr. Rutledge."

Adam was staring longingly at the comfortable bed. "I am," he said, unable to suppress a yawn. Amy turned back the quilt, then lighted a candle from the fire and carried it to the bed-stand.

"It will be over an hour before supper. I plan to have it late to-night for Harmon," she explained. "I'm sure a little sleep won't hurt thee. Don't worry, I'll call thee." Amy Husband left the room and closed the door quietly behind her.

Adam took off his coat and hung it on a peg near the fire. He stretched and yawned again. He could hear the rain beating steadily on the roof. He looked at the bed. It was too inviting. Finally he sat down in the chair and took off his riding-boots, walked to the stand and blew out the candle.

A moment later he was on the soft feather-bed and pulling the quilt over his shoulders. The fire-light danced and glistened on the polished floor boards. Adam watched for a moment and then his eyes closed.

The sound of a man's voice and the banging of a door woke him. Outside there was only darkness; the rain beat steadily. Adam had no idea how long he had slept. He stretched comfortably. He wanted to turn over and go back to sleep. Then the pleasant odour of spices and cooking meat seeped into the room, reminding him that he had had nothing to eat since breakfast at the Star Tavern. He lay for a while musing on the chance of fate that had led him to Harmon Husband's home. Hunger and curiosity overrode his thoughts soon enough, and after a short while he sat up in bed. He carried the candle to the dying fire, lighted it, and returned the candle to the bed-stand.

He was sitting on the edge of the bed rubbing the sleep from his eyes when Herk knocked at the door. "Master Adam, you wake? You wake yet?"

"Come in, Herk. I'm trying to rise."

"These folk are mighty kind, sar," Herk said as he entered. He was carrying a ewer of hot water which he placed on the wash-stand. He took Adam's riding-coat from the wall-peg. "A sad-iron is in the kitchen on the stove," he said. "I'll bring these back, sar, in a minute."

"Good, Herk. Good, if I ever wake up. I slept like the dead. What time is it?"

"Past nine o'clock, sar. Mr. Husband, he just come home. He says the rivers, they all high. He says maybe no one can cross them to-morrow if it keeps on raining."

"That's bad."

"He says maybe even a week before they go down."

"Well," Adam said, rubbing his hand over his chin, "we can't wait a week. I must have a talk with Farquhar Campbell at Cross Creek and get back to Rutledge Riding."

"Yes, sar," Herk said as he left the room with Adam's coat.

Adam washed himself at the stand and at last felt fully awake. He had to admit that he was rather pleased with events. The Hillsborough affair had been satisfactory, and the rain, though it had made him miserable, had led him to find shelter at Harmon Husband's.

He stood by the embers, looking at the glowing wood, wondering about Husband's character. It was strange how they had always seemed to miss each other in the press of events. They had missed each other, yet they had always seemed to be working for the same ends, and seeking to better the world about them. But, he suspected, at bottom they were moved by very different springs.

Herk knocked at the door once more and entered; he held the freshly pressed coat before him. "They got a good sad-iron, too, sar. If you look close, there's not much wrong with this home."

Adam smiled as he dressed. "I shan't look too close, Herk. But if I did, I'd probably agree with you. Did you see Mr. Husband?"

"Yes, sar. I done helped him from his horse when he came riding in. I took it to the barn for him 'cause the boy he was asleep. A very nice gentleman, sar."

Adam felt better after his rest. He stepped into the hall, hesitated for a moment, and then went back to pinch the candle. He had left the door to his chamber open, and Harmon Husband's voice came clearly down the hallway.

". . . good man, Amy," he was saying. "He has stood for us in the Assembly many a time. An honest man . . ."

Adam glanced once more to the fire. The embers flickered. He turned quickly, not wishing to hear more of Husband's conversation without his knowledge. He closed the door behind him with a slight noise and walked down the hallway to the main room.

He found Harmon Husband standing by the fire, his arm around his wife's shoulders. He was dressed in rough clothes. His thick hair was damp; a stray lock hung over his left eye and he brushed it back with one hand.

"The rivers are well up. I doubt if anyone can cross the Deep by morning. Even fording the creek here would be chancy."

Harmon saw Adam over Amy's shoulder. He walked

toward him with hand extended. Adam took the hand in
a firm grip. He was immediately impressed with Husband's features—a strong, craggy face, rough-hewn. It
was the eyes that gave him his character. They were
deep-set, large and dark; they seemed to penetrate.

Lord, Adam thought, how often had he warned
against a judgement from features alone! Let a man's
actions speak for him. Yet before him was a man whom
he already trusted. He saw kindness, strength and honesty in the face of Harmon Husband.

"Ah, Mr. Rutledge, you are very welcome in our
home. I've just been telling Amy that we owe the honour and pleasure to a storm which we had thought could
bring no good."

"I'd been thinking the same thing myself, sir. For
some time I've wanted to meet you."

"To find out what manner of man?" Husband's deep
eyes twinkled.

Adam laughed. "Exactly. One has a certain curiosity."

"As I. But I'm letting my curiosity rest for a moment.
I'm too hungry. Shall we sit at the table? Amy tells me
we're about ready for the meal." He indicated the table
which had been spread at the end of the long room, to
the right of the fire-place. Amy went to light the candles.
A young Negro boy entered with a large covered dish
which he placed carefully on the side table.

Harmon took Adam's arm. "Tell me, Mr. Rutledge,
have you any news from Hillsborough? I left early this
morning with deep misgivings. I'm worried about things
there."

"So am I. There were many country folk there this
morning before I departed."

"I hope and pray nothing happens. I left James Hunter in charge. I know he'll do his best . . . but with the
court opening . . ."

When they were seated, Adam's host and hostess
bowed their heads and sat in silence. Adam did likewise,
noting that they still followed the Friends' custom of silent prayer. He had heard that Husband had been ruled
out of the Friends' meetings and that his wife had been

disowned because she had married him. Pious people, he judged, but independent and unorthodox.

In a few moments Husband raised his head and unclasped his hands. The Negro serving-boy placed an earthenware tureen in front of Amy Husband, and she ladled out a thick soup into the dishes.

Amy was saying, "I hope thee enjoys pea soup, Mr. Rutledge. We're just country-folk, and we must eat what .we raise. Black-eyed peas are one of our best crops."

"And good for man and beast," Harmon added.

The soup was followed by baked ham, rice and gravy with a salad of cabbage. Hot corn bread and milk, with a sauce made of apples, completed the simple meal.

As soon as the two men were seated by the fire, pipes in hand, they began to talk about farming. Neither seemed to feel obliged—nor, it appeared, even cared—to bring up the subject of the Regulators and the controversy that raged between the East and the West. Their common bond was the land, and they respected each other the more for it.

"You know," Harmon said, "I've managed to get together a considerable number of grants here. It's good land, Mr. Rutledge, quite as good as the land I inherited in Maryland. You might enjoy it yourself if you should consider taking on more—oh, wait now, perhaps it isn't so fertile as your part of the country, but it's still good land. I like it here. It's not so settled as the East. A man can think unhampered by all the uproar of the present and the rattle of the past. It's a great help when a man can lay his own pattern of living, plow his own fields, instead of being forced by tyrannous custom or a ruler's decree to follow an ancient way."

"You mean instead of being forced to follow a pattern laid down by politics?"

Harmon glanced at Adam shrewdly. "Yes, that's more what I meant."

"I'd agree."

" 'Tis a grand land," Harmon said. "When the Redeemer comes, when there is that second coming, it must be to a land such as this: one He will find young, strong and vigorous, with a great capacity for the freedom of each man. Aye, Mr. Rutledge, it must be to a land even better than this."

Adam looked deep into the fire and then at the craggy-browed Husband, who had leaned forward, his elbow to one knee. He was not a politician, nor a soldier, in a way not even a farmer, Adam was thinking, but, rather, a mystic. He was a man who dreamed a dream, saw something beyond the world of ploughs and bolts, shot and guns, glory and papers of state; a man who saw something that he, Adam Rutledge, did not see. Perhaps in his turn, Adam thought, he held a more finite vision of life, one that Harmon could not live by. How rare it was that two visions ever were the same!

"Aye, the Lord must come to a grand land," Husband said.

"Let us hope."

"Amy says I shouldn't speak of my visions. She assures me that folk will think me mad." He laughed gently. "Is it madness to know that Christ will come again?"

"That I cannot say, Mr. Husband, but it would be madness not to hope He may come."

"True. I find no argument with you."

They sat for a long while in silence, both men looking into the fire. At length Harmon Husband spoke. "You were curious about me when you came, Mr. Rutledge, curious as to what manner of man I am. Let me explain myself to you."

Adam pressed tobacco into his pipe, took a light from the fire, settled himself to listen to Husband.

"When I was young I was like many lads in that I felt it necessary to keep a journal of my activities. I was quite faithful in keeping the record, but soon discovered that nothing of importance ever happened to me. Soon enough I realized that there was another world beyond the world of action, and it was then that I began to set down my thoughts on religion. My thoughts were meagre, but in time my horizon spread, and when I besought the Lord, I was answered. Prayers became my shelter, but they were not my salvation as I had hoped them to be.

"I have had several religions, Mr. Rutledge. In Maryland where I was reared, I held with the Church of En-

gland. When I was fifteen, a preacher from England visited America. His name was Whitefield." Husband
smiled, a dreamy look in his eyes as he recalled those
days.

"He had power, Mr. Rutledge. I was like the others
he conquered. I wanted to leave my few belongings and
to follow him—but I did not. Whitefield spoke as I imagine the prophets did in the olden days. He was my
prophet. He told of a strange new time to come. He told
of the Day of Judgement. I think then, truly, the spirit
of the Lord came to me, for then I began to understand
His meaning. And I walked with the spirit then, and
with hope.

"But I had the temptations of man still in my soul.
Once, in the dusk of evening when I was returning to
my father's home, a maiden appeared on the path in
front of me. She had golden hair, and she undid the
clasp which bound it, letting it fall loose to her waist.
She motioned for me to come to her. And I heard a
voice beside me, telling me to take the woman into my
arms and lie under the trees with her. There was a
springtime in my soul, for she came and touched my
hand. She put her hands to my breast, and the voice
commanded me to satisfy my body, saying my spirit
would be renewed afterwards.

"But I drew back from her warm touch, knowing it
was the devil commanded that I lie with her. I comfort-
ed myself with the words of the Lord, and I fell to the
earth.

"Then came a burst of light and a mocking laughter,
a breath of hot wind on my body. Yet I did not rise, and
I said the words of the Lord to myself. Of a sudden
there was a calm, a peace. The night air was fragrant
again, and the vision had vanished.

"That was my curse and my saving. That was the
devil of mine own flesh passing from me.

"I have had many religions and one God.

"With that negation of the flesh I was left hollow, like
a reed at the water's edge. Then the Quakers brought
me to them. They taught me truly of the spirit, for, once
I was cleansed of the curse of the flesh, I was ready to
accept their ways.

"St. Paul preached the revelation of the spirit for seventeen years. The revelation was the Truth. For a long time I followed the Quakers. But at last I could not stay in their footsteps. My vision carried me beyond them, searching always for the secret of the second coming of Christ. I search now—not for the transient, but for the eternal."

Husband paused, his eyes reflecting the fire-light. Then he said softly, "O ye daughters of Jerusalem, He will come in the time that will please Him, and it will be as a wind in the forest."

The room was silent except for the crackling of the logs in the fire-place. Harmon Husband was looking beyond the blaze, his eyes and heart in strange countries of the soul.

The sound of a door closing broke the silence, and presently Amy Husband came into the room. Her eyes were on her husband. She walked to him and laid her hand gently on his arm. "Harmon, Harmon," she said softly, looking into his eyes with love and understanding.

He turned to her slowly. "My dear one?"

In a moment he was talking about the harvest and spring planting, much as though another thought had never entered his head. A short while later he and Adam parted for the night.

Adam Rutledge did not sleep comfortably in spite of the feather-bed which had been heated with a warming-pan. He was tired, but sleep would not come.

Adam was thinking it was well enough to decide that Harmon Husband was a mystic more interested in the coming of Christ than in the politics of the poor farmers —well enough to decide this; yet still he could not sleep.

Adam perceived that Harmon Husband was a complex individual, not easily typed, not to be dismissed offhand as an impractical visionary. His very other-worldliness lent fire to his political "advertisements," his manifestoes. Moreover, he had acquired vast land-holdings. He had a very practical benevolence, and their good works must have accounted in part for his being attracted to the Quakers. Yet, by his entire unwilling-ness to resort to physical action, he was obviously unfitted to be the leader of a revolutionary movement. For himself he rejected even the name of Regulator.

What then bothered Adam? Why couldn't he sleep? He turned uneasily on the bed.

What should bother him other than that the work was left to the men of action, to the Rutledges, the Caswells, the Howells. And to them all, in the days of their trial, would come a wind in the forest.

20

Rain

The rain came down in torrents. Long grey streamers of rain beat against the windows and wakened Adam Rutledge from his uneasy sleep. He found himself tangled in the blankets. His head ached. He pulled the covers straight, waited until his mind cleared and then sat up in bed.

Herk was kneeling before the fire-place, teasing a small blaze into life by blowing on it. Slight tongues of flame leaped up the blackened chimney. Presently the pitch and pine splinters caught the logs, and a cheerful fire was alive.

Herk's giant proportions seemed magnified in that small room. Years ago, Adam remembered, when he had bought Herk, the slaver had told him that the man had been a prince in his own country. There was no reason to doubt that story, for Herk's ways were kingly; the other slaves seemed to recognize his superiority.

Herk dusted his hands, stood up and, seeing that Adam was awake, said *"M'vumbi,* master. A heavy, heavy rain."

"And a heavy, heavy headache," Adam said.

"You talked to yourself the last night, sar."

"I believe it. Even my throat's dry."

Adam climbed out of bed and put his arms into the sleeves of a dressing-gown that Herk held for him. "Has it been raining like this all night?"

"Yes, sar. Most of the night, they say."

Adam frowned. "Now the rivers ought to be higher than ever. I hope the storm struck only west."

"In the night, sar, Master Hillary come, and he have with him a woman with a cover." He made a gesture to show that they had had blankets over their heads.

"Hillary? I'm surprised he finished so quickly in Hillsborough. And if he was done there, why didn't he go east?"

"Sar, he bring the woman, and I think he bring bad news. He talk to Mr. Husband, and Mr. Husband, he have a mighty long face."

Adam frowned deeply over Herk's words, then began to wash and dress hurriedly.

When he reached the main hall he saw Hillary Caswell and Harmon Husband standing by the fire. He noticed the gash of red across Hillary's cheek, and could tell by Husband's tightly pressed lips that something dangerous had happened in those brief hours at Hillsborough.

Harmon glanced up distractedly. "Good morning, Mr. Rutledge. We have the honour of a visit from a friend of yours."

"I'm not so certain it's to your pleasure, though," Hillary said, and then he explained to Adam: "The fords across the rivers are well-nigh impassable, and Mr. Husband has been kind enough to ask me to stay until the rains are gone."

"Mr. Caswell," Husband said, "you brought my niece safely from the village, where she was in danger from the militiamen. You brought her through the hazards of the swollen streams. Our gratitude joins with common hospitality to make you doubly welcome."

"How did you get the cut on your cheek, Hillary?" Adam asked.

"It's a token of my bad news from Hillsborough."

"Rioting?"

"And worse. They made a fairly good attempt to hang Colonel Fanning. If it hadn't been for James Hunter and a farmer named Rafer Panky they'd have done it."

"He says the Judge is fled," Harmon interrupted.

"Lord!" Adam said. "Sit down and tell me all about it." His voice was weary.

Hillary sank into a chair by the fire and related the happenings since he had last seen Adam at the Star Tavern. When he had finished there was a momentary silence in the room.

Husband had been walking nervously back and forth as Hillary spoke. He had heard the story earlier in the morning. The second telling was salt to his wounds.

Now he said, "I should have been there. I should have stayed. I knew it."

"It sounds as if there's nothing you could have done," Adam said. He was quite frankly in no mood to hear self-accusations. He was trying to reason out the issue of the action.

"Mr. Rutledge, whether I could have done anything or not is immaterial—the fact remains that I should have been with my people."

Hillary's feelings were much the same as Adam's. He had already told himself that Husband's business concerned souls, not the walk and talk of the streets. He had discovered this much in the morning's talk. He turned to Adam and asked, "Where does it leave the whole case? Fanning's going to have his revenge. I'm sure of that."

Adam was still weighing the factors of the situation, and when he spoke it was with deliberation, as if he were feeling his way through a maze. "They've had their riots before. That much we know. And we know that Fanning's always passed word of them to the Governor —no doubt with considerable embroidery. In the past the Governor has taken no action, but the question is— will he in the present case? This riot will need no embroidery."

Harmon interrupted. "Action or not, Mr. Rutledge, we've lost any chance we might have had for redress. When Fanning gets back to Hillsborough it will be to crush us completely. He won't be pressing money out of us; he'll be pressing out our lives."

Adam continued with his own line of reasoning, oblivious of Harmon's interruption. "But I rather think the

Governor won't act in the present case, either. I don't think the time is ready for him."

"Time?" Hillary asked.

"Of course. You mustn't forget that Mr. Husband and some of his friends are in the Assembly. It puts the Governor in an awkward position. So long as they can tell the truth about Hillsborough affairs, it weakens whatever use Tryon might want to make of Fanning's hyperbolic reports. In some quarters, Mr. Husband——" Adam turned to the slender, nervous man—"there's a goodly respect for you. As long as you hold that respect I don't think Tryon would dare use the militia against the Western people. He would have to feel assured of the full support of the East before he could launch any sort of attack."

"You mean an actual attack? Troops marching from New Bern?" Hillary asked.

"Hillary, the moment Governor Tryon has the sympathies of the Eastern men behind him, he won't hesitate to crush what he believes rebellion. I'm certain of that."

Husband's face was lined with worry. "Now he has all the excuse he needs for that."

"Not yet," Adam said. "He has you to contend with. The riots may be enough to frighten some men to his side, but there are many who know Fanning's methods. They won't trust him or take his word for what's gone on. No," Adam said reflectively, "there'll have to be something on a grander scale—something that touches the Assemblymen directly, something they can see, hear and touch."

"What would that be, Adam?"

"I won't venture my guess yet."

"But you have an idea?" Harmon asked.

"Yes."

It was Hillary who asked: "When were you last in Hillsborough, Mr. Husband?"

"Exactly the same question I'd ask," Adam said. "Are we driving at the same point, Hillary?"

"I don't know. It was what you said a moment ago that made me ask."

"I was there day before yesterday," Harmon said. "I was with James Hunter when he submitted his first petition to the Judge, but I left early yesterday morning."

"Before there was any hint of the riots?" Adam asked.

"Yes, yes. I'd have stayed if I'd suspected any."

"It would be bad business if one of our Assemblymen were found to be a leader of a riot which threatened death to a county official and fellow Assemblyman and drove a judge from his court-room. . . ."

"Mr. Rutledge, I am *not* a Regulator. I write pamphlets; yes, that's true. And those writings are used by the Regulators . . . but I am not one of them. I don't condone their methods."

"I know that, Harmon. Hillary knows it. But tell me, do other Assemblymen know it?"

Hillary Caswell stood up and walked to the bookshelves. The same line of inquiry had been pressing on his own mind. He touched the backs of the books: books on doctrine, on history; two tomes on parliamentary law. On the desk next to the shelves were two piles of blank paper and a folder of written pages. There were also many pamphlets, some bearing the name of Poor Richard. To one side was a small work entitled *An Impartial Relation*.

Adam Rutledge was saying, "Certainly what happened in Hillsborough will lose any support you might have had from Richard Caswell. He has recognized the need of reform, but now he'll see the need of safety. Law and order must come first, he'll say; reform later. He'll swing more than a few of the planters with him— men who might have gone along with the redress of your grievances."

"Thomas Person will stand with me, Mr. Rutledge."

"Certainly. That's one man. How many others? And don't forget the fact that your power is virtually divided now that Fanning's elected from the borough Tryon made for him."

"But, Mr. Rutledge, I deplore the riots as much as any other man in the Assembly—perhaps more than any other. But the fact that the poor men resort to such violent courses only shows how desperately they need redress. One can't just say, 'Because they have violated some laws we shall press them until they become outlaws.' One can't say, 'We shall crush them with taxes until they are driven to such desperate measures that we may attack and kill them under legal sanction'!"

"One *can* say just that, Harmon. Mind you," Adam said, "it would be wrong to believe, wrong to act on it; but wrongness has never stopped men from pursuing their desires."

Outside, the rain had slackened, and in the east the sun glimmered through the clouds. Hillary stood by the window, vaguely listening to the argument. Adam Rutledge had brought him to the clear realization that battle lines were being drawn.

"I suppose, Hillary, you'll be conveying a report of the happenings to the Governor?"

Hillary turned from the window. "Yes. It's my obligation."

"It won't be a pleasant one."

"No. Nor will the Governor find it pleasant to listen to me. I've heard so many stories of oppression that I can balance every act of riot with an act of incitement."

"But the Governor will listen only to the riot. He'll shut his ears to the incitement," Harmon said with bitterness.

Amy Husband called that breakfast would soon be ready; if they could ignore the problems of the Colony for a spell, she might agree to feed them.

"By the way, Harmon," Adam said as he rose, "Do you intend to bring up the matter of representation in this coming session of the Assembly?"

"I'd planned to, but I don't think I'll find much support, after——" He broke off, then added, "Everything I say seems to turn on the trouble at Hillsborough! I can't dismiss it from my mind."

"Thee will have to," Amy said good-naturedly as she entered from the kitchen.

Charity Allen appeared just as the men were about to be seated at table. Her face was radiant. Her eyes were a vivid blue. She was dressed in Quaker grey with a fresh white fichu of soft mull around her neck and crossed on her breast. Her soft, blond hair was in braids about her head.

"My neice, Charity Allen. Mr. Rutledge of the Albemarle," Harmon said.

Adam bowed low over her hand. "A great pleasure, Mistress Allen."

Amy said, "Won't you all sit down? The meal grows cold." Again they bowed their heads in silent prayer. Hillary stole a glance about the table. Harmon, Amy and Charity were absorbed in prayer; Adam Rutledge had closed his eyes, then opened them.

There was a look of reproach—gentle, yet definite reproach—when Charity had finished her prayer and raised her eyes to meet Hillary's. He could almost hear her voice: "Thee did not pray." But as he continued to look at her, a delicate blush came over her fine, clear skin. He caught himself comparing her with Cecelia. In beauty they were even—unless Cecelia's vivacity gave her the advantage. As for their hearts, their dreams of life, they must be worlds apart.

The same feeling came to Hillary when, after the meal, he sat with the others around the fire-place in the main hall. The sound of rain was dying away when Charity and Harmon fell into a discussion of religious doctrine. Amy sat knitting; Adam smoked a pipe and stared into the fire.

Husband was saying, "I found in the Quakers one thing that I confidently affirm: the belief which denies the Scriptures to be the only present word of God. In part the Scriptures were written as prophecies. Many of them may not yet be open to our understanding. But we have an Inner Light that is God-given, too, and that may be trusted as a present guide."

"True, Friend," Charity said. "The Scriptures may be past our understanding if we do not evoke the Divine Spirit through the power of prayer. We needs must have a strong sense of our unworthiness."

The rain had stopped. From the window could be seen the glistening of the drops which covered the land. The group around the fire fell silent as they listened to a lone bird sing.

Harmon said then, "I should tell you of some of the

adventures Charity has had in this back country. I promise you, they're more than a man should have experienced."

"The Lord has protected me," Charity said. "I did nothing alone."

"True," Harmon said, "even to the sending of this young man to watch you safely from Hillsborough."

Charity nodded.

Hillary confessed to himself that he felt like anything but an instrument of the Lord. He did not say as much. He was searching Charity's face for some sign of mundane interests; but she was a mystic like Harmon Husband, as unorthodox a Quaker as he, though she might keep the name, more interested in a world which stretched beyond the rainbow, beyond an arch through which Hillary himself would never pass. Yet, as he and Charity sat in the room together, he felt a warmth for her, an eager kindness, that seemed inexplicable. They had nothing in common; there was no reason for the feeling. The striking young dreamer preached a world that was beyond to-morrow; he himself was involved in the joys, the treacheries, the high passions of to-day.

"I'm afraid I must try to ford the rivers," Adam Rutledge said. "Now the rain has ended I must make a start." He had been lazily watching the flames in the fire-place, apparently content to rest at the Husband home.

Amy looked startled. "But the men say it's impossible."

Adam smiled. "It may well be, Mrs. Husband, but it's equally impossible for me to rest here any longer, pleasant though it is."

"Where must you go?"

"First to Cross Creek, where I have business to discuss with Farquhar Campbell. From there I should like to go down the river for a day or two in Wilmington, but my plantations need me badly at this season. I won't have much more than a month at home before I must go to New Bern for the meeting of the Assembly, so every day is precious."

"He's right, Amy. You'd best not argue with him. We'll need him at New Bern." Harmon shook his head.

"I have the same problem, Mr. Rutledge. Between planting and politics, one scarcely has time to live."

The thought struck Adam as strange. Harmon Husband had never lived fully in *this* world—not for all his pamphlets nor for all his harvests.

Charity had excused herself from the group and gone to her room.

Hillary had listened idly to the conversation. Then Adam asked, "Will you be riding with me, Hillary?"

"I should like to, Adam, but I'll be going in the opposite direction. I want to go down to New Bern with a report—an honest one—before Fanning has time to fix his story in the Governor's mind. Then I shall go on down to Manor House for a short visit."

Adam Rutledge nodded and, turning to Harmon Husband, he said, "I suspect our young friend—" he motioned toward Hillary with his pipe—"was sent to Hillsborough in order to gain a low opinion of the Regulators. He's met you, Mr. Howell and Mr. Hunter, and so I'd say his trip was a failure."

Hillary was looking out the window as he answered, "Not quite a failure, Adam. I have no love for a mob, and I like it no better because it calls itself Regulator."

"But those are the very men we're trying to save from themselves," Husband said anxiously.

"From themselves and Fanning and his gang. Yes, I understand that. But which evil shall a man choose? The Regulators—or the Courthouse Ring?"

"It's not a matter of choice between the two," Harmon objected.

"It is for me. Somewhere in all the perverted law— even the law behind Fanning—there is a form, a mould, which should shape something decent. Say one ingot was cast badly; say the gold was dross—it doesn't mean one should break the mould."

"Then perhaps I was wrong," Adam said. "From Richard Caswell's standpoint, or Edwards', your trip was a success."

"Partly," Hillary said, facing the two men again. "If the battle which you predict, Adam, should come, then I shall know only that I fight for nothing. It's after a battle, I think, that the work must begin."

"Any physical battle is for nought," Husband said.

Adam Rutledge held his peace, but he was wondering if a man who would not devote himself to the world of the present had any place in trying to solve the troubles of the present—to solve them through the enjoyment of his own dreams.

"Will you excuse me for a while, gentlemen?" Hillary asked. "Since the rain has stopped I'd like to walk outside a bit."

"Go right ahead," Harmon said. "Will you be leaving soon, Mr. Rutledge?"

"There's nothing to hold me now."

"Oh, but, Mr. Rutledge," Husband said, "I'd hoped that you'd have time to look over a petition that I've been preparing."

Adam had glanced through the window into the garden. He had seen Charity Allen walking quietly down the path and he knew that Hillary wanted to speak with her. "Certainly, Mr. Husband, there's time for that. I'd be honoured."

The two others went toward Harmon's study, and Hillary walked from the house into the garden fresh with rain.

Charity Allen was standing at the end of it. She had stooped to look at a rain-beaten flower and did not see Hillary until he had nearly reached her side.

"Friend Hillary!" she said in surprise. "But I thought thee was still speaking with the men. Has all the sound of trumpets gone?"

"For the present—at least for me. I wanted only a chance to bid you farewell. I'm leaving for New Bern and the East soon."

"And to ford the rivers?"

"One has no choice."

"I heard Mr. Rutledge say that he would go south. I did not think thee would be going at the same time."

"I suppose one could rest here forever," he said.

Again the crimson flush of embarrassment came to her face. "I am sorry that thee must leave." She turned away from him and walked slowly along the garden path, pointing to the flowers which had been beaten by the rain. "Even the shrubs," she said. "Look at them."

He nodded as he walked beside her.

"Nothing so cruel as rain," she said.

"Nothing except men."

"Ah, they are not cruel, Friend Hillary—only helpless." She turned toward him, surprised at his nearness,
and she looked up into his eyes.

"That's the wish of all women," he said.

"Shall I see thee again, Friend Hillary? But, 'tis not
my place to ask. If it is the Lord's will, then I shall."

"I might be able to help that will."

She frowned, and puckered her lips as if to say something, but thought better of it. "Thee can make no difference in the Divine will, but still thee must say thy
prayers." She reached her fingers to touch his cheek.
"Thee will have a scar from that," she said. "Thee did
not take care of it properly."

The touch of her hand thrilled him, and at the moment he wished to take her in his arms. He wondered if
it was only from compassion, a knowledge of her loneliness. She drew away as if she had read his thoughts, and
once again turned to walk along the path.

He took her hand in his. She glanced at him with
something like fear, and then was passive as they
strolled.

"But I do not count it right, Friend Hillary, to touch
hands like this."

"And your heart objects?"

"No, my spirit." Her lips formed the words, but as
Hillary looked at her, he knew that she wanted him to
embrace her, that she needed comfort for her physical
loneliness. She talked in order to keep from showing this
feeling. Hillary was thinking that women were made for
love and a home—not to be ministers and prophets of a
visionary realm far beyond the County of Orange.

"We shall see each other again," Charity was saying,
"if it is His will. Now 'tis day, and a shame."

"Why?"

"Thee could read it in the stars, Friend Hillary. Thee
should know by the stars if we were to meet again. I
shall look to-night and pray."

"Read it in the stars?"

"Oh, yes! Harmon will tell thee that all is revealed

in the stars if one can but search them. If one would read their meaning along with the Scriptures and meditate in prayer—then even the future of the world would be unfolded." Her eyes were intense as she gazed at him.

She had drawn closer to him as she spoke, taking her hand from his, then resting it lightly on his arm. Her eyes were wide as she was caught in the emotion of her own words and the first breath of her love. That passion was new and strange to her; she could not understand herself.

"Thee could read it too, Hillary. All that would happen would be in the stars for us to see."

Hillary reached out and held her gently about the waist. "Sweet Charity, can you believe that? You, with a heart and sincerity? Do you really believe there is a portent in the stars?"

She still had not caught his incredulous tone, and as she touched his chest gently, curiously, as if to hold herself from him, she said, "Oh, yes, with all my soul I believe it."

He kissed her on the lips more from sympathy than desire, more from desire than from love.

"Hillary, I mustn't . . ."

She started to draw away. Then impulsively she put her hands to his cheeks and whispered his name.

"Charity," he said, "you mustn't believe this nonsense about the stars. Surely the Quakers do not believe it. They will tell you to read your own heart. That is well. Why look to the skies?"

She broke away from him. "Thee calls it nonsense! Is that thy true feeling?"

"I only tell you what——"

"Don't speak now. Has thee made enough fun of me?"

"I told you the truth."

"No. No. Thee has not." She turned away. "Let's go inside now. The wind makes me cold."

Only a fool is honest with a woman, he thought as he walked toward the house. But to meet sincerity with sincerity, how could he have spoken otherwise? He thought for a moment that he had seen tears in her eyes, but when she greeted Adam Rutledge and Harmon as they came from the study, there was not a trace of emotion in her voice.

Adam and Herk departed within the hour. Hillary and Andrew went their way soon after. Amy and Harmon Husband stood on the narrow stoop and waved farewell to them, but Charity Allen was not to be seen.

A heaviness of heart remained with Hillary for a long while as they rode along the rain-soaked trail. It was a presentiment that a precious moment in his life would not return, a moment forbidden by forces impossible to change.

21

Two Declarations

It was dark on an evening two weeks after his departure from Sandy Creek when Hillary Caswell rode up to Manor House. He had stopped only for a night's sleep in Hillsborough, then pushed on for New Bern. As he had travelled he had marshalled his thoughts for the report which he would have to write for the Governor. He had resolved to set down nothing but facts, taking care to exclude his own feelings and sympathies. Pieces of what he would write had arranged themselves in his mind. He knew that the Regulator leaders would be blamed for the Hillsborough outbreak, but around the Courthouse he had seen the leaders working feverishly to hold back the volcanic anger of the mob. He had seen with his own eyes how they had saved Fanning's life, and yet it was they who would be held accountable for his humiliation.

At New Bern he had spent several days putting on paper his account of the troubles in Hillsborough. Isaac Edwards had received him nervously, his eyes returning hypnotically to the half-healed gash on his cheek. Hillary had told him baldly the upshot of the affair, then settled down to write a full account while the events were clear in his memory. On this pretext he had thrust aside every attempt Edwards had made to question him more fully as to particulars, but he had been aware of Edwards' uneasiness.

Finished at last, his account had gone to Governor Tryon. After some hours the Governor had summoned

him for a testy interview, questioned him closely and
sometimes scolded him for taking an attitude too favourable to the rebels. When Hillary had had an opportunity
to defend himself he had coolly insisted that he had fa-
voured no one in his report; he had set down only what
he had seen. He had pointed out that he still bore the
marks of the mob's violence and had no reason to feel
kindly toward the rioters. The Governor had accepted
this with a mixture of impatience and absent-minded-
ness. The mob was not his quarry. He had questioned
Hillary shrewdly again and again about the leaders, and
particularly about Harmon Husband. Time after time he
had tried to manoeuvre Hillary into a statement which
would place Husband at the Courthouse during the riot.
He had finally given up in disgust. Almost scornfully he
assented to Hillary's request for a leave of absence to
visit his relatives in Tyrrell County.

New Bern had not been pleasant. Hillary had felt a
weight lifted off his spirit as he had mounted his roan
and started for Manor House.

He had hoped that Cecelia would have returned from
Charleston, but Angela, who was the first to greet him,
settled that matter quickly.

After standing on tiptoe to kiss his cheek, she said,
"Oh, Hillary, I'm so glad to see you! You don't know
how I've suffered here. Cecelia's in Charleston, and the
boys are absolutely no help to me. . . . Mother!" she
called toward the drawing-room. "Hillary's come
home." Then to Hillary she said, "When the boys come
home at night they have time only to eat their supper
and run off to bed. Father has them working *all* the
time, and they leave at six o'clock in the morning. Can
you imagine anything worse?"

Madame Caswell came from the drawing-room and
greeted him warmly. "Is the poor baby already filling
your ears with tales of her neglect? Come into the hall.
We've much to hear."

They entered the large cheery room and took seats by
the fire-place, Angela next to Hillary.

"Really, Hillary, Mother jokes about it, but I have
nothing to do but work on a sampler, and——"

"Pathetic," Madam Elizabeth said, and then to Hillary: "Now are you going to stay with us for a while? No . . . don't answer. I can see it in your eyes."

Hillary laughed. "A short while, but soon I must go back to New Bern."

"Ah!" she said, "I'd hoped that you were giving up politics and the little world of New Bern."

"Mother!" Angela said in horror. "How can you think for a moment that Hillary would give up New Bern? It is so much better than this frightful plantation life."

Hillary ignored the comment and said to Elizabeth, "I'm at the point where I'd like to give it up, but there's some business brewing, and I ought to be about to help stir the kettle."

"Or take it off the fire," Madam Elizabeth said. "Your cousin Richard just went to Joseph Chapman's home. He looks worried. Robin said that he was coming to visit us to-night to see Matthew. You're all so busy that I'm sure there *is* a pot on the boil."

"I'm afraid so," Hillary said as he shifted his position slightly.

Angela had crowded very close to him. "Yes," she said thoughtfully, ignoring the trend of the conversation, "perhaps you're both right. Hillary should stop going to New Bern, and should settle down and get married."

"Whatever brought that on?" Madam Elizabeth asked.

"Oh, I was just thinking. And I'm old enough to get married, am I not, Mother?"

"My dear, you have several years of school before you. One must gain a little education."

"Do I need education to get married?" she asked ingenuously.

"It will help you," Hillary said.

"Help me to get married?"

"Well . . . yes."

"I certainly don't see how! Mrs. Blankenship has been married twenty years and has seven children, and she's never been to school at all."

"Well, that's not the same thing," Hillary said. "I mean you just can't—— Whom do you intend to marry?"

Elizabeth Caswell raised her eyes for guidance. "I don't want to go through this again. You two children will have to excuse me."

"I haven't really decided yet," Angela answered Hillary. She began to count on her fingers. "There are the Blount boys." She turned down two fingers. "And there's always a Davenport about." Down went another finger. "Three Spruills." She dropped her two hands in her lap. "But of course I can't marry a real first cousin, so I haven't counted the Chapmans—though I do rather fancy Robin, and first cousins do sometimes marry."

"I'm sure he'd be flattered."

She rattled on happily: "Yes, he's quite handsome . . . and after all, he's been to Boston!"

"A splendid qualification," Hillary said.

"I should think it's better than the qualifications of most men I know. Except perhaps you, Cousin Hillary. You're not a *true* cousin, are you?"

"As true as Robin is, I've reason to believe."

"There's a nice thing about both of you. You and Robin don't go about talking always of ploughing straight rows, or how much manure to spread to an acre, or how to make the cows give more milk."

"But is there anything so wrong in that?"

"Hillary! You don't mean it. You know it's perfectly wretched to speak of those things. How can I ever count you on my fingers if you talk that way?"

"I guess you can't."

"I can so. Sixteen is a very fine age at which to get married. And anyway, you didn't mean what you said about planting. I can count you very easily."

Hillary laughed. "Why, that's the first proposal I've ever had!"

A look of consternation came over Angela's face. "That's dreadful of you. You're just trying to be mean. Ladies never make proposals of marriage. Never. Never. Never."

He patted her shoulder. "Ah, I wasn't serious. Neither of us will be married for years and years."

Angela shrugged and pouted. "You're just thinking about Cecelia. And you'd just as well forget her, too.

She has all the boys thinking they're in love with her. I've seen her kissing Tommy Blount right here in the garden. And she and Godfrey Spruill went out riding every morning for a week, and I saw them in the woods together, and he was lying down with his head in her lap!"

The mere retelling of the story made Angela angry, and she convinced herself as she spoke that Hillary was in love with Cecelia. She had seen the look of dismay on his face when she mentioned the two boys, and was quick to pursue her advantage. "And I know more about her, too, things I won't even tell you. So there! Now what do you think of your little Cecelia?"

"I think you're telling me stories," Hillary said. He said it lightly, certain she was lying to him, but in his heart he could not help wondering. He thought of autumn mornings, and of Cecelia riding with Godfrey Spruill, and of her warm lips, and of the way she would look stretched out on the grass, her auburn hair spilled like light. He tried to shake the vision from his mind.

"I'm *not* telling you stories," Angela said. "You just want to think I am. Cecelia's a flirt!"

"Angela!" Elizabeth Caswell entered the room with a severe look of reproach. "How in the world can you say such untrue things about your cousin?" She shook her head as if she could not understand her daughter, and then to Hillary she said, "Robin Chapman's just come from the shipyards. He is leading his horse around back."

"Good! I've many things to tell him."

"I suppose you've been meeting girls since you left us?"

"Angela!" Madam Elizabeth spoke with increasing annoyance. "What did I tell you about that sort of talk?"

Hillary smiled. "Oh, that's all right! As a matter of fact, I have met some interesting people—men and women. Madam Elizabeth, you used to be interested in the Quakers, weren't you?"

She smiled and said, "I *was* interested, yes. But I never could go far with it. I've too practical a turn of mind.

I shouldn't say that, for I'm sure there are many very practical Quakers. But anyway, I have little time for religion now, it seems. Life keeps me so busy."

"Life seems the best religion," Hillary said.

Robin Chapman stood for a moment in the passageway before the hall listening to the conversation, a slight smile on his lips. Then he stepped into view saying a single word, "Quakers."

"Robin," Hillary said coming forward to greet him, "it seems a long time."

"It does, but the better for seeing you now."

Madam Elizabeth motioned to Angela. "We two are going to supervise the baking of a ham."

"A ham!" Angela said, mortified.

"But I have a hundred things to say to you, Aunt Elizabeth," Robin said. "And, of course, to Angela."

"But, Robin, Angela has to get a kitchen education sometime. Do excuse us. It's the sort of education even Mrs. Blankenship had," she added dryly to her daughter.

Angela followed her mother toward the kitchen. It was impossible for her to understand that the two young men might have matters of their own to discuss.

Robin slumped in the chair across from Hillary. "Begin with the beginning and tell me everything. I got your letters. Oh, and I have one for you." He stood up and handed the letter to Hillary. "From my sister," he explained. "But don't bother reading it yet. I want to hear what you have to say."

Hillary sketched briefly the trouble at Hillsborough. As he listened Robin frowned. He weighed the story but made no comment when Hillary finished. Instead he said, "When is the Governor's Palace officially opened?"

"Early spring. I don't know exactly. You know, they're planning a great ball and all the celebration that should go with such an affair."

Robin nodded slowly. "Early spring. Well, I suppose that should be about the time."

"What do you mean?"

"That's about when everything should explode. All roads meet in April, or something like that."

"If you're speaking of the Regulators, Robin, haven't

we already had the explosion? What more do you want?"

"You mean you haven't heard about the Johnston Bill?"

"No. I get my ear off the ground once in a while."

Robin took a pipe from the rack by the fire-place, lighted it and returned to his chair. "It's a grand bill. Wonderful!"

"You sound as though you despise it. Tell me."

"If a group of people should meet to discuss, sanely, the problems of the Colony of North Carolina, and if those people are told to disperse by whatever magistrate happens to be about at the time, they have an hour to do so. No more. If they don't disperse, they can be sentenced to death as felons."

"That can't pass the Assembly!" Hillary said.

"You mean it *shouldn't*. It will, and there's more to it. They plan to put it into effect in February, but under its provisions they'll be able to punish any persons who have disobeyed it since last March!"

"That means all the Regulators."

"It means anyone the Governor doesn't take a fancy to—in particular, of course, it's directed against the Regulators. You say that you have met Harmon Husband? I'm sorry that he pleased you, because he'll be the first to go under this act."

"I don't see how. Tryon may get rid of some of the others—for instance, Butler and Howell; damn it, I'd hate to see anything happen to Howell. He's been good to me. Besides, I like the man. As for Husband, he has the immunity of the Assembly. They can't arrest him."

"They could if they expelled him from the Assembly."

"On what ground?" Hillary asked.

"Oh, maybe the riots you just told me about. I don't know."

"Impossible! He wasn't even there."

"You say that. Who else will? Do you expect Fanning to stand up in the Assembly and say that Husband is innocent of inciting riots? Will his militiamen say that Husband wasn't there?"

"No."

"Who will?"

"I can't believe the Governor would let it happen. Neither would Richard Caswell, nor Adam Rutledge, nor Buncombe—nor any other decent man in the East."

"Rutledge? I might agree with you. Buncombe, too. But not your cousin Richard. He's almost as eager as Tryon is to get rid of Husband. He believes what the Governor tells him."

"How can you hold such a low opinion of Governor Tryon?"

"And how, in God's name, can *you* hold such a high one?"

Hillary hesitated a moment before answering. "I suppose, because in my heart I want to believe he means well."

"Has he done anything to help the Westerners?"

"No. But he hasn't crushed them either."

"No, it's not yet time."

Hillary frowned. Those were almost the same words that Adam Rutledge had used when he spoke to Harmon Husband.

Robin continued: "Now with this act and with sufficient prodding by Fanning, it will only be a short while before they try to force Husband out of the Assembly. Then he'll have no immunity from arrest. Tryon will have severed the leaders from the people. Then—" Robin snapped his fingers—"he'll go for the throats of the people themselves."

"You carry it too far."

"Wait and see. First it'll be Husband: mark me. If that doesn't precipitate matters, then the grand opening of the Palace will. We'll have a pleasant spring."

"And you see Tryon marching on the West?"

"What else? Tryon's a military man. So's Fanning to some extent. Would you expect anything less of them?"

"All your reasoning depends on a great many men being taken in by Tryon."

"They will be."

"No. It won't be deceit that pitches us against the West. The fact remains that one can't give in to rioters. I mean it, Robin. Do you know what most of those men are like? Have you seen those ugly faces getting ready for a hanging? If I hadn't met Husband, Howell and Hunter, and a red-headed farmer called Rafer, I swear I'd be dead against the whole West. Richard won't ever have a chance to see those people. He'll see only the wrong in violence, and that wrong isn't deceitful contrivance on Tryon's part."

"Contrivance all the same. Haven't we ground the Western men under taxes? Haven't we cheated them out of fair representation in the Assembly? Haven't we ignored their petitions? Haven't we let their courts rot under our eyes? By God, why shouldn't they riot? They're breaking no law when there is no law!"

Hillary did not answer. Why shouldn't they riot? The answer seemed easy for him: because they had nothing to gain. What they might win, they would be sure to lose.

"Well, for you there's nothing to do anyway except wait," Robin said less seriously. "I *did* hear you talking about the Quakers when I came in, didn't I? By any chance have you met a very unorthodox young Quaker preacher?"

Hillary smiled. "Do you spend *any* time aboard that ship of yours?"

"Of course I do. But in my spare moments I make a visit to Richard Buncombe. He takes an inordinate delight in telling me of affairs of which I know nothing."

"Charity Allen is the preacher I know."

"I thought as much. Buncombe was talking about her, and then Meredith sent me a letter in which he mentioned her. He says she's a wonderful young woman —but I gathered she was a bit too holy for my brother. He said that he saw her with Rednap Howell when he was last near Hillsborough. You know Rednap and like him. He has all a poet's fancies but you'd scarce expect a lady preacher to be one of them. Meredith was curious and at last found means to meet the lady. He was surprised that Howell could have passed for a disciple."

Hillary laughed. He stretched back in his chair. "My feeling, too. I met her in Hillsborough and rode with her to Sandy Creek. If it's possible, I think she's too human to be a minister. But she'll try to be."

"You mean she didn't capture your heart?"

"She took my fancy, not my heart. I find most of my thoughts always turning to one particular woman."

"Do I know her?"

"Rather well, I'd imagine."

"Then I hope your letter is good news. Tell me, how soon are you going to New Bern?"

"In a few days."

"Then why don't you sail as far as Bath with me? I'll put you on the south shore and you can make the trip easily from there."

"A bargain, then. But it's all in my favour."

Robin had stood up. "Thought I just saw Matthew and the lads. Shall we go out to meet them? We have enough to tell him to put him on his ear with worry. It might be good for him, though, since he's been concentrating his fears on a possible break with England. He and my father spend their nights strengthening our outer walls while we crumble from within."

The evening was passed in a discussion of England's growing restraints on colonial trade. Matthew Caswell showed an unwillingness to speak of the differences between the East and West of the Colony. They could wait, he said, and talking of them had ceased to do any good.

Hillary was thankful when the night's arguments finally came to a close and he had a chance to read Cecelia's letter. He opened it with doubts, for it had been a long time since he had seen her.

My dear cousin Hillary,

I have started many letters to you, and torn them all up. I never seem able to say to you the things really on my mind. Each time the words come out twisted and nothing at all is the way I meant to put it.

Perhaps it will be so with this letter, but I shall chatter on, and if you can make any sense out of it, then the better for us both.

Charleston is still a frightful bore. I have been proposed to, and bored again. I think I would have accepted if you had written one more word about Esther Wake.

Now and then we receive news from New Bern telling

of this happening and that—all confusing, all exciting. More information came from one of our friends who travelled all the way to Orange County. I wonder what you are doing in the confusion of the capital, and I wonder if we shall ever see each other again.

You can see how depressing this letter is. That has been the way with the others, too. Of course that was really why I destroyed them.

I told Robin about a rumour we heard in Charleston, and I'm certain he told you. They say Governor Tryon is to be sent to New York. Nothing is definite about it, but the words are repeated more and more often. If he is, will Mr. Edwards go with him? And if Mr. Edwards leaves, will you?

In Charleston I feel divorced from everything I know and care about. The convent school is supposed to be very good for one, but I do not think it good for me. I care nothing for what I learn, and less for what I don't learn and am supposed to.

If I wish to talk about the problems of New Bern and our own Colony, I have only girls to speak to. None listen—or at least the few who do, think I am utterly foolish. Betsy Clark Hannah, who lives in Bath, tells me only her father's views—and they're ridiculous. She knows nothing of what goes on about her. At least I have Robin and Meredith and you to tell me a little, and I'm sure you all see more clearly than her father.

There was a line across the paper, drawn impatiently and angrily. Then the words seemed written in haste, as if there were only seconds to speak.

Cousin Hillary, this is so stupid. I write all this nonsense trying to find the courage to say I love you.

Another line was drawn across the blue paper.

Now that I've told you, I'd best go on and say all that has been bothering me. Do you remember the night of the fire when we stood by the summer-house? Do you remember the first time at Manor House? I tried to make you think me a terrible flirt, that I went out with all the boys in Charleston and that kissing meant nothing to me.

Cousin Hillary, you were the first boy I ever kissed. You were the first boy ever to hold me in his arms.

Now I have said it all. I have read it over and it looks terrible and sounds as terrible as I thought it would. I am going to post it anyway.

Have you fallen in love with Miss Wake or one of those girls in New Bern? If you have, will you tell me honestly and quickly? I think I'd marry Emory Little if you have. Small consolation, but I would do it, if only for spite.

Cecelia

Hillary folded the letter carefully and put it in his coat pocket. The sensation which had come over him was strange. It was almost as if at that moment he embraced her. Then the feeling passed, and there was only a hungry longing inside him—an emptiness which a scrap of paper could not fill. Charleston! How far away it seemed! He reached for the letter again, unfolded the pages looking for a date. There was none. How could she have been so careless?

What she might have done since she wrote sent a chill over him. He must write to her at once. Even then, would he be too late?

On the morning Hillary was to sail with Robin a house slave wakened him. The boy held a cup of hot tea in his hand. "The cook she say your breakfas' he be ready, Massa Hillary."

Hillary thanked him sleepily, took a gulp of the hot tea which almost blistered his throat. That was enough to bring him wide awake.

"It's hot, Massa."

"Thank you," Hillary said, holding one hand to his throat. "Tell cook I'll be right down."

"Yes, sar. I'll tell she I waked you."

Hillary dressed and went down the stairs to the main hall. Apparently none of the family was yet up and about, so it was as well he had made his farewells the night before. Andrew had started for the Chapmans' anchorage an hour earlier, carrying the saddle-bags. There seemed enough time, but still Hillary ate his breakfast hurriedly; something pricked him to be on his way.

A false dawn was streaking the east, and the mockingbird in her nest by the thorn bush seemed about to burst her throat with happiness. The stable-boy brought up his horse. He smiled and said, "Massa Hillary, is you ever goin' to stay with us for some time? Massa Matthew, he done tell me to let your horse 'scape if'n I can."

"It's kind of the master," Hillary said.

"He want you to stay."

Hillary smiled and then mounted quickly. He waved to the sleeping Manor House and was off down the avenue of cedars.

It was a splendid autumn morning. Perhaps, he thought, the letter in his pocket might have something to do with his elation, with the pleasant turn of the wind and the breath of pine sharpness in the air. A wonderful autumn morning if it were not too late!

He was crossing the little brook beyond the turn of the road when he saw a woman rider. Her mount was directly in his path at the far side of the ford. He had nearly reached the bank before he recognized Angela's pale blond hair. She made a beautiful picture in the setting of the dark-green pines, in the splashes of the first morning sunlight along the path.

He reined his horse beside her. "Whatever are you doing here at this hour? A sane person would be in bed sleeping."

"I'm not sane," Angela said. "And besides, Mother said I must apologize to you. But you stayed so long talking with Daddy and Robin last night that I had to go off to bed. I decided to do my apologizing this morning."

Hillary dismounted and went to her side. He took her hand gently. "Why, there's nothing for you to apologize for, child. I can't remember anything you said out of place."

"But I must. She said I must. I told you unkind things about my cousin Cecelia. I *love* my cousin Cecelia." She paused. Tears were gathering in her round, blue eyes, and her red lips were trembling. "Mother says I must say I'm sorry, even if Cecelia *does* draw the boys to her. And anyway I *did* see her kissing Tommy Blount in the moonlight and she had her arms around his neck and she was clinging like—like a—limpet!"

Hillary frowned. It hardly sounded like an apology. He wondered if Cecelia had told the truth in her letter. "Now, Angela, you know you shouldn't say things that aren't so."

"But it *is* so! I saw her. Cecelia *does* kiss the neighbour boys—and maybe she does even more!" Her tone indicated superior knowledge.

"What in the world are you talking about?"

"Maybe she even lies down with them like the wild girl who lives in the charcoal-burner's hut."

Hillary could not hide his shock. "What do you know about that wild girl?"

Angela's emotions seemed to change like the mockingbird's song. A silvery laugh rippled from her lips. "Don't be a nincompoop. Don't you suppose I know why the lads ride off into the forest? I'm not so stupid."

Angela slid from her mount and, holding the reins, began to lead it down the path toward the Chapman shipyards. "Come along," she called to the stupefied Hillary. "Walk with me. I can go as far as the docks and then I'll ride over to Aunty Chapman's for breakfast."

Hillary led his roan forward. "We can walk a little way," he said, "but we'll have to do it briskly. I don't want to keep Robin waiting, because he'll want to sail with the tide." He could think of nothing else to say.

Angela laughed. "You *are* a stupid. Don't you know there's no tide in Albermarle Sound? There's only a wind tide, and a northeaster isn't blowing this morning. It's just a lovely fall breeze, so you have to walk with me."

She slipped her arm through his, and they walked the trail in silence. Not content with that, she put her arm about his waist. Hillary drew away. "Angela! What in the world has come over you?"

"Is anything wrong?" she asked. "If you're my cousin I ought to be able to put my arm about you if I please."

"We settled it last night—you didn't want me to be a true cousin."

"Well, that makes it all the easier," she went on happily. "Then there's no reason on earth why I can't put my arm around you."

"There are several," he said.

"All right, tell them to me." She led her horse from the trail, dropped the reins, and strolled to a fallen log where she sat down as if waiting for his answer.

Hillary hesitated, not certain what he should say.

"Surely you're not afraid of me," she teased. "Come along. Sit down and I promise not to bite you. You've plenty of time and the horses won't run away with all that tender grass to nibble."

Reluctantly he dropped the reins and sat down on the log beside her. "Now listen to me, Angela." He tried to be stern. "You're much too young to be acting this way. For one thing . . ."

He felt her lovely blond hair brush against his cheek. She turned toward him. "Go on, Cousin Hillary. I'm listening."

"I was trying to say . . ."

She put her arms about his neck and pressed her lips against his, hard and urgent. Hillary struggled to his feet, but with her arms locked around his neck, he only pulled her up with him. "For the good lord, Angela!"

"Kiss me, Hillary," she said softly. "I want you to kiss me."

He held her at arm's length, both hands resting on her shoulders. "Angela, Angela, for heaven's sake use a little sense!" He strove to put humour in his voice, hoping it would relax the tension. "After all, it's six-thirty in the morning, we're first cousins, and Robin's waiting."

"But I like to kiss. I want to kiss you." She slipped toward him and had her arms about him again, pressing her body tight against him, and lifted herself to kiss him full and warmly on the mouth. "Don't be afraid, Hillary. I know you could be as passionate as I. Let us have love to its fullest. I am no virgin, dearest Hillary."

Her words were like ice water dashed in his face. He felt both shock and an incongruous desire to laugh. They were not her words but something she had read. Where had he seen them? Was it in *Clarissa?* Surely it was something by Richardson.

He pulled her arms away from his neck and looked down at her indignantly. "My God. Have you been reading your father's books?"

"What's the harm in that?" she asked petulantly, knowing she had been discovered.

"Don't do it again," he ordered, bending to pick up the reins of her mount. "And don't ever say that again. It's a wicked untruth, and you have no idea what it means." He hoped he was right about what she knew. His voice softened. "Promise me you won't talk that way again."

"I still don't see anything wrong in it," she said. "And it feels nice to hold you. I like it. What's wrong in it?"

"Never mind what's wrong in it. Just take my word for it that you've no business saying such things, and no business kissing boys that way. As a matter of fact, young lady, you're not old enough to be kissing boys at all."

He led his mount onto the path again and Angela followed him reluctantly. "But it seemed like such fun," she said.

"Well, it isn't," he said. He went on more firmly, "I assure you it isn't." It was strange and perhaps a little ridiculous for him to be giving moral instructions to a young girl rashly seeking another sort of instruction. Still his words seemed to have an effect on her. "Don't you believe me?" he demanded.

"Well, yes, I guess so . . . if I have to."

"And you'll do me that one favour? I ask it seriously."

"Not to kiss any more boys like that?"

"You haven't done it before, have you?"

"No. But I've wanted to. I've thought about it a lot."

"Don't think about it again."

"You'll kiss me good-bye, won't you? I'm not going to the docks with you now."

"A nice cousinly kiss," he said, bending forward and pecking her lightly on the forehead.

"That's horrid," she complained. "That's no fun at all."

"You've given your promise."

She sighed. It was a sigh full of the sorrows of a sixteen-year-old girl. She mounted her horse easily. Over her shoulder she said, with triumph in her voice, "Anyway, I'll wager Cecelia's never kissed you that way."

"I'd turn her over my knee and spank her if she did," Hillary answered slowly, but the memory of the summer-house transfused him.

"Would you really?" She asked the question seriously, but he answered only to himself: "No." He knew he'd have no such resolution, and no wish for it, with Cecelia.

He watched Angela ride down the trail and into the shadows of the pines before he mounted his roan. He shook his head. Lord, he thought, she's going to be a wild one!

He was still thinking over the incident when he reached Joseph Chapman's shipyards. From his point on the knoll he could see the trim lines of the *Laughing Girl* as she lay at anchor in the Sound.

22

An Interview
with the Governor

Richard Buncombe sighed happily. He settled himself comfortably in the great chair in the west wing of the Governor's Palace. His generous, cheerful features were flushed, partly from the exertion of walking from his carriage into the hall, and partly from the extra glasses of Canary wine he had allowed himself at the Swan.

The lovely Esther Wake sat on the divan before him. Her pink skirt spread like flower petals about her. She toyed with the bow which decorated the front of her low-cut dress. Sukey Cornell sat on Richard's right, leaning slightly forward as if to catch all of his words, even though it had never been said of Richard Buncombe that he spoke in low, secretive tones.

Even while speaking to the young women, he was listening to a conversation on the far side of the room. A group of young ladies who were supposed to be writing invitations to the Governor's ball were chatting merrily. Their gossip touched each person to whom they wrote. He dismissed that talk: most of it was old.

As for the two young men whom he had deprived of Esther and Sukey, they were a different matter. The first was saying, "Richard Buncombe acts as if he's God." The second answered quietly that it was in the realm of possibility, but please not to speak so loudly.

"Now, Miss Wake," Richard said heartily, "if you were forced to guess, why would you say that the Governor sent for me?"

Esther gave a rich, full-throated laugh. "Probably," she said, "to ask why you insisted on voting like Mr. Rutledge in the Assembly."

Richard nodded, and puckered his lips thoughtfully. "Possible. Quite possible. Would you agree, Miss Cornell?"

"I know the Governor doesn't have too much love for Harmon Husband. It could be."

"Though somehow—" Esther put her finger to her chin—"one never seems to think of you as a defender of the West and all that."

"Yes," Buncombe agreed. "It would be a bad reputation to get. I ought to be careful." Then turning to Sukey and motioning to the sideboard with a wave of his hand, he said, "My dear, would you be kind enough to fetch me a glass of Canary? I seem to spy a decanter on the table. If it's not Canary—don't put yourself to any trouble—it'll be all right."

To the utter amazement of her former escort, who still pouted near the window, Sukey Cornell rose and hurried to do his bidding.

Richard directed his attention to Esther Wake again. "If I were ten years younger, Miss Wake, I'd give these lads a race for you. As a matter of fact I'd start right now if it weren't for my gout and my charming wife."

"The wife doesn't, but the gout spurs us on," Sukey commented as she returned with the glass of wine. "It gives you a helpless air and brings out the mother in us."

"Even the wife adds to his fatal attraction," Esther said. "She makes him all the more unattainable, and, of course, all the more desirable."

"I didn't have a chance to speak with Adam. I suppose he's to be a guest to-day also?"

"So I'm told," Esther said. "You arrived early."

"I know. I know. It's a terrible habit," he answered seriously. "But I live in constant fear that something important will happen before I arrive. . . ." He turned up his hands, showing that there was nothing he could possibly do about his little irrationalities. "It might even be the cause of my gout," he added.

"But I've heard nothing *does* happen until you arrive," Esther said.

"Ah, you flatter me. But I won't be badgered into competing with your young fellows." Richard began to shift uncomfortably in his chair.

"It's only three-thirty," Sukey said. "Are you impatient?"

"Oh, no, my dear. Thank you." He bit his lip and shifted position again.

"Is there something wrong?" Esther asked. Then she smiled, realizing it was the question he had wanted.

"My foot only," he said. "You know how the blood rushes to it when I sit like this—feet to the floor."

"It's your turn, Esther." Sukey pointed to the footstool under the great table.

Esther Wake glanced across the room, and with a languid smile she caught the eye of Henry Furneau, a handsome young man who had been courting her in vain. "Henry," she called, "be a dear and bring the footstool for Mr. Buncombe." She smiled again to assuage the wound.

Henry grabbed the footstool by one leg. One could see that he ardently wished it were Richard Buncombe's throat. He carried it across the room with distaste. "Here you are sir," he said grimly.

Ah, thank you, my lad," Richard said. "Here, I'll lift up my foot."

It seemed such a magnificent act, such a splendid thing for Richard Buncombe to lift up his own foot, that Henry knelt readily and placed the stool under it. He remained a few seconds on his knees, adjusting it according to directions, as Richard settled himself to comfort.

When Henry returned to his sulking place by the window he did not think Richard nearly so annoying as he had thought at first. And Richard was musing that the first indignity must be the greatest, and, after that, all else seems a positive favour.

Adam Rutledge arrived at the Palace promptly at four o'clock. He was directed by the doorman to the wing where Buncombe waited with the young ladies for the Governor's audience. Adam's handsome face was severe.

He walked forward with hand extended to Richard Buncombe. "They've got you, too?"

Buncombe nodded and made as if to struggle to his feet, but Adam motioned him to remain seated. Buncombe sank back happily, a grin on his face.

"I should make you stand anyway," Adam said, realizing that Buncombe had never intended to get up.

"Miss Wake . . . and Miss Cornell," Richard said with a wave first to one lady and then to the other. "They've graciously consented to keep me company during my last hours."

Adam bowed over their hands. "The two most charming women in New Bern."

"And the handsomest Assemblyman,". Esther returned. "It's a pity we are both nearly wedded to Mr. Buncombe."

"He has an art," Adam said.

The Governor's messenger entered the room hastily and made for Adam and Richard. "Sirs, the Governor will see you now, if you will just follow me. . . ."

Now Buncombe got to his feet with surprising agility. "Shall we?" he said to Adam.

Adam nodded. "By all means, Richard. Let's not keep him waiting." They bade good-bye to the young ladies and followed the messenger to the hall.

Esther turned to Sukey. "Well, they're gone. Shall we return to our boring admirers?" She motioned toward the two young men who still sulked by the window.

"Any port now that the storm is on," Sukey replied, and then after a moment's hesitation she added, "You know, those were rather nice gentlemen."

"From the Albemarle, dear," Esther said. "Caswells, Buncombes, Rutledges—they grow men in that region, you know."

Richard Buncombe, in spite of his pretenses to complete invalidism, carried himself well. He was not so tall as Adam Rutledge, but his shoulders were broad. His almost coarse features disguised his subtle mind, and his easy step made him appear a simple, lovable fellow, of not too much account.

The messenger who led them down the hall had the feeling that he was leading two giants by a string to the pit of a sharp-toothed, unblinded bear. He announced them as he opened the door. Then he closed it quickly and quietly and hurried back to tell the doorman there was about to be a stormy session in His Excellency's office. The Governor was irate, and word was about that neither Adam Rutledge nor Richard Buncombe was a man on whom to vent one's spleen, even though Richard Caswell was present. The messenger posted this information with the doorman and then ran to His Excellency's office again in order not to miss a word. The oak panelling was thick, but if one had sharp ears . . .

Governor William Tryon was seated at his polished mahogany desk. He had just placed a red quill pen in its holder, and shoved aside the letter he had signed. "Good afternoon, gentlemen. I'm glad you were able to come." He smiled and motioned to Richard Caswell, who had been seated on his right and was now standing. Richard shook hands with his friends. "Won't you sit down, gentlemen?" Tryon indicated the two chairs directly in front of his desk.

"How are the plans for the ball coming along, Your Excellency?" Buncombe asked.

"Prosperously, Mr. Buncombe. It should be a grand affair." Tryon looked down to his desk, pursed his lips, and drew the letter before him again. "I've no desire to be anything but straightforward with you, Mr. Rutledge, Mr. Buncombe." He nodded to each as he mentioned his name. "I'll be frank with you. How long has it been since I asked my first favour of you? Six years ago, 1765? Do you recall the dinner we had together about the business of the Stamp Act."

"Quite well, Your Excellency," Adam said.

"Since that time I can't think of any serious disagreements we've had over the business of the Colony—oh, minor things, small affairs, of course. I expect such.

You expect them. But on the major issues we've seen eye to eye, have we not?"

"Until to-day, Your Excellency," Buncombe said heartily.

"No, even to-day I can understand your viewpoint. I personally might like to share it, but I have no choice but to see that the Government itself is protected. I don't feel you've given the matter of Husband thorough consideration. Now do you? Do you honestly?"

"Your Excellency," Adam Rutledge said before Caswell could stop him, "I gave the matter my most careful consideration."

"Mr. Buncombe, are you of the same mind?"

Richard Caswell interrupted. "Are we certain we're all speaking of the same issue? I don't think we are."

"All right, before you answer, Mr. Buncombe, it might not be unreasonable to lay the matter out neatly. I prefer not to go at these things with a hammer," Tryon said. He nodded to Richard Caswell, but the Speaker had no chance to state the case.

Adam Rutledge, in even and clipped tones, said, "Your Excellency, the two of us voted *not* to expel Harmon Husband from the Assembly. The majority overruled us, and Husband is out. Furthermore, he's been clapped in the gaol. I said in the first place that to deny our people, let alone an Assemblyman, the right of petition is the grossest injustice. In the second place, to cast that Assemblyman in the gaol is a—" Adam saw the glint in Tryon's eyes, the haughty uplift of his chin—"is yet another abuse of that man's rights."

"You might clear up those points for Mr. Rutledge, Mr. Speaker Caswell," the Governor said icily.

"Adam, look at the facts. Harmon Husband was dismissed from the Assembly for causing to be published James Hunter's letter making libelous statements about Maurice Moore—Moore, an associate judge and an Assemblyman! You know the rules as well as I."

"You know that wasn't the reason he was dismissed. What was behind it?"

"Adam, Adam, quiet down. I know how you feel, but look at it purely from the legal standpoint. The proof was there that Husband published a letter against Moore

—it doesn't even matter if he wrote it—and he knew full well what he was doing. That's enough in itself to have him dismissed. You know enough law, Adam. It's true."

"All right, Richard," Adam said wearily. "I'll grant the point that to the majority the action taken was technically correct. I don't approve of the spirit in which it was taken."

"Nor do I," Richard Caswell snapped back. "But it's done."

Richard Buncombe sat slumped in his chair, pampering his foot and studying his fingernails. To the Governor he seemed only a disinterested observer, but Tryon could not see how he was digging his thumbnail into his flesh.

"Take your second point, Adam," Caswell was saying. "Husband lost his immunity from arrest the second he was dismissed from the Assembly, and you know quite well that the Johnston Act gives sufficient ground to clap him in gaol. His writings have incited men to riot. The Act forbids it. And there's nothing else to it— now, damn it, Adam, I'm speaking only on the law. I've said nothing about the spirit of it all, and it's to that you're objecting. Now, if you'll grant me its legality, I'll consider the spirit with you."

"*Was* it legal, Mrs. Speaker?" Richard Buncombe asked quietly. "I'd always thought that His Majesty's courts refused to uphold *ex post facto* laws."

"It's for the court to decide whether it is or not—I mean, whether it's legal. Of course, it's after the fact and I know it."

"Gentlemen," the Governor's voice cut in, "do not think I lack appreciation of the struggle within you about this whole affair. I know it's painful to you. But if you'll agree on the *temporary* legality of our actions, then I think we can discuss the matter that's been bothering me."

"Your Excellency," Buncombe said, "I'll agree it's *temporarily* legal, but I'm truly curious how we can salve our consciences."

"I can't do that for you, Buncombe," the Governor snapped. "I have no need to salve my own."

Richard Caswell spoke up quickly. "I think you took a meaning not intended by Mr. Buncombe, Your Excellency."

"I heard him clearly enough, Caswell. But strike my remark. I feel rather strongly about this, Mr. Buncombe. I can't help my feelings. I've received detailed reports from Colonel Fanning about the September riots in Hillsborough. I'm quite aware that you've received reports too, though not directly from him. I won't stand by while the Government of the Crown . . . nay, even of the Colony, is thwarted, is flouted."

"What is it you expect of us, Your Excellency?" Adam Rutledge asked. "We've already cast our votes in the Assembly and wouldn't take them back if we could."

"I'm aware of that also, Mr. Rutledge. What I want to know is this: If we should be attacked by the Regulators, where would you stand?"

"I'd have no choice; I'd be forced to stand with the Crown against them."

"And I'd rather you didn't look at it that way. I'd like to think, Mr. Rutledge, that you would go willingly with the militia, not that I had forced you. I'd like to believe you wanted a government stable and respected. I can't have our officers threatened with death and our judges driven from the bench by the populace. If I let that stand, then nothing is left to us."

"Your Excellency, I think Adam would wish to see the government of the Western counties purged of abuses. He would see honest grievances redressed. Then at the first threat of insurrection he would gladly march to crush it."

Tryon's eyes flashed. "Mr. Speaker, I'll be damned in hell before I redress the grievances of a mob."

"They weren't a mob for several years, Your Excellency," Buncombe said.

"You might dismiss Fanning, and then there'd be no rioting, though God knows there'd still be reason for it," Adam said.

"Do you object to Colonel Fanning because as the representative of a military man he would impose a military discipline? I rather fancy that behaviour myself."

"Gentlemen, gentlemen," Caswell said, "We'll solve nothing to-day. It's too soon after the meeting."

"And now's when I wish to settle it, sir," Tryon snapped.

Richard Caswell sank back in his chair.

"You realize that you two are the only representatives from the East who register objections to the Government's natural defence of itself? Mr. Rutledge, there'll be time to give redress to human beings when they are just that—human beings. Not when they're a mob. Cut off the head of a tiger, and the body soon stops moving."

"I suspect you'll be chopping off the tail, Your Excellency. Husband's not the leader of the Regulators. He writes for them, but he's not the leader. He's a part of your own Government."

Tryon touched his hand to his forehead, closed his eyes, if trying to control his temper.

Richard Caswell leaned forward again. "Our main purpose, Adam, Richard, is to make certain that, no matter what your sentiments as to the spirit of the Act, you will still follow the letter of it."

"I'll go with the militia *when* and *if* it's called out. I suppose that's why Husband is in gaol. It should bring the Regulators together—the better to destroy them."

"Mr. Buncombe, will you be with the militia?"

"Mr. Caswell, I'll be with them. Of course, if I plead that my gout will be the death of me, I'll——"

"Confound your gout, Buncombe! Yes, it'll release you from service . . . but I have my doubts as to its seriousness," Caswell said.

"Very well, gentlemen," Tryon said. "I'm glad I can count on your support."

Richard Caswell stood, signalling that the interview was at a close. Buncombe and Adam Rutledge rose to leave the room, but Buncombe stopped at the door. "Your Excellency, I meant to ask you one question."

"Yes?" He looked up from his desk testily.

"There's a rumour circulating which has an interesting touch. They say you are to be transferred to New York as Governor. Is that true? It's a most excellent promotion."

Tryon with surprise and yet with pride noted all of the implications of the word "excellent." He looked evenly at Buncombe. "I have heard something to that effect, sir."

"If your transfer were to take place soon, would you still be in the mood to pursue the Regulators? I assume that is uppermost in your mind?"

"Gentlemen, there is *no* flouting the law of his Majesty's Royal Governor. That is *my* law, Mr. Buncombe. *Mine,* Mr. Rutledge. I hope I've finally made myself clear on that point. Don't let me detain you any longer."

23

Governor Tryon
Baits a Trap

"But, my dear Hillary," Esther Wake said, "you can't go back to your office. There's simply too much to do here. Why can't you just sit there like a proper gentleman and not think about your desk work?"

"She's absolutely right, Hillary." Sukey Cornell brushed her hair back. "The amount to be done here is overwhelming. You can't just walk away."

"I suppose you two are setting the example of industry?"

Esther Wake and Sukey Cornell sat by the grand parlour window in the Palace. The noise in the room was of laughter, gaiety, and a general chattering of the young people who were busy with the final preparations for the grand opening of the Palace and the ball.

"My dear, we're supervisors," Esther said. "Somebody has to see that affairs are handled properly. Half of the invitations aren't even written."

Hillary shook his head and sat down in a chair next to Esther. "Very well, I'll help you supervise for five minutes. Then I must go. Do I just have to sit here?"

"You have to look serious. It's not an easy occupation."

Two servants in green livery began to carry tea-trays into the room and to arrange cups and saucers on the long tables near the doorway.

"Harmon Husband . . ."

There was a burst of laughter from the young people who were crowded about the round table writing invitations.

Sukey Cornell was saying, "Have you seen the fabulous Lady Caroline, Hillary?"

"Lady Caroline?" he was trying to discover why Harmon Husband had been mentioned.

"She's that creature who——You're not listening!"

"Certainly I am, Sukey . . . 'she's that creature who' . . . Don't I always listen to you, no matter how foolish you may sound?"

"He'll be worse than Richard Buncombe if we let him live as long," Esther said.

"I don't think we should. But anyway, Lady Caroline just moved up from Wilmington with her entourage and has taken a house here. She claims she's the Queen's sister, Lady Caroline Mathilda." Sukey leaned forward confidentially, putting her hand to her low bodice. "She has a houseful of servants and a blackamoor dressed like an Oriental potentate who sits at her feet nearly all the time. She's plumped in a chair most of the day. And with her about it makes New Bern seem positively *countrified.*"

"One could hardly accuse you two of being countrified," Hillary said.

"That's sweet of you, my dear," Esther said, "but Sukey's right. One feels terribly inferior to Lady Caroline." Esther leaned back in her chair in her most languid manner. She surveyed herself, the full, warm curves of her body, and then caught Hillary's eye similarly appraising. "Well, not *quite* inferior," she said. "That was a poor choice of words."

"I should like to have three Chinese slaves from far Cathay," Sukey mused. "All of them would follow about with those frightfully large fans. I suppose that would put Lady Caroline into a rage."

"I see you love the lady," Hillary said.

"I can't bear superior people," Sukey answered.

"That's it!" Laughter burst again about the round table. A young man's voice said, "We'll have Jenkins carry it this evening."

"Put more frills on it," another suggested.

Hillary frowned. "What are they talking about?"

"Invitations to the ball," Esther said. "Young Borncamp—he's the dark-haired chap who's standing—insists on having one sent to Harmon Husband while he's in the gaol."

Borncamp raised his hands for silence. "Now tell me truly, do you think Jenkins is the one to carry it? Really, I don't think he has the good sense."

"He'll get it there."

"Try Hillary Caswell," one of the girls suggested. "He could always tell the gaoler that he's on official business."

"Excellent, Cindy," Borncamp said. "That should do the trick. Where is he?"

Esther was saying, "Hillary, do you think you could find a place for my South Carolina friends to stay?"

"You mentioned that earlier. I've already spoken to——"

"Hillary! Hillary Caswell! Come over here a minute." Borncamp's voice was officious.

Hillary ignored the interruption. "I've spoken to Mrs. Gilchrist. She said she'd have one room free and would be happy to put them up."

"I'm glad you remembered," Esther said. "They're really nice chaps, Emory Little and John Laurens—though I'll have to admit Emory's a bit of a bore at times. They'll be on their way to Philadelphia, so I asked them to stop for the ball." She laughed. "I wanted to be sure of having dancing partners."

That name! He remembered it from one of Cecelia's letters. Emory Little had proposed to her, and now he had found lodging for the young man.

"Caswell! I say there!" Borncamp, annoyed that he had been ignored, crossed the room toward Hillary with the invitation in his hand. He was followed by two young girls who were giggling, and a plump, rather oafish character named Alan Hartwig.

Borncamp tapped Hillary on the shoulder. "I say there!"

Hillary turned his head slightly. "What is it?"

Borncamp was completely oblivious of Hillary's tone.

"You've been elected to carry the invitation to Harmon Husband. I thought it would be a nice touch."

"Someone accused you of thinking?" Hillary took the invitation and glanced over it.

"You'll take it, won't you, old chap? It'll be a howler."

"Really funny?"

"Can't you imagine his expression?"

"Quite well." Hillary tore the invitation into four pieces and handed the scraps back to the astonished Borncamp.

"I say!"

"Your taste is as poor as your manners, Master Borncamp. I was speaking to Miss Wake when you interrupted."

Borncamp flushed with embarrassment. "What are you trying to be—a—a—Regulator? There's no need for you to get on such a fancy horse. You're just a little clerk."

A silence had fallen over the room. The invitation-writers looked up from their work.

"Please don't bother me, Borncamp. You may go write another. If you decide to have it delivered to Mr. Husband, don't bother to come tell me. I'll have found out, and will have already started after you to express my sentiments."

Borncamp hesitated. He started to take a step forward and halted. He had measured the size of his opponent and found the size not to his advantage. He said haughtily to his friends, "Come along. He's just a clod." He moved away.

"You're going to let him call you that?" Sukey demanded.

"From him it's a compliment."

"Precisely my feeling," Esther said.

"I know, but you can't just let him insult you like that! You're a man, aren't you?"

Esther broke in: "Of course, dear. That's exactly why he *is* taking it. It's rather pleasant to see one once in a while. Men are very rare, you know. My mother used to tell me they became extinct just before the unicorns."

"Perhaps," Sukey answered, "but it's strange to me."

Hillary had stood up. "Young ladies, you'll have to excuse me. I've done about all the supervising I'm capable of this afternoon. I *do* have some correspondence that I must copy. Shall I see you to-morrow?"

"You'll see me at seven—practically dawn," Esther said. "I intend to go riding."

"At seven then." Hillary bowed and walked from the parlour. He heard the buzz of conversation as he left the room. Master Borncamp's voice grew noticeably louder.

The work was waiting for him.

Edwards had stacked the papers neatly on the edge of his desk, and the correspondence book rested on his high stool. A green ribbon dangled as a marker at the place of the last entry. Hillary opened the book, seated himself on the stool and drew the first letter from the pile. The letter was from Governor William Tryon to the Earl of Hillsborough:

February 3, 1771

My Lord:

In my dispatch No. 60, I informed Your Lordship that an attempt to rescue Harmon Husband might be expected if we were to arrest him. This assumption was verified by an express from Hillsborough with the intelligence that were Husband to be clapped in the gaol—where he belongs—the insurgents would come down to New Bern and lay the town in ashes.

Bearing that information in mind I immediately dispatched orders to several regiments to make ready to defend our capital. I sent an express to Wilmington and appointed Colonel Waddell to take charge of the militia.

Mr. Edwards, by his great diligence and activity, brought down fifteen witnesses from Hillsborough who will hold for the Crown against this Regulator leader, Husband. All was completed under the protection of the Government.

I have lost no time in writing to each of the counties for a quota of men—if we should need them. I have written to General Gage to request that he send me two field-pieces for protection of the Palace.

In the Council minutes, Your Lordship, you will see an intercepted letter of Rednap Howell, another leader in the councils of the Regulators. It gives proof of the wicked designs of these people.

A principle of duty has launched me at this time into this service. The country seems willing to seize the opportunity of cleansing itself and I cheerfully offer my zealous services, relying that the motive of this conduct will be favourably accepted by the Most Gracious Sovereign.

Hillary finished copying the letter and then placed his pen thoughtfully on his desk. He stared out the window at the busy streets of New Bern but did not focus on any individual object. He saw only the sweep of movement. It was natural enough, he thought, that William Tryon should have taken measures of precaution even before the expulsion and arrest of Harmon Husband. One would expect that of a leader . . . still . . . He dismissed the matter from his mind, drew the second letter from the stack. It was directed to Edmund Fanning.

February 4, 1771

My Excellent Colonel:

I shall expect you to see that no copies are made of this letter.

I have informed His Lordship, the Earl of Hillsborough, that the militia has been notified it may be forced to defend itself— It is not willing to attack. In this wise we may secure its action toward the safety of the Government. Defence is the only cause which draws the militia to us. It would not be inaccurate to state that otherwise His Majesty's Colony might not expect support from its own people.

Harmon Husband is still in the gaol, and if your calculations are correct (though I assure you I reached the same conclusion long ago) matters should be brought to a head. The Eastern gentlemen are not solidly behind us. However, I shall expect their unanimous support if the rebels should attempt to free Harmon Husband—particularly at the time of the grand opening of our Palace.

We shall endeavour to make no efforts to impede the flow of rebels to New Bern. The greater their number, the greater will be the fear of our Eastern kinsmen. Naturally, all pains will be taken to see that no escape is effected, but to see that the attempt is made. The attempt to free the rebel leader will suit the Government's wish admirably. The rebel forces will be drawn into a single group—large enough to be visible to the most obtuse Eastern gentlemen. Moreover, the mass of the militia which now hesitates to act except in self-defence, can be easily enjoined to march upon the Regulators. One has no doubt that in the field of battle we shall be more than a match for the malcontents of the West.

My dear Colonel, I venture to say that your heart flames with indignation and anger at the rebels. It is a most natural feeling for a gentleman who has been set upon by a mob and been forced to flee his rightful home to preserve his very life. Your strong feeling does you credit, for I believe your every act is set in motion by a fundamental faith in sound government and an unwavering trust in the courts. I encourage you to continue in that trust and to hold that, wherever these actions may lead us, we must stand for the sanctity of those great institutions: the Crown and the Law.

I myself have a love of two things: my duty to the Crown and my duty to that high principle of government which demands that the functions of law be not disturbed by the madding crowd, that justice be not impeded.

I would be speaking with less than candour if I did not remind you that I expected you, as an officer of militia, a judge and protector of the courts, to preserve law and order by any means at your disposal.

My promotion to the Colony of New York as His Majesty's Royal Governor would make it appear that I might drop charges against the insurgents. Were I seeking glory, or the transient plaudits of society, I assure you, sir, that I would not risk danger on a battlefield. There are, however, things that a man cannot dismiss from his heart. When his deepest beliefs, his most sacred institutions are set upon, then he must take his stand. You need have no fear that I shall dismiss the case of the Regulators.

One might forget the past. One might say that a change of place brings new challenges, and that to part from place and position is to part from duty. It is not so.

None shall ever say, "His Excellency William Tryon is now the Governor of New York, but has left North Carolina in a state of rebellion." Nay, there shall never

*be a voice to speak those words. There shall never be
cause to speak them. Those who oppose law, those who
oppose the thousand years' labour of our forefathers
shall be crushed. The unnatural evil force which twists
and bends their natures shall be cut out as weeds in a
garden.*

*Nay, sir, once more, there shall be no voice to speak
those words. There shall be no rebels. A revolt against
the Crown and the express desires of the Royal Governor shall not be tolerated. I shall stamp out the rebellion
as one stamps out a small fire. It shall not be to my glory—I seek not that—but to the glory of Law and His
Majesty . . .*

Hillary threw his pen on the desk. Then it was true
that the entire affair had been planned—the expulsion
of Husband from the Assembly and his subsequent arrest, the deliberate infuriation of the Westerners—all
had been planned to force a battle for the glory of the
Crown and William Tryon.

Hillary turned on his stool as Isaac Edwards entered
the room hurriedly. The darkness under his eyes was accentuated. His fatigue was more apparent than ever before.

Edwards stopped short of his desk, noting the look of
anger on Hillary's face. "And what bothers you, Hillary?"

"This." He pushed Tryon's letter to the edge of the
desk.

Edwards walked slowly toward him, leaned over,
glanced at it and nodded. "Is that any cause for alarm?"

"It seems to me," Hillary said, "that I recall a letter
from the Governor long ago in which he said, 'The
grievances of the people cry aloud for and shall receive
the strictest attention.' I have not his precise words, but
that was the purport."

"And?"

"Doesn't this seem like an excellent redress? A separation of the head from the body to ease the pain of an
injury to the foot."

"You're working too hard," Edwards said heavily.
"We both are."

"Then it's time to stop working."

Edwards glanced at the clock on the mantel.

"I don't mean for the day. I mean completely," Hillary said.

"You mean to leave your place here?"

"The sum of it."

"Hillary, you promised to stay with me until May. We will discuss the future then."

"I don't recall that promise."

"It was implied."

"As everything else is here? Mr. Edwards, I had no idea of the type of man for whom I was to work. I'd guessed; I'd been told—but I wouldn't believe it until now. Can't you understand how I feel?"

Isaac Edwards walked slowly to his desk and sat on the stool. He toyed with his pen for a moment. "At times, Hillary, I've had the same feeling. Of course I understand—perhaps I understand better than you."

"Why do you keep working for him?"

"It would be difficult to explain to you now."

"You might try."

"Very well," Edwards said. "I understand the latter portions of that letter. I know he believes what he says about law. There *is* a principle of stability in government—the law has to obeyed. If there are flaws in government, then those flaws must be corrected by law."

"And if the law won't correct them? It doesn't always, you know."

"One has to be patient. One has to wait. Would you want everlasting strife, malcontents and rebels ready to overthrow every government that seeks to rule? You simply can't let such a pattern start. You can't suffer rebellion."

"Your logic doesn't impress me."

"Hillary, believe me, I can't afford to let you go now. I need you here. Please try to understand my position. Just think it over for a while. That's all I ask."

"It's a great deal to ask, Mr. Edwards."

"I know, I know, but think of me."

"Tell me one thing: Do you really believe Tryon seeks no glory on the field?"

Edwards paused, then said, "Does the motive make any difference?"

"I'd like to believe it did."

"You will give my request consideration, won't you?"

"I don't know," Hillary said as he rose from the desk. "I want an early supper. I'll speak to you later about my leaving. Perhaps I *am* too tired to think clearly."

Hillary walked into the streets of New Bern. Every thought carried a certain bitterness with it. He considered the grand ball. The Governor had said there would be barbecues and open-air dancing for the common folk. The ball in the Palace would be, of course, only for the gentry. And for the men in the hills—what would be for them? What could Harmon Husband expect, who lay in the New Bern gaol?

Hillary turned his feet toward the Swan. He glanced upward for a moment to the window of his office. Isaac Edwards was leaning forward on the sill, a sad expression on his face as he looked out to the slow-moving River Trent.

24

The Gaol

Hillary's decision to remain with Edwards was bitter. He had spoken to no one of the letters which he had copied into the correspondence book, though it had taken considerable will power to remain silent on the night he visited the gaol with Adam Rutledge.

Now, on the day of the grand ball and opening of the Palace, he relived that walk with Adam Rutledge.

From the Swan they had gone into the fresh night air and strolled down to the confluence of the two rivers, the Trent and the Neuse. The stars were brilliant in the unclouded sky. Riding lights of ships twinkled in the dark. Anchor chains rattled and clanked, and watchmen called the hour. Voices and quick laughter broke upward from the water front. Lanthorns bobbed up and down as sailors hurried toward the town and the taverns.

"The night air does one good," Adam had said. "It clears the mind."

"Of what?"

"The fog of all the Fannings and Tryons," Adam said easily. "I'm going over to the gaol and talk with Husband. No doubt he's a lonely enough man without a prison to confine him. Would you care to come along, or do you feel it would look improper?"

"The appearances make no difference to me. I'd be happy to keep you company."

"You talk like a man who has just bitten into a sour

apple," Adam said as they turned down the narrow street toward the gaol.

"An apple out of season, anyway. I might not have minded the taste in the spring. The apple's the same, only my taste has changed."

Adam did not question him further, perhaps realizing that it was a time to allow a man his personal feelings without question.

They had stopped at the entrance to a small stone building. Adam had rapped twice on the door before they heard a rattling of keys. Eventually the door was opened to the darkness and a thin wedge of light broke out to the street.

The gaoler squinted into the darkness. "Oh, it's you, Mr. Rutledge. Have to be careful, you know. Governor's not sending his guards until later." He started to open the door to admit the two men but hesitated and asked cautiously, "Have you got some sort of permit, sir?"

"I didn't come to release anyone, Hodkins, merely to see him."

"You be speaking of Mr. Husband?"

Completely at ease, Adam said good-naturedly, "Surely you haven't received orders to keep Mr. Husband in strict confinement?"

Hodkins scratched his bald head. "Well, no, sir. I guess I haven't. They just fetched him here and said to keep him."

"But certainly you can let me see him."

Hodkins opened the door wide, then closed it behind them, turned the key in the lock. "I suppose there's no harm. But they talk pretty strong about this fellow. They're giving me ten guards till after the barbecue and fancy doings."

"Quite a lot of trouble for one man," Adam observed.

"Well, now . . . I don't know. He seems a mite too quiet to suit me. We had a fellow here just like him, 'bout two years ago. He was a quiet one, too." Hodkins shuffled slowly to the wall and took down a ring of keys which was hanging on a wooden peg. He stopped. "That-there fellow two years ago had killed himself two men—cut 'em down with an axe. You think he didn't take a mite of watching. . . . I'll say he did, what with him sitting in there just as quiet as that Husband." Hodkins started to move down the dim corridor, which was illuminated by a single candle placed before each of the three cells. Again he stopped, turned and surveyed Hillary. He gnawed on his lip. "Say now, Mr. Rutledge, no offence meant, but you won't mind if your young friend stays without?"

"You've no objection, have you, Hillary?"

"Go right ahead. I don't think I'd care to see him in this state anyway."

Adam nodded and then followed the gaoler down the corridor to the cell. Hillary sat on the stone bench in the main room. The gaol was quiet as death, and Hillary decided that Husband must be the the only prisoner.

Adam Rutledge was not gone more than five minutes. There came the noise of a door being opened and closed, and presently the voice of Adam speaking with Hodkins. He was putting money in the gaoler's outstretched hand. "I want you to make a fire—the room's overly damp even for this place."

Hodkins tried to look abused. "There's not much you can do with a gaol, Mr. Rutledge."

Adam ignored the comment and continued. "I'd like him to have some extra food and drink as well. I'll be back to-morrow."

"Yes, sir. You're sure they won't mind that you come here?"

"That I visit? Of course not."

"You know how it is, sir. A man has to be careful. Especially here. It's sort of a habit with me. I mean——"

"I'm sure it'll be all right. Now don't forget the fire."

"No, sir. I won't."

As they retraced their steps along the narrow street Adam had said, "I found Harmon reading the Bible by a short bit of candle. I don't think he even realizes what is happening to him. As for himself, he wouldn't make any complaints, though I pressed him. I couldn't detect the slightest bitterness in his heart. By God, I don't think I could accept injustice with such a spirit!"

Just before they separated at the door of the Swan, Adam had said, "What do you think will happen when the word of all of this—the fact that Husband's in the gaol—is spread about Hillsborough?"

Hillary knew perfectly well what would happen if Tryon's plans were fulfilled. The Western men would march to New Bern, attempt to rescue Harmon Husband; and no doubt would fail because they were expected. Dubious Easterners would swing to the Governor's side and the field would be set for a battle somewhere.

"I don't know," Hillary said.

"But you could guess, I suppose."

"Not as well as you. You foretold most of this at Sandy Creek."

"Then we shall hope I am wrong about the ending of this, shan't we?" Adam had asked.

"We can hope."

No ending had yet come, but this day might bring a reckoning. This was the day of celebration, of the opening of the Palace, and the ball. Hillary stood on the board walk in front of the Swan before entering to see Adam Rutledge.

The whole Colony seemed to be moving in on New Bern. The streets were crowded with vehicles, carts and riding horses. The taverns, inns, ordinaries and boarding-houses were filled with people. The innkeepers were letting their rooms at high prices, sleeping three in the great canopied beds. The poorer folk were making camp in the woods beyond the town and along the rivers.

From the hurry and bustle in the streets of New Bern it might appear that Governor William Tryon was living up to his promise: food and drink and laughter for everyone who should come to the celebration. Hogsheads of ale and rum were being rolled up from the wharf and loaded onto high-wheeled carts; beef and pork were put to roast in great open pits.

Already young dandies, dignified gentlemen on horseback, and finely dressed couples were about the serious business of exhibiting themselves to the public. Hawkers and peddlers cried their wares from street corners: toys, kerchiefs, cups and china, pottery, a hundred household articles, gay kerchiefs and lengths of cloth.

The square beyond the Swan even at this early hour was thronged with men and women. Many of these people were dressed in the butternut-dyed clothes and homespun cloth of the farmers. Their women were clothed in gay calico with mobcaps and white kerchiefs, but the air of celebration had not seemed to catch the spirits of all those people.

Hillary left the porch and entered the Swan, pushed his way through the crowded hall to the desk of the innkeeper. That gentleman was busily scratching out bills and notes with his green quill pen. "No room. Sorry, sir," he said. "Completely full. Everything's full." He had scarcely looked up from his work.

"I don't want a room."

That brought the innkeeper sharply to his senses. "You don't?" The implication was that anyone not desiring a room was surely mad.

"You were to keep an eye out for Mr. Rutledge. Has he returned from the Palace?"

"I don't know at all. Just been too busy. Go see for yourself, please."

Hillary slowly climbed the stairs toward Adam Rutledge's room. For some time he had struggled with his conscience and at last had come to the decision that he would inform Adam of Tryon's plan. Though it made him feel a spy in the Governor's household, his resolution held. He knocked at the broad oak door.

"Come in." He recognized the robust voice of Richard Buncombe.

Hillary entered the room. Buncombe was seated, as usual, in a large chair by the fire-place. Adam sat at the writing-desk. He looked up momentarily. "Good to see you," he said and then went on with his work. Hillary sat on the bed.

Buncombe said, "I was just telling Adam about a delightful little happening in the committee room this morning." He turned to Adam. "It's all right for Master Hillary to hear, isn't it?"

"I assure you that he hears more than we, Richard," Adam said.

Buncombe cleared his throat. "In came His Excellency, plumped himself down at the head of the table, listened for a good two minutes until he had assured himself of a thorough understanding of our two-hours' discussion. Bam! He smashed his fist on the table so violently that I nearly went to my feet in spite of my gout. 'Gentlemen,' said he, 'if you don't pass my currency measures the Province will be bankrupt!' Maurice Moore, bless his soul, craned his neck to look out the window at those hundred fellows working on the greensward and the gardens. Dear William had turned so crimson we might have planted him with the roses, and there'd have been not a whit difference between them."

"And that was your morning?" Adam asked.

"And a lovely one. Tryon threatened to send the Assembly packing, and I was rather in favour of that. Oh, don't worry, he'll have his currency measures passed in spite of us."

Adam finished the note which he had been writing, folded it and sealed it. He regarded it thoughtfully before he walked to the door and called for Herk. "Deliver this message to the same place as the last one, Herk. I don't want anyone else to get hold of it. Can you do it?"

"Yes, sar," Herk answered. His huge body seemed to fill the doorway. Hillary suspected that there was slight chance anyone other than the man Adam had addressed would see the message. Adam returned to his chair by the desk. "And now we wait," he said.

Buncombe nodded in agreement. "Hillary, old chap, would you be so kind——"

Hillary was already busily pouring out a glass of Canary wine.

"I suppose you've noticed that there are a great many men from Orange and the West in the town," Hillary said as he carried the glass to Richard Buncombe. "At least I think I recognized some of them, Adam. One can tell from their speech and their dress."

"Do you mean in the town or along the river?"

"In the town."

"Perhaps that's natural enough. After all, the whole Province has been invited to this confounded celebration."

Hillary hesitated for a moment, and then suddenly found himself telling the two men of Tryon's letter to Fanning.

"I know it isn't proper, but I feel past the point of caring for propriety. I suppose that you are the only ones whom I can tell."

"What's this?" Buncombe asked.

"I copied a letter from the Governor to Fanning in the correspondence book. It seems that the Governor is hoping an attempt will be made to rescue Husband from the gaol. That will prod any Easterners who hesitate to side with Tryon to march on the Regulators."

Adam nodded slowly. Buncombe pursed his lips and stared at one foot. He asked, "Adam, shall I clarify matters for the young man?"

"Yes. It might be better if he knew."

Buncombe scratched his chin, shifted in his chair and began by saying, "We appreciate your telling us this. For myself, I hardly consider it improper. Nor you, Adam?"

"Not at all."

"There's another piece of information which you haven't gathered. At least I have to assume you haven't. We got hold of it quite by the usual series of accidents. If Harmon Husband doesn't escape, the Orange Ring has a scheme to have him hanged in a fortnight." He waited until he was certain Hillary understood the implication of Husband's death. Then he explained: "I don't think the Governor's aware of the Colonel's scheme, but that's neither here nor there. One has no choice. Either Mr. Husband escapes and consolidates the Eastern people against the West, or else he hangs and consolidates his people against the East. Either way the Colony loses, but in the second instance Husband loses his life as well. A very pretty trick on the Colonel's part, wouldn't you say?"

"It's a pity that the mob didn't have their way with that man."

"Perhaps," Buncombe said, "but then this would have only come sooner."

"The Governor's timing might have been thrown off."

"It might have been, but Husband would be taken on one charge or another—let me assure you of that." Buncombe drained his glass of wine.

Adam Rutledge had risen and walked to the window. "Or put it this way, Hillary: Between Fanning and Governor Tryon, which man is the more intelligent, the stronger?"

"Tryon, of course."

"Then do you believe the tail wags the dog? For myself I can't believe that Fanning manages these schemes by himself. He's not man enough to manipulate the Governor. I prefer to think that Tryon seeks glory, is hungry for it, and doesn't realize himself how far that hunger drives him. He travels far from the country of his ideals to satiate himself." Adam pulled aside the flimsy curtains. "It seems they always decorate these windows for women," he said as he looked down into the street. Then he added casually. "Richard, since I've been visiting Husband at the gaol, I've yet to see the guards Hodkins spoke of. Do you think it could have slipped the Governor's mind?"

"It might have, but I don't think so. I'll admit he's rather preoccupied with the opening and the ball, but those things aren't enough to make him forget."

"I wish I could be certain the guard won't be there to-night." Adam Rutledge let the curtain fall into place.

Buncombe nodded. "Life would be easier."

"You two will excuse me for a while?" Adam asked.

"Certainly."

Hillary had leaned back on the bed and closed his eyes, trying to picture in his mind the peculiar situation in New Bern. Adam had reached the door when Hillary sat bolt upright. "Mr. Rutledge, one word before you go."

Adam turned. "You sound serious."

"I think it would be prudent," Hillary began, "if you would let me go to the gaol instead of you."

"How's that?" Richard Buncombe said in surprise.

"Now I really have no idea of your plans, so you'll excuse me for speaking this way, but if they concern Mr. Husband, they concern also the Western people and Husband's release from the gaol. Am I right?"

Buncombe was regarding him skeptically. Adam was smiling.

"The Governor is aware that the country people intend to free Mr. Husband. I only suggest this—I don't mean to sound too stupid—but I suppose he is not pleased with the attitude of either of you. After all, how you both voted on the expulsion of Husband is common knowledge. And it's well known that you don't favour the Johnston Act."

"You must keep your eye on this lad," Richard said. "He's been thinking again."

Hillary continued: "Old Hodkins made quite a point of telling us that he expected to have guards at the gaol. But we haven't seen any in readiness. Mr. Rutledge, if you were to go there this afternoon when one ought to be preparing for the grand ball, and if by chance there were a plan to release Husband at that time, I'd think Tryon would have you in a very compromising position."

"If one were going to release Husband," Buncombe said, "one would have to know about the guards."

"Of course, you *might* act on the assumption they were there," Hillary said.

"Too difficult," Adam answered.

"No," Buncombe said, "the lad's right: someone other than you must discover the situation, Adam."

"Well, Hillary, can you do it?" Adam asked.

"I'd consider it an honour," Hillary said, standing. He saw that Buncombe's glass was empty and reached to take and fill it.

Buncombe raised his hand. "No. Don't bother. I'll do it myself."

Hillary laughed, knowing it was Buncombe's way of paying a compliment. Then he was on his way from the room, down the steps and into the crowded street.

The sun had passed the zenith. The air was mild. The faces of the men and women in the lanes, gossiping about the taverns, standing in the square, gazing into the shop windows, were studies in contrast. The lesser folk of the Eastern counties were highly pleased with the spectacle of New Bern. They were at their ease, smiling, laughing, scarcely taking note of their rudely dressed counterparts from the West. Yet any observer, Hillary thought, whose mind was not torpid from the night's revelry should have taken note of the multitude of Western men in the town and found cause for alarm in their grim-faced, resolute regard.

He turned down the street which led past the church, hoping to avoid the crowd near the square while making his way toward the gaol.

He was surprised to hear his name called. He turned to see a group of Western men standing slightly apart from the press of the crowd. It was a moment before he recognized Hiram Whitlock and advanced to shake his hand. "I'm surprised to see you, Mr. Whitlock. You always seem far from home."

Whitlock laughed grimly. "Home? Why, Mr. Caswell, I figure I've paid more money to New Bern than I've put on my own farm. I guess I could sort of call this my home."

A man in the group interposed: "We come to eat barbecue and look at the Palace."

Whitlock said. "This is James Few. . . . Mr. Caswell, James. He's a friend of Adam Rutledge."

"Oh, that's different then." Few's tone had changed radically.

"And this-here's MacMahon," Whitlock continued.

Hillary shook hands with the two men. He observed them both closely. Few was a lean, cadaverous fellow; a shock of iron-grey hair stood like a rooster's comb on his head. MacMahon was short and plump; his heavy jowls shook vigorously when he spoke.

"You haven't seen Adam Rutledge lately, have you? I mean sometime today," Whitlock asked.

MacMahon interrupted: "You two go on and have your talk. Me and Few are a-goin' to get ourselves somethin' to eat down to the barbecue pit."

"My ribs are fair clappin' together," Few said. "We'll meet you by the Courthouse later." The two men moved into the crowd.

They were dressed as true men of the hills. Hillary had noted their butternut-dyed coats and buckskin breeks, their home-knitted stockings and wooden-buckled shoes. He turned his attention to Whitlock. "I saw Adam at the Swan less than thirty minutes ago."

"Look, Mr. Caswell, I can't see him just yet. I've got some affairs here to tend to. You think you might see him again—soon?"

"Yes."

"You're sure of that? I've got to be sure, Mr. Caswell."

"I promise you that I'll be seeing him. I take it you want me to tell him something."

"Tell him Whitlock said not to turn in before one o'clock."

"No more than that?"

"That's all. He'll understand."

Hillary nodded, motioned good-bye to Whitlock and turned again toward the gaol. The message could not have been clearer to Hillary. One o'clock was the hour when the Westerners planned to release Harmon Husband from the gaol.

He made his way slowly through the crowds. The number of idlers about the gaol surprised him at first; when he looked at them closely he realized that they were not Western men but the country-folk from the near-by regions. Few of them probably knew or cared about Harmon Husband, the sole occupant of the gaol. They were merely curious: for this building, along with the Courthouse and the Palace represented law and order to them. It was an interesting and necessary part of Government—and of course, they must see it.

The single guard in front of the gaol leaned back easily against the wall, apparently disinterested in all about him. Hillary approached him confidently and said that he wished to speak with Hodkins.

"And what's yer business with him?"

"I'm Edwards' assistant over at the Palace. Private message for Hodkins."

"I don't know if'n I remember seein' you there."

"Let's have Hodkins decide if it's important."

"All the same to me. Go knock yerself."

Hillary stepped to the heavy oak door and rapped loudly. When there was no immediate answer he knocked again. Finally the door was opened a few inches. Hodkins' raspy voice sounded from the interior. "Oh, it's you! You're the one who came before with Adam Rutledge."

"Rutledge?"

"You were with him, weren't you?"

"Oh, that fellow. I just happened along."

Hodkins appeared unwilling to open the door wider than a crack, and it was impossible for Hillary to see inside. The brilliance of the sun blinded him to the prison's darkness.

"What ya want? You can't see Husband."

"I don't want to see him. I'm supposed to report to Edwards on the state of the prisoner. Your word will be enough."

"What's he want to know for?"

"Mr. Hodkins, I have no idea what Mr. Edwards says to the Governor. I just follow orders. Now if you'll——"

"Prisoner's all right," Hodkins snapped, and started to close the door.

Hillary's foot blocked it. "Hold on a minute, man. What kind of report is that?"

"Get yer foot out of there!"

Hodkins' unwillingness to open the door farther made Hillary certain that extra militiamen had been brought inside the gaol to wait for the attempted rescue. He wanted to be certain.

"I said get yer foot out of there."

"Hold on, I've got something for you. My God, man, you're jumpy!"

"Never mind what I am. What ya got?"

Hillary had reached into his jacket pocket and drawn out five shilling pieces. The sum was immense, but he thought it worth the object. "This is for any special trouble you might have gone to on Husband's behalf. Might not be wise to mention it. You might not keep it." He held out the money casually, still groping into his pocket with his other hand as if to find more.

Hodkins eyed the coins glittering in the outstretched palm, and his unwillingness to open the door became less apparent. The five shillings were too tempting. It was evident that with only a slight struggle his allegiance to duty was yielding to his greed. "Edwards sent you?"

"I'm reporting to Edwards."

Hodkins opened the door enough to reach out his pale, scrawny arm. As Hillary dropped the coins into the eager hand he let the last one fall to the street. "God, you're clumsy!" Hodkins snapped. He let the door swing open, came down the single step and stooped to snatch the shilling from the dust. Then he hurried back and slammed the door shut. Hillary heard the bar fall into place.

The guard in front of the gaol had moved closer. " 'Pears he's through talking to you. Better be movin' along now."

"Yes, certainly. Not a very friendly chap, is he?"

"He ain't so bad."

Hillary scarcely heard the last words as he moved away and down the street toward the Swan. He had much to tell Rutledge and Buncombe. It was the fifth shilling that had given it away. Hodkins had opened the door wide enough for the sunlight to make a shaft into the dimness. It had glinted on sabres piled on the gaoler's table. It had revealed the astonished eyes of one militiaman sitting at that table, and illumined the hands of another across from him. Hillary did not know how many guards in all lurked inside the gaol: it was enough to know that some were there. Whatever plans had been made for Husband's release would have to be revised with this in mind.

He wondered if Hodkins had been convinced that he had no connection with Adam Rutledge. There was cause enough for fear. It might be best, he decided, to cover his actions carefully. He turned his steps away from the Swan and toward his own office, while he devised the story he would tell Edwards.

"I grew worried, Mr. Edwards, when I saw the number of Westerners in the town so I took the liberty of going to the gaol and seeing how the situation stood. More than a few were gathered there. I hope I didn't do wrong. I told the gaoler I'd see you and report the state of affairs."

Edwards asked with obvious alarm, "Did Hodkins let you inside?"

"No, sir. I saw no cause to go in."

"Very well."

"Was I wrong?"

"No, no. But don't bother yourself about those matters again. I assure you Husband's been taken care of."

Hillary made his way to the Swan. He was quite certain that Hodkins would not mention the five shillings. They would be a safe secret.

Only as he climbed the stairs to Adam's room did it occur to him that now he deserved the name of traitor. He knocked at the door, and again the thought came to him—a traitor, but not to his conscience and convictions, a traitor to his office and his disbeliefs.

25

Prelude to the Ball

From Orange and the other counties west a thousand men had slashed through the forests, crossed the broad fields, forded rivers, plodded their lonely way through swamps to the town of New Bern. They were trappers and hunters, farmers hardened by poverty, frontiersmen roughened by the icy blasts of winter, burned by the summer's sun. They were lean, angular men with packs on their backs and rifles crooked in their arms.

They came in quiet anger. They had heard of throne chairs for Tryon and his lady. They had heard of jewels, satins and silks, the hundred luxuries brought by ships from the Indies. They had paid their fees and taxes, and they had come to see what their labours had bought.

They had reached the end of their patience long before the messengers brought word that their spokesman had been clapped in gaol for the pleasure of a Fanning and the tyranny of a Governor.

New Bern, then, became a cross-roads: the many elements of power were to meet there.

Although it was still a secret to many, a "great personage" had arrived unexpectedly that morning on H.M.S. *Jupiter* which now lay at anchor at the confluence of the Trent and the Neuse. The elect of New Bern, such as Master Cornell, Robertson Hope, Esther Wake, Richard Caswell and members of the Governor's inner circle had been instructed that in no circumstances were they to address that person as the Duke or the Sailor Prince. He had chosen to travel under the name of

Baron Cotswold, refusing all suggestions that he hold a special levee, and emphasizing his desire to meet the good people of the Colony as informally as possible.

Some doubted that he really desired to remain anonymous, for the guests were always forewarned of his status in England. The pretence of informality was not truly calculated to put at ease those with whom he conferred.

It might have been, as Adam Rutledge observed, "only another means of magnifying his importance: a simple thing blown up to greatness by a whisper." Or perhaps Richard Buncombe might have been correct in saying, "It's only another way to satisfy his appetite for play-acting. He's a rather fat, homely man who likes to fancy himself the dark designer of the universe; a man who tries to hide his meanness in the gallantry of a mask."

It made no difference: he *was* an important man in England even if one of his titles was dropped—for he had many. The Baron was on his passage south from Edenton where he had attended another great ball given in the panel room of the Courthouse. He had obviously enjoyed himself at that town for he had been treated as if he were a well-loved king. He had been a guest at Hayes and Pembroke; they had danced, dined, and flirted in a rather clumsy fashion with the belles of Edenton, paying marked attention to Mistress Blair. He had been a god on holiday.

One would not have been surprised to see him dance his way the length of the Colonies, but he insisted that his visit was truly to discover the temper of the Provinces. To that end he had decided to call a conference on board the *Jupiter* to which he invited such prominent men as Samuel Johnston, James Iredell, Joseph Hewes and Stephen Cabarrus.

"Gentlemen," he said as he adjusted his corpulent body in the great chair at the head of the table, "I want you to tell me the precise state of affairs in this most excellent Colony of North Carolina." He toyed with the medallions which hung from a silver chain across his vest. He seemed always to forget to remove those marks of rank. "The Edenton gentlemen were delightful at parties, at dinners, at dances, but they had the most abominable habit of speaking platitudes rather than the truth —the full truth, that is, for of course there's a great deal of truth in a platitude, but 'tis difficult to husk it free. From you I desire nothing but complete honesty. Well? Well? Well?" He raised his eyebrows slightly, looking from man to man as he demanded the state of affairs.

He gave no one a chance to answer, for he hurried on to say, "I've heard there's a dissatisfaction here. Mind you, I didn't hear that from the Edenton people. Let's get down to cold facts. How do you feel about your Royal Governor? What have you to say of him?" He paused only to catch his breath. "You have, I trust, no objection to him. I'd find it difficult to imagine that those of you who associate with William Tryon have any reason to doubt either his capability or his integrity—or, for that matter, his leadership. Well, if you have, out with it. Let's hear your complaints."

It was not an introduction designed to bring out the most candid appraisals. The gentlemen at the table shifted somewhat uneasily.

The Baron sank back in his chair, blew through his mouth, fluttering his lips. He had no desire to encourage small complaints. One could hear them voiced at any street corner by merely suggesting all was not well. They weren't worth listening to. It was better, surely, to put up a barrier, a wall against them. If these people had major grievances, strong hatreds, they would try to batter down the wall. He would be certain then that affairs were very much askew.

Perhaps, the Baron thought, his little wall had not been strong enough in Tyrrell County, or perhaps the leaders were seriously aroused. He had heard complaints there, quiet but purposeful. It had been when the *Jupiter* crossed Albemarle Sound and put in at Joseph Chapman's shipyards for minor repairs.

"Well, gentlemen? I hear no answers. Mr. Iredell, how think you?"

Judge Iredell began to speak with clipped precision as if his mind were a fine watch ticking out thoughts. The words were well chosen, in perfect order. He offered, of course, no complaints. He had too good sense. The Baron leaned slightly forward as if to hear better, encouraging the Judge with his overwhelming interest. In truth, his mind was on the discussion at Joseph Chapman's Another man had been there, a man named Matthew Caswell.

To Caswell he had said, "So you don't approve of your Government?"

"In some ways I do, but I think that our Governor hasn't reached the heart of this Regulator business. He leans too much on Colonel Fanning's opinion. I fail to understand that."

"You feel these—these Regulators are in the right?"

"No, sir, I don't. But I feel the Government's partly in the wrong."

"I see. I see. Well, I shall look into this Fanning matter. Perhaps it's just as well that Tryon's being sent to New York. . . . Ah! There I've let the cat out of the bag! Can I count on you gentlemen not to divulge the fact that Mr. Tryon has been considered for that rather important Governorship?"

Matthew Caswell had smiled. "Sir, we've forgotten it already."

"Excellent! I become careless in good company."

"Kind of you, sir. But one can't help feeling that you held the strings of the bag a bit loosely."

"Fie! You suspect me, Mr. Caswell? No. I assure you it was only a slip. I'd as well add now that the new Governor strongly dislikes the Regulators. It's only honest to tell you that."

"And who is he?"

"That I can't tell you, I'm sorry to say. I suppose I shall see you both at New Bern?"

"A touch of the gout prevents me, sir," Matthew said.

"And you, Mr. Chapman?" the Baron asked.

"Profoundly sorry, sir, but I'm in the midst of loading a ship of mine for the West Indies—and then for England, of course. My son Robin and my daughter will represent the family. They're coming up from Charleston. There's been a yellow plague in that city, you know."

"Not serious, I believe, from what I've heard."

Yes, the meeting at the shipyards had given hint enough of the disturbances in the Colony. Why should one press to find more alarm? "Fine, Mr. Iredell," the Baron said. "I'm glad to hear a man who speaks his mind. Now as to this Colonel Fanning—you have no objection to him, do you? His Lordship the Earl of Hillsborough seems pleased with the things he's heard of him."

"No, sir," Iredell said immediately. "I can't think of any specific complaints. The Colonel has had difficulties at times with the rabble from the hills. Some of his measures might seem harsh, but one must protect the rights of the Crown and the colonial Government."

"Yes, yes. That's what I like to hear," the Baron said, relaxing in his chair again and surveying contentedly the other men about the table. "I suppose you've all had your fears about a civil war, haven't you?" He held up his hand to preclude any remarks. "One *would* have to crush any rebellion, of course, were there such overt trouble. And one *can't* go against the wishes of one's Governor, can one? Since Mr. Tryon will be on his way to the Governorship of New York—oh my! I can see by the looks on your faces that I've let slip a secret! Of course, you won't disclose it to anyone, will you?"

There were murmurs of "No," and "We wouldn't consider it." Samuel Johnston shook his head vigorously.

"Well, since I've gone that far, I might as well add that I'm not at liberty to mention the name of your new Governor. . . . But I've been led to believe that he strongly favours crushing the Regulators. They're quite a threat to the Crown, you know. I speak now with perfect candour when I suggest that from your point of view it might be wise to stand firmly behind William Tryon should he be forced to take action against them. The new Governor—at least the one I'm thinking of—would probably look with a good deal of disfavour on those who refused to support his predecessor in such a conflict." The Baron yawned, fluttered his lips again. "Now tell me frankly, have you any complaints?"

"The currency issue has been giving us some trouble,

sir." Stephen Cabarrus' voice was low-pitched and smooth.

"Yes, yes. Do tell me about it, Mr. Cabarrus." The Baron leaned forward with a look of profound interest. In truth he wanted to look from the port window to see the ship which was gliding by them in the harbour. He could make out the name *Laughing Girl*. It seemed to him that Joseph Chapman had made mention of that ship. Well, it was of no import. His own seeds had been planted. Tryon had told him that the gentlemen gathered in New Bern might require a slight prodding to take his side; he would need them all in a battle with the Regulators.

The Baron closed his eyes, placing his finger-tips to the lids as one in deep concentration. Didn't men always like to place themselves in the good graces of the powers of this world? Now he had given them a hint as to a predilection of their Great Unknown: he didn't enjoy the Regulators. Surely these men would now strive to accord with it.

26

The Laughing Girl

The *Laughing Girl* with Captain Robin Chapman in command was seven days out of Charleston when she reached the port of New Bern. Lines were thrown ashore and the ship was tied to the dock.

She had a heavy cargo, and among the many wares of trade was a special gift from Josiah Martin to Governor Tryon: three hogsheds of rum from the islands and two pipes of Madeira. The main load of the *Laughing Girl* had been consigned to Merchant Cornell and that gentleman was on the docks in person, calling up to Robin in a shrill voice, "You have the consignment from Antigua?"

"Aye, Mr. Cornell," Robin called from the helm. "And ready to unload her. You can send your stevedores aboard in a moment."

"Good! Good!" Cornell shouted. He hurried beyond the kegs and crates stacked on the wharf to signal to his foreman.

Robin strode to the rail and looked out at the busy dock. He was a fine, bronzed, seafaring man. His cap was tilted back on his brown hair; his eyes were eager and alert. The water front before him was alive with country-folk; he had never seen so many at New Bern before. He turned and called to Scipio. The Negro came forward quickly.

"Take charge of the unloading for the time, Scipio. Make certain the stevedores keep Master Martin's gift separate from the rest of the cargo."

"Yes, sar."

"And tell Thomas to go ashore and hire a cart to take the gifts to the Palace storage rooms."

"Yes, sar. Does you want Ambrose to take Mistress Cecelia's things ashore?"

"I'll speak to him about it."

Robin stayed a moment to see that the Madeira and rum for the Governor were safely marked and put to one side on the dock. Then he strode down the deck to the master cabin and knocked on the door. "Cecelia? Are you ready?"

She opened the cabin door almost immediately. He surveyed her with appreciation. "Well, if you're not the belle of the ball tonight, I'll know the landsmen are poor judges of women."

She smiled and stepped out onto the deck. "I didn't even get to watch us tie up!" She looked over the ship's rail with curiosity. "Anyway, I don't care if I'm the belle or not. I have to please only one landsman. Will I suit his taste?" She twirled, her dress spinning wide.

Robin laughed. "I should hope so. After all, you're *my* sister." He paused a moment. "Are you packed? As soon as I see Mr. Cornell I'll take you up to the Swan. I'm sure we'll find Mary Warden there. She can take you to the Palace to-night, and she may be able to give you a seat in her carriage for the trip back to Manor House."

She looked at him in surprise. "But can't I go on the *Laughing Girl?* I thought you were going back to the shipyards."

"I was," he said thoughtfully, "but I may tarry here in New Bern for a few days. The news we heard in Charleston bothers me. After all, things happen while a man sails to Antigua."

She walked from the rail back to the cabin, hesitating at the door. "I don't object to the bumpy roads so much as I do to that dour man, William Warden."

"I don't blame you. But it'll be easier for me. Don't you like to see your brother comfortable?"

She gave in, entered the cabin to pack her clothes for the journey. It took her some time to arrange her things, and at least twenty minutes had passed before Cecelia stepped onto the deck again to look for Robin.

She saw him standing at the stern. Two rudely dressed men, looking much like poor farmers, were beside him. The one with a long, bitter face was doing the talking. The shorter, heavy man was nodding vigorously in agreement. His jowls quivered in emphasis.

She saw Robin nod, and noted the brief and bitter smiles that came to the faces of the two men.

"Mistress Chapman! Cecelia Chapman!" Master Cornell had come aboard amidships and was advancing toward her. He wore a brilliant blue silk coat and was carrying a handful of papers. "All for your brother," he said, waggling them. "You look beautiful, my dear, beautiful. You'll even have my Sukey jealous. Is Robin in the cabin?"

Before she could answer, he had glanced toward the stern. "Ah, there he is!" Cecelia frowned slightly as she walked aft beside Master Cornell. She had a foreboding that something was wrong even before Cornell said, "Now what business should those backwoodsmen have here? They've been all about my docks this morning," he added in explanation. "You'd think they'd never seen a ship before."

As they approached, they could hear Robin saying, "I'm sorry, men, but I don't think you understand. I couldn't take a woodsman aboard as a hand on this ship. We carry a small crew, and none of them is a free-man."

"We're tired of the land, Captain."

"I know the feeling, men. But I just couldn't take you on. Did Mr. Cornell give you permission to come aboard?"

"I certainly did not," Cornell said as he joined the group.

The taller of the two farmers said, "There weren't nobody stoppin' us, so we just come."

"Well, you try some other ship. They may take you on." He gave them a wink which Cecelia saw but Cornell could not.

They seemed reluctant to leave, but under the stern eye of Cornell they finally thought it best. When they were gone Robin said, "I felt sure you'd given them permission to come aboard."

"Not I. I was surprised to see you talking to them."

"Landlubbers trying to hire aboard." Robin shook his head. "I'd say that all those farmers seem to be going crazy."

"True," Cornell answered. "Very true. I'm not surprised to see that you feel as the rest of us do."

"Did you finish packing?" Robin asked Cecelia.

"I'm ready whenever you are."

"You have the papers for me, Mr. Cornell?"

"Yes, except that I haven't finished checking my own consignment of rum. I imagine you're in a hurry for the ball. We can manage everything to-morrow."

"No, I'd like to . . . but I'll return after I get Cecelia safely to the Swan. I'll be sailing to-night."

"To-night!"

"I know, I know," Robin made a motion with his hand. "I feel the same way, but there's nothing I can do about it."

Cecelia kept herself from showing any astonishment at Robin's abrupt change of plans. She had a vague suspicion that the Westerners whom Robin had appeared to refuse had much to do with his departure. She said, "He's terribly cruel, isn't he, Mr. Cornell? I've begged him ever since we left Charleston to stay at least until one day after the ball so I might go along with him. . . . He'll have to stop at the shipyards *some* day."

Robin smiled. "You know, Mr. Cornell, the captain of a ship has little to say when his father orders him to Edenton almost before he's reached New Bern."

"A father'd get nowhere if he had a daughter like my Sukey."

"Perhaps not, but he'd be very proud of her, sir. I'm told she's quite *the* beauty of New Bern."

Joseph Cornell was in good spirits by the time Cecelia and Robin managed to be free of him. They had flattered him with talk of Sukey, since it was a subject he dearly loved, and by the time they parted at the dock's end he appeared to have completely forgotten the incident of the two woodsmen and accepted the early sailing as quite understandable.

Cecelia did not mention her fears to Robin until they were well away from the ship and walking along the path to the Swan.

"Robin, why did you tell that lie to Mr. Cornell?" she asked.

"There was no lie. I'm sailing to-night."

"You know perfectly well what I mean. You've no orders from Father to go to Edenton."

"No, you're right. Thank you for using your head about the sailing, though. You sounded so giddy I nearly believed myself that you'd been begging me all the way from Charleston."

"Why are you sailing to-night?"

"It's better you don't know that."

"I want to know. What did those frontiersmen ask you to do?"

"To take them aboard," he answered simply.

"In Charleston they said the Westerners were going to tear down the New Bern gaol for Harmon Husband. Are you going to be mixed in that? Answer me."

"If I were, Cecelia, then the best thing you could do to protect me would be to say nothing to anyone about what you've seen or guessed."

Cecelia lowered her eyes. "I was afraid I was right."

"Forget the whole affair, Sis. I've made my promises. Look! From here you can catch a glimpse of the Palace."

"Yes, I see it." The tone of her voice was dull.

"Now, cheer up, Sis." He stopped and took her hands. "You're the prettiest girl in New Bern and you're going to the finest ball in the Colony—in all the Colonies."

"Should that make me feel better? It doesn't."

"Would I make you feel better by giving up my honour and breaking my promises?"

"I'd detest you for it."

"Well?"

"Very well, I'll change the subject. What colour, my dear brother, do you think Lady Tryon will wear to-night? Yellow doesn't suit her at all, I'm told."

Robin laughed at her mimicry and suggested green. So they talked as they made their way through the streets of New Bern toward the Swan.

Hillary Caswell, having delivered his information to Adam Rutledge, emerged from the crowded hall of the inn. He stood with apprehension on the broad front stoop and surveyed the people moving slowly down the street. In that space before the Swan it seemed as though the first bustle and excitement of the crowd were gone; this was more an hour of promenade. As their curiosity waned, the visitors had become more conscious of themselves and of how they might appear to the town people. The undercurrent of hate and rebellion which had been so pronounced in the Square was less apparent. He decided most of the Westerners must have gone to sample the Governor's rum and stand around the barbecue pits. Was this a lull before the storm?

"Quite a show, sir. Never have seen so many in New Bern," commented a portly gentleman who had moved to Hillary's side. The purple velvet of his coat was slightly faded. There were ragged edges on his cuffs.

Hillary barely glanced at the man. "Why, yes, it is." For a brief moment he thought he had seen Cecelia Chapman in the distance. A slow-moving carriage blocked his view.

"Doubt if we'll ever see the likes of it again," the gentleman continued, oblivious of Hillary's disinterest.

"I doubt it, too." Hillary moved part way down the steps. He paused, wishing that the cart which followed the carriage would move more quickly. He knew he should return to the office, but he delayed. Edwards had wanted to give the office an air of out-and-out business, should the Governor by chance drop in for final arrangements.

"Yes, sir, we'll never see the likes of it again." The overtures to a conversation persisted.

"Now I'll agree with you there!" A spry old farmer nodded in accord with the man in the purple coat. "But I remember once . . ."

He *had* seen Cecelia! There could be no mistake

about it. A moment later he caught sight of Robin Chapman walking beside her.

He had never thought it would be like this: how strange to know suddenly that you are in love, to know it after gradual groping, to know it for always and beyond all peradventure. The laughing, moving crowd was only a setting for her beauty. As Hillary stepped down into the street and pushed toward her he felt a tension within him. The press, the voices which had grown excited again, his own heightened senses, made him acutely aware of the threatening swing of events, which might sweep them apart. With someone to love, he was given the pain of something to fear.

He avoided a prancing grey mare, and then a narrow cart drawn by mules. He sidled by an elderly woman who carried a basket of shawls, hurried around a lanky gentleman who wore a tall green hat, dodged a young boy who carried his hoop, and then was behind Robin and Cecelia.

"Mistress Chapman," he said quietly.

Cecelia turned. She looked at him for a second in astonishment, murmured, "Hillary," took his hands and impulsively kissed him on the cheek. Her warmth filled him with happiness, and then the cold fear of losing her swept over him again, and in spite of all the people around them he pulled her toward him, wanting to take her in his arms. She turned her cheek to him, blushing at her own impetuousness.

"Come now! Don't I get a greeting?" Robin demanded. "But not that sort, of course."

Hillary laughed and shook hands with Robin. "You're really here! I didn't think it would be my luck to find you in New Bern."

"You thought we'd miss the ball?" Cecelia asked.

"I thought I would, the way my affairs have been going."

The three of them stepped up onto the broad porch of the Swan. The man in the purple coat and the old farmer were still discussing the size of the crowd.

"We hope to find Mary Warden," Cecelia said. "Robin claims that I must have a chaperone."

"And he's absolutely right," Hillary said. "Are you

going back to Red Bank after the ball?"

"I am to-morrow. Robin is leaving to-night for Edenton."

"To-night!" Hillary said. "You mean you won't stay for the whole celebration, Robin?"

"Shipment for Edenton—I've no choice."

Hillary looked back to Cecelia; even in his heart he had not believed her so beautiful. Life flowed through her like a flame. "I saw Mary Warden a moment ago," Hillary said. "She was speaking to the innkeeper Maybe she's still there. You're not yet committed for all the dances, are you?"

They entered the inn as she answered, "A few, only a few." She laughed. "And there's the gentleman to whom I've promised them!"

Mary Warden was standing in the main hall talking to a tall, handsome young man. Perhaps there was character enough in his straight nose and firm chin to compensate for his eyes, bright but vacant. He was dressed immaculately in a brilliant blue suit; the ruffles of his sleeves had been pressed with extreme care; his silver shoe-buckles gleamed.

Mary saw the three as they entered, and she touched the young man's arm to call his attention to them. "Cecelia and Robin," she exclaimed, "how wonderful to see you! Now the ball will be perfect. Tyrrell County is here in force." She smiled at Hillary, and then asked Cecelia, "Do you know Mr. Emory Little?"

Cecelia lowered her eyes. "I've had the pleasure of meeting Mr. Little in Charleston."

He bowed low over her head. He said to Robin, "A pleasure to see you again, old fellow." His voice was deep, assured. He nodded to Hillary.

Mary Warden was saying, "Of course, from Charleston. I should have guessed that you know Cecelia. As always, she looks charming to-day."

If Emory Little had heard about Hillary, he gave no sign. His handclasp was firm and cordial. "Mr. Caswell is in the Governor's household," Mary said. "He's one of the secretaries."

"A clerk?" Emory asked. The edge of condescension in his tone was barely discernible, but Hillary felt it.

"Only a clerk," he replied.

Robin took Mary Warden aside and explained that Cecelia would need a chaperone, a room and a thousand little things. Mary laughed and answered, "Certainly. I'll be delighted to help. But as for a chaperone, I'll probably need one myself. William seems to be finding much to occupy him to-day."

"What exactly *is* a clerk's function, Mr. Caswell?"

"It's dreadfully boring," Cecelia said before Hillary could answer. She brushed back a lock of her auburn hair.

"Well, in that case, I shan't press him," Emory said.

Hillary bit back the words that were forming on his lips. He glanced toward Cecelia, infuriated with her, with himself, with Mr. Emory Little of Charleston, and not admitting that the cause of his anger was a sudden, piercing jealousy.

"You remember the dances you promised me?" Emory said.

"Certainly I remember, Emory." Cecelia smiled at Hillary, quite aware that he had reached the boiling point. Well enough, she was thinking, if it loosens his tongue to-night. Letters are pale things, and it seems one has to make a man jealous before he will commit himself.

Mary and Robin returned to the group and Mary said, "It's all settled. Cecelia, you're staying with me, and we shall ride back to Red Bank and Manor House to-morrow afternoon. Is the baggage here, Robin?"

"Should be here now. I saw Ambrose pass us on the street."

"By the desk," Cecelia said. "I see my hat-box."

"Then we'll be going upstairs to prepare your young belle." Mary smiled to both Hillary and Emory. "How long do you intend to stay, Robin?"

"Only a few hours."

Emory Little asked Hillary, "And in which direction are you going? As a clerk here you ought to know New Bern rather well. I'll walk along with you and let you point out the interesting spots."

Hillary was taken aback. He saw Cecelia's red lips

part in amusement. He wondered if she could possibly know his anger.

"I'd like to show you New Bern, Mr. Little, but I have some details to clear up at my office. They have to do with the ball, and I can't let them slide."

"I'll go along that far with you," Emory said pleasantly.

"My path isn't very interesting."

"That's nothing. Everything will be new to me. Don't forget, you're a bit more provincial than Charleston. The country festivities I find quaint. I like all sorts of people."

"They are nice, aren't they?" Hillary said dryly.

"Always interesting."

There appeared no way out of it. Hillary wondered if he hadn't made things clear enough to the gentleman. They exchanged a few more banalities and then bade good-bye to Robin, who was returning to the *Laughing Girl* to check bills with Mr. Cornell. Hillary and Emory both turned to watch Mary Warden and Cecelia climb the stairs to their room. Mary waved, Cecelia threw a kiss, and they were gone.

"Charming girl," Emory said. "Charming. I'll tell you frankly, I've every intention of marrying that lass."

Hillary walked from the Swan with Emory trailing slightly behind him.

"Don't you think she's lovely?" Emory was persistent.

"Quite."

Emory pulled at a ruffle of his sleeve. "Seems to be quite a crowd of ruffians here. I don't know if I like the idea of Cecelia being in the midst of them. I'll have to watch her closely."

"Yes, by all means try to do that."

"Now what do you think of that crowd by the Square?"

"I try not to think of them."

Emory laughed. "I've heard about New Bern." After a moment's pause he said, "Well, I suppose you wouldn't have to worry about them. Being a clerk doesn't put any great responsibility on a man, does it? No offence meant, old chap, but I should imagine it rather leaves one to oneself."

It was not until they had passed the Square that Hillary managed to get himself separated from the garrulous and overbearing Emory Little. When that young gentleman was hopelessly lost in the crowd, Hillary started toward his office. He took the path along the Trent.

The sun had set, leaving its flaming trail of crimson across the western sky. The river still reflected the afterglow, a stream of blazing gold. As he walked along the bank Hillary thought he had never seen a flow of such quiet splendour. It made a violent contrast to the swirling eddies of humanity. Now the night-birds were skimming over the water; fish leaped, leaving a spray of golden bubbles in their wake. Beyond the river the cattle lowed as they crossed the young green meadows.

The noise of the town seemed far behind him. When he looked back he could see little fires alight where the people were waiting for the great barbecue which the Governor had provided for their enjoyment. Lights were beginning to show in the river façade of the Palace, and the Governor's office was already ablaze with many candles.

In the state ballroom, Negro slaves and bewigged servants in the Governor's livery were scurrying about to complete the decorations, to give the last polish to the floor, to place the Chippendale chairs against the walls and to light the myriads of candles.

At the far end of that great room was a dais covered with a red Turkey carpet. Two high-backed elbow-chairs were waiting for the Governor and his guest the Baron. At a slightly lower level were two smaller chairs for the Goveroor's lady and Esther Wake.

A canopy of red velvet fringed in gold and bearing the arms of the Colony of North Carolina hung from the ceiling. Flags and banners were draped across the walls giving a military flavour to the great room.

The preparations for the spectacle could be seen clearly from the river. Hillary wondered how many paused to look, to stare at the splendour; how many angry glares were cast on that Palace by the frontiersmen who streamed into New Bern in ever-increasing numbers. This, he thought, must seem a mockery of their ordeals. Their leader lay in gaol, and their cries for relief and redress fell on deaf ears.

In the Palace was a throne for their heedless god.

27

Dancing for the Gentry

After leaving the Swan, Robin Chapman returned to the *Laughing Girl*. His servant Scipio was waiting for him at the head of the plank when he stepped aboard.

"Did two men ask to come on, Scipio?"

"Yes, sar. They come just after dark."

Robin glanced down the deck. "Where did you put them?"

"I tell them they wait in front of your cabin, sar. I don't knows 'em. So that's all I say."

"Good."

"Mr. Cornell, he want to come aboard after they here, but I say to him I ain't 'lowed to let no one on. He mighty mad at me, but him leave some papers for you, sar."

"Did you put them in my cabin?"

"Yes, sar."

"Good enough. Now remember, you're still to let no one else aboard. If the dockmaster should trouble you, just tell him I'll be here at one o'clock, and if he wants to talk, he can see me then."

"Yes, sar. Nobody on board."

Robin took the lanthorn that Scipio offered him, and made his way down the deck. He swung the light before him and saw the dark figures waiting by his cabin. He held the lanthorn high to examine their faces. They were both dressed as farmers. The first had hair white as cotton, and his cheeks were lined by age and weather; the other was much younger, sturdier, his face angled and handsome, his brown hair queued neatly.

"Did you men come aboard to see me? We're not taking on any hands," Robin said cautiously.

"If you be the captain," the first said, "my name is Whitlock."

"I'm the captain."

"This be Enos Dye, sir. He's a friend of Adam Rutledge."

"Perhaps there's something I can do for you then. Mr. Rutledge is a good friend of mine, too."

"We're looking for passage, sir," Dye said.

"Usually I carry no passengers, gentlemen."

"But New Bern is crowded."

"Too crowded," Robin said. "I'll agree to that."

"Then you're of the same mind as we, Captain."

"Come into my cabin, gentlemen. I believe we can talk better there."

Robin drew a key from his pocket, opened the cabin door, entered and hung the lanthorn over the round centre table. He motioned to the men to draw up chairs.

Once they were seated and Robin had had time to observe them more carefully, he said to Enos Dye, "I believe I've seen you on one of Mr. Rutledge's plantations."

"Rutledge Riding, perhaps."

"It might have been," Robin agreed. He adjusted his chair and leaned forward on the table. "Have you made your plans?"

"Yes, sir."

"Are your chances good?"

"We think so. They depend on too many people, though. That worries me," Whitlock said.

Robin shrugged his shoulders. "If that's the only way it can be done, we'll have to make the best of it. For myself, I've arranged to sail at two o'clock. If that fits your plans it's a good time. If not, I think I can delay longer. My men in town . . . something like that will do."

Dye glanced to Whitlock. "No need for that. Two o'clock ought to be just about right." He added to Robin: "We're planning our part for one o'clock."

Robin nodded. "I'll be at the ball till about then. It would make things look better."

"Aye, that I can understand," Whitlock said.

Robin hesitated. "Now, when you bring him aboard, don't come from the dock side. If they should discover he's escaped they might well send some militiamen to the docks. Our bulwarks are low; a man could step up easily and quietly from a boat—or better, I'll leave the stern window open in the cabin. It's a good size."

"Much better," Dye said. "Whitlock, didn't Jennison say he had a flat-bottom boat up the river a piece? We could use that."

"Is one of you going with me?" Robin asked.

"Dye is."

"Very well. My servant Scipio will show you the place to hide."

"Where will that be?" Whitlock asked.

Robin hesitated; Whitlock had no need to know the exact spot on his ship. Then he smiled at himself, realizing that, with many people aware of the plans, one slight precaution meant nothing. "I'll be keeping you both in my cabin for the start of the voyage. I don't think my ship will be searched, but in any case, my cabin will have a sort of sanctity."

"That's why I asked, sir," Whitlock said. "I'm not in favour of it. If he's discovered elsewhere aboard, you might be able to talk your way out of it. But if they are really after him, they'll find him in your cabin—and you'll never be sailing from another port in these waters."

"I'm aware of that."

"Very well, sir. As long as you want it that way . . ."

"Then it's decided," Dye said. He shoved back his chair and stood up.

"Try to avoid the dockmaster on your way to the town. He's usually asleep, but it wouldn't be good to have him see you about."

"He'll not see us." Whitlock spoke with assurance.

They shook hands, and then the men walked out onto the deck. The April breeze was mild. The moon was down, and they stood for a moment looking at the water.

Whitlock pursed his lips thoughtfully. "Well, I wish you Godspeed on your voyage, Captain, and that I see you again."

"Aye, the same," Dye said, and laughed. "For I'll be with you."

"I think my course this night will be easier than yours, gentlemen."

"Maybe," Whitlock said, "but we've less to lose."

Robin watched as the two men departed from the ship. Then he called to Scipio and told him that two passengers would be boarding through the stern cabin window sometime after one o'clock.

"Don't question their right to be aboard. See they remain quietly in my cabin, and, above all, don't mention their presence to anyone—not even to the Governor himself."

"Yes, sar."

"I'll bring you the key to the cabin when I've finished dressing for this confounded ball. It's been a long time since I've danced."

He walked back along the deck, wondering ironically how he might dance—in the air—if he were caught with Harmon Husband aboard his ship—a fugitive from the will of Governor Tryon.

The ball was in progress by the time Robin Chapman reached the Palace. He stood in the great doorway for a moment, watching the first minuet.

Such a splendid pageant, he thought: the lacy precision of a grand minuet; the billowing dresses of the women—the elegance of the gentlemen; the brilliance of a thousand candles illuminating the great room. He could not suppress a certain pleasure that arose from it all, nor at the same time deny a cross-current of bitterness flowing in his heart toward the injustice of many of those most excellent people.

In the gaol of New Bern lay one who spoke for the rights of a different sort of men: men who swore and laughed loudly, who were noisy, yet inarticulate; men who now stood in front of great barbecue pits waiting to be served like animals, who were given a sop of pork and rum to fill the gap in their hearts.

Robin discovered Cecelia dancing the minuet with Emory Little. They made a splendid couple, he thought. There was no denying that he was proud of his lovely young sister. Her blue satin gown swirled about her. Her auburn hair was like a flame of autumn. He smiled. He was quite certain that she was as beautiful as Esther Wake.

Governor William Tryon was seated on his throne at the far end of the room. He was dressed elegantly, and he smiled as he viewed his subjects, evidently pleased at the opening of the Palace. Beside him on another throne was Baron Cotswold, to whom the Governor kept speaking in light asides. The Baron looked more portly than ever. He nodded in agreement with the Governor's word. His face was puffy and pale; his nose short and upturned; his lips too red, too full: in short, he was inordinately ugly. His dress, fortunately, distracted from his features. He wore a white satin waistcoat under a brocaded coat, and his orders and ribbands blazed on his broad chest. He continually sipped a glass of wine. His heavy eyelids were already drooping. He fluttered his lips like a horse.

"Robin Chapman!" At the sound of his name, Robin looked about and saw Joseph Hewes of Edenton approaching. "Your charming sister told me I'd see you here to-night. I was afraid I'd miss you. Tell me, sir, have you heard anything of my ship *Mercury?* She's long overdue."

Robin shook hands. "You've no cause for worry, Mr. Hewes. I saw her riding safe last week in Charleston harbour."

"Ah." Hewes breathed a sigh of relief. "I don't mind telling you, sir, I had my fears. And the delay?"

"From what I gathered, she'd run into a storm off Antigua. Lost a mast and had her canvas riddled, but all hands and the cargo are safe."

"Good news, good news! My night shall be pleasant then. Could you join me for a drink in the supperroom?"

"I'd enjoy it. Give me one minute to pay my respects to the throne, Mr. Hewes."

Joseph Hewes raised his eyebrows slightly. "Aye, you're excused for that duty. It's true royalty up there. I'd think the King himself might feel a bit nervous were he matched with them."

"Tch, tch, Mr. Hewes. You sound like a man who's been burned by a few taxes."

"I have," Hewes said grimly. "Well, go along. Don't let it be said that I ever kept a man from a sacred duty."

Robin smiled and made his way toward the throne through the dancers dispersing after the first minuet.

Lady Tryon, seated on the dais below the Governor, held her powdered, elaborately coiffed head regally. She smoothed her wide-spreading green dress, then folded her hands in her lap as she surveyed her "people." For her this night was, obviously, the zenith of her ambition. She held out her hand gracefully for the provincial gentlemen to kiss; she tilted her head slightly to one side to acknowledge the curtsies of the ladies.

Robin was pleased with his brother provincials; they made an excellent showing. Their dress, for the most part, was simple: dark-blue satin coats and white breeches held in place at the knee with silver buckles. They wore white silk stockings, and the buckles of their shoes were silver or paste. The ladies made an even braver picture. Their silks and satins flowed and billowed. Their varicoloured skirts were like a garden of flowers.

But any pride Robin might feel in the splendour of the Palace and the dress of the guests was a troubled pride, a surface pride blown rough by ever-invading memory of the Western men and their vain protests. Had not their labours paid for the well-proportioned room, the highly polished floors, the candlelight that blazed from the crystal chandeliers and wall sconces?

Robin Chapman knelt to the Governor's lady, bending his head over her extended hand. "Mr. Chapman," she said. "Someone told me you were away at sea. It's good to see you again."

"You flatter me to remember, Lady Tryon. You look most beautiful this night."

"My dear young man, it's because of such words that I remember you."

Robin smiled and moved on to make his bows to the Governor and the Baron.

"Captain Chapman?" The Baron puzzled over the name. "Ah, yes! I've spoken to your father. We put in for repairs at his shipyard, William." He closed his eyes and yawned. "Quite an honest man, your father."

"Thank you, sir."

"I didn't say that his candour pleased me," the Baron said. "Sometimes I prefer my subjects dishonest. Then they may be much easier to get along with. You've noticed that, haven't you, William?"

Tryon caught the implication, and he said casually, "Mr. Chapman, doesn't your father approve of the way the Colony moves? Has he another fashion in mind?"

"I can't speak for him, Your Excellency."

"No, no, I suppose you wouldn't."

The Baron tapped Tryon on the shoulder. "Observe that gentleman by the window." Tryon looked that way. "Interesting face," the Baron said. He took another sip from his wine-glass, ordered it refilled, then settled back apparently to sleep.

Robin stepped back from the thrones and walked to the supper-room where he had promised to meet Joseph Hewes, but instead he found Adam Rutledge.

"Good to see you, Robin." They shook hands and Adam said, "Joseph was accosted by Lady Caroline a moment ago, which is just as well, since I've been trying to find you."

"About what?"

"Let's go into the garden to do our talking. I don't think too well with a multitude of people about me."

They took the centre path through the gardens to the river front. The softly lighted palace was outlined by the red glow of the tall fires where the plain folk drank and danced near the Courthouse. The voices of the countrymen at their festival sounded particularly loud on the night air. Now and then a single voice could be heard above the others. The words would be sharp and distinct for an instant like a fal'ing star, and then vanish into the wide sky of sound. The scent of syringa and sweet shrubs was in the air, and from the Palace came the hum of light voices and laughter. Robin Chapman and Adam Rutledge, hands behind their backs, walked the dividing line in the darkness.

When they were well away from any listeners Adam asked, "Did you speak to Enos Dye or Whitlock?"

Robin was surprised. "Why, yes, I did. But I didn't suppose you'd know of it."

Adam nodded, understanding. "I told them to use my name if they felt there was need."

"They used it, but told me nothing of you."

"I'd hoped that there'd be no need for the plan, Robin. I've been talking to Tryon about the whole affair for the past week. I've literally begged the man to release Husband before there's rioting, but I'm sure I haven't done any good."

"If you've any hope of stopping it, you'll have to hurry. It's nearly eleven o'clock now."

"I know. It worries me. Believe me, I don't know of any way to make Tryon realize the seriousness. He honestly believes that he has well-laid plans, and I think he's in for a shock."

"What do you mean?"

"He wanted to draw the Regulators together, to frighten the Eastern gentlemen to his side. . . ."

"Hasn't he done that?"

"I don't think he meant to gather quite so much power at his doorstep. Dispersing those frontiersmen isn't going to be easy. The way it's going now he'll be lucky not to lose a Palace."

"You believe that?"

"I fear it. Robin, I can even picture it a slaughter-house."

Robin gazed again at the brightly lighted Palace. Adam was saying, "If we could persuade the Governor to give amnesty to Husband I'm sure it would save us from a riot, and it might even keep him from later trying to march on the Regulators."

"But he won't give it."

"And if he doesn't, then I pray Husband makes good his escape. Even that would lessen the chance of the Palace's destruction."

"And if the escape isn't successful—or in time—then I suppose we must look for the worst?"

"At least be ready for it. I've Mary Warden and Lavinia to watch over. I've begun to doubt William Warden's ability to—well, that's of no import. You have a sister in there. I'll see that she and Mary are safe if anything should happen."

"We could send them off now."

"I'd rather not see a flood of people leaving the Palace suddenly. It would only precipitate the thing we fear most."

"We? I wonder how many are aware of the danger."

"Not enough. Perhaps I *should* try the Governor again."

"Would it be better if you told the Baron? Tryon would listen to him. After all, he represents the home Goverment, the Crown. I believe Tryon would stand on his head in the centre of the court if it pleased the Baron."

"I've considered it," Adam said. "I've considered it —and dismissed it. They're both the sort of men who must think of things themselves or an idea's worth nothing to them. It's their insufferable pride."

Hillary led Cecelia through a side door of the Palace into the cool of the garden. She was laughing. "I hadn't imagined that New Bern could be so gay." She faced him. "Well, why is it you're so serious? Come now, you're as bad as Robin."

"New Bern's gay?"

"Just look at the light!" She motioned toward the brilliant Palace.

"I'm afraid you're only seeing half the light."

"What?"

"The fires over there. That's another New Bern," he said. "But perhaps it's a New Bern I'd rather not have you see." She did not answer as they strolled down the path. He continued: "I talked to Mary Warden. She's leaving within the hour. I rather encouraged her. I decided to stop your evening early."

"You decided! But the ball's only started." She hesitated by a syringa bush, touched the buds curiously. A burst of shouting echoed across the fields and died away. A single voice broke through with jumbled words and the shouting rose again.

"No, the ball is nearly over."

"Can't you forget all that for a moment?" she asked.

"No," he answered simply.

"In the garden at night, with a girl—oh, if you had any feeling in you, you'd be telling me about the spring, and the night, and that it's been so long since we've seen each other! And . . . well, it's my fault. I should have known better than to follow after a man who loves to shut himself within four walls. When you sit there, don't you dream of the country just a bit?"

He smiled and put his arm about her slim waist as they walked the path to the river.

"For me," Cecelia said, "I can hardly wait for the pocosin to turn green, to see the colours of the cypress and the lace it makes against the sky. Do your walls have seasons, Hillary?"

"You love the land so much?" he asked, stopping her then, his hands on her waist as she turned toward him.

"Of course I love the land! Is there anything better? Hillary, Hillary," she chided, "why must you be the only boy I care for? Even that stupid Emory Little—"

"Spare me that name, please."

"—even he at least pretends to love the land. He doesn't——"

Hillary drew her close to him and pressed his lips against hers. She tried to draw away but he held her close, and then he felt the softness of her arms about his neck, and the sweetness of her lips against his.

Another burst of shouting rumbled toward them, a prolonged shouting more angry than before.

"Cecelia," he whispered, "I love you with all my heart."

"With all your heart?" she repeated, looking into his eyes.

"My dear, within the two months I swear I'm through with this world of New Bern."

She looked at him in surprise. "But this was to be your life. It's not your place to change for me."

"Change? No. I'll only be where I should have been all along. I've paid my promise."

"Promise?" She drew away a little.

He did not want to explain it then, but only to hold her in his arms and wish the stormy time had passed.

"I'll tell you about it when this is over and done. . . . Cecelia, will you marry me?"

She hesitated for a moment, searching his eyes as if the answer were to be found in them. Then she slipped her arms about him again and kissed him gently, drawing her body close to his. When they finally drew apart her eyes were shining, her body alive with warmth. She whispered, "Yes, yes, I will marry you, my dearest."

"Cecelia! Cecelia Chapman!" Emory Little's voice called from the side entrance into the garden.

"Can I do violence to that sprig now?" Hillary demanded.

Cecelia laughed. "No, my darling, you must be kind to my old suitors. They're very useful, you know." She leaned forward, kissed him warmly, impulsively on the lips.

She took Hillary by the hand and led him from the garden toward Emory Little. That tall, arrogant young man was framed in the light of the doorway.

"Gainsborough should have that man—and keep him away from other people," Hillary said.

"Dear, he does look noble."

"I see you! There you are." Emory stepped forward. "Oh, you're with the clerk, Caswell."

"No longer a clerk, Emory," she said. "He's decided plantation life is better."

Emory laughed. "Good decision, but not on a clerk's salary. Come, my dear," he said. "They're about to begin another dance."

"But, Emory, didn't it occur to you that he might already have his plantation? And that I might already be promised for this dance?"

From the expression on his face it was obvious that neither thought had occurred to Emory Little. And in spite of his father's pool of information, he demanded, still rather stunned, "What's the shouting in town about?"

"They're celebrating our engagement," Hillary said.

Emory Little hesitated for a moment as if he believed it to be true. Then a look of revelation came to his face. "Oh, you're joking." He gave another glance at the river. He shook his head, certain that there was too much of a rabble in New Bern. "Not at all like Charleston." He followed Hillary and Cecelia into the room and across the floor. As though it had just occurred to him, he said, "By the way, Caswell, a Mr. Rutledge was looking for you."

Hillary stopped short. "Are you sure of that? When?" he demanded.

"Of course I'm sure—a few moments ago, old fellow."

"Stay with Cecelia," Hillary said. "When this dance is over, make certain that she finds Mary Warden."

"I say, that sounds like an order," Emory said, slightly angered.

"It is." Hillary took Cecelia's hand. "Look, darling, after this dance—no matter what—keep near Mary. I'll be back as soon as I can."

She nodded, her eyes wide. "Hillary, please take care of yourself."

"There's a reason for that—now. Will you do the same?"

Again she nodded, her eyes bright.

As Hillary left toward the main door, Emory escorted Cecelia to the floor, saying, "Aren't you getting awfully friendly with that chap, Cecelia?"

"Oh, yes, I am," she answered. And the dance began.

28

Barbecue for the People

When Robin Chapman left the Palace he hurried down the crowded lane toward the Square and the road that led to the docks. The image of Palace grandeur was still in his mind's eye; the powdered heads of the ladies, the irridescent satin of the dresses, the gentlemen's brocaded coats, the sparkling music, the dancing feet, and the brilliance of the thousand candles.

That image persisted until he reached the Square, then shattered like glass. The farmers had vanished. In their place were the grim-faced frontiersmen, hundreds of them packing the Square and trailing into the side streets. Their faces were alive with hate.

A rickety table had been placed at the centre of the Square. Now a tall, angular backwoodsman jumped onto it, stood with his legs wide and raised his hands to silence the crowd. "Can you hear me back there?"

Shouts of "Yes" and "No" and "Louder" came from the fringes of the mob.

"Then be quiet so's you *can* hear me!"

Robin worked his way along the edge of the crowd, keeping his eyes focused on the distant speaker.

"Now you've got yerselves here to a great barbecue," the speaker shouted. "But I been kind of wondering about somethin': Who's gettin' barbecued? You? Or that-there pork?"

Robin stopped short.

There was a little laughter, a few coarse shouts. Then

the crowd grew silent again, except for a rustle of clothes, a click of metal, an undertone of whispers.

They sensed that this was the speaker for whom they had waited. The others had harangued them, built them up, aired their wrongs, then quieted them. None had suggested action.

This one would: they knew it. They could tell it from the way he stood spread-legged on the table; the way he held his head; the way he hooked his thumb in his belt. His words cracked out like rifle shots.

Suddenly his manner grew easy, and his voice more quiet, as he continued: "Now, I'm a-goin' to take a little time talkin' to you folk. And don't you go gettin' restless and jumpy. Ain't no cause for it. You ain't been bothered much for the last five years . . . so . . ."

He waited until the protests had died down. He began again. "So, like I say, hold yer horses for a while. We've had some men talkin' to you for quite a spell. I don't aim to repeat much they've said."

"Give 'em hell, Panky!"

"There's a friend who knows my name. He's right. It's Rafer Panky, and I ain't ashamed of it before you folk. Reckon maybe some of you know me from Hillsborough. Reckon maybe some of you remember I done asked a favour of you-all. I didn't want you to hang Fanning! You remember that?"

"Shoulda done it!" someone shouted.

Rafer turned slowly in the direction of the voice. He pointed a long finger. "That man down there says we should have hanged Fanning! Men, I ain't so sure he's wrong. I kinda figure now we should have done it."

There were scattered shouts of agreement.

"Men, I come here to see a Palace that I done paid for. But I'll tell you somethin': I sure ain't got to see nothin' 'cept the outside. Did they let you folks in when I wasn't lookin'? Maybe some of you done got down on yer hunkers outside them gates and got to look in. Anybody here get a look? Shout it out! No? I don't hear none of you.

"Well, I sure want to congratulate you folk. I want to tell you, you're pretty damn good about not complainin'.

I want to tell you, you're a right smart bunch of folk, just paying all you can, just breakin' yer backs and starvin' yer kids for the good of our Colony. I think yer doin' a real nice thing to buy this-here Governor Tryon a Palace so's he can have his fancy friends to dance in it, and bring their womenfolk in there to have 'emselves a good time. That's mighty nice of you. I got a question, though: What's the matter with you men? You got yer own womenfolk. Don't you want them to see nothin' fine? No! Course you don't. Hell, you men don't care who yer buying this stuff for! You don't give a damn why you're workin' in them fields or tearin' them rocks out of the dirt!"

"We sure as hell do!" a man shouted.

"You do, friend? Well, why don't you go up there a right smart way and ask 'em what they've done with yer corn and yer wheat and yer sweat? Maybe you want to stay here and have me tell you? I can. They've done some nice things with that stuff. They done turned it into gold! Don't you want to see it?"

"What air we a-goin' to do about it?" a voice shouted.

Panky hooked both thumbs in his belt and smiled. "Friend, you ain't a-goin' to do nothin'. You never have done a thing. Reckon you never will. What's the matter with you folk? I thought a Carolina frontiersman had some guts in him. I didn't know anyone could just walk the hell all over him. You're a-goin' to let 'em dance up there and laugh at you. By God, that's what they're a-doin'! They're laughin' at you 'cause they're gettin' you sloppy drunk and happy so you'll go home. That's all they want. Get you drunk and happy so's you'll go home and slave for 'em some more.

"Did I say *home?* Pardon me, friends. I mean you'll go back to a little chunk of land that, by the good Lord, you *don't* even *own!* Fanning owns it. Tryon owns it. Lady Tryon owns it. The King owns it. But, by the good Lord, you don't own one acre of it! And to-morrow you're a-goin' back and work yer damned heads off again. You're a-goin' back with a belly full of rum, all ready to break yerselves in half to pay some more for that Palace, and them fine silks, and that pork and rum you been gettin' yerselves sick on. Is everybody real happy?"

"You tell us what to do, Rafer!"

"Come on! Give us the word!"

"Let's go take a look at that Palace!"

"Easy, friends! You've heard this all before. Why get excited? You've heard three different men before me stand up here on this same table, right here, and they told you the same blessed things. Why get excited? There ain't no reason.

"Shucks, men—" Rafer scratched the back of his head—"you don't want to go doing somethin' out of place. You keep talkin' to yerselves and yer liable to go burn that whole damn Palace down. And you boys just can't afford to do that 'cause Tryon'd go build himself another, and you'd be havin' yer kids pay for that one. Why get excited?

"You used to have yerselves a fine man in that Harmon Husband. You won't find a better one. He used to tell you how to get yer rights. Told you how to assert yerselves. And you ain't got no reason to get yerselves worked up over one little Palace!

"Judas—is that the name for you? How many of you done sold him? Who raised a finger to help him when Fanning had him thrown in that bloody gaol? Who thinks about him now? Three hundred yards from here, by God, he's lying in a stinkin' gaol, and you go about yer drinkin'!"

"Hell, what kind of men are you! They grub in yer pockets and rob you blind. And you smile. They grub in yer breasts and tear your damn hearts out, and you grin. What's it take to get you mad? What do I got to tell you? Do I got to tear that damned Palace down with my own two hands? Do I got to beat the gaol in with my own bloody fists?

"Some of you came here for business!" Rafer Panky's voice had risen steadily. "Some of you came here to settle a score. Some of you came here to show you was still men. But what's happened to you? What's happened to yer friends?

"Look about ye!

"Look! Look at the man next to ye. Go on! Everybody! See who's got a smile on his face now. Who's grinning. Who's proud o' hisself. Who's nice and drunk,

and fat, and happy, and not carin' they've robbed him
and his neighbours, and not carin' he's played Judas to
the only man who loved him. Look at the man next to
you. Now, by the Lord, look at me.

"I'm tired of waitin'. I ain't a-goin' to wait. First, I'm
a-goin' to see that Palace. I'm a-goin' to see that-there
Governor. I'm a-goin' to see Harmon Husband. I'm
a-goin' to get my rights or, by God, I'm a-tearing the
whole town apart brick by brick! Who's a-comin' with
me?"

Rafer Panky leaped down from the table. At the same
moment, to the roaring of the crowd, a dozen flares
burst into light. The torches had been soaked in oil long
before.

The Regulators surged toward the Palace. Rafer Panky had run to their head and taken his place beside
James Hunter.

Robin hurried down a side street, away from the advancing mob, toward the dock. Quietly he cursed Tryon
for not having given amnesty before the rebels had begun their march on the Palace. Then both the people
and the Palace would have been saved. There was still a
chance that Tryon might save the Palace if he acted
quickly. But the people were lost. Nothing now would
stop him from attacking the Regulators in his own good
time.

Isaac Edwards strode quickly into the ballroom, his
eyes searching everywhere. Hillary excused himself from
Adam Rutledge when he saw the pallor of Edward's
face, and he hurried to the secretary's side. "What's
wrong? Can I help you?"

The music almost drowned Edwards' voice. "The
Governor! I must find the Governor quickly." He kept
looking for him in the crowd. "A messenger just arrived.
He says that there's a mob forming at the Square.
Where *is* the Governor?"

"Isn't that he with Mary Warden?"

"Where? Quick, man!"

"Far side of the room," Hillary said, "by Mr. Cabarrus." Edwards started toward the Governor and Hillary
returned to Adam Rutledge.

"What's the matter with Edwards?" Adams asked.

Hillary told him, and Adam said immediately, "Find Richard Caswell and Iredell. Tell them to meet me at the Governor's office. I'll try to find some others and I hope to God we can talk some sense into Tryon."

Before Edwards could reach him Governor Tryon had started to dance a minuet with Mary Warden. His elegantly dressed figure in broidered white satin advanced, retreated, bowed low, advanced again in the intricate patterns of the dance.

Edwards worked his way as close as he could and stationed himself where the Governor must notice him as he moved toward Mary. "Your Excellency," he said, "a messenger's arrived with most important news. He's waiting in your office now."

The somewhat insipid smile on Tryon's face gave way to petulant anger. "Let him wait! Let him wait, Edwards!" He turned, bowed to Mary Warden and stepped away in the design of the minuet.

Edwards did not move. He rubbed the tips of his fingers together nervously. The Governor approached again, his expression of anger more pronounced at the continued impertinence of his secretary. Edwards, surprised by his own boldness, drew him to one side, "Your Excellency, I beg you, this is of the utmost importance!"

"I said not to disturb me. I told you——"

"An armed mob is about to march on the Palace. There's no time to be lost," Edwards whispered.

The Governor's look of anger vanished. A stunned perplexity came to his face. A second later his manner changed to brusqueness. "You're certain of that, sir?"

"Yes, Your Excellency."

"Very well, I'll be with you." To Mary Warden and the others in the set he said very calmly, very graciously: "I must beg you to excuse me. I have a boring matter to attend to." He glanced to the throne where the Baron appeared to be sleeping peacefully. There was a trace of amusement in his smile at that sleeping figure, a trace of contempt. William Tryon walked leisurely across the ballroom floor, nodding first to one couple, then to another. That air of complete assurance made him certain that none of the dancers would guess.

Hillary had found Judge Iredell and his cousin Richard Caswell, and both were soon on their way to the Governor's office. Adam Rutledge was already there. Maurice Moore, Joseph Hewes and Colonel Waddell followed a few moments later.

Hillary had searched the ballroom for Cecelia, but could not find her. He asked himself angrily why he'd been fool enough to trust Emory Little to see to her safety. He was on the point of yanking that suave young gentleman off his feet when he caught sight of Mary Warden and Cecelia standing by Dr. Armitage. He walked toward them with a sense of relief.

Governor William Tryon was standing in the centre of his office, and the gentlemen of the Colony of North Carolina stood around him, awaiting his decision. Tryon's lips were taut, his jaw was firm, as he looked to the face of each man.

"What is this nonsense that makes you all come running here? I'm told there's a mob at the Square, that several men have harangued them. So you suppose they'd march on the Palace? They wouldn't dare! My guards are at the wharves. My soldiers are at the walls. My sentries are posted at the gates. My cannon are loaded. Well? Why do you stand there gawking?"

Caswell spoke up. "Your Excellency, this is no place for cannon fire."

"No place, Mr. Speaker? Can you think of a better place? That is, *if* the rumours are true."

"But, sir, they're your own people."

Edmund Fanning, dressed in a brilliant green coat and white breeches, stepped into the room. A few eyes turned to him, then looked quickly away.

"You have no right to rail at me, sir," the Governor said to Caswell. "It's not your place."

Adam Rutledge said, "Sir, that mob has formed to take Harmon Husband from the gaol. I think they'll appeal to you first."

"You think, Mr. Rutledge? You *think?* If so, please

consider the fact that I don't intend to release him."

"I agree with His Excellency," Fanning said. "You give an inch to a mob, and they'll smash down the Government. Aren't there cannon posted and in position?"

"You're going to man the cannon yourself, Colonel?" Adam asked dryly.

"If I must, sir, I shall do it gladly."

"Iredell, Hewes," the Governor snapped, "what think you? Do you believe a mob would march on the Palace? I say they'd stop at the gates. I've had no other reports from my men."

"I think as Adam Rutledge does," Iredell said. "Wait until they appeal to you for the release of Husband, and then *give* them the man."

"By God, are you all against me?"

Hewes spoke. His long face with its dark, deep lines about the mouth was grim. "Your Excellency, we're aware there've been complaints in Orange." He glanced at Colonel Fanning as he spoke, and Fanning turned away contemptuously. "Isn't it possible they're using this occasion merely to place another grievance before you? If you should placate them ever so slightly, I'm sure they'd intend no violence."

"Do you suggest hurling me to them as you would a bone, Mr. Hewes?" Fanning asked, his face livid.

From Joseph Hewes's expression it appeared that this was the correct assumption.

Governor Tryon turned his back to the men, walked to the Palace window and stared out on the slow flowing River Trent. He appeared to be trying to control his anger.

"A mob in any form, gentlemen, is a rebellion," Fanning said. "Haven't we the Johnston Act?"

"My dear Colonel," Iredell said, "you were one of those who invited the frontiersmen here. With a stretch of the imagination one might even call you a leader of them."

"Quite a stretch to call him that," Hewes said.

Tryon whirled from the window, his face flushed with the wrath he could no longer restrain. "By the Lord, I say insolence should be met with what it deserves! Violence with violence! You say they march on me? Then I say I'll cut them down. Edwards, call my adjutant. I want Colonel Weavly here at once."

Richard Caswell held out his hand, protesting. "Your Excellency, I beg you not to call the militia into action. We can't have a civil war in the Colony!"

"You fail to make a distinction between civil war and insurrection. I will crush an insurrection, sir."

"When there's no need?" Adam Rutledge asked angrily.

"By God, I'll thank you to keep your place, Rutledge! Edwards, I told you to bring the Colonel."

Edwards, who had hesitated a moment in hope a settlement might be reached, hurried from the room.

Once more Richard Caswell attempted to restrain the Governor. "Sir, even to release Husband is preferable to war. I hate to see him set free as much as Your Excellency does, but——"

"If you hate it, you'll prevent it, Caswell."

"Am I the only one to agree with the Governor?" Fanning asked with raised eyebrows. "When the Government is faced with destruction, you men seem to wish merely to precipitate its fall. I have faith in the Governor's ability to decide this affair."

"I, too," Colonel Waddell said, speaking for the first time since he had entered the room.

"*Two* men, two out of the pack of you gentlemen!"

"Sir," Iredell objected, "We're thinking of the Colony and the people."

"The people!" Tryon's face was inflamed. "Damme, they're my *only* thought. You rail at me as though I were inhuman. I'm not to be driven that way, Mr. Iredell. Do you hear me?"

"But the people——"

"Good God, sir, what call you those beings in our hall? Aren't those gentlemen and ladies people? Do you wish to sacrifice them to a mob?"

"We ask only for the release of Harmon Husband," Adam said.

"Pipe me another tune, Mr. Rutledge. That air makes me sick."

There was a light knock at the door and one of the

Governor's aides, Captain MacLeod, entered. He was followed by a young lieutenant.

Tryon spoke icily. "Why didn't you report that an armed mob was preparing to advance on the Palace? Have I to trust civilians for my information?"

MacLeod appeared bewildered. "But, sir, there is no mob."

Tryon's manner changed instantly.

"Captain Macleod, you tell me there is no mob? My good sir—" Tryon placed his hand on the shoulder of the astonished officer—"would you please explain it to these gentlemen. Go on, go on, my good man."

MacLeod was hesitant. He began slowly: "Well, sir, I was just at the Palace gates . . . and well, nothing seemed out of place there. I mean, there was a goodly crowd about, yes, but certainly no mob. They're shouting in praise of Your Excellency for feasting them and dispensing rum so generously. The dancing goes on. . . ." He consulted the faces of his listeners as if to be sure they believed him.

Tryon let his hand drop. He was smiling particularly at Adam Rutledge. "Gentlemen, you may go back to your dancing. In the future, please try to hold your imaginations in rein."

Iredell and Hewes started for the door. They stopped when they heard the voice of the young lieutenant who had followed the captain into the room. "Sir, your pardon, may I make a report?"

"Who the devil do you think you are?" Tryon snapped.

"Moray, sir, acting Officer of the Day."

"I sent for your superior, Colonel Weavly. Where is he?"

Moray hesitated.

"Never mind, never mind. Weavly's drunk. That's your report, isn't it?"

"No, sir, My report is that a thousand men from Halifax and Orange have gathered at the town's edge. Five hundred more are in the Square, shouting that they'll burn the Palace to the ground."

"Report? Who reported it?"

"I heard them, sir. They mean it."

Fanning said, "That's rebellion. Is it clear enough for you, Mr. Rutledge, Mr. Hewes? Now we'll use the cannon on them."

"Order the guard to surround the Palace," Tryon said. "Train the cannon on the front gates."

Edmund Fanning started hurriedly from the room, but he was blocked at the doorway by the rotund figure of Baron Costwold and two men in livery who held him erect. The Baron's face was red with wine.

He raised his hand with great effort toward Fanning. "Stay," he said simply.

Fanning tried to move past him regardless of the injunction. The Baron's voice was surprisingly harsh. "I told you to stay, Colonel Fanning."

Farquhar Campbell and John Hawkes, the swarthy architect of the Palace, stood behind him in the doorway, prepared to enter after the Baron. The Great Person was suppressing a yawn. That affair finished, he directed the flunkies to aid him to the Governor's chair.

He settled himself comfortably. When he spoke his accent was heavy and Germanic; excess of wine accounted for the slurring of his words. "A rebellion." He yawned again prodigiously. "So you've a rebellion on your hands, William. I thought as much. Ah, William, you shouldn't try to keep such things from me. I've been through these little incidents many times in London." He clasped his hands over his rotund belly, blinked, and resumed: "Tell me what's going on here, Caswell. William's too distressed to speak clearly."

Richard Caswell explained the situation as succinctly as he could. The Baron's head began to nod after the second sentence; his eyelids closed; his double chin sank low on his chest. Suddenly he roused himself.

"Gaol? Did I hear you say the word *gaol?*"

"Yes, sir. There's a man—"

"Careless of me. I'd completely forgotten, William."

The men in the room looked at one another in perplexity. Their lives might be the balance, and the issue hung on an irate Governor and an obese madman.

"Gaol! A beautiful word. That's what one always has to do. *I* always do it. Release all the prisoners from the gaol. A Royal gesture of good will. A Royal visit and—"

he fluttered his lips, raised one hand to show how simple it was—"all the prisoners are set free. Go among them, William. That's the only way to do it. Go among the stupid folk. They're always searching for a god, and you're the brightest, shiniest piece of tinsel we have about the Palace. You'll do."

He closed his eyes again, opened them momentarily. "*Have* to release them! It's the only way. *We* want it, William. We, the people, cry for it. One simple token of your affection. Throw open the Palace doors to us, William. Let us walk about and touch your clothes. We beg it. Can't you see why we're here, raging in front of your Palace? We want no rights, only love! Let us touch a god!"

The Baron sank back, exhausted from his mimicry. His star and other orders glistened in the candlelight.

"And you really suggest it, Baron?" Tryon demanded.

"I advise it. I command it, William. Oh—" he waved a languid hand—"I don't command anything of you, William. Do as you please." Baron closed his eyes and in a moment was snoring comfortably.

Silence, and then Tryon said to Lieutenant Moray, "Saddle my horse and have it at the front gates within the minute."

The lieutenant rushed from the room.

"You're going alone, sir?" Fanning demanded. "I won't allow it! You'll need protection, sir. Mayn't I order the guard to mount?"

"Leave the guards at their posts. Order the crier, the buglers and two torch-bearers to follow me. Edwards, come along with me. I'll have need of your quill."

William Tryon left the room without looking at the Assemblymen again.

Caswell, Campbell and Hewes remained in the room after the others had left. The servants prepared to lift Baron Cotswold from his chair. The Great Person had opened his eyes again. He was smiling. "Now, gentlemen," he said, "it would be prudent to plan for the invitation to the commonalty. They'll be all through your Palace like pack rats. You'd best inform those who have remained in the ballroom. I promise you the people will be grateful. They always are. It really takes so miserably little to make them happy and send them home. Our family's quite adroit at it—you may take my word for it. Of course, you'll have to ride against the mob on another day, but it's really not wise to do it so near to your Palace—and your wives—and with so beastly many of the commoners about." He paused, stifled another yawn and asked, "Now, where's that secret passage to the river? I'm sleepy, and William might fail—though I doubt it. He'll make them happy. It takes so little."

29

Act of Royal Grace

"Find Whitlock and Dye and tell them to hold off," Adam Rutledge said.

"I'll try," Hillary answered.

"You've got to find them. The Governor's pardon can settle the whole affair peacefully, but if Husband's released by the mob Tryon will still have the excuse to march on them. Hurry!"

Hillary rushed down the broad hall to Edwards' office, pulled open the drawer of his desk and took the pistol which lay there. He stuck it in his belt, threw his cape about his shoulders and ran from the Palace.

The crowds before the front gates were still dense. An open space had been made for couples who wished to dance. The music of fiddles and the skirl of pipes were cheerful. Hillary made his way quickly past the dancers and down the lane.

A wind was blowing from the northeast, whipping young tender leaves from oak, myrtle and gum trees. Beyond, in the dark night, the fires blazed from the river camps. Ahead, near the Square, he heard the shouting of many voices.

He approached the gaol from the west, taking the narrow side lanes that were free of people. The visitors to New Bern had kept themselves on the main route or grouped in one or another of the three meeting places about the town: the Palace gates, the Square, and the gaol.

The press at the gaol seemed, strangely, the most orderly. The raging bonfires at the Square, two blocks down the lane, could be seen from there, and the raucous cries were carried on the air. Hillary emerged from an alley half-way between the two meeting places. He paused for an instant. The words of one man rose above all others at the Square. In the dim light Hillary could see him standing on some makeshift platform. His arms were raised. Vaguely Hillary remembered the voice; somewhere before he had heard it, but then the tones had been less strident. Then the words had been meant to pacify. Now he knew it—the voice was Rafer Panky's. Abruptly he turned toward the gaol.

The crowd there was silent, in strong contrast to the one at the Square. All eyes stared at the gaol. The militiamen whom the Governor had secreted inside had now taken their posts about the building. They had been reinforced from the direction of the wharves. The troops held their guns at port and looked directly at the sullen faces before them. Hillary recognized the lieutenant in charge, a man named Bartleson. He was walking back and forth between his men and the crowd, keeping a semicircle free in front of the gaol.

Hillary pushed his way through the silent people and stepped into the open space. When he had noted how many were assembled, he knew there would be no hope of finding Whitlock or Dye. The best thing would be to see Husband and tell him not to let himself be freed.

"Get back there!" one of the militiamen shouted. He lowered his gun, pointed it at Hillary.

"I want to see the lieutenant."

"Keep your place, man."

"And hold your fire, soldier. Call the lieutenant."

Lieutenant Bartleson's attention was attracted by the voices. He walked over at once and recognized Hillary as a member of the Governor's household. He motioned to the guard that all was well. "Do you bring news from the Palace?" Bartleson was anxious. "This crowd won't hold still much longer."

"Yours looks much better than the one at the Square."

At that moment a tremendous shout echoed from down the street.

"But there are no orders?"

"None, none yet."

"We can guess from the haranguing what may happen down there. But look at these people! These don't need to be worked up. They're so damned mad now they can't even talk."

"Husband's still inside?"

Bartleson looked up quickly, "Why, certainly. But I tell you I couldn't hold these people. If they wanted Husband—or us—they could move in any time they pleased. We might fire once, but there wouldn't be a chance to reload. Lord, if they made a rush, I don't know if we could fire even once."

"But no one's tried to rescue Husband?"

"Not yet. He's there all right. Come and see for yourself."

It occurred to Hillary, then, that the young lieutenant was a bit too anxious to display the prisoner. There was no need for it, but he made no objection since it fitted his plans. The only problem would be to speak *alone* with Husband. Then the escape might be forestalled.

Bartleson rapped twice on the gaol door, calling, "It's Lieutenant Bartleson. Stop shaking and open the door."

Hodkins, the gaoler, lifted the bar long enough to admit the two men, and then slammed it into place again. There was a blood-stained bandage about his forehead. Two militiamen, corporals, sat at the broad table in the centre of the room. They kept their eyes on Hodkins.

"What happened to him?" Hillary asked the lieutenant. Bartleson was taking a lanthorn down from the wall-peg. "Oh, he got——"

"I'll tell you what happened to me," Hodkins interrupted. "I opened that damned door and walked out 'cause this-here lieutenant says he wants five more armed men and I'm to go get 'em. Says he, it'll be safer, he won't be puttin' me in what he calls jeopardy. I got about two steps into that nice quiet bunch of thieves and somebody brains me."

Hillary glanced toward the lieutenant.

"That's just the way it happened," Bartleson said. "He had tried to reach the men coming up from the wharves. We brought him back inside."

"I practically had to crawl back by myself. Passed out right here by the door. Don't know how long I was out." He glanced suspiciously at the lieutenant. "Anything could have happened with me gone."

"You were only out for a minute."

"They might have killed me."

"Should have . . . should have. Watch your words." The lieutenant carried the lanthorn toward the corridor and Hillary followed him.

"He's in the last cell," Bartleson said, "a quiet fellow."

"I know."

"Here. You can hold the lanthorn." Bartleson stopped at the farthest door.

Hillary took the light and stepped forward. He had been trying to decipher exactly what was wrong in Bartleson's behaviour. He held the lanthorn high and looked through the grating. It cast a feeble glimmer onto the cot against the wall. Hillary could see a figure wrapped in a blanket, face turned to the wall. The man appeared to be sleeping, and even in the dim light Hillary thought he could discern the rhythmic rise and fall of the blanket.

Bartleson had started to return down the corridor, evidently expecting Hillary to follow, now he was satisfied Husband was there.

"Harmon, Harmon," Hillary called.

Bartleson wheeled round. He was suddenly infuriated. "Who gave you leave to speak to the prisoner, Caswell?"

Hillary, surprised at the violence of the outburst, turned to face the lieutenant. "You didn't forbid me."

"I shouldn't have to! I asked you if you wanted to see him—not speak to him. I'm sorry, Caswell."

"He's in strict confinement?"

"Those were my orders."

Hillary nodded. There was nothing he could do except be thankful that the escape had not yet been made. He knew his chances of finding Dye and Whitlock were nearly nil. But how had they planned it? Surely, he thought, they couldn't have wanted a frontal assault on the gaol. Adam Rutledge and Buncombe would never have agreed to that.

"Had your eyes full?" Hodkins asked when Hillary returned.

"I saw him."

"That's more 'n they'll let me do. Me! Keepin' me out of my own gaol!"

"Look, Hodkins," Bartleson snapped, "you've heard my orders. I let this man in because he's a messenger of the Governor. You're a gaoler—but I never knew you before now."

"You don't trust me?" Hodkins demanded. "My God, I *am* the gaol!"

Bartleson spoke wearily. "Remember this, Mr. Hodkins: you're in no way responsible for the prisoner. Remember that." He turned to Hillary. "You're a witness to that."

"Very well, but it hardly makes sense."

"Never mind that. You'll have to be going now, Mr. Caswell. I'm giving the order only for your own safety."

"I understand."

"It's useless, but tell the Governor to send us more men."

Hodkins lifted the bar and the two men passed into the semicircle before the crowd. The bar slammed down.

Suddenly out of silence came a voice. A fine, rich baritone sang out an ancient Scotch ballad:

> "The news was brought to Edinburgh,
>   Where Scotland's king did reign,
> That brave Earl Douglas suddenly
>   Was with an arrow slain . . .
>
> "With that there came an arrow keen
>   Out of an English bow,
> Which struck Lord Douglas to the heart,
>   A deep and deadly blow . . ."

The song was caught up by many voices, and a measured stamping of feet and clapping of hands followed the singers.

Hillary twisted through the press and started for the lane which led toward the Palace. Then, above the song, there came another angry outburst from the Square. Its violence rocked down the street. A dozen torches burst

into light. The speaker had leaped down from his perch
above the crowd and run to the head of the mob that
surged toward the Palace.

"Who never spake more words than these:
    'Fight on, my merry men all;
For why, my life is at an end;
    Lord Percy sees my fall.'

"Then leaving life, Earl Percy took
    The dead man by the hand;
And said. 'Earl Douglas, for thy life
    Would I have lost my hand.' "

Part of the mob from the Square filtered into the lane
leading to the gaol, poured down it like water rushing
through a gorge. The words of the song were drowned in
their shouting.

A bugle burst high above the clamour. A second blast
sounded on a yet higher key. Hillary looked to see what
was happening. Coming from the Palace and riding directly toward the onrushing mob, were four men on
horseback. The first two carried blazing torches.

A voice at the edge of the crowd called, "It's the
Governor! Tryon's coming!"

"Give way! Make way for him!"

Light from the torches fell full on Tryon himself
mounted on a white charger, riding just behind the
torch-bearers.

The foremost of that angry crowd made a solid wave
filling the width of the street. As the torch-bearers came
close to it, the angry men spread apart, and Governor
Tryon, stiffly erect on his mount, advanced slowly between them, the flickering light gleaming on his splendid
figure. He raised his hand high for silence.

At a signal from him the crier advanced beside him.
His stentorian voice rose above the muttering of the
crowd: "Hark to the beneficent words of His Excellency, the Governor. Oyez, Oyez! A noble visitor of great
importance to our Government has made request that
the doors to the prison be opened, and all prisoners, ex-
cepting only murderers, be released at once. His Excellency grants this request. Oyez, oyez!"

A violent cheering broke from the crowd—the same mob that moments before had been ready to fire the Palace and shackle the Governor himself.

An emotion of thankfulness, and yet of disgust, swept over Hillary as he listened. The mercurial mob began chanting, screaming, "Tryon! Tryon! Tryon!"

"Oyez, oyez!" the crier went on. "I, William Tryon, Governor of the Province of North Carolina, declare that the doors of the Palace will be opened this night at one o'clock. I, William Tryon, invite all loyal subjects of the Crown to walk through the public rooms and see with their own eyes their Government building. Oyez, oyez!"

William Tryon, elegantly erect on his white charger, reined his mount, saluted the people, then turned back toward the Palace with the crowd surging after him in jubilance.

Hillary did not move. He stared in anger at the men pushing past him toward the Palace. Unable to restrain himself, he collared a lanky, red-faced farmer. The two stood for the moment as in an eddy of a swift current.

"What about Husband?" Hillary shouted to him. "Don't you want to see him? Don't you want to wait for his release?"

"Aye, friend, aye—Husband. Surely, friend." And the farmer shook himself loose from Hillary's grasp and moved on with the delirious mob.

A stern-faced captain manoeuvered his horse through the meagre few who had waited to see Husband appear.

"Why the delay, Lieutenant?" he called out. "Governor's orders to release the prisoner. Look alive there!"

Bartleson entered the gaol reluctantly. He was gone a long time, and when he finally emerged again there was a look of dismay on his face, although he led a dark-clad figure.

"Bring him forward," the captain called. "Be quick about it!"

Bartleson's eyes were evasive. "He's gone. Husband's gone. They've taken him away."

"Who's the prisoner?" someone shouted.

Hillary felt a touch on his arm and turned to find

Whitlock. "My God, how could we have known the Governor would order a release?"

"You couldn't," Hillary said wearily.

"Who *is* the prisoner, Lieutenant?" the captain shouted.

"It's a woman, sir," Bartleson answered. "She took his place."

Hillary moved forward to see, but he had guessed what had happened even before the dark cape dropped from her head, and her pale, ash-blond hair fell to her shoulders.

A guard moved quickly behind Charity Allen, his gun in readiness.

"We couldn't know," Whitlock was saying.

Hillary shouldered his way to reach Charity. A cordon of guards kept him from her.

"Charity, Charity," he called.

She turned for a moment, seemed to recognize him, but moved her head in negation. Whitlock had grabbed his arm. "Don't speak to her. Don't!"

"Woman," the Captain shouted as he guided his mount forward, "who helped you to do this? Speak up!"

The bystanders had fallen silent. Charity spoke in clear, ringing words. "My faith is not built on man; the fall of man did not make me stumble, for my faith is in Truth and in God."

"Clap that woman in the gaol," the captain shouted.

"Let her speak!"

Bartleson made no move to obey his superior.

"The Governor ordered all prisoners released," a man yelled.

"And *I* order her arrest," the captain said.

Charity spoke again; her eyes were raised toward the black sky. "O ye daughters of Jerusalem, stir the Son of my devotion, that my soul may live. For He will come again in the time when it shall please Him, and be as a wind in the forest."

Before the Captain could shout his order again, Lieutenant Bartleson, with a peculiar gentleness, took Charity by the arm and led her quietly toward the darkness of the gaol.

30

A Resignation

Two days had passed in spring, and Tryon's ball was a matter of history. The story of his beneficence was on the tongue of every Eastern farmer. That mercurial mob who called themselves Regulators were returning to their woodlands and pastures, still blinded by the flash of Tryon's ride into the streets, still deafened to their own hearts' desire by his proclamations.

Now to them the fact that Husband had been forcibly released from the gaol seemed of no import. One way or another, he was freed—what difference how it had been accomplished? The Governor had been forebearing. There was no cause for alarm.

After all, some said, Husband *is* a strange creature. Might not he truly be in league with the devil? Why, it might have been old Lucifer himself who had changed Husband into a beautiful maiden. Had they not seen her only once? Had she not uttered strange and imcomprehensible words before she, too, vanished?

Then suddenly the dreams and the laughter were gone. The hard grind began again: the soil was still there to be worked by the sweat of their brows, the taxes remained, the courts opened their doors, and the lawyers reached out their greedy hands.

Life would be the same.

They had barely settled to their tasks when riders thundered up the trails from New Bern.

The word was let loose: William Tryon had announced that he was marching the militia west to crush rebellion! If the Westerners had lost their former urgency, their bright spark of noble insistence on freedom, still this did not keep them from gathering. Bravely they sent notices to the Governor that were he to visit Orange to correct the abuses of Government, they would gladly join him, but if he came in arms, bent on their destruction, then it was *they* who would destroy *him*.

"We should be ready to march soon," Edwards said, wiping his forehead with a large, blue handkerchief.

Hillary Caswell sat at his office desk and continued his writing.

"We're expected to go with the Governor, you know," Edwards went on. "Everyone's needed. . . ." A hacking cough shook his frame. He was pale, an obviously sick man. "Haven't you anything to say about that?"

Hillary put down his pen. "I don't feel that any comment's necessary, Mr. Edwards."

"What's that you're copying?" Edwards walked toward his desk.

"I'm not copying. I'm writing it—my resignation," Hillary said.

Edwards eyes were wide. "But you can't!"

"That's strange. I just did it. It seemed easy."

"But we've been through this before. You promised me. I can't accept it—not now at least. I can't."

"I'm afraid you'll have to. I don't care to be a part of this war."

"Hillary, this isn't the time to desert! The Governor needs every man to follow him. There are more than two thousand Regulators ready to take arms against us."

"It seems that we're the ones taking arms. Didn't they go home peacefully enough?"

Edwards began coughing again. He hunched his shoulders in pain. Hillary looked down on his desk. He felt a sympathy for Edwards: a little man, a man with slight imagination, a man who was often afraid—yet a man who held himself loyally to the Governor; Edwards, who had raised his voice only in mild protest against the state of affairs, and was never strong enough to make himself free. The coughing continued.

"You've no business going with him either. You ought to be in bed."

Edwards caught his breath. "My dear sir, he's given me my position, and I owe him my loyalty, regardless of what I believe." After a moment he added, "And you owe him yours, whether you like it or not."

"I like it not."

Edwards returned to his desk, seeing it was useless to argue. Hillary sealed his letter of resignation and began to straighten his papers. He had copied a letter earlier in the day from the Earl of Hillsborough to Tryon. The original still lay spread before him. He picked it up and read it again.

Your letters 57 & 58 are received and laid before the King. It has given His Majesty great concern to find that the peace of the Government has again been disturbed and the execution of laws obstructed by violence.

It is to be hoped, however, that the same zeal and spirit in His Majesty's well-disposed subjects in North Carolina, which had the effect to put a stop to the like riots on a former occasion, will again be exerted on the present emergency, and will have the same success, and that the Assembly will concur with the measures you have recommended for the support of Government against the lawless and savage disturbers of the Public Tranquillity, and for bringing the ringleaders to Justice.

I have the pleasure to acquaint you officially that I have by New York packet transmitted to Lord Dunmore His Majesty's Commission under the Great Seal, appointing you Governor of the Province of New York, together with His Majesty's instructions for your guidance in the administration of that Government.

It is His Majesty's pleasure that you lose no time in repairing to that Province, where I doubt not you will meet with that favourable reception to which you are so justly entitled by your character and conduct.

Hillary placed the letter inside the correspondence book. He glanced at Edwards who was leaning forward on his desk, his hands pressed against his head.

"I had it in mind," Hillary began evenly, "to leave this work and go to my own plantation long ago. I should have stopped when I realized that the Governor and Fanning had planned the affair against Husband only to stir up the Eastern men against the Regulators. I didn't quit then, Mr. Edwards. I stayed on because of a promise to you."

Edwards had begun to cough again.

"You've had that cough for months. For God's sake," Hillary said irritably, "why don't you take some rest?"

Edwards did not answer.

"Now I read that Tryon's going on to New York as governor. I find an official announcement of it, and, still he gathers his forces to crush the men who returned to their homes in peace."

"And who broke wide the gaol! And who would have burned the Palace down had he not stopped them," Edwards said.

"That makes no difference to me."

"Have you ceased to believe in punishment?"

"My dear man, why don't you get some rest?"

"I shall, I shall. Anyway I have to go to His Excellency's office this evening. The Governor is in a fever to justify all his actions. He's sure he's right—and equally certain that no one believes him."

"And you're going to make the march with him in your condition?"

"Yes. There's nothing wrong with me."

"Are you trying to kill yourself?"

Edwards looked up quickly, anger flashing in his eyes. "Mr. Caswell, I believe you're moved by the best of feeling, but you have no business in my personal affairs." Edwards got up from his desk, put on his jacket. He began coughing again. At last he got his voice and asked, "When does this resignation go into effect?"

"I suppose I'll move my belongings in the morning."

Edwards paused at the door. "I can help you with that. Then may we have a glass at the Swan in parting?"

"I'd enjoy it—if you have the time."

"For that, yes, I will." Edwards left the room quickly, unwilling to say more. The echo of his coughing came down the hall.

Hillary sat at his desk for a long while, staring out the narrow window. The sun had gone down, but the afterglow reflected on the river—the same picture he had seen the night of the ball. He lighted a candle and set to work finishing a letter which he had started to Cecelia. He wrote that he would soon be returning to Manor House and would speak to her father for her hand in marriage. He sealed the letter. Again he looked out to the river.

What a strange little man Edwards was, he thought. Alone, ill, working desperately for the Governor on this final campaign, he would surely kill himself. Could he want that? What longing drove him on? Ah, surely it was the hope that after going to New York he might return to England with the Governor—return in a certain minor glory, receive the plaudits and preferment of the home Government, a certain recognition that would of course come to the attention of his wife and children. No, why give the man credit for loyalty, when it was certainly a selfishness, a fulfilling of his own desires, that was carrying him to the brink of death? Well enough, that was his own business.

Hillary tucked the letter to Cecelia in his pocket. He stood up and stretched. There would be no more of this for him! He was through with the office forever, and through with deceit. The good Lord knew there was no lie, no hate, no war in planting. No, in earth there was a touch of heaven.

He walked idly to Edwards' desk, saw an open letter, and curiously, almost before he knew it, he glanced over its contents. He thought it strange that Edwards had not given it to him to copy. It was from William Tryon to Colonel Fanning.

My Dear Colonel:
In recognition of your support through the ordeal of the mob which was about to march on the Palace, I give you my warmest thanks. You believed in me and stood with me when the hounds of the Assembly were in full cry. Your loyalty shall not go unrewarded.

My appointment as His Majesty's Governor of the Province of New York is official. I should consider it an honour to have you accompany me to that Province as my assistant and secretary.

Mr. Edwards, my loyal assistant through these trying years, has accepted his dismissal with an attitude con-

sistent with his unfailing devotion. I have, of course, promised to give him the best of recommendations to the new Governor of this Province. There are some hopes that he may meet with approval. He will accompany me on the campaign against the Regulators as his last official service to me.

From our words together, my good Colonel, I am led to believe that you will not refuse my offer. Therefore, you may make your plans accordingly. On your return from Wilmington we shall put in train our plan to pacify the Province of North Carolina, and embark for New York thereafter.

William Tryon

Hillary dropped the letter on the desk; he lowered his hands slowly to his sides.

A recommendation! That was the only recompense the Governor was offering to the one man who had served him faithfully, sacrificially, without question.

Hillary sat down on the bench between the desks. Isaac Edwards was to be dismissed—but only after he had succeeded in killing himself on a final campaign. Now he obeyed Tryon's orders to his own destruction in the face of dismissal.

Hillary frowned as he looked out to the darkened River Trent. He took off his jacket slowly. He realized that he had not been just to Isaac Edwards. He could not leave him in the lurch. He drew the letter to Cecelia from his pocket and deliberately tore it into pieces. He would have to write another and explain to her that he must follow the Governor for one more month. There would be no point in telling her why he had made this choice; she would have to understand that he did not wish to stay with Tryon. She would have to understand by herself that he had no other course.

Hillary stepped into the hallway and called to a servant, "Will you see that they bring some dinner up here to me?"

"Yes, sar, Mr. Caswell," came the reply.

Hillary entered the room again, took the file on the Regulator leaders from Edwards' desk and carried it to his own. He opened it slowly, checking the papers one by one. This was the packet the Governor would want to carry with him on the march. He would save Edwards a little work.

He completed the file just before the clock struck midnight. He had resolved to write the letter to Cecelia in his own room. The office was a maddening place; the knowledge that he must continue work for a Governor whom he despised dismayed him the more the longer he thought about it. His bitterness was sharpened by the realization that Edwards was not only a loyal man, but a loyal fool. So he should be saved from himself. Hillary walked through the quiet streets, still brooding on the character of Isaac Edwards. He strayed for a while along the River Trent in spite of the lateness of the hour. It was then he realized why there had been the sudden bitter outburst from Edwards when he had asked him, "Are you trying to kill yourself?"

The answer might have been quite simply, "Yes. I am." It would have been the truth.

Hillary threw a pebble into the River Trent. How Edwards must have felt himself deserted! How lonely he must be now! Because of his foolish loyalty and his frailty he had more often than not gone against his own convictions. Now he was without those convictions, and without friends.

But it was not right to leave a man alone to his final weakness.

Hillary returned to his room, tiptoeing up the steps, carefully avoiding the ones that creaked. He was tired to the very bone, sick of his own confusion. The last shred of illusion about Tryon was gone.

When he lighted the candle on the dresser he saw that a note had been propped against the mirror. He opened it with curiosity, glanced first at the end, and saw in surprise that it was signed by Charity Allen.

Friend Hillary, Thee must have wondered why I signalled thee not to show recognition of me at the gaol. It was for thy own protection. There seemed no other way to ensure thy safety, and I could never stand to see thee harmed.

We decided that it must be I to take Harmon's place in the gaol. He objected, but we were able to convince him that no harm could befall a woman. A man might be beaten, or left forever in that dismal place.

The very kind officer, Lieutenant Bartleson, after leading me into the gaol, unlocked the side door. He occupied a Mr. Hodkins until Isaac Cox was able to see me safely on my way.

I should have liked so much to see thee again, but it was not to be. If thee should ever think on me, thee need have no fear. I return to England to complete my work for the Lord.

I value thy friendship, Hillary, and can never forget how thee brought me through the floods.

The moment has passed between us. My work is now for the Lord. I pray for thee, Friend Hillary. If I have seen a meaning in the stars, thee will not laugh at me again, for yet I pray for thee.

                                                   Charity Allen

He folded the letter and placed it on the desk. He knew that Charity had written the truth: they would not meet again. It had been a tender moment, and had passed. Now the work of the Lord would lead her through strange paths alone, perhaps into a darkness, but perhaps into a glorious light.

It was in the early hours of the morning when he finally began again the letter to Cecelia Chapman. He told her of Charity, and of his own feelings—he could do no less.

Tired, discouraged, dimly aware of all that had transpired, groping in shadows of love and regret, of knowledge of the things life denies, of foreboding of the battle ahead of him, at last he laid his head down on the desk and went to sleep even as the candle guttered, even as a bird of dawn began to sing.

31

To the West

The *Laughing Girl* lay waiting for a breeze at the mouth of the Scuppernong. The schooner had slipped down the Neuse unmolested and headed northwards up Pamlico Sound. In the Albemarle, Robin had got his passengers out of sight and risked putting in at Edenton. There his father had sent word he was to bring the schooner home. Edenton was buzzing with discussion of the events at New Bern, and several people told him about Tryon's plans to march on the Regulators of the West.

Robin Chapman was depressed by the news. He realized that the Eastern men were solidly behind the Governor, but his own resolve was to support the Regulators.

Two days before, while still out in Pamlico Sound, he had told Enos Dye which side he would be on if it came to fighting, and Dye had immediately voiced a painful thought. "I suppose it's already occurred to you, Captain, but with the East behind Tryon, you'll be fighting your own kin."

"It has occurred to me."

"Just wondered."

"I know . . . there'll be Richard Caswell, Hillary—though he may not stay with the Governor." He paused, not wishing to pursue the list of his relatives. After a moment's thought he added, "Won't Adam Rutledge be forced to follow the Governor? He's an officer in the militia. How are you going to feel, Enos, going against him?"

"I didn't say I would."

"You didn't have to. You will," Robin said wearily.

Enos scratched his ear. "Yes, I suppose so. There's nothing else I can do."

Harmon Husband had come onto the deck at that point in the conversation. Sleep and good food from the galley had made a change in him. It was a peculiar change. The return of health and spirits seemed to have turned his mind wholly to faith in the divine Spirit: the Regulators were broken bits of the past. When told that Tryon was going to march on the Western people he had merely nodded, and said, "I knew it would come to this. I felt it in my heart."

Sitting on the deck, he listened quietly to their conversation. Now and then he would write an entry in his leather-bound journal; more often than not, however, he would be reading his Bible, a book worn with the use of many years.

Enos Dye shifted his position on the deck, trying to make himself comfortable. "Now, Robin," he said, "just how do you plan to get Harmon back to Orange?"

"I thought we could let Matthew Caswell choose our path. He should know the best way."

Dye laughed. "A farmer, a captain and a preacher cutting through the woods. Aye, we'll make a good three!"

"There'll be horses down at the shipyards," Robin said. "We can use them to reach Manor House. I'd rather you waited there until I make certain the path is clear."

"And we'll leave immediately after that?"

"To-night, I hope."

Dye rapped his knuckles on the rail. "It would be our luck to meet Tryon's men on the march."

"Hardly this soon. Anyway, so far the luck's been good."

Enos Dye looked at Husband, who had just closed his Bible. "You know, Harmon, if we *do* meet any of the Governor's men there'll more than likely be violence. I've no mind to be captured."

"Enos, all violence is wrong and worthless."

"Aye, Harmon. I won't disagree with you. But sometimes a man can't avoid it. Just like us. We'll all be marching with the Regulators soon."

It seemed a long time before Harmon Husband spoke. At last he said softly, "I shan't be marching with the Regulators, Enos. I cannot."

Enos looked up quickly. "You don't mean that, Harmon."

"With all my heart and soul."

Enos spoke reproachfully, "Now, see here, Harmon. That's no way to go talking. I figure you had a fairly good hand in starting all this, and it just isn't right to go quitting in the middle. Those men are going to expect you to be with them. You're going to have to fight."

"I don't believe in fighting."

"You're just going to take the easy way out?"

"It's a much more difficult path than yours, Enos." Harmon paused. "I know what they'll think of me. I've still the curse of pride in me, Enos. Do you think I want to hear the words that will be said about me? Do you think I'll be happy to know that my old friends are friends no more? That they'll mark me down a fool, a coward and a deserter, and think my words were windy nothings because I would not stay to fight? I don't believe in their wars. I believe in the Spirit, and the Spirit has taught me my way of peace." He shrugged his shoulders. "What should the thoughts of man be to me? Should I fight, and be a coward in the eyes of God? No, I cannot."

Harmon had looked out to the half-visible shore, and when he spoke again it was as though he were ending a dispute with himself, one that he had waged silently and for a long time in his soul. ". . . so I went on squabbling with my playmates when I was young and put off doing what was right and good and true. I put off living as the Spirit commanded me, and I lived my animal youth. Each day I said I would correct myself, that when my short youth was done, why, then I would become good, and then I would act as the divine Spirit commanded me. I told myself that when I came to my age I would follow Truth. . . ."

"You prick yourself too much," Robin said. "Your religion is too demanding for plain men."

"Religion is difficult for *all* men. There is no easy path."

Enos Dye had been slightly angered when he heard Harmon was not going to fight for his people. He had wanted to argue, but restrained himself. Finally he said, " 'Tis a difficult thing. Each man has his own idea of that good and truth of which you speak, Harmon."

"True, friend, very true." Harmon adjusted the Bible on his lap. "One time there was a Presbyterian minister who came to my grandfather's house when I was young. He said to me, 'Say the Lord's Prayer for me, child.' I did so, and he was pleased. Then he said, "Repeat the Hundredth Psalm, child." Again I did as I was told, and he said, 'Ah, perfect to the word! You're a very good child. You love God.' I was not a good child. I knew the passages word-perfect, but I knew nothing of the Spirit."

"Now, Harmon," Enos said, "you can't expect too much of a child. Anyway, the minister was just complimenting himself because he knew them too."

"And, Harmon, you know a minister is searching all through his life just like the rest of us," Robin said. "They're foolish and human, too, or they wouldn't be here with us."

"You just expect too much from a child," Enos said again.

"Then when am I a man? Even as a young lad I knew that I was not 'good' because I knew the prayer and the psalm, but I continued to delay in seeking the Spirit. I put things off. I would say, 'Monday I shall be good.' But Tuesday came, and I was no different. There are always Tuesdays. And so it went."

They all fell silent. Robin's hands on the wheel were light and gentle. He loved the pull of the sea. He breathed deeply of the salt air. With a deck under his feet and a fair breeze, he supposed he would always be contented. Harmon worried a lot. As the comfortable silence stretched out, Robin wondered idly whether Harmon would have taken things less hard if he had followed the sea.

"A man *must* seek the Spirit," Harmon began again. "There is nothing else in this life."

Robin Chapman had no choice but to leave Harmon and Enos at the shipyards while he rode to Manor House to speak with Matthew Caswell. Husband was a hunted man, and his very presence in a home threatened the welfare of his hosts.

Matthew Caswell was in his study reading a pamphlet by a Scotsman, Adam Smith, and scribbling notes in the margin. But when Robin entered, he quickly put the book aside.

Robin told the full story of the New Bern affair, and Matthew listened without comment until the end. Then he lighted his pipe as he always did before discussing a problem. He puffed slowly, thoughtfully. At length he asked, "How does this man Husband impress you personally—out of all association with the movement he represents? I know where your sympathies fall, and I don't want them mixed in with your judgement. Is he honest? Is he sincere? Or does he just qualify as a talented fanatic? We don't hear the best things about him, you know."

Robin's thin, ascetic face was serious. He ran his fingers through his brown hair. "I can answer 'yes' to the first and second questions. He's honest and sincere. As for his being a fanatic—I suppose some might call him that. But to me the word always suggests some violence or extravagance in the person's nature. There's none in Harmon's. So what can I call him? A Quaker in his love of peace, though the Quakers have expelled him. A mystic. He's torn by some inner fire, but it never flares into violence, or any desire for it."

"Where is he now? At the yards, you say?"

"Yes. Enos Dye is with him."

"And I take it that you want me to meet him?"

Robin smiled. "I do—but I couldn't bring him without asking you first. You know he's hunted by Tryon now."

"Of course." Matthew waved his hand.

"I intend to help him on his journey back to his

Sandy Creek plantation. If you've any ideas about the best route—the one where we're least likely to meet any of Fanning's men—I'd like to have them."

"I can help you with that," Matthew said. "Why don't you ride back to the yards now and send Husband and Dye here? You can visit your mother before you return. If you're really set on going to Sandy Creek, it would be best to have done with it quickly. You'll want to travel at night, of course?"

"Yes."

Matthew nodded. He had asked no more questions, for he suspected that Robin might become yet more deeply involved with the Regulators. He did not pose the problem as Enos Dye had done aboard the *Laughing Girl*. . . .

Robin directed Dye and Husband to Manor House and then rode on to his own home. It was as he knew it would be—his mother was reluctant to let him go west, but in the end he persuaded her that it was the only thing for him to do.

"Cecelia will be back to-morrow," she said. "That will be a help anyway. And the lads ought to return from New Bern within the week. I have some news I might tell you." There was a lightness in her voice.

"Do tell me," Robin said.

"No. It can wait until you return. It won't be more than ten days, will it? I worry so for you." She had been about to tell him that Cecelia had confided before she went to visit the Spruills that Hillary had asked her to marry him. Ah, but she had promised to say nothing of it, so she kept silence.

"Is it good news?"

"Of course it is," she said. Her smile was gay. "Do I ever have any other?"

"No. You're the best woman in the world for that." She paused. "But I *am* loath to lose you."

"To lose me?" he said with surprise.

"I lose you when you go to sea. I lose Joseph when he leaves. I wonder if I shall ever have the peace of knowing that all my children are safe and at home."

"One at a time we return, Mother," he said lightly.

"For how long?" He detected a sad note, an almost bitter tone in her voice. "They are already talking of war to come—not just with the West, but with the Crown itself. Is there truth in that, Robin? Tell me."

"I don't know, Mother. I don't know."

"I pray every night that God will not let us come to war with England. England is our mother, and we are her children."

"Wayward children. Wayward as I. But you forgive me, don't you?"

"I love you."

As he kissed his mother good-bye he was shocked by the lightness of her body. A surge of deep feeling came over him. How uncomplaining she was, she who was always hurt to be left behind. His father was on the sea half the year, and now there were his own frequent voyages since he had a ship of his own.

She pressed her cheek against his. "Oh, Robin, Robin, you'll never know how much I can hate the sea!"

He left her and rode back to Manor House, a heaviness within him that he could not dispel, no matter how hard he concentrated on the rightness of his plans. As he entered Manor House and saw the three men bending over a map, the vague feeling came to him that there were forces stronger than truth, better than right.

The men greeted him and then resumed their study of the map. Matthew was saying, ". . . well north of the road from New Bern to Hillsborough. Follow Fishing Creek through Halifax. You can cut south about here—" Matthew's finger touched the map—"and pass to the west of Hillsborough."

"It seems the best route," Dye said. "We know houses where Harmon will be safely hidden. We can draw near Sandy Creek, but we can't go directly there. Fanning will have his men watching."

"You've decided then?" Robin asked.

"This should work out fairly well," Matthew said. "It is imperative that you be on your way, though. Tryon's sergeants were in Tyrrell yesterday trying to muster men."

"They'll get none here," Robin said. "The Governor will have to rely on the South and Fanning's few men in the West. The East won't support him in this war."

Matthew shook his head. "I think you're wrong, Robin. They may not like to, but they will support him. You'll see." He was positive.

Husband had moved away from the map, seeming inattentive, careless of his own safety, as if his thoughts were on some faraway land. He examined the books in Matthew's library, caressing them lovingly with his fingers.

"It should be dark within the hour," Matthew said. "I've sent Eb to pack food for you. I'd imagine you could start this first portion of your journey as soon as you wish."

"Sooner the better," Enos Dye said.

"Then the horses are waiting."

Matthew put his hand on the collar of an old hound who had gone eagerly to the door. "You're not going, Puddles. Back to the fire for you!" The dog turned and went back to the fire, tail wagging slowly.

Dye and Husband mounted their horses immediately, but Robin lingered a moment. "Did you see, Uncle, why I *must* go with him?"

"I understand," Matthew said. "There *are* people who have to be protected."

"Then you felt the same as I about him?"

"Perhaps. He spoke about the Regulators and their aims, but I rather think the aims were his own. It gives me pause. His dream of a man's right to be free is different from mine. He may have gone farther, or he may only have gone in a different direction. Who's to say?"

The morning was fine and the air balmy five days later when the travellers arrived at the caves beyond Maddock's Mill. Their journey had been without event. Enos Dye had made several attempts during the long ride to convince Harmon that his place was beside the Regulators. Husband had only shaken his head. Finally Enos had dropped the matter.

Robin Chapman rode on to Sandy Creek. When Amy Husband met him at the doorway of her home, she said before he could speak, "Thee brought Harmon."

It was a statement, not a question, but he answered, "Yes."

"And we're leaving Sandy Creek?"

"They've decided it's the only safe thing to do."

"I understand. I understand."

"He's near Maddock's Mill. He'll need some clothes and provisions for a time."

Amy immediately set about packing a few clothes and possessions, and within the hour the two of them were riding back along the trail. The woods were starred with the waxwhite blossoms of the dogwood. Cardinals flashed scarlet through the trees, and mockingbirds broke the silence of the forest. The green of the pines and the deep pink of the redbud flared through the land.

Amy Husband sighed. "God has given us a world of beauty, but we've turned the paradise into a devil's forest."

"Do you know where Harmon wants to go now?" Robin asked. "With the proclamation of treason against him there'll be nowhere in North Carolina that's safe."

"I don't know. I'll follow him."

"To Maryland, perhaps. He's mentioned that Province."

"Oh, it would be good to go to Maryland! . . . It would be good to stay here. I think Harmon would stay at Sandy Creek if it weren't that the others want him to leave. He'd never fight, but he would stand and face them."

"And it would accomplish nothing," Robin said.

On the slope of clear ground ahead he could see the mill, and beyond it the hills where Husband and Enos Dye had made their camp. On their last night's stop, a Friend had warned them that even the mill was not safe, but that the caves beyond would afford good shelter.

"I know thee is right," Amy said to Robin. "It would be for nothing. They would kill him. Isaac Cox told me he'd make certain Harmon left. He's a kind man; he can talk to Harmon."

Isaac Cox, his brother and Enos Dye were waiting at the mouth of one of the caves. Harmon sat a short distance from them, brooding and alone. Without a word he got to his feet the moment he saw Amy, and he held out his arms as she went to him.

At night they built a small fire by the cave, and the men made their plans for Harmon. They had already decided against his going to Maryland, for he might not be safe there. They looked out over the trees of the hillside to the broad valley and the gently rising hills beyond, hills burning in the moonlight. Beyond the Piedmont in the darkness were the high slopes of the Virginia mountains. It was into that country Husband must go first.

At midnight Hiram Whitlock arrived with a woodsman named Allan Brackett. Whitlock drew a map in the earth with a stick from the fire which still smouldered. "You'll take this direction, Isaac. It's an old Indian trail. It follows a little stream called the Eno. That'll give you plenty of water, and you shouldn't meet any people along there. Later on, you might."

Cox tapped the pocket of his shirt. "I've a pass from Fanning's office which might serve some good. We've one friend there, you know."

Robin noted that Husband was staring at the bright moon and the stars dimmed by its brilliance. Amy was leaning her head on his shoulder. Robin wondered what Husband was thinking: of a new earth to make blossom like the rose, of the new world where the Lord could come to His kingdom in triumph? It was enough to know that this was his Gethsemane.

Toward morning Amy Husband left to return to Sandy Creek, guided by Whitlock. Isaac Cox and his brother had gone to find horses and more provisions for the long journey ahead.

The stars were gone. The sky was washed with dawn; a pale light from the east flooded the sky. Robin and Enos sat by the dying embers, waiting for the other men to return, and for Husband's final departure. Again Harmon sat alone. When he spoke, it was to neither of them, but to something that filled the morning beyond their eyes.

"Will all think that I leave because I fear? I do not fear. I do not fear. And I must be called fool and coward? . . . There is no other way."

When Isaac Cox returned with the horses and final

provisions, and when he and Husband had disappeared down the trail into the forest, Robin stood by the fire and reflected.

How strange were the separate paths of men! Harmon must vanish northward from a battle that his words and spirit had inflamed; and he, Robin, must stay and fight in that battle against his own friends and kinsmen.

Drums thundered.

Governor William Tryon of the Province of North Carolina rode to the head of the militia. The bands were playing; banners and flags were flying.

The Governor's lady and Miss Esther Wake were on horseback, their long velvet skirts caught by the wind. They had ridden ahead to the point where the road turned westward. And when the militia reached that turn, the Governor reined his horse to one side and dropped out of the formation to bid them farewell.

"You look glorious, William, every inch the noble soldier," Lady Tryon said proudly.

Esther Wake laughed. They did not catch the irony in her tone when she said, "You make a very brave show, William. One only wishes, though, that all this weren't so necessary."

The Governor kissed his wife's hand. "I thank you, my dear," he said. "There is little enough glory to be earned in overmastering a crowd of untaught yokels. But these Orange rebles require a sharp lesson, and I shall administer one they'll not soon forget."

Esther Wake asked, "May we begin our packing, William? I long to be on the voyage to New York."

The Governor smiled at her. "Everything is arranged, my dear. As soon as this unpleasantness is behind me we will sail on one of Mr. Cornell's ships."

"I praise God for our leaving," Lady Tryon said. "After a twelve-month in this muddy village, New York will seem almost as civil as London. It will do me good to see officers in red coats in my drawing-room once more."

The Governor lingered a moment longer, watching the columns of militiamen march down the dusty April road. "Red coats! I swear you're right, my dear. I long to command men who can march smartly. Then for the three of us let me say 'Praise God, the King and the Earl of Hillsborough!' "

He turned his horse to ride toward the head of the troops, but his wife detained him. "William, even the King will be most interested in the outcome of this march. Be just but not over-generous to your lieutenants. Remember, victory belongs to the General in Command, not to Fanning nor the Assemblymen like Caswell nor anyone else. To you, William Tryon."

The Governor smiled, sat taller in his saddle, his shoulders and head erect. His face set in sterner lines. He was immensely conscious of the cheering people who lined the road. "My dear, I shan't forget that something is owing to William Tryon."

From the roadside came a few scattered cheers of "God save the King!"

Tryon cantered to put himself in the vanguard.

"God save them all!" Esther Wake said. "They'll need His protection."

Lady Tryon did not hear the words. Her eyes were on her husband. He made such a brave show!

32

On the March

On April 23, 1771, the troops of Governor Tryon, pennons and banners unfurled to the wind, drums beating, began their long march to the rendezvous at Smith's Ferry and thence to Hillsborough. From the south, General Hugh Waddell led the Cape Fear militia; the plan of campaign was for his troops to march to Salisbury and discourage the Rowan Regulators from taking part in the insurrection. Then they would join Tryon at Hillsborough.

Tryon's militiamen did not reach Hillsborough until May 9, and their total number was only slightly more than a thousand. The Governor was disappointed by the small muster of his force. The bounty of forty shillings had not been enough to lure more. Of a consequence, he was in a foul humour.

"You'd think it was sinning against my countrymen to save them," he told Adam Rutledge.

"Perhaps we feel little need to be saved, Your Excellency."

"*You* feel that way, don't you, Rutledge?"

"I feel there's a need to preserve order, sir. If that's the true purpose of our march, I'm satisfied."

Tryon snapped to an orderly, "Is my tent ready?"

"Yes, sir."

He returned to Adam: "Pray tell, Colonel Rutledge, what other purpose would there be?"

"I'm sure I don't know, sir."

A lone rider galloped down the road, dust rising into

shafts of sunlight. A captain in charge of the guard about Tryon's headquarters intercepted him, took his dispatch case and hurried into the broad tent which had been stretched by the roadside. The Governor stalked after him. A moment later an orderly said to Adam, "Colonel Rutledge, the Governor would see you after your meal, sir."

Adam nodded wearily. He noted how quickly the sun fell behind the mountains, then strode past the guard to his mount. He had made camp a quarter of a mile down the road.

"Adam!" He turned at the call to see Dr. Armitage dismounting. "Stay a moment. You'd as well come to my camp for dinner. I take it you're coming back here immediately after."

"Kind of you, Doctor." Adam waited impatiently while Armitage finished writing a list of ailments the men had and the names of those too sick for duty.

Up and down the dusty road cooking fires gleamed in the dusk. To how many of the men, Adam speculated, was it merely a forty-shilling march? Would they have felt differently going out after Indians? Did it disturb them now to be in arms against men very like themselves, people they might have rubbed elbows with around the Governor's barbecue pits at New Bern, and who used the very same words to complain about taxes?

At another camp fire Hillary Caswell was asking himself the same sort of questions. He had loyally stayed close to Edwards during the long way to Hillsborough. He had taken on most of the work: making a dozen copies of the orders of march, compiling inventories of the equipment, writing a multitude of letters, dispatches and memoranda, and taking care of the records the Governor wanted kept. He had snatched only a few hours' sleep each night, and the strain was beginning to tell on him. The work seemed for nought: Edwards' health steadily declined.

They used a rough wood table for writing, for meals and, more often than not, for a place to rest their weary heads a few minutes. Some days that was their only rest. Hillary saw to it that their meagre equipment was loaded each morning and unloaded each night from the rude Devon cart assigned to them.

He had just finished his evening meal at the Hillsborough encampment when Edwards returned from the Governor's headquarters with another handful of orders to be copied and sent to the various commanders. Edwards dismounted slowly, his face pale, and walked to the table. He slumped down on a three-legged stool, eyed his meal with distaste, put his head in his hands, and murmured, "God's blood, will that man ever slow down?"

Hillary knew perfectly well to whom he referred, but in his own state of exhaustion he was given to answering rhetorical questions. "The Governor?"

"Aye! William Tryon. These orders must be out by midnight. How much sleep have *you* been getting?"

"If there's sleep about to spare, I'll take it."

"There's little to spare."

Edwards bent forward to his food, wolfed it down as if his life were measured in seconds.

"Have they heard from General Waddell yet?" Hillary asked. "He should be on his way to meet us by now."

"Heard to-day. Messenger said he left Salisbury with about two hundred men."

Edwards began coughing violently as he had so often in the past few days.

Hillary could feel the raking pain in his own chest. "My Lord, wash it down with some water," he said, shoving his mug toward him.

When the coughing stopped, Edwards wiped his eyes with a large handkerchief. "Do you think you can keep this pace and even speed up a little more?"

"I doubt it. Do I have to?"

"You may. I've been feeling worse. I may not go with you when we leave for Hillsborough. I might have to stay here." There was exhaustion in his tone.

Hillary pushed his stool from the crude board table. The night was brilliant with stars. He could hear the laughter of the men in the camps by the roadside. He saw the twinkling of a hundred small fires like a bridge

across the flat of the land—fires of comfort. Somewhere
in the brush a group was singing an old Scotch ballad.

"You'd think those men were going to war, would
you?"

Edwards did not answer.

Hillary tried again. "Listen to them! Do they know
they're marching to fight their countrymen?" Edwards
would usually answer on the second query, but this time
he did not. Hillary was slightly annoyed that he should
break a pattern.

Isaac Edwards had slumped forward at the table. His
arm dangled down and his fingers touched the ground.
His mouth was open. His eyes were shut. His breath
came in short gasps. His face was like carved ivory.

Hillary ran to the table. He put one arm about his
shoulders, the other under his legs and carried him
quickly to his blankets. He loosened his tight-fitting
jacket. He called to him, but there was no answer—only
short gasps. Hillary was painfully reminded of fish that
died in his father's aquarium, their bodies floating, their
mouths half in the water, gasping for something neither
air nor water could give them.

"Soldier! Soldier!" Hillary shouted toward the fire
on the opposite side of the road.

After a moment's hesitation the sleepy reply came:
"Aye, what do you want?"

"Sick man here! Give me some help. Quick!"

A young, red-bearded private strolled across the road.
He was scratching his side. "What ya got there?"

Hillary motioned to the cot. "Governor's secretary.
Very ill. I'm going to fetch the doctor. Watch him, and
don't let him try to get up."

The soldier had stepped to the cot and looked curiously at the figure of Edwards. He scratched his neck.
" 'Pears he's jest sleepin.' "

"Look at him again, soldier," Hillary said as he
swung onto his mount. A slight trickle of blood came
from Edwards' mouth.

"Well—" the private scratched his ear—"maybe
you're right."

By that time Hillary was off, cantering down the road

toward the Governor's tent and Dr. Armitage at the head of the line.

The small camp fires, the men laughing and singing along the road, the light guard about the brass cannon, all made the thought of war impossible. This was a comic play, Hillary thought, much like pieces he had seen on the London stage, with a little make-believe thunder. A farce of war. But a careless playwright had unfortunately sketched in a line of tragedy by mistake.

The Governor's tent was the one well-guarded spot along the road. Only there was Hillary challenged—by a much too eager young militiaman who seemed bent on shooting someone, no matter who; he must make the world aware he was a soldier of importance. The guard, though he remembered Hillary, would not let him pass without a small storm of officiousness.

He found Dr. Armitage and Adam Rutledge standing by the fire outside the Governor's tent, and he explained quickly what had happened.

"It could be almost anything," Armitage said. "A black humour? Who can say? By the Lord, I'd not be surprised, though. What *can't* happen here?" He motioned to one of the messengers who waited by the tent. "Bring my mount!"

"Edwards! Edwards! Is that he?" The voice of William Tryon sounded impatiently from the tent.

A second later the flap was opened and a captain, his countenance angry, glared into the darkness. "Is that you, Edwards? The Governor wants you immediately."

"He's not here," Hillary said. "He has collapsed at his tent. We're sending the doctor now."

"Who are you?"

"His assistant, Hillary Caswell."

The name Caswell softened the captain's tone. "Oh, I see. Will you wait there? I'll see if the Governor can use you instead."

By now Dr. Armitage had mounted his horse and started it toward the road.

"Who goes there?" the officious young guard called out.

"Armitage. Keep blocking the road and I'll run you down."

The guard must have jumped clear. The sound of hoofs diminished in the night. Hillary joined Adam Rutledge, who was standing with feet wide apart at the fringe of the fire. "I don't understand this," he said tiredly.

"Is there anything in particular?" Adam asked kindly. "Or are you just discouraged about the entire affair?"

"The whole thing, I suppose."

"Try getting more sleep. It's the only thing one can do—even if dreams do disturb you."

"But the purpose in this? There's no point to it that I can see," Hillary objected.

Adam put his hand to his cheek. "No. But the Governor *will* have his little war. A few lives—a cheap price for glory, don't you think?"

Hillary sat down on a log at the edge of the camp fire. "And we support him," he said bitterly.

"That we do. How else would you have it? I'd rather not be branded as a traitor. One's either tricked or forced into this . . . or bought with a trifling bounty. For myself, Hillary, I intend to make something of this country long after Tryon has passed. I can wait—angrily, I'll grant—but I can wait."

Hillary picked up a stick and dug it into the ground. "Look at the lights along the road," he said.

"Not too many," Adam said. "There'll be twice as many in the Regulator camp."

"If we knew where they were."

"West of Hillsborough," Adam said simply. "So it's reported, and they're strong in that area. I doubt if they'll move far. And if they do, they won't move fast."

"But to fight our own people—and fight them over nothing!" Hillary shook his head. "I pray the Lord I don't know any of them."

"Does that make killing easier?"

"Certainly. Certainly it does. Without knowing them I can pretend they're animals. The Governor *believes* they're animals . . . there's our difference."

"Perhaps."

"But I *do* know them. There are Howell and Husband. One saved my life and the other gave me shelter. My God, I hope there are no more!"

"Look at it merely as crushing a rebellion," Adam said. Then he laughed bitterly. "No, I don't ask you to do that. I can't even see it that way myself."

Again the hoofbeats.

"Who goes there?"

Hillary looked through the glaze of fire-light. Adam stepped to one side and shielded his eyes.

The voices were rough. "Yank him off! No, wait his hands are tied."

"Who gives a damn? He's a Regulator, ain't he?"

"Call the sergeant of the guard!"

"There ain't none. Here! Give me a hand."

A scuffle of feet, another shout. A corporal came from the opposite side of the road. Two men waiting in front of the Governor's tent left their places quickly. The figures were dim in the fire-light. The new guards held the reins of the horses which now stamped nervously in the road. Two riders dismounted and a third was pulled down from his horse. His hands were tied behind him. The guards grabbed him by the arms, one on either side, and half dragged him past the fire and to the tent. A moment later the flap was opened and they were admitted.

"He looked like a young boy," Hillary said.

"You mean a young prisoner," Adam said. "From now till the finish we make no distinction in age."

Again the tent flap was pulled back by the captain. "Colonel Rutledge, the Governor would see you now, sir. Caswell, you come along, too. You'll have to take Edward's place."

The tent was wide and deep. Lanthorns were set on either side of the Governor's desk which was directly opposite the flap. Tryon sat with his hands clasped on the table before him. His eyes were dark circles from lack of sleep. His face was stern; his mouth a straight line of anger. To his left, at a smaller table, sat Richard Caswell; and to his right at another narrow table, a duplicate of the first, were Colonels Edgerton and Barton. A slim-faced lieutenant stood behind them.

The captain had just given his report to the Governor.

He motioned Hillary to the table next to Richard Caswell. "Take down everything His Excellency commands." It seemed a rather superfluous order. Adam Rutledge took a chair next to Colonel Barton.

The two privates who had brought in the prisoner stood to one side of the entrance-way, keeping firm grip on the boy's arms. The lad was dishevelled, mud-stained, his hair hanging loose from its queue. His face was pale, and his eyes were wide with fright.

"Speak up, private!" Tryon snapped. "You say the prisoner's so damned important. What's to be said?"

"Sir, I was scouting with the advance party. We found ourselves a few chickens, and this one—" he motioned with his thumb—"was trying to hide in a tree. So we plucked him down and sort of encouraged him to talk to us." The private grinned. "He says he's been a-riding a piece. And he tells us some men with burned cork on their faces stopped Colonel Waddell's ammunition wagon and blew them up. Did it just the other night, sir. Just afore the place where them Regulators is holdin' up the Colonel's army."

"God's death!" Tryon said quietly. His face reddened in anger. He circled his desk and approached the young prisoner. Suddenly he grabbed the boy by the shoulder and shook him violently. His voice boomed out: "What's this about a powder train? Speak up! Speak up, you fool!"

The lad struggled to keep his lips from trembling. His mouth opened to speak, but no words came forth. He was in a state of mortal fright.

"Damn you! *Will* you talk?"

Words came tumbling out. "True, sir. It's true, I swear by the holy evangelists of Almighty God. Colonel Waddell—his army—held back by the——"

"Damn! I know that. Tell me of the powder train. Can't you hear me?"

"I hear you, sir, I mean to. . . ."

"Colonel Caswell," the Governor said, "question this idiot. I'm too angry. And you—" he motioned to Hillary—"take it all down."

Richard Caswell went to the boy. "Let the prisoner sit down on that stool," he said to the guards.

The first guard gave the boy a shove. He stumbled. Richard caught him and helped him to the stool. He noticed that the lad's hands were still tied. "Cut the bonds," he ordered.

The guard seemed reluctant. "I said *cut the bonds,* Private."

A long-bladed hunting knife flashed and the cords fell to the earthen floor. The boy looked like a small, frightened animal, wide-eyed, shoulders hunched forward, his hands rubbing his wrists.

"What's your name, boy?" Richard asked.

"James Ashmore, sir."

Richard pulled a chair from the table and sat down close to the youngster. "Now, Ashmore, we want you to tell us exactly what happened to the powder train."

The lad hesitated. He saw the Governor's scowl, and the way he clenched his fists on his hips.

"Yes, sir. It was on Andrew Logan's plantation, sir. An advertisement . . . there was an advertisement to meet there. And I went because most of my friends said they were going . . . and then there was this man— that's the one who was at Logan's place—and he asked me if I thought there would . . ."

"What was the man's name, Ashmore?" Richard Caswell's voice was kindly but firm.

"James White, Junior, sir."

"And what did he want?" Richard asked.

"And he asked me if I thought there'd be any harm in burning some powder that the militia was bringing through. He said his father was with the Regulators and he thought he could help save him some harm."

"Are you getting all of this?" Tryon demanded of Hillary.

"Yes, sir. I'm getting it all," Hillary said. He knew that a "Yes, sir" would have been enough, but somehow those additional words let him feel that he had expressed his growing hatred of Tryon.

"Go on," Richard prompted.

"Well, I said I didn't think burning the powder was any harm. I guessed it was better than leaving it 'bout to kill people with."

"I don't want your philosophy. Just tell your damned story," Tryon stormed.

Richard Caswell twisted in his chair to look at the Governor. His eyebrows were raised. "Do you want me to question this man, sir?"

"Continue," Tryon said evenly, trying to control his impatience.

"I went home after the meeting, and then they came and got me the next day."

"Who are 'they'?" Richard asked.

"The fellows from around home who'd smeared burned cork on their faces—I guess to look like Indians or something. I don't know. I'm not sure, but they called 'emselves the 'black boys of Carrabust.' "

"What were their names?" Richard asked patiently.

"Must I tell you, sir?" the lad implored.

"The names!" Tryon snapped. "The names, or I'll have you whipped."

For the first time the young boy raised his eyes to meet the Governor's. "I can stand that, sir. I've been whipped before."

"By God, not like the whipping I'll give you!"

"Your Excellency, I'll ask once more: do you want me to finish this interrogation, or not?"

"Finish."

Caswell turned again to Ashmore. "Never mind the names. You can tell them to us later. Now we want to hear what happened."

"Well, I said I'd go with them. I didn't want to at first, but they were all my friends. So we went to a little rocky place about half a mile from my house. Oh, we stopped once to take Joshua Hadley with us."

Tryon caught Hillary's eye and raised one finger to note the name.

"Anyway, when we'd all got together there were nine of us. And we made sure the cork was good and thick on our faces and we went to Captain Phillips' muster ground. Well, the wagons were there and I guess we sort of scared away the guards. Then we got the powder."

"What did you do then?"

"You won't do anything to Joshua, will you? I mean you won't have him whipped or nothing?"

"Just go on and tell your story," Richard said.

"But I want to know."

"Don't worry, just tell us the story."

He was reluctant, but he went on. "We broke open the powder kegs, that's all. Then we put a fire to it along with some other stuff."

"What other things?"

"Oh, some blankets."

"That's all?"

"No, some leggings and things like that."

"And that's the whole story?"

"Yes, sir. That's all. I swear to it."

"Now tell us the names of the other man, and we'll let you go free."

"You aren't going to whip me?"

"Not if you tell the names."

Tryon half rose from his chair, and then settled back when Richard motioned to him.

"I don't know if I should. I guess you know me, though. And I told you about Junior and Joshua. . . ."

"Go on."

"Well, John White, too."

"And?"

"William and Robert Carruthers . . . Robert Davis." He took a long breath. "Cochran, and Widow White's boy—that's all we ever call him. I didn't know the last one."

The young boy continued to rub his wrists nervously where the ropes had made their mark. Richard Caswell ordered a drink of water for him and then motioned to the Governor that the interview was over.

The boy asked suddenly, "You're not going whip my friends, are you? I mean it's not right to let me go free and then whip them. Say you won't beat them because of me."

Tryon was standing. "No," he said, "I promise not to have them whipped."

"Thank you, sir. We didn't——"

Tryon interrupted. "There'd be no point in whipping them after we've hanged them."

The boy opened his mouth to speak, but was struck dumb in horror.

"Take him under guard," Tryon ordered.

Richard Caswell stood up and shook his head. "I promised this boy his freedom."

"I don't care."

"Under my authority as Speaker of the Assembly I promised him. Now I order him released."

"You're not practical, Colonel Caswell."

"Promises are seldom practical, sir." He turned to the privates who had prodded the boy to his feet. "Take him to the sentry limits and set him free."

"Yes, sir."

"But I don't want to go. I don't want to go free now. I didn't think you'd do that to them."

"Take him outside," Tryon ordered. "Do as the Speaker said."

Hillary and Adam rode back to their camps, but they did not speak of the affairs in the tent. They parted for the morning with a salute, both feeling depressed.

Hillary found a note from Dr. Armitage on the board table by the dying fire. A heavy rock kept the spring winds from blowing it away.

Hillary:
I have ordered Isaac Edwards to his home in Hillsborough where he may find the proper rest and care which he will need in order to survive this illness. I shall speak with you further on the march of the morrow.
                                    Armitage

Hillary threw two pieces of dry wood on the fire before he sat down at the table. He drew a piece of paper from his file box, and in spite of his exhaustion, tried to write a letter.

My dearest Cecelia,
To-night a young lad was captured and brought before . . .

He cut off the top of the page with his hunting knife and began again.

My dearest Cecelia,
The wind is fair. The march, like all marches, boring and tiring. This evening I was called to the Governor's

tent where a young prisoner was held and forced to tell . . ."

Again Hillary cut it with the knife.

My dearest Cecelia,
  Is there ever a time when a man will be free to plough the earth, hold the sky in his hands, and make springtime in his heart for his life and his love?
  I hear the breach-locks snap about me; and a bird sings. I see the powder wagons roll; and beyond me the fields are green. I smell flint, oil and leather; in the air is the fragrance of rain.
  What do I fight now? When can I fight for something I believe in?
  Our hollow drums echo in the hills.
  Someday . . .
  The only world I've seen built has been with a plough and love. I have the love for you, and the earth is waiting for my plough.

Hillary

33

Alamance

On the eleventh day of May, Tryon's little army marched westward to rescue General Hugh Waddell. Scouts reported that his Cape Fear militia had already retreated to Salisbury and the Regulators had not pursued.

In the afternoon of May 14 the column reached Alamance Creek, and Tryon let his weary men rest by the creek all the next day.

While the men took their ease, Tryon dictated orders to Hillary for the next day's operation. His voice was crisp. His assurance had steadily increased as he approached the insurgent forces.

"The troops will be prepared to form a line of battle on command. The front line will be formed as follows: Left flank, Carteret company; next, Orange; then Dobbs —no, change that. I want the artillery in the centre. Carteret, Orange, artillery, then Beaufort and Craven. The Rangers will be on the right flank. In close support, four companies, as follows: Onslow, Dobbs, Johnston and New Hanover. This is from left to right as in the front line, of course. Do you have all that?"

"Yes, sir."

"Read it back."

When Hillary had read it, the Governor ordered copies for each of the ten commanders. Then he called, "Orderly!"

"Yes, sir." The canvas tent flap was pulled back and

a trooper entered smartly, came to attention before the Governor and saluted.

"I want Colonels Fanning, Rutledge, Ashe and—that's enough for the time. Get them here at once." The Governor turned back to Hillary. "Call the messengers yourself as soon as you've completed your work. I want the orders dispatched to the county commanders as soon as possible."

Tryon placed both hands on his table and surveyed the map of the Salisbury road spread before him. When Hillary had copied three sets of the orders, he rose, went to the entrance of the tent and called a messenger.

Tryon asked, "Have you already sent out orders for the *time* of formation?"

"Yes, sir."

"Good! Edwards trained you well." He looked down at the map again. Hillary noted that it was the only time Edwards' name had been mentioned since the secretary had fallen ill before they had reached Hillsborough. Edwards was a thing of the past; the Governor's mind was entirely on the task ahead.

Colonel John Ashe arrived first. He was dressed as handsomely as a soldier on parade. Tryon surveyed him for a moment. "You're a credit to your command, Colonel. You're to take charge of the scouts from now on. The rebels should be— Come here, come here, over to the map where you can see, man! Now, look. This circle represents the probable position of the rebel camp. By morning I'll expect to see the exact position marked here. Do you understand? I'm not asking you for strategy, merely for facts. Caswell, let the Colonel examine a set of orders. He'll mark our own positions as well."

An orderly opened the tent flap to admit a scout. He was unshaven, dressed in the buckskin clothes of the hill country.

"Speak up!"

"Sir, sentry lines of the enemy are about five miles down the road. Their sentries don't seem to pay much mind to watchin'. Anybody could just walk through."

"How far behind the lines is the camp?"

"Don't rightly know, sir."

" 'Don't know' would be more accurate. Ashe, did you hear that? You should have men through those lines and back before dawn."

Adam Rutledge and Fanning came into the tent then. Hillary tried to catch Adam's eye, but both men were intent on the Governor as he waved them to seats at the big table.

"You took your time coming, gentlemen."

Adam said nothing, but Fanning began to protest. "Your Excellency, I came the moment the messenger reached me."

"No doubt, Edmund, no doubt. But you should learn that every statement is not a criticism."

"But you . . ."

"Colonel Fanning, your suggestion that a hundred men be detailed under your command to seize what property you can carry and burn the homes and barns of rebel leaders is a good one. You will understand, however, that I can't spare any men at present. After we have put down the insurrection, we shall see. I may march most of the army through Sandy Creek and other rebel strong points."

While Tryon was speaking, Colonel Ashe had been studying the copy of the battle orders Hillary had given him. He started to put it in his pocket and leave the tent.

"Colonel!" Tryon halted him. "Leave the orders here. You are to be within the enemy lines to-night. If you should have the bad fortune to be captured, you wouldn't want those orders to be taken with you." He watched while Ashe sheepishly handed the orders back to Hillary. "Good Lord, haven't any of you men fought a campaign before? If the rebels could see you it would be a comfort to them. You'd never win a war by yourselves."

Hillary sent off the other copies of the battle formation and returned to his table. He cut a new quill.

"Caswell, are you ready with your pen?"

"Yes, sir."

"Listen to this," Tryon said to Fanning and Rutledge. The tent flap swung aside and Richard Caswell stepped in. "You, too, Richard. I want your opinions on this—

though I won't promise to follow them. All right, Caswell, take this down.

"The rebels are reported to be concentrated about five miles ahead. We shall march in column by the road for three miles, then form a line of battle, each contingent taking the place assigned by orders already delivered to its commander. On making contact with the enemy, our right will demonstrate against the enemy—a mere feint—and hold as a pivot. The men of Carteret and Orange on the left and the artillery in the centre will press home a strong attack on the enemy right, driving it back and in on its centre in a turning movement."

He paused and, looking at Richard Caswell, said, "I like not fighting behind rocks and trees. These rebels must be half Indian from what I hear. I plan to hit them hard at one point, on their right, and drive it into disorder. Though they outnumber us, they have no training, no discipline. Once we break their spirit we may count on a complete rout. In that way there will be no Indian fighting. You men agree, don't you?"

Richard Caswell nodded.

"Rutledge?"

"The sooner the battle is brought to a close, the better."

"You treat the rebels too lightly, Your Excellency!" Fanning protested.

"Colonel, there is the difference between us. You would be a tyrant; I wish to be only a master." Then, his voice firm, he said, "I intend to crush them, Colonel. But, to be quite frank, it does not serve my purpose to butcher them."

"I prefer the Governor's logic, Colonel Fanning," Adam said.

Tryon smiled. "For the first time, sir, I'm quite certain. Nevertheless, it pleases me."

Hillary leaned forward on the table and rubbed his eyes.

"Let me see your work," Tryon ordered. Hillary blinked, stood up and carried the paper to the Governor. "Scarcely legible. Get yourself some rest. Colonel Fanning, you will send me one of your assistants."

"Yes, Your Excellency." Fanning hurried from the tent, and in a moment they could hear him dispatching a messenger. Hillary waited until the man returned with Fanning's clerk.

It was the same scrub-faced lad whom Hillary had seen that day in Fanning's office: the same man who had betrayed Fanning to the Regulators. He entered the tent hesitantly. His eyes darted from one face to another. At sight of Hillary he started. When he saw Adam Rutledge, too, he blanched.

Tryon, intent on the notes before him, missed his recognition of Hillary, but he noticed the lad's uneasiness with Adam. "You've met Colonel Rutledge before?"

"Yes, Your Excellency."

"And where was that?"

"At Hillsborough, sir."

"And you weren't pleased with the meeting?" Tryon persisted.

Adam broke in: "There was merely an argument about a land deed. In the end Colonel Fanning and I settled the matter but not without sharp words along the way. And both of us vented some of our spleen on the lad here. I'm not surprised he winced at the sight of me."

"I can imagine. Very well, take Caswell's place."

The clerk walked slowly to Hillary's table. He sat down and stared numbly, still uncertain if he were to be exposed.

"Your Excellency," Adam said—the clerk's shoulders hunched forward as if he'd been hit—"since I'll be on the right flank, my men and I may have need of a messenger. Might I have one of these two clerks—Caswell or the new fellow—on the morrow?"

"Have you none of your own?"

"None, sir."

"And what have you used up to now for your detachment?"

"One James Carper. He broke his hand this morning while loading a cart."

"I saw no report. Well, that's normal. You may take Caswell." He turned to Fanning's clerk. "You've had enough sleep, I hope."

"Yes, sir," the boy said. He gave Adam a grateful glance, but Rutledge, who was studying the map, missed it.

"Then you'll not be sleeping this night."

"I'll take him if you feel Caswell would do better for you," Adam said, looking up.

"No need of that. If he's Fanning's man, he'll do a good job. Why are you still here?" Tryon asked Hillary. "Get some sleep. You need it."

Adam and Hillary walked from the tent into the warm night. The fire in front of the Governor's tent was low. The road to Salisbury stretched like a stream of fog to the west. Adam stepped toward the fire and shook Dr. Armitage awake. The doctor rubbed his eyes, straightened himself, and yawned. "My Lord, Adam, let a man get some sleep! I was called here three hours ago and haven't been admitted yet."

"You'll be with the Governor's group to-morrow?"

"I suppose so. Personal care of his staff, and such things."

"Do you have a pistol?"

"Adam," he said reproachfully, "you shouldn't ask a doctor that. Of course I do."

"Are you awake enough to listen?"

"Yes."

"There's a clerk with Tryon now. As long as he stays with the Governor don't bother him. If he should try to leave the Governor's side, stop him. Shoot him if you must."

"But as a messenger?"

At that moment the tent flap opened and the young clerk appeared. "Colonel Rutledge, the Governor wants to see you again." Adam put his hand on the youth's shoulder. "Don't leave the Governor to-morrow. Do you understand that?"

"Sir, you and Caswell saved my skin a moment ago by not speaking what you knew. I give you my word I will make no communication with the Regulators."

Adam nodded slowly. "I believe you."

"Colonel Rutledge!" Tryon called.

The clerk started to stammer out his gratitude, but Adam took him by the arm and led him to the tent.

"Come, we can't keep the Governor waiting." Over his shoulder he said to Hillary, "In the morning you'll form with the Rangers. Bring your weapons. We shan't be communicating with a quill."

It was full morning. The troops had been marching for over an hour. A steady roll of drums beat as the long column deployed into line of battle. The brass cannon were rolled down the dusty road to centre position. Supply carts and wagons rattled across the uneven terrain with last-minute supplies. Messengers rode back and forth between the companies and the brave flags of battle streamed in the light wind of May. The proud horses pranced nervously as if eager to go into action. The men of the Carteret contingent talked a little among themselves. They were more restless than the others, for they were to carry home the first thrust. At the far end of the line, the Rangers were well out to the right, not in contact with the Craven men on the right of the line. Their task was to guard against a rebel flanking movement and to keep any of the frontiersmen from slipping through or around. Since the Regulators had the superior numbers, Governor Tryon was taking measures to protect the flanks of his own force, though he doubted the enemy had the skill to take advantage of its numerical superiority.

Hillary spurred his mount and gained Adam's side. They were on a gentle rise of ground that gave them a good view of the field before them. From that vantage point they could see a lone rider galloping down the road toward the provincial artillery, which was getting into position athwart the road. The man's black cape blew out behind him.

"Seems that Caldwell is back again," Adam said.

"Who's he and what's he doing? Remember, I spent a few hours sleeping."

"David Caldwell is a minister. He's been shuttling back and forth between the two camps most of the night and all morning, trying everything to arrange a last-minute peace. I think his hope is vain. There'll be no turning back now."

The rider came headlong along the road straight to

the waiting cannon, swerved by them, and galloped toward the Governor's staff. They were already mounting their horses when he arrived.

A bugle blast shattered the still air, and the Craven company on their left, which had been sprawled out on the ground, climbed grumbling to their feet and began to form ranks.

"Almost ready, almost ready," Adam was saying.

Hillary rose in his stirrups and peered over the scrub trees and rocks which spread before them. "Have we two Caldwells?"

"What do you mean?"

"Isn't that another rider coming?"

Whoever he was, he was now directly in front of the Rangers' position. His horse moved slowly, picking its way through the low brush and over the rocky ground. The rider reeled as if he were about to topple from the saddle.

For a moment Adam watched him intently. "Come along, let's see." He urged his mount forward.

Hillary brought his horse to a trot beside him. "Can you make him out?"

Adam nodded. "I'm afraid so. In any case, he's alive." They broke their mounts into a gallop to reach the horseman.

Colonel John Ashe, who had been listed as missing since four o'clock that morning, held weakly to the reins of his horse. His uniform had been half ripped from his back; the rest hung in shreds about him.

"Take the reins," Adam commanded Hillary, as at the same time he eased his own mount beside Ashe's.

The Colonel's face was drawn and pale. He wavered in the saddle. His back was raw, cut and bleeding. Adam took his arm to steady him as they rode slowly back to the advancing lines of Rangers.

"They caught me this morning," Ashe said. "About five of them."

"And Captain Walker?"

"Hasn't he come back yet?"

"No."

"He should have been here. They turned him loose at the same time as me."

"Don't try to talk now," Hillary said.

"I might as well. Talking doesn't hurt the back."

Adam said, "No, the lad's right. Rest easy for the time."

Ashe bit his lips. "I'm damned if I can! Find one of the doctors and let him salve me. Then I'm riding."

"Don't be stupid, John. You can't see your own back."

"They caught us both. Took John Walker first and tied him up to a tree. They gave me the honour of watching while they whipped him raw. I think they wore themselves out on him."

A trooper from the Craven company cantered through the brush to them, and Adam told him the story quickly. "Relay it to the Governor, and tell the boys to keep looking for Captain Walker. He's somewhere out there."

"Yes, sir!" The trooper wheeled and started back.

"I had no heart in this fight, John," Adam said. "I'm sorry your back had to be the spur I needed. God, I *have* to fight for something! Even a back."

John Ashe managed a grin. "Felt the same way, Adam. Works for me, too. Can you loosen what's left of the shirt? It's rubbing."

Adam unsheathed his long knife and cut the shreds free.

"When they'd finished with Walker they put me up and went to work. I don't think they'd half done with it when somebody stopped them. Man who didn't talk like a woodsman. I suppose they'd still be laying it on to me if it weren't for him. He brained the whipper with his pistol."

"And the others?"

"Said he'd kill the first who moved to stop him. They didn't move."

"You were lucky enough," Hillary said. "Did he give you the horses, too?"

"Stole them for us."

They were close to their command when two more riders came out from the lines. A messenger from the Governor's staff followed hard on them.

"Name was Robin," Ashe went on, "or something

like that. Two of them were all for tying him up in my place. Is that coat free? It feels like it's still rubbing."

Dr. Mattheson from the Craven Company, his assistant and the messenger from the Governor arrived almost at the same time. The messenger spoke first. "His Excellency wants to see Colonel Ashe immediately."

Dr. Mattheson directed his assistant to take the Colonel to his own detachment. He said to the messenger, "You tell the Governor that the Colonel can't see him —not till I've ministered to him."

"Yes, sir."

Adam and Hillary rode back to the Ranger lines. Bugles were sounding the advance. Drums beat. Tryon's militia was picking its way forward through the rough, broken country, trying to keep its formation in line of battle.

Hillary finally asked the question that was troubling him. "The name Robin—it couldn't be Robin Chapman?"

Adam raised his eyebrows. "Do you want an honest opinion?"

"Yes."

"I rather imagine it was he."

Hillary stared at the lines of Rangers who worked slowly through the brush. Ahead, scouts picked their way gingerly, keeping prudently behind cover when they could.

Turning back to Adam, he said, "I can't fight *him!*"

Adam glanced to the artillery far to his left. He raised his hand to slow the advance of his horsemen. "There's no battle in which you fight every man." He shouted to his men, "Hold in your horses! The artillery can't keep pace with you!" He resumed to Hillary, "No battle in which you fight only against enemies. If I were to fight total strangers I would still be killing friends."

Hillary suddenly felt the weight of the gun in his hand.

The six units that were spread out in long lines on each side of the road advanced slowly, picking their way through the woods and brush, their officers labouring to keep them abreast and centred on the road. Occasionally Hillary caught a glimpse of a man or a group of men falling back before the militia's advance. The main body of the Regulators must be close now, he decided.

The line surmounted a low wooded ridge. Ahead lay more open country, rocky, patched with brush, but with only an occasional tree. Near woods farther on, small in the distance, stood a crowd of men. They lounged about carelessly in groups but not in military formation. Some of them seemed to be wrestling and skylarking.

"It looks as if they are still expecting us to treat with them rather than fight," Adam said after a slow survey. "They aren't ready for the sort of attack the Governor knows how to drive home."

Hillary felt a dryness in his mouth.

At that moment a messenger summoned Adam to Governor Tryon, who was just behind the artillery company in the centre. Adam motioned Hillary to follow.

Tryon was abrupt. "An hour ago, through that minister, Caldwell, I sent the rebels a message offering them a choice: to return peacefully to their homes or be fired on. The hour is up. You'll be better received than anyone on my staff. Go and bring back their answer. Better go alone."

While Adam performed his mission, the lines were halted. The gunners readied the swivel guns for action. Hillary could see Adam reach the Regulators, talk briefly with them, and start back at a slow trot. His return seemed agonizingly slow. At last he came past the cannon and reined in his horse beside Tryon's. "The message is: 'Fire and be damned.'"

As Adam and Hillary rejoined the Rangers, the advance was sounded and the long line of militia began to move forward. Two shots broke from the distant brush. A horse near Hillary reared in fright. Intermittent puffs of smoke appeared from the brush and from the edge of the woods. A soldier in the Craven company spun, fell, and picked himself up clutching his shoulder.

"At this distance," Adam said, "they're wasting most of their shots."

The militia continued its steady, relentless advance. From the edge of the woods men in buckskin opened a thin, irregular fire. The line pressed on. A bullet winged past Hillary's ear with a whine like an angry mosquito's.

At last came the command to halt. The drums were stilled. The red silk colours flapped idly in the breeze.

In the sudden quiet, Colonel Edmund Fanning came forward. "Front ranks, kneel!" His voice carried out over the field.

"Aim!" he shouted.

He held his sabre aloft for a tense second. His arm dropped. "Fire!" he cried.

The milita line was dead still.

"Fire!" he screamed again.

The rebels waited in silent suspense, realizing that the troops were reluctant to fire on them.

"Damn that Tryon!" Adam said. "Why in the Lord's name did he have Fanning give the order? They would obey anyone else."

Fanning looked helplessly at his troops. He started to ride back toward the staff. The companies wavered.

Now shots burst from the Regulators.

The kneeling men rose. It was the second before panic.

William Tryon, mounted on a coal-black charger, cantered through the breach between the Beaufort unit and the artillery. He raised his gleaming sabre and shouted to all the field: "Fire! Fire on them, or fire on *me!*" He swung his sabre down.

Now the militia let go with a thundering blast at the rebels. The artillery delivered its salvo. The troops jammed home powder and ball.

The men of Carteret and Orange, assisted by the cannon, pressed the attack on the Regulator right. Some of the rebels fled for the woods, but others took shelter behind rocks and trees and kept up a stubborn fire—Indian style. They did not seem awed by the roar of the cannon. Some fifty or so, at close range behind rocks, so harassed the gunners that many were hurt and others had to take shelter. The cannon stood silent. But the attack mounted in fury and, little by little, in spite of spirited resistance, the rebel right was pushed back.

Governor Tryon rode back and brought up the Onslow and Dobbs contingents to throw their weight into the attack beside the Orange troops, where the fight was most intense. Almost two hours had passed since the fighting started, and the rebel resistance was crumbling at last.

On the right the Rangers had repulsed some feeble attempts of the rebels to get around the militia's flank, but they were still waiting their moment. A lean-faced farmer out of the ranks edged his horse up beside Hillary. "Let's go in!" he shouted. "They're a-runnin'." He started off at a gallop.

"Keep in line!" Adam commanded.

Even as he called, the farmer's horse reared. The man clutched his chest, dropped sideways from the saddle, and the horse ran frantically back through the ranks.

A moment later Tryon was beside Adam. "They're breaking. Go into the woods after them before they hide like Indians. Pursue them and they'll run."

The Rangers advanced at a trot. Hillary found himself knee to knee with a young lieutenant. Three shots, almost simultaneous, flashed at them from the woods ahead. The lieutenant's mount sank to its knees, throwing its rider to the ground. He rose to his feet groggily. Hillary raised his gun, aimed at the rebel before him, fired, and saw the man topple.

"Down! Get down!" the lieutenant was shouting.

Shots broke from the thicket again as Hillary swung from the saddle. A mounted man made a perfect target for brush country sharpshooters.

Hillary was dimly aware of a bugle sounding far to the centre of the field. He saw the lieutenant ten paces ahead, crouched behind an age-old rock, one that had been rounded by the sand winds. He ran low and threw himself on the ground beside the lieutenant.

A rebel darted from behind a rock and ran for the safety of the forest. In a second the lieutenant fired. The rebel plunged on drunkenly for ten steps, then dropped suddenly.

"There's another at that triangular boulder. I saw him. If he comes out while I'm reloading, be ready for him."

"Right," Hillary said.

"I'll push him your way." The Lieutenant fired again, and the solitary rebel, who had been deserted by his companions, edged around the rock. Hillary could see the arm of his jacket. He seemed unwilling to make the final dash for safety. He slipped farther around, now certain that only one militiaman waited for him. He exposed himself clearly to Hillary.

Hillary raised his gun. He aimed carefully along the sights. The rebel crouched to run.

"Can you see him?" the lieutenant whispered.

"Can you?"

Hillary did not squeeze the trigger. He lowered the rifle. The rebel at last darted for cover.

"Get him!" The lieutenant was still engaged in reloading. "Get him!" At last the lieutenant fired himself, but it was too late. The rebel had gained the dense wood.

"My God, didn't you see him?"

"Just after you fired."

"But he was on your side. You had a clear shot!"

"Damn you! Are you calling me a coward or a fool?"

The lieutenant did not answer. The two men separated, Hillary gaining his mount again and the young officer hurrying to the rear to procure a new horse. No, Hillary thought, he could never have shot the rebel in the back—never have shot him at all—not when he could see that the rebel was Robin Chapman.

Most of the Rangers were back in formation again. Hillary found Adam at the head of them. His mount was still wet with sweat.

"Good! You're alive," Adam said.

"And you," Hillary responded.

"In one piece for the day. The fight has gone out of the Regulators. If you'll take a look, I think you'll see the end of the battle." He pointed toward the centre of the field.

Just beyond the artillery stood some fifteen prisoners guarded by troops of Colonel Fanning.

"Let's ride over," Hillary said.

"No. I prefer to wait. Do you see what they're doing?"

One of the prisoners, a man with a shock of iron-grey hair, was mounted backwards on a roan. The horse was being led by the Colonel himself.

William Tryon and his staff were at the top of a small hill, surveying the field. Two drummers had been dispatched from the colour guard to accompany Fanning. The prisoner was led in full view.

"What are they going to do with him?" Hillary demanded.

"What does it look like?"

"But they can't! He's a prisoner of war!"

"The Governor would prefer that you said a prisoner of rebellion."

Fanning led the horse under the wide-spreading oak which stood before the Orange company.

"Isn't the Governor going to stop him?"

"I rather imagine it was the Governor who ordered the execution."

The field of battle was still.

Fanning moved toward the prisoner and said a few words. The prisoner spat on him. Fanning stepped back, wiping his face with his hand. He motioned to the orderlies, who slipped a noose over the prisoner's head and pulled it tight about his neck. They threw the other end of the rope over a limb of the tree and fastened it securely.

The drummers from the colour guard began a quick roll.

Fanning moved forward again, and shouted something unintelligible at the man on the horse.

The answer was a hoarse, wild laugh.

Fanning lashed his riding crop across the rump of the roan. It bolted toward the green forest.

The drums stopped beating. The body swung on the rope from the tree, jerked for a moment, and then was still.

Adam Rutledge motioned to Hillary, and the two cantered to join the Governor and his staff, who had remained stationed on the hillock.

Governor Tryon was in high spirits. After the hanging there had not been another shot fired from the scattered ranks of the rebels. "Gentlemen," he said, "the field has been won!" The commanders of the various companies had gathered about Tryon. "Appoint two officers and four militiamen from each of your groups. They shall carry the word of amnesty to those who will swear allegiance to the government."

To Dr. Mattheson he directed, "Take your men and scour the field for our wounded. When they are cared for, you may return and gather the rebels'. Submit a list of the names of all the captured. Our dead will be interred at five o'clock this evening."

His eyes searched the officers. "Major Pryor, you will prepare court-martial proceedings against all the present prisoners and any man captured two hours after amnesty is offered. We will try them at Hillsborough."

"Colonel Rutledge, I should explain for your benefit why the hanging of the rebel James Few was necessary. You were on the flank when the decision was made."

"There is no need to explain to me, Your Excellency."

The Governor continued, a cold fury in his tone. "I commanded that the rebel be hanged in full view on the field to strike terror in the hearts of his fellows. I believe I succeeded. I wanted no more of our brave men killed in this folly. Does that suffice for you?"

Adam hesitated before answering. "I asked for no justification of your actions. You are the Governor and the General."

"Am I to infer it does not suffice?"

"You press me, Your Excellency. A few minutes ago, when I was in the woods, I saw rebels running. I saw no resistance left. Has the man Few's execution just now further reduced resistance?"

The Governor's rigid face paled with anger. "Rutledge, you'll hear of this insolence again. I may make an example of you." He paused. "You, the clerk . . . Caswell!"

Hillary looked up, meeting the cold blue eyes of the Governor.

"Repair to headquarters. I'll be in presently to dictate dispatches for New Bern."

Hillary, infuriated, did not move. Tryon turned to speak to Colonel Bergson. "Send a rider to General Waddell in Salisbury informing him of our victory and——" He broke off, realizing that his clerk had not started for headquarters. "Did you hear my orders, Caswell?"

"Yes, sir. I heard them."

"Move!"

"In a moment, sir. I beg to inform you, however, that the battle is over, and with its close the resignation I long since gave Mr. Edwards takes effect. I want no more of this idiocy."

Tryon stared at Hillary in amazement. At first he appeared ready to laugh, then his face twisted in anger.

"Also I beg to remind Your Excellency that I'm a civilian. I have no official connection with your militia."

"You're also a fool, Caswell," Tryon snapped. Then to Fanning he said, "Clap that man in with the prisoners. Brand him as a traitor."

Richard Caswell said, "You have no authority!"

"Well let a military court decide that, Colonel Caswell."

Armitage turned in his saddle toward Adam Rutledge and said softly, "Aye, he's a fool for speaking his heart. I wish there were more fools like you and Caswell here, and fewer gentlemen."

Adam merely shrugged his shoulders. "He'll be free in a fortnight, I promise you."

34

The Next Night

Robin Chapman and Whitlock trudged wearily toward the Piedmont and the mountains until they reached Deep River Crossing. There they camped, and during the long night after the battle, streams of men poured in and lay down to sleep: the tired, the wounded and the broken.

In the morning new groups swelled the camp, among them Enos Dye. The farmer, Rafer Panky, took charge and sent out hunting parties to bring in meat for the camp.

Once during the night had come an anguished scream from a young lad of Orange who had walked the many miles from Alamance with a gunshot wound in his stomach. He had kept moving when well men had wanted to stop, and he had led a small group of survivors out of range of the light-horse troop of militia that searched the countryside for prisoners. He had died during the night; and his choked and startled scream of pain had been the voice of those defeated men. They had lost their cause; they had lost their homes. That cry in the night was an echo of their own despair.

Whitlock crouched on the ground beside Robin. He plucked a blade of grass and put it in his mouth. "It's dawn," he said. "Aye, there'll be many a man takin' the trail to the Northwest country now." As he spoke he looked over the camping grounds. Men were sprawled beneath the oaks. Fires burned low in many spots. The faces of the men were haggard, worn, dirt-smeared. A few horses had been tethered in the green grass plot beyond the oaks, but the number was pitifully small. A shot sounded through the forest as one of the hunters flushed game.

Robin leaned back against a tree. He tightened the rag about his arm by using his teeth to hold one end of the crude bandage.

"Did that thing go deep?" Whitlock asked.

"No. Just grazed the flesh."

Enos Dye saw them from his bedroll beyond the third fire. He rose sleepily and carried his belongings toward them, dropped them on the ground with disgust.

"You look hale, Enos."

"Hale and angry. That's the way the saying goes, isn't it?"

"Aye, for a well man. I've been telling Robin here that we're goin' to make the west country wide open now. We're driven to it." He laughed and added, "It's the one thing that I been saying is good to do. If I weren't so damned mad at that Fanning and the Governor, I'd get right down on my knees and thank 'em."

Enos Dye frowned. "Mighty poor beginning for a new country."

Whitlock shook his head. "Nope, Enos, I don't figure it is. Maybe I'd have felt that way last night. But not this morning. Hell, Enos, look around you. These men just lost a little battle—that's not a war, they tell me."

"What's this, friend?" A man who had been sleeping at their fire suddenly wakened. "You say we're gonna have another battle with the militia?"

"Don't reckon so, brother," Whitlock said. "We got a whole new land to open up and battle for. I guess that's our next fight. We ain't much more than farmers. We ain't so handy with guns, but I use a pretty mean plough, myself."

Robin looked out over the camp, and he was thinking the greatest crime that could be laid to Fanning and the Governor was not the battle at Alamance, nor even the trampled rights of the frontiersmen—but, rather, the threat of prosecution that would send the best of them out of the Colony of North Carolina.

Almost as if he had been thinking the same thoughts,

Enos Dye said, "Aye, it's God's shame to see the Colony bled."

"There are men who'll stay," Robin said.

"Who?"

"There are always the Moores, the Buncombes, the Caswells—men like them will stay and fight in their own way. And others who'll come back."

In the deep of the forest they heard five shots.

"Some more game . . . maybe."

Above the morning rustle of the camp, they heard a rough country voice in the distance. It was joined by the voices of other hunters as the morning sun broke clear.

"Sounds like young Rafer Panky," Whitlock said.

"Where's he going?" Robin asked.

"Rafer?"

"Yes."

"Why, hell, Robin, you couldn't move him out of Orange with three kegs of powder."

"What about yourself, lad?" Enos Dye asked.

"Me? I'm going home, too. Tryon couldn't drive me out. I've a ship to be sailed. My people have been here for a century. This is *my* country. No Crown-made Governor can drive me from my home."

"Good talk," the sleepy man said. He had rolled from the blankets and was listening with interest.

"If you're bound to go back, lad," Whitlock said, "let me advise you to make your way to the Virginia border and then go east to Princess Ann County. You could catch you a ship there to the Albemarle. You'll not be safe going through Fanning's country right now. He'll have you on a list. You can be sure we've been marked by some of our own. They grow them skunks everywhere. What's more, there'll be a bounty for us, I'll wager."

Dye was sitting on his haunches, picking his teeth with a brown pine needle of last year's autumn. "Yes, you're likely to be in trouble, Robin. Maybe you ought to come out West with us till everything simmers down."

Robin shook his head. "I'd like to see the land, but I've got a cargo to carry to Antigua in June—" he laughed—"and a lass to bring back with me."

"By God, that's worth getting hanged for!" Enos said.

"She is."

"I'll not doubt it for a second," Enos said, "but I've been thinkin' you'd be a fine man to captain a boat—say, from St. Louis to New Orleans. Now *there's* a trip for you."

Robin gazed out over the rolling hills covered with tall pines, chestnuts and hardwoods. He shook his head slowly. "The Mississippi River—they say she's a mighty body of water—for a river. I don't know, Enos, but I've got a taste for salt. It sort of cures me of land-sickness."

"Wonder how old Harmon's making out," Whitlock mused. "I felt sort of bad letting that fellow go off with Isaac Cox. I mean, Isaac is a good man, but Harmon needs a lot of carin' for."

"Pennsylvania country," Dye said. "They say it's wild up there in the high hills. I figure he'll get along, though. He's got himself a good wife. He's got God on his side, too. They help a man make out. Doesn't take much more."

Robin thought briefly of that strange man whom he had carried to safety from New Bern, of the peculiar conversation they'd had. Then his mind turned to his voyage to Antigua, and to Cynthia Martin. His thoughts were interrupted by Whitlock. "Now, if you ever decide to give up this sea-going foolishness, you want to let me be the man to lead you 'cross the mountains. I can get you quicker to the Northwest than you'd sail to England —well, maybe a little longer."

"Don't forget you're an outlaw now."

Whitlock grinned. "I've been an outlaw most of my life. This is no time to change. Anyways, I'll be perching on the high ridges. Don't know a body that'd take the time to come fetch me to a court."

"And you, Enos? What will you be doing?" Robin asked.

"Oh, I'm Mr. Rutledge's man." He spoke as if that settled things, but went on to explain. "He has a mess of land in the Illinois country that he's clearing, a beautiful country where the corn grows—" he looked about for a marker, and then pointed to a high notch on the pine— "Corn grows that high. I swear it does. His place is just about where the Missouri meets the Mississippi. He's got a superintendent working there right now building a grist-mill right on the river. God willing, I'll be working there for the rest of my days."

Robin did not go until the sun was high. He felt drawn to the strong men with whom he had fought. At the last, Whitlock gave him instructions on how to reach the sea. He drew a map with a stick on the ground.

"You've a mess of rivers to cross. The Haw is *there*—" he pointed with the stick—"and there are a lot of others before you get to Virginia and come to the upper Roanoke. I don't rightly know the country to the east, but they tell me there's some big rivers—the Meherrin and the Blackwater. That's all before you get to the sea at Norfolk County."

When they were done with the discussion—several other frontiersman having offered advice—they all shook hands.

Others were departing, each to his separate fortune. Some turned to the south, a few to the north along Robin's path, a very few headed directly for homes in the East, but most turned toward the western mountains.

Robin slapped his grey mare gently on the neck. "I hope she holds out," he said.

"She'll make it," Dye said.

"You can remember you struck one good blow for freedom, lad," Whitlock said. "It may be we'll have to do it again. I'll see you then."

"Aye," Robin answered, "then we shall meet."

He left, guiding his mount through the camp of disarray and hope, the camp of the broken yet undefeated, and with sadness in his heart he heard shouts of farewell from the western-bound.

35

Homecoming

Y ou expressed the desire. Your Excellency, to leave our Colony in peace and tranquillity. You convinced me that a stroke against the Regulators was necessary to the well-being of the Province. These gentlemen and I have followed you to those ends." Richard Caswell fell silent.

The Governor ticked off the names of the men standing before him. "Caswell, Armitage, Iredell, Hewes. If the Cape Fear men were not in Salisbury, I suppose you would have brought the leading gentlemen from that region. And is not the Province pacified?"

"In the West, Your Excellency," Richard Caswell conceded. "I fear, however, your successor may encounter some discontents in the Albemarle. Adam Rutledge is much esteemed there, by rich and poor. They will think it harsh that his name appears with those of the rebel leaders as an outlaw. He served well in the heat of the battle, and his one offence was an effect of virtue, a candour that trespassed at once on politeness and discretion. We beg you, sir, to show the men of Albemarle that you have the generosity to forgive; the greater the injury, the greater the generosity."

The Governor considered. A faint smile relaxed his stern lips. "Many things I shall be glad to put in the hands of my successor but not the occasion to excell me in largeness of spirit. Pray inform Mr. Rutledge—but not too quickly—that he has my pardon."

Richard Caswell bowed, but to the Governor's evident surprise, the group did not retire.

"What!" he exclaimed. "More?"

"You've granted us an ell. Now add an inch. We speak for my young kinsman Hillary Caswell."

"Young Caswell? There's a spirit of dissent about him." His expression was frosty. "I don't trust his loyalty, not fully." He stepped to the doorway and called, "Ask Colonel Fanning to come in."

Fanning appeared promptly. "These gentlemen are interceding for young Caswell, Colonel. Does he deserve my mercy?"

"I scarcely know him, Your Excellency. You are better acquainted."

Richard Caswell took a step forward. "Your Excellency, if the Colonel will jog his memory, he may recall that the young man ventured his skin to save the Colonel's life during the riots in Hillsborough."

"Perhaps . . . perhaps he may have done something to open a path for me as I left the Courthouse. It would have been the natural thing to do."

"Natural!" Richard Caswell smiled sardonically. "Natural to put oneself at the mercy of a mob?"

Governor Tryon's face was a mask, hard as stone. "Those who serve need not expect to go without reward," Tryon said. "Have you gentlemen served me? Even in the days when I should have joy in my heart that the Government is whole again, that the threat to peace is gone, I have my doubts of you."

Richard Caswell said, "There's much pride in youth, sir; you can forgive a spirit that is not alien to yours."

The Governor smiled faintly. "You're beginning to speak more boldly, Mr. Caswell." He paused. "Very well, I release the prisoner."

That had been seven weeks ago, and now the warmth of July spread over the land, and the path along the pocosin was a tunnel of green. The cypress standing knee-deep in the black water had sent out their feathery leaves. The oaks were green, and the swamp maples made a canopy so heavy that only a few rays of the evening sun could penetrate to the dark waters.

Birds were singing joyously. Cardinals, bluebirds and parakeets flashed their brilliant colour through the Great Dismal. White cranes and ospreys moved along the verge of the bank and were reflected in the black water. A blue heron, head under its wing, stood on one leg in a pool, sleeping.

His horse quickened its pace when it came to the long avenue of cedars that led to Manor House. A feeling of urgency came over Hillary, a hunger for the land and for his own home. The swift-moving events of the past year presaged no end to rebellion, but the beginning of greater unrest. There seemed only a few scant years to build a world.

He saw Madam Elizabeth's garden ablaze with a bloom. Rows of purple flags and yellow lilies lined the brick walks. Great syringa bushes were covered with waxen bloom as white as the dogwood in the forest. Pink, crimson and yellow roses bloomed in beds among the boxwood. The climbing rose grew in profuse splendour over latticed arches. The air was fragrant with jasmine and sweet shrub.

At the last turn of the avenue the old house came in view, and Hillary saw the young people, some sprawled on the green lawn and some apparently playing a game. He could hear them laugh.

Gregory was the first to see him, and he shouted. The lads ran across the lawn to the riding-block. Angela lifted her white skirt daintily, and broke into a run, calling, "Hillary! Hillary!" Ann followed her. Only Cecelia moved slowly toward him, her lips parted in a smile, her eyes shining with deep happiness.

"Welcome home, Hillary, my dear," Madam Elizabeth said in a husky voice.

Matthew, standing on the broad stoop, called, "Welcome to Manor House, son."

Hillary gave the reins of his mount to the smiling Negro boy who had come at the shouting. He took Madam Elazabeth's hand in greeting and heard the barrage of questions from them all as he walked toward Cecelia. Angela held onto his arm, "Oh, Hillary, I've so many questions to ask. Don't you think I'm quite grown-up now? Will you ever——"

"Did the Governor sail for New York?" Gregory asked.

"How about Fanning?"

"I want to know about Esther Wake," Ann said. "Is she really as beautiful as they say?"

Hillary had taken Cecelia's hands, felt their warmth and gentle pressure. "Welcome home, my cousin," she said. "I've worried over you for so long."

"Oh, Hillary *do* answer my questions," Angela said. "And Esther Wake?"

Hillary could not take his eyes from Cecelia. He answered quietly, "Esther Wake is a wonderful woman— but she has her peer, believe me."

"Hillary!" Angela stamped her foot. "You're paying all your attention to Cecelia. That's not fair."

"Give way! Give way!" Matthew called, walking down the front steps. "The lad must have *some* peace. Come along, Hillary. We'll have a drink together in the study."

"Daddy!" Angela pouted. "You're mean. Between you and Cecelia, I'll not get to speak to him even for a moment."

"You have not changed your mind?" Hillary asked Cecelia.

"Could you ever think I would?" she answered.

"Only fear."

"What in the world are you two talking about?" Angela demanded.

Hillary laughed. "Just an agreement we made long ago. We promised each other we would live up to it." He turned to follow Matthew Caswell into the house.

"You talk like two . . . two lovers . . . or something."

"Angela," Madam Caswell said reprovingly, "are we going to go through all that again?"

"Well, they do."

Madam Caswell could not restrain a smile when she glanced at Cecelia's radiant face. "I can't imagine where the child gets all those wild ideas."

Matthew was saying, "As usual I have to rescue you. The girls—including Madam Elizabeth—will persist until you've told them every detail of Palace living, and the lads will want to fight the battle of Alamance over again." Matthew poured whisky from a decanter.

Hillary, tired from his travel, sank into a chair. "With all the questions, I'd like to ask one myself: Has Robin Chapman returned yet?"

Matthew shook his head. "No, he hasn't come back, and we've had no word about him. I was rather hoping you'd know. Joseph's sore worried, and his wife fails a little more each day. I fear sorrow will kill her if he doesn't come home."

"He escaped from the battle—that much I can say. You knew he fought with the Regulators?"

"I guessed as much before he departed, but I said nothing. At least your news will cheer Mrs. Chapman to some extent." Matthew frowned, and shoved his glass aside. "Ah, the crime of it! Do you realize how many hundreds of North Carolinians are making their way over the mountains into the Tennessee country?"

"I know," Hillary said. "I pray they can build as free a land there as they sought here. But perhaps they left us better off than they knew. Fanning and Tryon have sailed for New York."

"So I heard. Cornell's ship, wasn't it?—Cornell, the man who advanced the money for the Governor's nonsense at Alamance."

"Aye," Hillary said, "there are many who don't understand what happened. The Reverend Mr. Reed held service in Christ Church to give thanks for the outcome of the battle. The whole town met in a body and waited on Tryon at the Palace: magistrates, freeholders, merchants, Eastern farmers. Somebody even tendered him an oration, which began, 'At the expense of fatigue and great danger to your person, at least equal to that experienced by the private soldiers . . .' Needless to say it pleased Tryon greatly."

"And I suppose all the leaders of our Assembly were there?"

"Many of them. But I don't think that they all shared his feeling that he had 'left the Colony at peace.' "

"They rode with him, didn't they?"

"You know some of them were forced to—Richard, for one. There were many others like him."

"And many who weren't forced."

"True, but they had convinced themselves that the preservation of law and government was the most important thing." Hillary bit his lip. "You know, though, I observed something strange happening. Many of those men felt they were fighting to preserve *their own* government—not the Crown's. How do I say it?"

"You *really* noted that?"

"Aye. It was a pregnant battle."

"But only a slight storm—how can we count it more than that?"

"For the moment I suppose we can't, but even a hurricane must begin from some small twist of leaves on the ground. I think we have seen the beginning."

Matthew Caswell puffed strongly on his unlighted pipe, the habit he had when troubled. "And Husband, perhaps, was the man—or the spirit—to make the leaves whirl. Could that be it?"

Hillary thought for a moment. "It might be," he said. "He had a power, but I think it was no more than many men have. I think it takes a spirit in many men, and in one place or another the spirit finds a voice in its own time."

Robin Chapman came home to Tyrrell in the dead of night. He had not dared to venture to the shipyards, for he had been warned the militiamen were still searching for him.

He came as an outlaw, with a price on his head. The Governor had been told that it was on Robin Chapman's ship that Husband had made his escape. One of his last official acts in the Colony had been to place Robin on the blacklist of rebels—those to whom he would give no pardon.

Robin climbed the tulip poplar tree whose branches jutted near the window of the guest room. In the light from the window he could see the figure of Hillary Caswell outlined. He breathed a sigh of relief, worked his way to the window ledge and called softly, "Hillary! It's Robin."

Hillary yanked the thin curtains aside. "For God's sake, where have you been?"

Robin climbed through the open window, grasping the proffered hand to make the final step. "A long, long story," he said. "I lost." He grinned. "At the moment I want nothing but food and a drink and to get out of these evil clothes."

Hillary poured a drink from a decanter on the mantelboard, handed it to Robin, and then walked to the wardrobe to find a dressing-gown. "There's water in the ewer. Strip and bathe. I'll see what I can find in the kitchen."

When he returned a short time later, Robin was seated in an easy chair with eyes closed. "I made my way to the coast in Virginia. At Williamsburg I found a schooner bound for the Albemarle and begged a passage. They had nothing to eat aboard but weevily corn-meal and rancid bacon. I'm half starved."

Hillary set the tray on his lap. "This may not be elegant but it is substantial."

Robin smiled, opened his eyes. He began to eat. After the second bite he asked, "How are my father and mother?"

"Your mother's been worried to sickness, but I think you can cure her. And Joseph's in Annapolis with your ship. He's expected back to-morrow."

"And Cecelia?"

"Beautiful, wonderful . . ."

Robin waved his hand. "She's fine, I see. And Meredith?"

"Well."

"Good!" Robin did not eat heavily in spite of his claim to hunger. "I think my stomach must have shrivelled to nothing." He set the tray aside. "Now I'm for that bed. I've never seen a more handsome object. What a waste!" he said as he sank into its softness. "You have been having two beds in this room—for how long?"

"One day." Hillary laughed.

"Beds are so nice," Robin said.

Hillary had begun to undress. "You know, yesterday I . . ."

Robin Chapman was already asleep. Hillary frowned

as he looked at the sleeping figure. He must have lost fifteen pounds or more, he thought. Robin's face was more thin and drawn than he had ever seen it. There were deep circles under his eyes, and the lines about his mouth were accentuated.

Two nights later there was a conference in Matthew Caswell's study. Robin said, "I have only two choices for the time being—Boston or the Indies."

Joseph Chapman stroked his chin. "North would probably be better. Next week I'll have a ship sailing with full cargo for Boston. If it's with you aboard, I'll take it up myself. You could remain there, and, anyway, it's about time we had an agent in the north. It won't be too long before we have no more cargoes for the Indies —or England either."

Matthew frowned. "Do you think war is imminent?"

"Not imminent, but not too far off either. Everything's pointing that way. Oh, yes, and I brought back a Boston paper about our battle of Alamance." He drew the folded paper from his pocket, laid it on the table and pressed it flat. "Skim it for me, Hillary—only the gist of it. I think my eyes must be getting bad."

Hillary pulled a candlestick nearer and scanned the article. "This is the *Massachusetts Spy*. 'Leonidas' is the writer. He denounces the tyranny of the British Royal Governor of North Carolina and the 'murder' at Alamance."

Matthew Caswell raised his eyebrows and nodded in agreement. "Well put," he said.

Hillary continued: " 'Leonidas' claims that the North Carolina press didn't print a true account of the Regulators. He says Tryon managed the Assemblymen and deceived the people about the Palace appropriations—says he impoverished the Colony. He accuses Tryon of disregarding the rights of common men for his own glory. It's quite a storm he kicks up. Here, Matthew." He handed him the paper. "After all, you'd better assure yourself."

Matthew held it in his hand for a moment, glancing over the article.

"As you see," Hillary said, "they're sympathetic enough. Boston would be safe for Robin."

"Safe from Tryon, I'm sure. But with that son of mine he'll be in the thick of things there."

"Sirs," Robin said, "would you want my own feelings on this matter?"

Matthew laughed. "We did rather leave you out of it, son."

"My object is Antigua for the time being. There's a maiden there who interests me mightily."

Joseph Chapman looked at his son, a gleam of mischief in his eyes. "Your mother may not like that, son."

"I've already talked to her, Father. She's given me her blessing. Now I seek yours."

"You have it, of course. You're a man. But would you mind telling your father who *is* this lass?"

"Cynthia Martin, sir. I fear she's kin to the new Governor—a far kin. And she's also related to Samuel Martin—the one who duelled with John Wilkes. But don't let her relatives keep you from liking her."

"And what will you do if we go to war with England?" Hillary asked.

Robin was thoughtful for a moment. "A wife must stand by her husband and, anyway, the islanders are far from the Mother Country."

"Well, then, sirs," Matthew said, "I'll call for brandy, and ask the honour of proposing the first toast."

He motioned to Ebenezer, who brought forth the decanter and the glasses.

Matthew stood. "To Robin and the Lady from Antigua!"

They raised their glasses and drank. Joseph Chapman coughed slightly to get attention. "And I would propose the second toast."

"Another?"

"To my daughter Cecelia Chapman and to my son-in-law Hillary Caswell! Hillary has asked permission to marry her and I've granted it with pride in my heart."

Three days later when the *Laughing Girl* sailed from Albemarle Sound for Charleston, she made an unscheduled stop off the banks of Ocracoke Inlet. It was a short stop, only long enough to take aboard an outlawed man, Robin Chapman.

"They will have little time," Joseph Chapman had said to Matthew. "Let the young folk have a moment together. I tell you, Matthew, the times are rushing on us. I can measure out the hours of their happiness."

"Could we give them more?"

"I don't know, I don't know. I feel myself getting old, Matthew."

36

A Time For Planting

Midsummer brought the growing days. The fat cattle were knee-deep in lush green grass. The corn was tall and heavily laden. The limbs of the orchard trees, peach and pear and winter apple, were bent low, bolstered up with braces to keep them from breaking. Figs were abundant, and the cotton ready to burst into fields of white.

In the turpentine woods the shrill whine of the saw and the ring of axes broke the silence of the forest. The smell of tar was in the warm, hazy air.

The Negro slaves were singing as they chopped weeds along the field's edge. They were a happy folk, thinking of August, a fine harvest, and rest. An old white-haired Negro sat on a log and thumped out the rhythm of a song that the ancient ones had brought from Africa.

> *"Ndi Lem Bere, malire*
> *Ndi lem bere, malire*
> *Kwanga, ndi, dzadye, msonte."*

From the fields came another voice, that of a young Negro, singing,

> "Draw out the boundaries of the garden for me.
> Give me a garden
> That at my own place
> I may eat my grass seeds."

Cecelia Caswell put her hands to her husband's cheeks and kissed him warmly on the lips. She took his hand. Together she and Hillary walked toward their new home.

From their path they could see the family house, built many years ago, and beyond rose the strong heart-pine posts of their own home, a frame now almost completed. Tomorrow the final work would be done on the roof. The house would stand against a background of heavy forest and before the gleaming river.

"I thought you would never come to the land," she said.

"I could never have stayed from it."

"But I didn't know. Twice I was ready to give you up —to find someone else."

"And now you can never do it," he said.

"Never," she said, slipping her arm about his waist.

They turned from the house and walked down toward the river. "Next year," Hillary said, "we'll clear a hundred acres of the forest, and the year after that a hundred more."

She laughed. "How could I have thought you would do anything but that?"

"Come," he said, "sit by the river with me."

She held his hand as they passed down the gentle incline to the river's bank. There she found a place to sit and spread her skirt like the petals of a flower. He sat beside her and put his arm around her.

In content he looked out across the water at the fair prospect before them. After a time he looked down at Cecelia's auburn hair. "I can't suppose," he said, "that the Governor intended me any kindness. As for Harmon Husband and Rednap Howell and the others, they were kind enough, but too preoccupied with other matters to intend my personal happiness. But the wind in the western forest blew us together. If I had been too quick to become a planter, I might never have come to Manor House, never have seen you in time and fallen at once in love."

He looked off into the distance. "There will be another wind, a greater one. Please God we have some time first. Give us only so much as four years and we'll have a family coming on and we'll have a respectable plantation."

Cecelia shivered faintly. "Where will the new wind blow us? For we must be together, no matter where it carries us."

Hillary sighed. "God knows. But let us have a breathing time first. Four years is little enough to ask for us to be at peace together."

But when four years had passed, the thunder of cannon rolled across America. Men marched to the beat of drums and there was war in the land.

Yet here and there a man stood aside and took no part in war and killing. Here and there the thud of an axe could be heard clearing the forest for the days of peace to come. In the Allegheny Mountains of western Pennsylvania an exiled man who called himself Toescape Death but whose real name was Harmon Husband hacked away at the deep forest.

He was not a young man making a home for himself in the wilderness, but a tousle-headed old man who was fashioning a place for his dream to be made manifest. He had believed that men who walked in freedom could look up to God in quiet. He had striven for peace, good will and justice. Man's lust to fight and kill had forced him to relinquish that task and go into exile. Now where the encircling mountains held back the winds he was clearing a fit place on earth for the coming of the Prince of Peace, according to the vision of Ezekiel.

ABOUT THE AUTHOR

INGLIS FLETCHER'S greatest fame rests on her books about early North Carolina, although her first two novels, *White Leopard* and *Red Jasmine,* were about Africa. Travel was long one of Mrs. Fletcher's chief enthusiasms. With her mining engineer husband, or often alone, she journeyed to remote mountain camps in Alaska and into the interior of Africa, where she went to study witchcraft and native customs.

Once back in the United States, she began, haphazardly at first, to hunt through records in California's Huntington Library for information about her early North Carolina ancestors. As she searched through the colonial documents, her interest grew until the names became live, vivid men and women and eventually the characters in such stories as *Raleigh's Eden, Men of Albemarle, Lusty Wind for Carolina, Toil of the Brave, Roanoke Hundred, Bennett's Welcome, Queen's Gift, Cormorant's Brood* and *The Wind in the Forest.* The Fletchers lived in an old plantation house called Bandon, right on the scene of the historic events that come alive in Mrs. Fletcher's writing.

ENGLAND'S "MISTRESS OF ROMANCE"
GEORGETTE HEYER

Georgette Heyer, England's best-loved novelist, combines history and romance into an enthralling blend of drama and emotion. All of her enduring stories will bring you many hours of enjoyment and satisfaction.

- [ ] ROYAL ESCAPE   (5620—95¢)
- [ ] A BLUNT INSTRUMENT   (5692—95¢)
- [ ] DEATH IN THE STOCKS   (5995—95¢)
- [ ] ENVIOUS CASCA   (7118—95¢)
- [ ] BEHOLD, HERE'S POISON   (7694—95¢)
- [ ] LADY OF QUALITY   (7779—$1.25)
- [ ] COUSIN KATE   (7861—$1.25)
- [ ] REGENCY BUCK   (8302—$1.25)
- [ ] FREDERICA   (8308—$1.25)
- [ ] THE CORINTHIAN   (8321—$1.25)
- [ ] DEVIL'S CUB   (8361—$1.25)
- [ ] THE CONQUEROR   (8473—$1.25)

Catherine Cookson

For years a bestselling author in England, Catherine Cookson's readership today is worldwide. Now one of the most popular and best-loved writers of romantic fiction, her spellbinding novels are memorable stories of love, tragedy and courage.

☐	THE MALLEN LOT	6323	$1.50
☐	THE DWELLING PLACE	7246	$1.25
☐	FEATHERS IN THE FIRE	7289	$1.25
☐	OUR KATE	7599	$1.25
☐	THE MALLEN STREAK	7806	$1.50
☐	THE GLASS VIRGIN	7962	$1.25
☐	PURE AS THE LILY	8079	$1.25
☐	THE FIFTEEN STREETS	8174	$1.25
☐	THE MENAGERIE	8331	$1.25
☐	THE MALLEN GIRL	8406	$1.50
☐	KATE HANNIGAN	8646	$1.25
☐	FENWICK HOUSES	8656	$1.25
☐	KATIE MULHOLLAND	8678	$1.25

Bantam Book Catalog

It lists over a thousand money-saving best-sellers originally priced from $3.75 to $15.00 —bestsellers that are yours now for as little as 50¢ to $2.95!

The catalog gives you a great opportunity to build your own private library at huge savings!

So don't delay any longer—send us your name and address and 10¢ (to help defray postage and handling costs).